Man of War

Man of War

An Eric Steele Novel

Sean Parnell

HARPER LUXE

An Imprint of HarperCollins*Publishers*

MAN OF WAR. Copyright © 2018 by Sean Parnell. All rights reserved. Printed in the United States of America. No part of this book may be used or reproduced in any manner whatsoever without written permission except in the case of brief quotations embodied in critical articles and reviews. For information address HarperCollins Publishers, 195 Broadway, New York, NY 10007.

HarperCollins books may be purchased for educational, business, or sales promotional use. For information please e-mail the Special Markets Department at SPsales@harpercollins.com.

FIRST HARPERLUXE EDITION

ISBN: 978-0-06-285946-4

HarperLuxe™ is a trademark of HarperCollins Publishers.

Library of Congress Cataloging-in-Publication Data is available upon request.

18 19 20 21 22   ID/LSC   10 9 8 7 6 5 4 3 2 1

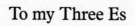
To my Three Es

Man of War

Chapter 1

Algiers

Khalid arrived at his commander's house before first light. At fifteen, he was built like a Great Dane puppy, all legs and feet except for the wisp of hair growing around his upper lip. The facial hair marked him as a man, but it was the pistol in his waist that made him feel invincible.

Khalid was a *jundi*, what the men of the Algerian Liberation Front called a gun boy. Armed with Kalashnikovs, they were street thugs who took what they wanted. Khalid's only loyalty was to Commander Cheb Massi.

Massi ran the Bir Mourad Raïs district, the strategic strip of land that ran from the plateau of western Algiers to the Hydra district where the westerners had their embassies. He also controlled the docks where

Khalid traded hashish and opium for guns and RPGs. It was because of the docks that everyone called Massi the emir, and as long as Khalid worked for him, he was untouchable.

As he always did when summoned to the emir's house, Khalid went straight to the fridge for a beer. The kitchen was dark, and he yanked at the handle. The seal gave way with a wet pop, and the harsh light hit him in the eyes, dilating his pupils. He was twisting the cap off the bottle when a voice said, in Arabic:

"A bit early."

Damn. Khalid jumped, and the bottle slipped out of his hand and shattered on the tile floor. He stepped back, reaching for the pistol stuck in his waistband, glass crunching under his feet. A match flared at the table, and a pair of scarred hands appeared in the circle of yellow light. The man leaned in to touch the end of the cigarette against the flame, and Khalid froze.

His face was gaunt and skeletal, and suddenly Khalid had to pee. It happened every time he got nervous or scared.

"You pull that piece"—the man paused to drag smoke into his lungs—"and I will blow you out of your shoes."

It was too dark for Khalid to make out if he had a gun, but if he did there was no doubt that the man would kill him right there. So he raised his hands, palms out like they did in the American movies, and prayed that Commander Massi was close by. He thanked Allah when the lights came on and his boss stomped into the kitchen.

"Khalid, why are you standing like that?"

Massi nodded to the man at the table.

"This is the boy I told you about."

The man calmly brought his right hand up, his eyes freezing Khalid in place. They were black and emotionless, just like the Egyptian cobra that had bit his cousin, but instead of fangs the man was holding a large revolver centered on Khalid's gut.

"Do you know who I am?" he asked.

Khalid nodded. There was no mistaking the face. It was the burned man. His voice cracked when he answered. "Yeeess . . . yes."

"Cheb says you have the *hadia*, is that true?"

The gift. It was the name his mother had given his ability to find things. When he nodded again, the burned man put his thumb on the hammer and eased it forward.

Khalid hadn't realized he was holding his breath until his head began to spin. His legs trembled beneath him, and he could hear his heart hammering like a drum in his chest. *He would have killed me*, he realized.

At that moment Khalid understood that he knew nothing about death. He had been strong before walking into the kitchen, and now he was weak, helpless to control the shaking that ran up his legs.

"Have a seat before you fall down," Massi snapped.

Khalid walked to the table. He heard the refrigerator open behind him when he sat, and forced himself not to jump when the man pushed a photograph across the table.

"Can you find this man for me?"

Massi had to thump the fresh beer against his shoulder before Khalid realized it was there. He took it and poured half the bottle down his parched throat, stopping only when he ran out of air.

As a *jundi*, Khalid spent most of his time running errands for Massi and his lieutenants. He knew the city like the back of his hand, but the gift he couldn't explain. Somehow he was able to find people even if they wanted to stay hidden.

The man in the picture was an Arab, light-skinned but not like the Berbers. He had soft features, short black hair, and a thin nose. Khalid focused on the eyes and the nose; they were the hardest to change. Finally, after memorizing the face, he nodded.

"Okay."

Massi took out an old flip phone and handed it to Khalid.

"If he finds him before noon, I will give you an extra hundred thousand dollars," the burned man said to Massi. "My number is the only one on this phone. You call me as soon as you find him. If you tell anyone I will kill your father first. He is still working at the oil fields in Gassi Touil, correct?"

Khalid didn't feel right again until he was riding through the bazaar. He wanted to stop and smoke some hashish, but then he remembered the burned man's gun. He drove around for two hours before ending up back at the bazaar. *This is where he is,* he thought, so he drove back and forth until his stomach began to rumble.

He was so hungry that he almost didn't notice the silver van creeping down the road.

Shit, police.

The cops in Algiers were dirty, and if they stopped him they would want money. Money he didn't have. Khalid was about to scurry away, but then he got a good look at the driver of the van. He was white—a foreigner—and Khalid realized that he had seen him before.

"The American embassy," he said aloud.

Something told him that the van was looking for the man in the picture. So instead of cutting through one of the alleys that led away from the bazaar, Khalid released the handbrake and aimed the motorbike at the vehicle. He happened to glance toward the sidewalk, and that was when he saw the man in the photo.

The target was walking toward him, head low and unaware of the van creeping up from behind. Khalid couldn't believe his good fortune. He pulled the motorcycle to the curb and dug the phone from his pocket.

"That was quick."

"He is at the bazaar. The Americans are here in a van."

"What is he carrying?"

"Uh . . . he has a bag."

"Are you sure they are Americans?"

"Yes . . ."

The van sped forward so fast that Khalid almost dropped the phone. It jumped onto the curb amid angry shouts from pedestrians. Three burly men jumped out.

Khalid relayed what was happening in real time. "Three men, they have beards and rifles."

"Breul, don't you fucking move!" one of the men yelled in English, pointing at the man Khalid had been sent to find.

"They are yelling at him. He is running."

Behind him tires screeched and another car flashed around the corner. Khalid barely got out of the way, and almost dumped the bike in the street. The man in the picture tried to run, but one of the Americans pulled out a yellow pistol and fired.

The Arab ran into a woman carrying a bundle of oranges, a pair of wires trailing from his back. The fruit went flying and then there was a *tick, tick, tick* sound that sent the man to the ground. He dropped like a bag of stones and flopped around on the pavement like a fish in Khalid's cousin's net.

"I told you not to run," one of the men said before kicking the Arab in the face. They grabbed his hands and forced them behind his back.

"We got him," one of the Americans said into the radio.

"They are binding his hands and carrying him back to the van."

"Follow them. I need to know where they are going."

"Yes, of course."

Khalid shoved the phone into his pocket and waited for the two vehicles to pass. He turned the bike around and hurried after them, his hunger forgotten. The only thing he remembered was the burned man's eyes and the pistol leveled at his stomach.

He would not fail him.

Chapter 2

Beirut

Four thousand miles to the east, Eric Steele turned into the alley, the headlights of the stolen Mercedes playing across the cinderblock wall. He cut the lights, and before stepping out of the car made sure the dome light was disengaged.

Steele was an Alpha—a clandestine operative assigned to a unit known simply as "the Program." It traced its lineage to World War II and existed because there were enemies that the President of the United States couldn't handle with diplomacy or all-out war. In these events the Commander in Chief needed a third option, and that was why Steele was in Beirut.

Eric gingerly reached back and touched the throbbing lump at the back of his skull. It felt like someone had embedded a golf ball beneath the skin and even the lightest of touches sent a shard of pain radiating along his jaw.

The blood staining his fingers looked black in the dark. "That sucker-punching bastard," he muttered while wiping his hands on the leather upholstery. The center console rattled when it hinged open, and after futilely pawing around for a bottle of aspirin, Steele settled on the FN Five-seven instead.

Most of the time Steele carried a modified Colt 1911. The .45 was an old gun, and the only thing his father left at the house before he disappeared. It was Steele's most cherished possession, but not the right weapon for what he had planned.

The FN, on the other hand, was designed in Belgium around the SS190 5.7×28mm round; hence the name. Its sole purpose was to punch through body armor, and it was the cartel favorite. Steele press-checked the pistol and after ensuring it was loaded, screwed a suppressor onto the threaded barrel. When it was snug, he pressed a wireless earpiece into his ear, stepped out of the vehicle, and eased the door shut behind him.

In the darkness the only sound came from the raindrops on the roof and the gentle swishing of traffic that drifted from the highway. Steele let his eyes adjust to the darkness.

"Radio check," he said, stepping around the car and

angling for the building to his right. At six foot two, he moved with a predatory grace that seemed impossible for a man of his build. Steele hadn't seen the inside of a gym in years. His physique, like his light, measured step, had come from the mountains of Afghanistan, where he had hunted terrorists as a Green Beret.

"Took you long enough," came the response.

The voice on the radio belonged to Demo, Steele's handler. They had been together since Eric became an Alpha and it was a tight bond, forged by countless operations.

"Traffic," Steele replied.

It was the understatement of the year. The ride over had been a white-knuckle nightmare. Rain in Beirut is like snow in Florida, and it didn't matter if it was an inch or a foot—it made the locals drive like maniacs.

Steele paused at the door and tested the knob. It was locked. He had the picks ready in his shirt pocket and went to work. Sweat beaded up on his forehead—it was hot, and the rain had made it worse.

Lock picking was a perishable skill, one that Steele knew he had neglected. During phase two of the Program's selection course it would have taken him thirty seconds. "Damn you, lock," he hissed through gritted teeth.

"Take forever, mano," Demo quipped.

Steele gritted his teeth and fought the urge to just kick the door in, but a second later the last tumbler clicked into place and he was able to turn the knob.

"I'm in."

He cleared the house, fully aware that he could be walking into a trap. He took his time, slipping from room to room. The street side of the structure had a row of windows, and now and then a passing car cast its oblong shadow across the wall. Most of the buildings in Beirut had been built in a rush after the civil war ended in 1990. The fighting had been close and personal and the city had taken a beating. Steele had seen the same damage in Fallujah, and he knew that tanks and artillery had destroyed eighty percent of the structures in Beirut.

In the rush to rebuild, contractors cut corners. Steele hadn't been in a building yet that didn't swell during the day and pop and creak each night when it settled. Usually he didn't notice, but moving through the final rooms was unnerving, and by the time he got to the last one on the second floor, his shoulders were on fire.

He wiped the sweat off his forehead and bent to look out the window. It was amazing how heavy a 1.6-pound pistol could get if you weren't relaxed. He knew better and chided himself, but forgot the pain the moment he saw the target building.

The neon dragon dancing on the roof glinted off the puddles in sparks of yellow and red. Outside the Dragon's Door the line stretched back around the block. Steele set the pistol on the ledge and checked the Rolex Submariner on his wrist. It was 11:25. He pulled a magnifier from the inside pocket of his Manning and Manning jacket and pressed it to his eye.

"I'm on target," he said.

"Uploading the feed, stand by," Demo replied.

While his handler remotely connected to the magnifier's Bluetooth so he could watch the feed, Steele went over what he knew of the operation. He had received the dossier three days ago by secure courier. Known as the "target package," the mission files and operations order contained in the dossier were supposed to provide him with everything he needed to plan and execute the operation. This one had the CIA's stench all over it.

There was no chain-of-custody slip on the front, so he had no idea who'd rushed it to the White House, but what made the hairs on the back of his neck stand up was the intel. Everything about the file, from the narrative explaining how the NSA had pinged the target's phone in Beirut to the exact time he was supposed to show up at the club, was too precise to be a rush. Someone had taken a great deal of time on the packet, and the first word that popped into Steele's mind was "convenient."

"Looks like we have company," Demo said as a silver Land Rover pulled up in front of the club.

Steele checked his watch. It was exactly 11:30. *Right on time.*

Two men got out, and the one from the front moved back and pressed his butt against the passenger door. The second man posted up on the street, hand inside his jacket. They were pros. Steele could tell that much by the way they handled the street.

Julian Burrows stepped out of the SUV without a care in the world. He popped his jacket, making a big show of the gold on his wrist. He was a small man, with stooped shoulders, and despite the half-million-dollar bounty on his head, he still dressed like a 1980s pimp with a red silk shirt open at the collar.

"You'd think a guy like that would *try* to keep a low profile," Demo said.

Burrows had started out as a Ukrainian pimp before graduating to trafficking cocaine and heroin from Afghanistan. He'd been a pissant before the dope, not even a blip on Steele's radar, but then he started moving weapons.

Should have brought the rifle up with me, Steele thought as he waited for Demo to run the man's face through the facial recognition program. *I could hit him right here, and by the time the check cleared I'd be in Ibiza, sipping mai tais on the beach.*

"It's him," Demo said.

That was all Steele needed to hear. He returned to the Mercedes, moved to the rear bumper, and popped the trunk. It bounced open an inch, the light revealing a man with duct tape over his mouth.

"Easy there, Hamid," Steele said in Arabic, making sure the owner of the Mercedes saw the pistol before opening the trunk all the way. "If I take the tape off are you going to play by the rules this time?"

The man cursed at him through the tape, but changed his tune when Steele looked like he was going to shut the trunk.

"Well, what's it gonna be?"

Hamid shook his head up and down, an awkward movement considering the size of the trunk. It reminded Steele of a dog hamming it up for a treat. "You sure?"

The Arab tried to talk, but it sounded like a string of vowels because of the tape. Steele reached in and ripped it free so he could understand what the Arab was saying.

"I couldn't understand you," he said, shaking the duct tape by way of explanation.

"I said," Hamid began a bit too forcefully. He paused, taking the hint from the ice in Steele's jade eyes, and adjusted his tone. "I apologize for hitting you with the lamp."

"Fair enough."

Steele lifted the man out of the trunk with one hand and set him on the bumper. At his height, Steele was careful to appear unimposing. It was a skill drilled into him during training. He had his tailor cut his jackets wide in the shoulders to hide his bulk and keep his gun from printing. But the camouflage was only skin deep, and wouldn't hold up to the trained eye. No matter how he walked or what he wore, there was no hiding the fact that he was a hunter.

"So Burrows and Ronna in the same place, that's a thousand to one odds. Tell me what I'm not seeing, Hamid."

"I told you what I know."

Steele believed him and pushed the pistol into the front of his pants, *cholo* style. He slipped a blade from his pocket and held it up, looking into Hamid's eyes for any sign of deceit. It didn't matter if the man was lying or not, Steele realized as he cut his bonds, because he already had his orders.

He slipped the knife away, and when his hand came back into view there was a roll of cash. Hamid might be a piece of crap, but the man had a wife and a kid on the way. Steele knew firsthand what it was like to grow up without a father. *His* dad had walked out when he was nine, forcing his mom to work two jobs just to keep a roof over his head. It wasn't a life he would wish on his worst enemy.

"Get your wife the hell out of Beirut before that baby is born," Steele hissed.

Hamid obviously hadn't expected to be let go, and the relief was evident on his face, but the fact that Steele was helping him was too much for the man to bear. Tears formed at the edges of his eyes and his voice broke with emotion.

"I thought you were going to kill me," he said, taking the money.

"Give me a break. If I killed everyone who hit me with a lamp, I wouldn't have any friends left."

"That's for damn sure," Demo remarked.

Steele muted the earpiece and grabbed a duffel bag from the trunk. He tossed Hamid the keys and walked back to the building to get ready. He took off his jacket, unbuttoned his shirt, and pulled an ultra-thin Kevlar vest over his well-muscled torso. He cinched it tight, hearing the Mercedes start up outside.

Steele was under no illusions about what was waiting for him inside the bar. Men like Ronna and

Julian Burrows were killers, and Jean-Luc, the man who owned the club, would do whatever it took to protect his clients. Steele knew that if he wasn't on his game there was a good chance he wouldn't make it out alive.

He stuck his left arm through the loop of a bungee sling and stretched it across his back. At one end there was a magazine pouch; on the other hung a Brügger & Thomet MP9. The machine pistol weighed less than three pounds and even with the built-in suppressor was only ten inches in length. It fit perfectly beneath his arm, but Steele knew that it wouldn't slip the notice of the security guards at the door.

Finally he put his blazer back on and stuffed a can of CS, the military's name for tear gas, and two Belgian mini grenades into the hidden pockets sewn inside. He took the wireless headset controller out of his pocket and unmuted it. The device was built to look like a key fob, complete with a silver Toyota emblem on the back. Using the fob, Steele unmuted the earpiece and stepped outside.

"Loop the security channel onto frequency two," he said. There was a moment of silence.

"You're hot," Demo replied.

The secondary channel was "listen only," which meant that Steele could hear the guards' conversation through the earpiece but it would disappear anytime he or Demo transmitted over channel one.

"Got it. Here we go," he said.

Steele skipped the line, angling for the guards at the top of the stairs. One was patting down a man in a tuxedo with an ease borne of thousands of repetitions. But Steele was fixated on the second guard, a bald man standing next to the red door. The golden emblazoned dragon winked from the lights above.

The guard's name was Felix, and the bald ex-Legionnaire watched Eric's approach with a flat expression. Steele knew he was committed now. There was no turning back.

Time to play the game, he told himself.

When Felix waved him forward, Steele stepped up, hands raised and painfully aware of the MP9 under his arm.

"I'm with the band," he said in French, flashing the second guard a toothy grin.

The man grunted. Steele kept his eyes on Felix, tensing when the second guard ran his hands over his sport coat. He felt Steele's weapon and took a tiny step back, his hand reaching for the pistol inside his own jacket.

"Easy," Steele warned, his jade eyes cutting and cold.

There was no doubt in his mind what would happen if Felix didn't step in very soon. He might get some of them, but in the end Steele knew he'd lose.

"Hey, baldy, you going to put a leash on your mutt?" he asked Felix.

The second guard snarled, and Steele saw the pistol coming out. It was now or never.

Chapter 3

100 miles south of Tunis

Nestled among the boulders, beneath a section of
camo netting, Nathaniel West watched the highway through his night vision scope. The road looked
like a gray ribbon laid over black scrub brush and green
sand, and every time a car passed, West had to take his
eyes out of the scope to keep from being blinded.

As was the case with the rest of the cars he had seen
since getting into position, by the time the Citroën's
headlights found the bend in the road, the driver had to
slam on his brakes to keep the tires on the asphalt.

It was the perfect kill zone.

West rested his scarred chin on the buttstock of the
Barrett .50 cal and savored the breeze that blew in from
the desert. *I bet it's beautiful in the daylight.*

The radio came to life with a flash of static.

"Road Runner to Coyote."

"Go for Coyote," his spotter, Peter Villars, answered.

West didn't notice the rush of blood coursing through his veins until his face got hot. Most of the nerve endings had been burned away on the left side of his body, but he could still feel the right side of his face.

There was only one reason why the observation post he'd set two miles down the road would break radio silence. The target vehicles were in sight. He had to give it to Commander Massi. That *jundi* of his really did have a gift. Everything was coming together, just like he said it would.

"Coyote, target in sight."

West smiled, a rare moment of emotion that, because of the scarring, looked more like a grimace in the green light spilling from the night vision optic. In the last three days he had achieved the impossible. Not only had he played the CIA, but he had manipulated the Program into sending his old protégé to Beirut. The best part was that they had no idea.

"Roger that," Villars said before reaching into his pocket and extracting a wadded-up hundred-dollar bill. West reached for it, but at the last second Villars pulled it back an inch and said, "Double or nothing Steele's a no-show."

West's grimace shifted into a full-on grin. "It's your money," he said, his voice low and gravelly, like the rumble of thunder on the horizon. He plucked the cash from the man's fingers and shoved it into his back pocket.

"What time is it?"

"Twenty-three thirty."

Right on cue the Iridium satellite phone in West's pocket rang. He had the backlight turned all the way down so it wouldn't give away his position. "I wonder who *that* could be?" he asked with a theatrical smile.

"Damn."

"Oh, hey, Felix," West said in French, playing it up to the discomfort of his spotter. "You don't say." He pulled the phone away from his ear and whispered, "Eric Steele just showed up at the Dragon's Door. What are the chances of that happening?"

"Shit," Villars swore.

West went back to the phone. "Felix, be a dear and make sure he doesn't leave. Give Jean-Luc my regards while you're at it."

There was another rustle of cash and West put the bill with its partner. "Easy money."

He pulled the Barrett .50 cal toward him, while his spotter settled behind the thermal scope set up on the tripod. West adjusted the focus knob, maxing out the magnification, pressed his chest to the ground, and opened his legs until they formed a V behind him.

"Spotter up."

"Stand by," West muttered.

The road had been built atop a thick layer of gravel and the edges sloped down on each side. His men had hammered a series of range stakes into the low ground on the left side of the road. They were a hundred meters apart, and every other stake had a blue ribbon tied to the top that fluttered in the wind. The Barrett had an effective range of 2,000 yards and the last stake was set · at 800—a chip shot for the powerful rifle.

"I'm on the 8," he said.

They had preset the routine earlier in the day and both men agreed that ambushing the lead vehicle at an assigned range was the best course of action.

"Wind out of the east—full value."

"Check."

West had spent a lot of time behind "the glass" and knew the power wind had over ballistics. During the day he could have used the heat shimmering off the asphalt, what snipers called mirage. It was the same phenomenon you experienced when driving on a hot summer day. But at night he had to use the flags.

As a child, West remembered a road trip with his parents from Colorado to California. In the desert the heat made it look like there was water on the road, and he was always disappointed when the old station wagon passed the spot and it was dry.

When the lead vehicle appeared in the upper edge of his scope he adjusted for both wind and distance.

Aim small, miss small, he said to himself.

He had less than thirty seconds to finish his ritual. Using his toes, West loaded the bipod, pushing his body tight into the buttstock. He set his cheek on the rest, locked into the gun, his body set up to absorb the recoil.

His mind calculated the data needed to put a 750-grain armor-piercing bullet into the bow tie affixed to the grille. Hitting a target the size of a coffee can was hard enough. When the target was moving at 80 miles per hour West knew he had to be right on the money. He focused on breathing normally—even breaths in and out. The reticle was locked in high and to the right of the spot he actually wanted to put the bullet, and then he flicked the safety off with his thumb.

"Package identified. He is in the rear passenger seat."

West picked up the first of the three vehicles in his scope.

"Cleared hot in five, four, three . . ."

He wasn't thinking anymore. His mind was clear, and as he settled into the rhythm of his spotter's count his finger closed on the trigger. "Smooth, smooth," he said to himself, applying more and more pressure to the trigger.

At the bottom of his exhale the target vehicle appeared in his crosshairs. The big gun bucked to life, recoil shoving the rifle back into his shoulders, and with no place to go the muzzle traveled skyward. West lost the sight picture for a second even though his face never left the stock. His right hand worked the bolt, snapping the handle up and ripping it to the rear. Out of the corner of his eye, he saw the expended brass cartwheel from the gun. He was already shoving the bolt forward, stuffing a fresh round into the chamber.

By the time he got back on target the API, or armor-piercing incendiary, round had reached the end of its one-way trip. It exploded in a flash of light, the bonded core howling through the engine block like a freight train with a full head of steam. It punched through, ripping pistons and shearing cams, and still had enough velocity to blast through the firewall before dropkicking the driver in the pelvis.

The report bounced over the countryside, the sign for his men to engage. A nearside machine gun, nestled in a copse of boulders, opened up on the lead vehicle. The M240 Bravo chewed through the belt of 7.62

ammo. It fired a standard four-to-one mix, four steel-jacketed rounds per every tracer, and the six-second burst sounded like a buzz saw going off. The tracers hit the side of the vehicle and ricocheted skyward, a flicker of orange. The gunner worked the rounds across the door panel, killing the driver and sending the truck headlong into the desert. It didn't get far.

The driver of the rear vehicle slammed on the brakes. He turned the wheel to avoid the SUV stalled in front of him, but he wasn't fast enough to outrun the AT4 that screamed in from the road. The 84mm rocket crossed the distance in less than the blink of an eye, turning the SUV into a rolling fireball.

"Well, that escalated quickly," West said.

Four men dressed in plate carriers and carrying rifles rushed the target vehicle, a pair of jeeps bumping into view behind them. West grabbed his rifle while Villars took down the camo net.

"Jackpot. I repeat, Jackpot," a voice said over the radio.

West slung the Barrett and shot Villars a smile. "Let's go grab our nuke," he said before heading down the hill to join the rest of his team.

Chapter 4

E ric Steele felt the seconds stretching into hours. Felix just stared at him. He was imposing and dark, dressed in a black suit, the only spot of color coming from the long white scar that hooked over a mangled ear, down the side of his face, and into his shirt.

"*C'est bon*—it's good." Felix finally nodded.

Steele let out a sigh of relief and stepped past the guard.

"I wish I could say it was good to see you," Felix said, opening his arms.

"I get that a lot." Steele's hand slipped into his pocket, emerging with a black felt bag. The two men embraced, and Steele passed him the bag. "Played that one to the very end, didn't you?"

"Least I could do for a *friend*," the Algerian hissed, not an ounce of warmth in the words.

They both knew why Steele was here.

Felix bounced the payment in his palm, eyebrows arching as he took in the weight and then with a nod slipped it away.

"You need to go, *now*," Steele said.

"I have a wife. Jean-Luc will find me."

"I wouldn't worry about *him*."

Felix's eyes sparked with a feral glint.

Steele tightened his grip on the man's arm. "But before you do anything stupid, I want you to realize that there is no reason for your wife to become a widow tonight. You leave *now* and you will never see me again. But if you stay . . ."

The silence was deafening, heavy with the promise of violence that emanated like a live wire between the two men. Felix was the first to blink.

"*C'est la vie*," he said with a Gallic shrug. That's life.

"You got that right."

Steele forced him out of the way, grabbed the door's golden handle, and stepped inside. He found himself in the entryway, lights and sound pouring from the crack at the bottom of the door. He took a deep breath and stepped in.

What he saw inside made sensory overload feel like

a decaf latte, and he moved out to the side and scanned his surroundings. The house lights were turned low over the dance floor, which was about the same size as a 7-Eleven parking lot. Every inch was crammed with sweat-soaked bodies jumping, grinding, and bouncing in time with what Steele assumed was music.

The bass from the subwoofer reverberated off the far wall and palm-heeled him square in the chest. Ultraviolet lights strobed on and off, while green lasers oscillated through the fog rising around the DJ booth. A shirtless Arab hunched over a mixing board presided over the masses. He drove the music to a shrill crescendo, and when it could go no higher, he threw his hands into the air and screamed.

The crowd was frenetic.

Steele saw the bar to his right and stepped into the fray. The scene reminded him of a fishing trip he'd taken in South Africa, where the captain chummed the waters and laughed when the great whites rolled in.

The music was so loud that Steele had to turn the radio's volume all the way up to hear Demo say, "Sounds like my kind of party, mano."

Steele knew that right now Felix was outside, making a choice. The scarred ex-Legionnaire would either beat feet for the docks or alert his boss and then try to put a bullet in the back of his skull. No matter the decision,

Steele knew he was running short on time and needed to find Jean-Luc before the alert was given.

He scanned the faces sitting at the tables as he moved. Years of practice allowed him to easily separate the predators from the prey. Finally he saw Jean-Luc peacocking at the bar. The Frenchman was hard to miss even among the chaos, because of his signature silver fauxhawk. He was chatting up a young girl, most likely underage, whose glassy eyes were fixed on the bar. The girl picked a rolled bill from the bar, bent her head, and aimed the open end at a mirror with cocaine lined across its surface. Steele waited until her head was down and then slipped in behind Jean-Luc. He jammed his finger in the base of the man's back.

"DGSE, don't move," he ordered as the girl sucked the white powder up her nose.

"*Merde,*" Jean-Luc cursed. The Frenchman had good reason to fear the Direction générale de la sécurité extérieure, or Directorate-General for External Security, as it was known in the United States; they had been after him for years. But he quickly regained his composure and started negotiating. "Listen to me. I know what they pay you in France and I will double it right here, right now."

He was stalling and Eric knew it.

The girl looked up from the dope, a smear of white on her nostril, and Jean-Luc made his move. But Steele was ready and caught his hand creeping toward the bottom edge of the bar where a panic button was installed.

"Push that button and I will burn you down," Steele said, this time in English.

"Hey, where did *you* come from?" the girl demanded.

The Frenchman recognized Steele's voice and tried to play it cool. "Don't worry, Judith, dear, Eric is an old friend. Jesus, buddy, you scared me."

He tried to turn around, but Steele wasn't having it. "Get rid of her," he ordered, pulling the man away from the bar by the back of his Italian suit coat.

"Give us a second, love."

Steele didn't wait for her to leave. He muscled Jean-Luc a half step to the right, until they were both facing the mirror over the bar. In this position he could watch Jean-Luc's face and make sure no one snuck up on his six.

"What do you want?" Jean-Luc demanded, his eyebrows darting upward into sharp little Vs, giving him the look of a frosted Satan.

"What was our deal?"

Jean-Luc's tongue flashed nervously across his thin lips, eyes scanning for the help that wasn't coming.

"What was it?" Steele asked, switching to French so there would be no confusion.

"No more guns."

"That's right. No more guns. So imagine my surprise when I found out that you were facilitating a deal between Burrows and Ronna." Steele was lying—he had no idea what involvement the man had in the arms deal—but he knew that Jean-Luc got a piece of every deal that happened in his place. "Where are they?"

Steele had to get moving. Right now there was no sign that anyone was on to him, but when things broke bad, which he knew they would, it would happen in the blink of an eye. There were enough guns in the club to start a second intifada, and if there was going to be gunplay, *he* wanted to start it.

"VIP," the Frenchman hissed.

"Take me to them," Steele said, grabbing a handful of jacket and pulling him closer. He checked the mirror; no one was paying them any attention. He yanked the FN from its holster and shoved it into the back of Jean-Luc's waistband. He held him close, giving him a final warning. "You play it straight and I will let you live, but if I even think you are stepping out of bounds I am going kill you. Now walk."

Steele stayed close, an easy smile on his face. They were just two guys walking through a crowded club. He just hoped the ruse would hold up.

There were two guards flanking the arch leading into the VIP section. Steele tensed. If Jean-Luc was going to make a move it would happen here, but the man just nodded and walked past. Everything was going smoothly, and Steele thought he might just pull it off when Demo's voice filled his ear.

"Eric, we've got trouble."

Chapter 5

Virginia

It was 11:30 P.M. and CIA Director Robin Styles was standing barefoot on the balcony outside her bedroom. *God, the tile is cold,* she thought, curling her manicured toes against the chill. She had been up since four waiting for the team she had sent to Algiers to report in. The later it got, the more her sleep-deprived brain ran over the list of things that could have gone wrong.

No news is good news.

When she finally began to feel the effects of the Ambien she grabbed the empty wineglass from the table at her feet and stepped inside.

Her bedroom was well furnished and warm, a far cry from the one in rural Kentucky where she had grown up. Styles could still remember the sound of the leaking faucet and lying in bed listening to the *drip, drip, drip* reverberating off the steel sink.

She eyed the bed on the way to the bathroom, wanting nothing more than to dive beneath the comforter and go to sleep. The picture on the bedside table quickly dissuaded her.

The photo was of her mother and it was the only memento in the room. Everything else was replaceable. Styles kept the picture to remind her of what happened to people who took the easy road. Her mother had everything she needed to get out of Kentucky, but traded it all for a five-minute romp in the back of a rusted Ford pickup.

If you could see me now, Momma.

Styles went into the bathroom to wash her face instead of jumping into bed. As the first female Director of the CIA, she knew the importance of "optics." *It doesn't matter how good a job I'm doing,* she thought. *If I got caught on camera looking like a tired hag, the media would go crazy.* She followed up with a gentle toner and a nighttime cream. Only after she had finished her ritual did she finally crawl into bed and drift off to sleep.

A rattling on her nightstand woke her up three hours later. Styles came out of the sleep like a ship emerging from the fog, eyeballs burning, the room out of focus and hazy.

It can't be morning already.

The clock on the cable box said it was 2:30 A.M. Styles rubbed her hand over her face, trying to place the vibrating sound. *What is that noise?* Then it hit her: *my cell phone.* She snatched the offending device off the table, and cursed when the phone snagged on the charger.

"This better be good," she snapped.

"You need to get down here."

Jesus Christ, what now?

The line was unsecured, and as much as she wanted to ask what had happened, she simply said, "I'm on my way."

She got dressed and grabbed the keys to the Jeep on the way to the garage. As the Director of the CIA, Styles had a driver and a government-issued Suburban, but government vehicles were equipped with GPS chips, and the last thing Styles needed was someone finding out where she was going. In the last twenty-four hours she had broken enough laws to earn a free room at the black site of her choice. Treason was one thing, but what she had done, shit, they didn't even have a law for that. Styles didn't want to think about it and held to the mantra she had been using since President Cole took office.

Cole can't burn you if he doesn't know.

Robin Styles had joined the Agency back in the 1980s when America was still fighting the Cold War. While her colleagues were fixated on Russia, Styles got the Middle East desk. She quickly proved that she was more than just a pretty face, developing intel that Hezbollah and the PLO were an emerging threat. She tried to warn her boss, but the man laughed at her.

Then in 1983, Islamic Jihad blew up the Marine barracks in Beirut and the jokes stopped. Styles got a promotion and hadn't stopped climbing the ladder since.

Thirty minutes later, Robin Styles pulled across the railroad tracks, the Jeep's headlights spraying over the fractured concrete drive. The industrial plaza was a mix of warehouses in dire need of a pressure washing and squat office buildings that looked like gray pillboxes. It was not the place you'd expect the CIA to have an off-the-books listening station, which was why Styles put it there.

She pulled the Jeep into a spot next to a sign that read LOOKING GLASS SOLUTIONS. On paper, LGS was a telecom provider, but in reality it was a CIA shell company Styles had been illegally funding for five years. When she cut the headlights a man in light blue coveralls stepped out of the shadows. He was red-faced from the wind, and peeking out of his jacket Styles saw the rear sight of an H&K MP7.

"They are waiting for you inside, ma'am."

The building was a no-frills operation and the bare concrete floors were dotted with strips of carpet tape. The walls were also bare and the pipes were exposed in the ceiling. Styles had poured millions into the facility, but the only way you would know it was if you had access to the vault.

Styles hadn't kept an iron grip on the CIA by playing by the rules. Her job was to protect the United States from its enemies, especially those in the White House. She hadn't had these problems under the previous administration. President Bentley had been her ally. But Cole was a different story.

She badged herself through the steel door and stepped into a small room with tan walls and a desk surrounded by a bulletproof cubicle. The door closed behind her, causing her ears to pop.

The room was soundproof, with a lead insert that kept cell phone signals from coming in or out. Styles knew this because she had signed off on the plans and paid for the building using money siphoned from the black fund.

There was one more door, and when she stepped through, Styles was in a room smaller than her den.

It was cooler in here and the only light came from the two large monitors sitting on a desk. The temperature was kept low to protect the supercomputers that took up the rest of the space. About the size of a refrigerator and arrayed with a panel of blinking lights, the massive machines hummed behind a protective steel cage that kept anyone from ripping out one of the drives.

Unlike the guards, the man behind the desk was in his late twenties. He was dressed in a stained T-shirt and had a wispy beard. His workstation was clean, but the trash can was full of empty Red Bull cans and foil gum wrappers wadded into little balls. He rotated the chair toward the door, his face void of its usual cocky grin.

Above all the assets that made up Styles's arsenal, she liked the geeks the best. There was no guile in their motives, and as long as she made sure to give them the newest gear and the fastest Internet, they were happy. It was a lesson the NSA ignored, which in Styles's opinion was the main reason why Edward Snowden had developed a conscience and decided to leak reams of classified documents to the world.

Not that it mattered. Styles had managed to turn the fiasco to her advantage by stealing the STATEROOM program, one of the top-secret assets Snowden leaked from inside Russian custody. According to the Director's congressional testimony, STATEROOM didn't exist anymore. The satellite map covered in blue and green dots on the technician's monitor said otherwise.

In its most basic form STATEROOM was a clearing-house for government and commercial telecommunication assets, a database of audio and video recordings that was updated every second. Styles called it "the unblinking eye," and it was illegal as hell.

The blue dots were commercial platforms, and the government owned the green ones. The tech double clicked on a blue dot he had marked with a red pin and the UAV's heads-up display filled the screen. Styles knew it was a passive link, meaning that the tech could control the camera if the feed was open, but could not alter the drone's flight plan, and at 30,000 feet in the dark, the drone wasn't much.

"What is so important?" she asked.

The tech's fingers rattled over the keyboard and a satellite overlay popped up below the feed. It showed a highway and an antenna icon moving east. When he clicked on the icon a little box displaying the speed, compass heading, and lat/long appeared.

"I found Breul's phone," he said.

Styles was impressed. Two decades at the CIA had told her that locating Ali Breul was a fool's errand, a task she equated with finding a needle in a stack of needles. But her geeks had come through. The jolt of triumph was tempered as her sleep-deprived mind processed what the tech had just told her.

"How did you get the phone?" she asked, praying he was smart enough *not* to use the NSA.

Phone intercepts were the purview of the National Security Agency, who used their satellites and Intelligence, Surveillance, and Reconnaissance, or ISR, platforms to signal all over the world. The boys at Fort Meade had "turned over a new leaf" after Snowden went public, promising Congress that they had shut down their surveillance programs. Styles knew it was bullshit.

The NSA was still spying on the world. They just weren't sharing it anymore.

"I ran it through a few open repeaters and cell phone towers. Actually got a hit faster than if I *had* used the NSA."

"Well done," Styles congratulated him. It was good news, but she knew he hadn't gotten her out of bed to tell her that he'd found an asset's phone.

"This is a recording from the drone feed," he said, pointing at the screen. He hit the play button and activated the drone's thermal camera.

The darkness disappeared, replaced by a gray landscape and a convoy of trucks that glowed black from the heat of the engines. The tech leaned forward, finger outstretched, and pointed at the lead vehicle. In the next instant there was a flash of light on the screen followed by an ink-black fireball that suddenly flared.

"What the hell was that?" Styles asked, waiting for the thermal iris to refresh so she could see what was going on.

Instead of replying, the tech zoomed in, and when the picture returned a moment later, the director saw tracer fire slamming into the convoy, which was now stopped and on fire in the middle of the road. A group of men appeared from what looked like a ditch. They advanced on the convoy, muzzles flashing in the dark.

Oh my God.

The first thing that popped into Styles's mind was that in three hours the sun would be up and the President would get his daily intelligence briefing. The Director of National Intelligence would make sure the first thing he told President Cole was that Styles had lost a team in Tunis.

She knew how Cole's brain worked. The first question out of his mouth would be, "What were they doing in Tunis?"

I have to get ahead of this. But how?

The answer came out of sheer desperation. *You are going to call a briefing. Get your story on record before Cole and his lapdogs hear it from anyone else.*

It was a game called "controlling the narrative," and Styles was a master.

She knew what would happen if *anyone* ever learned the truth behind the operation she was running. *Going to jail would be the least of my concerns.* Once the decision was made, she didn't hesitate. "Kill the feed and erase the log," she ordered. "I was never here, and *this*"—Styles jabbed a manicured nail at the screen—"*this* never happened."

Chapter 6

Beirut

Inside the Dragon's Door, Demo's warning was followed up by Felix's voice on the security channel.

"Security breach, code one. Blue jacket, black hair. I am sending a picture."

"You are blown."

Well, that didn't take long.

Steele couldn't go back if he wanted to, the men standing guard behind him had seen to that. He knew there was an emergency exit on the back wall, but to get there he had to keep going.

The VIP section was divided up into little cubes with a walkway that ran toward the back of the building. The cubes to Steele's left and right were built on top of a raised dais and surrounded by a waist-high wall. He couldn't see over the wall because he was below it, but he assumed they were laid out the same.

A never-ending line of servers bustled back and forth with trays of food and drinks. Steele had to push Jean-Luc to the side to let one pass, which gave him an opportunity to look up the set of stairs and probe the layout. The stairs were the only way in or out, and when he looked up after the server, Steele saw that the back wall of each section was mirrored.

Got to go in fast and hard. The stairs are a kill zone and then three leather couches and a low table. One maybe two hard corners. Not good.

"Which one is it?" he demanded, shoving the Frenchman forward while the clock in his head ticked away. *Got to move.* He didn't hear his answer because of the noise, and Steele levered the pistol into Jean-Luc's back. A not too gentle reminder as to who was in charge.

Jean-Luc flinched from the pain and held up four fingers, then gestured to the right.

Steele imagined twenty seconds had elapsed since Felix dimed him out. It felt like forever. Being exposed like this made his back itch. He glanced behind him, checking his back trail. *Dammit.* One of the guards had stepped through the archway and was standing in the center of the walk, his face lit up by the phone in his hand.

Steele jammed his thumb down on the channel one button until there was a beep in the earpiece. The sound told him that the mike was now open and anything he said or heard would transmit to Demo without his having to push the button.

"Get the car, things are about to get ugly," he told his handler.

"Already on it."

Steele ducked down, hoping the ebb and flow of high rollers and servers would protect him. When things went sideways, and they often did, there was no cavalry waiting on the other side of the hill.

They were within ten feet when Jean-Luc made his move. He jumped forward like a sprinter coming out of the blocks, twisting his arm back to strike at Steele. "I see him," the radio crackled.

Steele yanked on the pistol, but the front sight got snagged on the Frenchman's belt. Jean-Luc's right arm hit him in the wrist, a painful bone-on-bone collision that wrenched the Five-seven out of his grip. Steele could make out Burrows's bodyguard posted up ahead, faithfully guarding his boss's booth.

Jean-Luc shouted a warning while trying to dodge the server who seemed to appear out of nowhere. The bodyguard turned to his left, reached into his jacket, and squared up to the threat. Steele's instincts told him that he was too far behind the eight-ball to get the MP9 into action fast, so he improvised.

He launched a kick at Jean-Luc's ankle that would have made an NFL punter proud. His leg muscles pistoned his foot toward its target like a hot rod on a quarter-mile track. The impact snapped the fleeing Frenchman's puny ankle, causing him to tumble into the server.

Now.

The bodyguard froze, trying to make sense of the tangle of legs that had appeared before him. Steele stayed low; he could see the pistol a few feet ahead, but knew he'd never make it. Instead he lowered his shoulder into the unsuspecting server, who was frozen in place by his boss's bloodcurdling shrieks. Steele hit him hard and sent him tumbling into Burrows's man. He snatched a beer bottle from the ground, and was swinging it when the bodyguard panicked and fired.

Orange flame erupted from the barrel, scorching the server's white jacket. There was a flash of blood; Steele kept moving toward the threat, shutting everything away. He was in the zone, the dark raging place he'd always gone when the killing started. Steele slammed the bottle against the bodyguard's skull. Glass and beer exploded in a cloud, mixing with the blood that erupted from the impact. What was left in his hand was a jagged shard attached to the neck like some primeval blade.

It was the only weapon Steele needed. He pushed the falling server into the bodyguard, and saw the man fold like a table when the dead man's head slammed into his solar plexus. Steele was so close that he smelled the bodyguard's cologne, a musky scent that made his eyes water. The man shifted, trying to keep his balance while pushing the corpse off him. His pistol was useless, but he cracked off another shot. It buzzed past Steele's ear like an angry hornet.

Ears ringing from the gunshot, Steele grabbed the pistol with his left hand and forced the guard's arm up, uncovering his armpit. He drove the makeshift blade into unprotected flesh, four quick jabs that had more in common with a prison shanking than a government-sanctioned hit. The jagged blade must have hit the lung and a jet of blood sprayed across the side of Steele's face, carrying the stench of the guard's breath. The blood smelled of old pennies, but the air of vodka and garlic.

On the fifth strike the blade hit bone and splintered, leaving a jagged haft in Steele's hand. He sunk it into the man's thigh and dove sideways for the FN. It wasn't a moment too soon.

Steele saw the wall explode in a puff of masonry dust and drywall and then he heard the shot. He landed on his side, grabbed the pistol, and rolled to the left. The shooter was moving toward him, firing on the move. His second shot hit the ground where Steele had been a moment before, and the bullet whined when it ricocheted up, striking a woman in the pelvis.

He fired three shots, engaging the shooter from his back. The suppressor sounded like a book being dropped onto a concrete floor. *Thwap, thwap, thwap.* Steele got up to his knees, turreted the pistol toward the bodyguard bleeding all over the wall, and put him out of his misery.

Steele switched the Five-seven into his left hand and jerked one of the mini frags from his pocket. The grenade was smaller than a racquetball, and he had straightened the pin beforehand for just this reason. He looped the ring over his left thumb and yanked it. The spring pinged the spoon free, arming the fragmentation grenade, and Steele bolted to the stairs in a crouch.

One thousand, two thousand, three thousand.

He saw his reflection in the mirror. Beneath the macabre mask made of glistening blood, his green eyes burned with the fire of impending violence. He could see five men in the center of the room and used the glass to bounce the mini frag into their midst.

Four thousand . . .

The frag exploded, and Steele came around the corner low, pistol up and firing.

The mini grenade had gone off under the table, filling the cube with smoke and the screams of the wounded. Steele worked from left to right, icepicking the full metal jackets through the bodyguard's soft armor with the kinetic energy of a rocket ship. The first shots were low, on purpose, and he snapped two rounds into one of his targets' pelvises, letting the muzzle rise carry the barrel up, while he pivoted to the right.

He gave Ronna a single shot to the eye, double-tapped a bodyguard whose shin had been blown open, and then settled on Burrows.

"Should have stayed away," he said with a shrug, and then he blew the man's brains against the back wall.

Bullets cracked over the VIP box and Steele dumped the Five-seven and yanked the MP9 out. He climbed up on one of the smoldering couches and ripped a burst into the shooters. He saw Felix rushing down the walkway, a shotgun in his hands. He aimed at his belt and stitched five rounds up to his neck.

The club was in chaos, the music mixing with the screams of dancers and drunken businessmen. Steele was careful with his shots, avoiding collateral damage like the plague. He only fired when he had a target, and after working through the magazine, he stepped down from the couch and pulled the CS gas out of his jacket. He surveyed the damage, and once he was sure that everyone he had come to kill was dead, he rammed a fresh magazine into the MP9 and calmly walked down the steps.

He ripped the pin from the canister and tossed it into the club, fixed his jacket, and headed for the emergency exit. Before the tear gas filled the Dragon's Door, Eric Steele pushed the door open and stepped into the alley.

A late-model sedan skidded to a halt where the alley opened up to the street. Steele jogged over, saw Demo lean across the seat and pop the door as he approached. Steele hazarded a final look behind him and hopped into the vehicle.

"Let's get the hell out of here."

"Best news I've heard all day, mano," Demo said, nodding to the red and blue lights screaming up the street behind them.

Chapter 7

Algiers

Meg Harden saw the kick coming, but wasn't fast enough to get out of the way. It landed with a snap, causing her thigh to go numb. She raised her gloves, wiping the sweat from her eyes in preparation for the onslaught to follow, but nothing happened.

"C'mon," her sparring partner taunted with a cocky little wave.

Meg's face got hot and it had nothing to do with the pain.

Her sparring partner went by James or Jack—she couldn't remember. The CIA Special Operations guys were all the same. Cocky ex–Special Forces who just wanted to fuck her.

At five foot five, Meg was a stunner. She had shoulder-length black hair, which she always wore in a ponytail, a perfectly upturned nose, and dimples that usually made her male coworkers forget how to talk.

Meg didn't mind the cockiness, or the fact that James kept staring at her tits. What pissed her off was that he was going easy on her.

She found that *extremely* disrespectful, and when he sent another halfhearted leg kick her way, Meg made him pay for it.

She shot in like a snake, left arm down, to block the strike. She hit him in the stomach, as hard as she could. The blow knocked the breath out of him, but she wasn't finished. Once her left foot was set, Meg scythed her right heel back and into James's calf. It hit like a hammer and sent him tumbling on his ass.

Oooomph.

Meg easily achieved the mount and dropped a few punches on his face before letting him up. James used his thumb to wipe the blood from his nose and raised his gloves. Meg circled to the left, and he closed the distance a few times, but it was obvious his heart wasn't in it.

If I were a man he'd be trying to beat my ass.

They sparred for another ten minutes, but the playful flirting was over, and now that sex was off the table, James just wanted to get on with his day. Meg knew she was intense, and while she expected to be treated like one of the guys, it always turned out the same way. Once a man lost his self-confidence, his interest in her quickly followed.

Meg left the gym, her flip-flops smacking against her feet, but slowed before entering the living quarters. Most of the people who lived adjacent to her worked nights and Meg didn't want to wake them up. She pinned the offending soles to the bottom of her feet by curling her toes and taking smaller steps.

It made her feel like she was sneaking into her parents' house, which brought a smile to her face.

She unlocked the door with the key that hung around her neck and stepped inside. The room was small and obsessively tidy. Along the far wall her bed was tightly made, and the only things on the desk were a laptop and a small lamp. The walls were bare and the same neutral brown as the hotel-size chest of drawers.

She tossed her towel on the bed and booted up the laptop before heading toward the bathroom. Before she crossed the threshold she felt something nagging at her. Meg stopped, her pretty face framed in the mirror.

"Just leave it," she told herself.

Being a neat freak was a daily struggle. In college her roommates would stage little messes, then run off and hide. It didn't matter if she was late for class or a date, Meg fell for it every time. And just as soon as she threw up her hands and started to clean up the mess, there would be a chorus of muffled laughter behind her.

The Army had just made it worse.

Meg had spent ten years in the Army and loved every minute of it. But the second time she was passed over for major, she didn't need anyone to spell it out for her.

She was done.

Just turn on the shower, Meg Harden.

She turned on the water and held her hand up to test the temperature. Once satisfied, she pulled the curtain closed and tugged her shirt over her head. She tossed it into the plastic hamper, before moving back to the mirror and eyeing the towel again. She absently rubbed her palm over the leg of her workout pants in an attempt to dry her hands.

Her face wrinkled into an *O*, revealing a dimple on her right cheek.

"Owwww."

Meg tugged her pants down around her ankles and heeled them back into the room. Taking a step back, she pointed her big toe, bringing her leg into view. The skin around her shapely thigh was red and angry, and a wine-colored bruise had begun to form. She gingerly fingertipped the puffy skin, all thoughts of the towel momentarily forgotten.

"Son of a bitch."

Standing in front of the mirror in her bra and panties, Meg was reminded for the hundredth time that being a woman in a male-dominated world was not for the faint of heart. It was lonely and something her mother and sisters still didn't understand.

"Don't you want babies?" they'd asked the last time she went home to Pittsburgh.

"You obviously haven't seen the men in the Army," she'd replied.

When deployed, it was easy for a girl to forget what it meant to be a woman. In Iraq she had a group of girlfriends who loved the fact that being deployed meant no makeup and an easy hair day, but that wasn't Meg. Sure, she skimped on makeup sometimes and liked to keep her hair up in a ponytail, but that was before she met Colt Weller.

The thought of the SOG officer made Meg aware that she hadn't shaved her legs in three days. She took the razor from the shower caddy and set about remedying the problem before washing her hair and turning off the water. She stepped out of the shower, toweled off, and dressed quickly in a gray bra, a black tank top, and a worn-in pair of Mountain Hardware pants. She typed her password into the laptop, which unlocked with a ding. Meg pressed her thumb to the biometric reader then toweled her damp hair while waiting for the server to connect to the encrypted CIA interweb.

An hourglass spun lazily on the screen, telling her that the computer was uplinking with one of the Agency's satellites. Before it could connect there was a sharp rap at the door.

"Yeah?" Meg asked.

"It's me."

Shit.

Meg had turned her head toward the door at the sound of the knock, but froze when she recognized Colt's voice. She saw her reflection in the bathroom mirror and it made her want to crawl under the bed and hide. Her cheeks were flushed below wet, formless hair. She saw the makeup bag sitting alone on the counter.

"H-hold on. I just got out of the shower," she replied, tiptoeing quickly toward the makeup bag.

"I need you to hurry it up. We have a mission."

Meg stopped in midstride, instantly forgetting about the makeup. She turned to the door and unlocked it with a twist of the knob.

"I um, I . . . Hey," she said, opening the door.

"I wasn't interrupting anything, was I?" Colt asked, making a show of looking around the room.

"What . . . no?" Meg quickly got hold of herself and

tried to play it off. "Don't tell me, someone crashed another iPad."

"No idea," Colt replied, stepping in the doorway but not entering her room. "You sure keep it clean in here."

"Thanks," Meg replied, grabbing a pair of socks.

"You know, I *should* be upstairs at the briefing, but for some reason when I told James to come and get you he suddenly had something really important to do. You know anything about that?"

Meg smiled innocently and finished tugging the final sock on. "Why would I know anything about that?" she asked, retrieving a pair of hiking boots from beneath the bed.

"Some of the guys said he's been macking on this little brunette who works in operations."

"What, are you jealous?"

Oh my God, why did I say that?

As the SOG, or Special Operations Group, team leader, Colt was one of the few men who knew what Meg really did for the CIA. He'd been around the block a few times, and with multiple tours in Iraq, Syria, and Afghanistan, he had a disarming manner that Meg found sexy. It didn't hurt that he was good-looking and believed she was an asset for the Algiers station.

The only problem was that he treated Meg like she was his little sister.

"Why would I be jealous?" he asked with a confused look that annoyed the hell out of Meg.

"It was a joke," she said, getting to her feet and heading to her wall locker. *Can I make a bigger fool of myself?*

She was excited to leave the wire. Since she was the only woman at the Algiers station, the station chief was loath to let her leave the compound. In fact, the only reason she had combat gear was because she had gone down to supply and scrounged it up herself.

She opened the locker and was reaching for the Glock 17 sitting on the top shelf when the wall started to vibrate. It was followed a moment later by a faint *cruuuump* that came from the north. The sound was as familiar as the smell of gun oil coming from the holstered Glock.

It was a mortar.

Meg grabbed the pistol, clipped it to her belt, and turned just as three more detonations erupted. Colt didn't flinch. He stood in the doorway looking up at the ceiling with a furrowed brow, index finger held to his lips.

"You hear that?"

"Kind of hard to miss four mortar rounds."

"No, listen."

Meg didn't hear anything at first, but then she made out a faint crackling in the distance. It was tentative, like the fireworks her brother used to shoot off before the big Fourth of July show, and just as distinctive.

"Those are AK-47s, and lots of them," she said.

"We should go," Colt replied. "Right now."

Chapter 8

Tyre, Lebanon

Steele and Demo split up outside Beirut and Eric took the coastal highway toward Tyre. He stopped twice to switch cars. Twenty miles north of his destination, he donned a pair of night vision goggles. He cut the lights and bounced the SUV off the road. Under NODs the desert looked green and flat, the amplified light killing his depth perception. Far to the east he could see the hint of dawn.

Soon the sky would turn pink and blue as the sun slipped over the Mediterranean, and if he didn't get to the landing zone soon he was going to have to remain overnight.

The GPS strapped to his wrist beeped and Steele hit the brakes and cut the engine. He grabbed his gear and stepped out of the Isuzu Rodeo before turning the radio on.

"Eagle, this is Stalker 7, how do you read?"

There was a moment of silence then a voice that sounded like it was coming from a tin can came up on the net.

"Stalker 7, this is Eagle, I read you five by five."

"Good copy, Eagle, I am activating my beacon now."

Steele flipped a switch on the radio, which activated the search and rescue that would give his location to the pilot.

"I've got you, Stalker 7, we are inbound at 98 degrees ETA zero five mikes, how copy?"

"Stalker copies."

Steele carried the radio with him to the back of the SUV. He popped the hatch and leaned in to arm the charge he had taped to the five-gallon can of gas. The wireless detonator beeped in his hand, telling him that it had a signal. Steele closed the lift gate and headed back to his pack, the growl in his stomach reminding him that he hadn't eaten in almost seven hours.

He was eating an apple when he caught sight of the MH-60 Pave Hawk coming low and fast over the water. He took a final bite of the apple before throwing it away. The special operations bird was almost on top of him and he stole a quick glance.

The pilot yanked the stick back and the bird rocked onto its tail. The engine screamed and the blades beat at the air, loading the tips with static electricity. Eric saw them turn yellow through his night vision and then ducked his head. A wall of sand, hot air, and dirt hit him in the chest, almost blowing him over, and he waited until the bird touched down before grabbing his pack and jumping to his feet.

The crew chief waited for him at the troop door. Eric noticed the double take when he saw what Steele was wearing.

"What? A guy can't get dressed up for an op anymore?"

The crew chief shook his head and Steele hopped inside, followed by the crewman, who was about to slam the door when Steele shook his head no and held up the detonator.

The bird jumped skyward and Steele's stomach rolled as the pilot banked the bird toward the sea. "Tell the pilot I've got to blow the car," he yelled, leaning in close to the crew chief's ear.

The crew chief nodded and pushed the transmit button on the internal radio. When he was given the thumbs-up, Steele leaned out the door and pressed the button on the detonator.

The explosion glinted orange, small at first, but it quickly grew into a towering pillar.

Not a bad day's work, Steele thought.

He nodded to the crew chief and walked over to the nylon bench. He pulled a pair of headphones from the hook above him and shoved them over his ears. The pilot was transmitting over the encrypted high-frequency net.

"Eagle to Cutlass," he said, using the Program's operations center call sign. "We have the package and are feet wet." Steele's eyes closed, and he let the vibration of the helo rock him to sleep.

He felt someone shaking him awake. The pitch of the blades told him that the helo was descending. His eyes flashed open and he saw the crew chief standing a few inches away. He checked the GPS on his wrist; instead of landing in Cyprus, it appeared that the helo was setting down in the middle of the ocean.

Something's wrong.

"Sir, a tasking just came over the satcom."

"Where are we?"

"Landing on the *Wasp*."

The USS *Wasp*, known in the Navy as LHD-1, was a multipurpose amphibian assault ship, basically a carrier for helicopters. Steele knew that the only reason they were landing on the deck as opposed to the base in Cyprus was because he was about to be redeployed.

The Pave Hawk touched down on the deck and when he stepped out the first thing he noticed was a Cobra attack helicopter spinning up next to a V-22 Osprey. The Osprey's massive tilt rotors were pointed skyward and dwarfed the squad of men checking over their gear near the ramp. At first glance, Steele thought they were Marine Raiders, but realized his error as he got a better look at the master chief who came hustling toward him.

Steele had mistaken the Marine camo pattern for the new AOR, or Area of Responsibility, pattern worn by the SEALs.

"Sir, if you could follow me," the master chief yelled over the whining engines. Steele fell in line behind him, dodging the aircrew that rushed out to refuel the Pave Hawk

"What's going on, Chief?" Steele demanded once they were inside.

"No idea, CENTCOM sent a flash telling the captain to expect a package, and to have a strike team ready and waiting. I assume they were talking about you."

"Don't look at me, Chief. I was asleep a minute ago."

The bridge was a hive of activity. Sailors were busy overseeing the Pave Low's refueling, while the air officer worked to clear the deck. Near a door with the word SCIF stenciled on it, a thin, weather-beaten man in a ball cap watched the proceedings with a stained coffee cup in his hands. Steele didn't need an introduction to know he was the captain; the man's silent command presence was all he needed to see.

The Sensitive Compartmented Information Facility, pronounced "skiff," was the most secure place on the ship. It was where the most classified information was held.

"Not every day I get a call from Italy telling me to stop what I'm doing and prepare for a visitor," the captain said with a warm smile. "Nice threads. Want some coffee?"

Steele knew the skipper was referring to Naval Support Activity Naples, where both the United States Naval Forces Europe, or NAVEUR, and Sixth Fleet were headquartered. The Sixth Fleet patrolled the Mediterranean Sea as well as Africa.

"Been a long night, Skipper," Steele replied.

"I can imagine," the captain said, gesturing for Steele to follow him into the SCIF. Inside there was a table with maps and overlays and a commander dressed identically to his master chief.

A sailor appeared with a mug of coffee and Steele didn't even have time to take a sip before the commander was handing him a red phone.

"Code in," a robotic voice said as soon as he pressed it to his ear. Steele rattled off his identification code and the line beeped and clicked as the crypto decoded his voice and secured the line.

"Stalker 7, this is Cutlass Main, we have a problem."

"Yeah, I gathered that much."

Cutlass Main was the Program's call sign at the White House, which meant that whatever was going down had just happened and that President Cole was personally activating an Alpha.

"We have lost a level one."

Oh shit.

A level one asset was the highest-value classification the Program had, and Steele knew that right now there were only three on the board. Two were in Europe, which was out of his area of operation. That left one.

"Breul," Steele said.

There was silence.

"He is supposed to be in Iran, what the hell happened?" he asked, making no attempt to hide the anger in his voice. Ali Breul was *his* asset, but more than that, he was his friend.

"The only thing we know is that the CIA called a meeting first thing this morning."

"Wait, what? How the hell does the CIA know about Breul?"

"We don't have *any* answers, Stalker 7."

"So what's the play?"

"We are activating you for this mission, and you have full authority. Get him back."

Steele hung up the phone, dropped his assault pack on the floor, and ripped open the main compartment. He took out a ruggedized GPS about the size of a paperback book and walked over to one of the computer terminals. "Is this thing hooked to the satcom?"

"Yeah." The commander nodded.

Steele plugged it in, typed in his password, and waited for the computer to link with the satellite. A map came up and he typed a string of numbers into the search bar and hit enter.

"What exactly are you looking for?"

"You know what a data pin is?" Steele asked.

"Hell no."

"It's like a tracker, and we have hundreds of them in the field. Each one has an address, what we call a pin code, and when you type it in"—Steele hit the enter key with a flourish and an hourglass popped up on the screen—"the satellite finds it for you. We use the tablets in the field, but they are slow and need a clear view of the sky to lock on to a satellite."

"So you put them in cars and stuff? Important things you want to track."

"No . . ." He paused when a blinking dot appeared on a map identifying the pin's location. "We put them in things we don't want to lose," Steele said softly, like he was speaking to himself.

That can't be right.

The data pin in question was assigned to Ali Breul, an Iranian scientist and in Steele's mind the most important asset the United States had in its inventory. He had checked on Breul two days ago and the scientist was where he was supposed to be—in Tehran waiting for him. There was absolutely no reason for him to be in Tunis.

Steele turned to the commander. "We are wheels up in ten. I need some clothes and a weapon."

Inside the Osprey, Steele plugged into the commo jack and turned to the pilot, who was staring back from the cockpit.

"You have the grid?"

"Roger that, you guys ready?"

Steele nodded and took his seat next to the commander before addressing the heavily armed operators watching him from the nylon bench.

"This is going to be a down-and-dirty smash and grab," he began. "We have a compromised asset in Tunisia. We go in hard, and if you guys do what I say when I say it, I'll have you back on the ship in time for chow. Any questions?"

The commander had one: "What's the ROE?"

As members of JSOC, or Joint Special Operations Command, the SEALs were used to working in the shadows, but not like him. Alphas were trusted to figure it out on the ground, and when a unit was assigned to them, it became his call.

"Weapons free," Steele called over the net. He was in charge of the operation now and wanted everyone, especially the Cobra gunship, to know that they were going in hot.

Chapter 9

Washington, D.C.

Vice President John Rockford was a big man with wide shoulders and blond hair worn long over his ears. In his hands the baseball looked tiny. It was a beautiful morning and he didn't want to spend it inside.

"You ready for this?" he asked, slamming the ball into the mitt so hard it sounded like a rifle shot. "Here it comes."

He turned and was about to let the ball fly, but his catcher wasn't paying attention.

"Emma, what are you doing?"

"A butterfly, Daddy," his six-year-old daughter said, forgetting the glove at her feet.

"Emma, I thought you wanted to play baseball."

"It's a big one," she said with a smile that melted his heart.

Rockford shook his head and looked at his wife, who was grinning at him.

"See what you did?" he accused.

"Rock, she's a little girl," Lisa Rockford said.

"Sir," a female voice said behind him.

Rockford turned to see the President's secretary. Allison was a little young to have her job, with mousy brown hair and thin glasses. But despite her age she had proven herself more than capable. Usually implacable, Rockford noticed something in her face and nervously waited for what he knew was coming next.

"The ambassador from Brazil is on the phone."

It was a code he and President Denton Cole had come up with, to be used when their families were present. Rockford tried to keep the smile from melting away. He didn't want to worry Lisa, and tried to play it off.

"Probably wants to talk about the price of bananas or something."

He bent to give his wife a peck on the cheek and could tell immediately that he wasn't fooling her. The sudden tension around her eyes reminded him that he wasn't the only one affected by his job.

He walked across the garden and ducked into the Oval Office. Allison was waiting there with a black folder.

"What is it?" he asked.

"Director Styles has called an emergency security brief," she said, handing him the folder. "I know it is last-minute, but I can't get hold of the President."

"It's fine, Allison," Rockford said. "I can take the meeting for him."

She nodded. "Thank you, sir, they are waiting for you *now*."

Rockford skimmed the folder on his way to the Situation Room. The workup was short, so short that he was able to stop outside the door and read through the entire packet.

Why would Styles call a presidential briefing if this is all she has? he wondered.

From the hall it was just another nondescript oak-paneled door, but inside was the most secure space in the U.S. government. Rockford took a breath and entered. He could feel the weight of the room as soon as he stepped inside.

The group seated around the walnut table represented every branch of the intelligence community and were the most powerful men in the country. He scanned the faces, wondering what each of them knew, or what part they had played in the string of events that had brought him here.

"Keep your seats," he said with a wave. He sat down

and everyone turned back to the large monitor fixed to the far wall. Rockford knew from experience that the feed was from a Reaper drone. It was a newer UAV, or unmanned aerial vehicle, and had a better camera than did the older Predators.

"Where's the boss?" William Harris, the Director of the National Security Agency, asked.

"En route," Rockford lied before addressing the table. "What do we have today?" There was no time for the usual banter. It was time to get down to business.

Rockford's gaze settled on Director Styles, who observed him with the detached coolness of an ice sculpture. The Director had her blond hair pulled up in a French twist, which framed her high cheekbones and piercing blue eyes. Around her neck she wore a simple string of pearls that contrasted perfectly with an ink-black dress.

Rockford had to admit that she was a striking woman, but the way she looked at him, almost like he was beneath her, was something that grated on his nerves.

Before becoming the second most powerful man in the United States, John Rockford had been a captain in the first Gulf War. During the battle of Wadi Al-Batin, he was wounded while dragging one of his soldiers from a burning Bradley Fighting Vehicle. He received the Distinguished Service Cross and a trip to Walter Reed for his trouble and was given a medical discharge. The CIA came knocking soon after, and by the end of his time at Langley, he had become the Director. So he knew all too well the pressure Robin's job carried, which was why he went out of his way to treat her with respect.

The stress that came with being the Director of the CIA was impossible to convey to anyone who hadn't held the title, but you wouldn't know it from looking at Robin. She managed to appear aloof even in times of chaos.

Rockford had shared his observation with his wife, who'd said, "I think you are reading too much into this, John. She is probably intimidated."

"Intimidated by what?"

"Rock, you guys have your little boys' club and as the only woman she probably feels left out."

Rockford had never thought of it before, but he took his wife's counsel to heart. As the VP, it was his job to make sure everything ran smoothly when President Cole was away—a task he accomplished with ease, because Rockford was at heart a natural conciliator. But it seemed that no matter how hard he tried, he found he couldn't break through the latent hostility that existed between himself and the Director of the CIA.

"So," he began, turning his full attention to Styles, "you have the floor."

"I was *expecting* President Cole," she began, her southern accent thick and smooth as unfired molasses.

"Like I said, President Cole is out of pocket."

Rockford wasn't sure what else to say. Unlike the rest of the people in the room, he wasn't a fan of the spotlight, and had told the President as much when he asked Rockford to be his running mate. "Sir, no offense, but I am just starting to enjoy the retired life," he'd said. "I don't think I'm the guy you are looking for." But Cole had chosen him anyway.

More than anything, Rockford wanted to be back in the shadows. The sudden increase in high-level briefings, and the fact that he was the only person in the room who knew the *real* reason why the President wasn't here, made him uncomfortable.

Two months ago, he and his wife were invited to a private dinner at the Executive Residence. It wasn't the invite that surprised him, because the two families were close. In fact, President Cole was his daughter's godfather, but the news he laid on him over brandy and cigars still festered in his mind.

The President of the United States was sick.

"So what do you say we start the briefing?"

"Very well, I called the briefing because of Tunisia," Styles replied, the ice in her eyes evaporating in an instant.

It wasn't the shift in attitude that threw Rockford off balance, it was the feeling that Director Styles had been sizing him up and had come to the conclusion that he wasn't worth her time.

Tunisia? What is the CIA doing in Tunisia?

Rockford looked again to Harris to make sure he wasn't losing his mind. "Director Harris, does the United States have an *active* mission in Tunisia that I am not aware of?"

"No sir, *we* don't, but apparently the CIA does," Harris said, looking at Styles. "Robin lost a team this morning."

"Where in Tunisia?"

"South of Tunis," Styles said. "It was a routine asset pickup. My team was murdered during extraction. At the moment we don't know who the players are, but—"

Styles stopped speaking when the door to the Situation Room opened and Allison stepped in holding a sheet of paper tight to her body.

"Sir, I apologize for interrupting, but I need to speak with you, *now.*"

"Excuse me," Rockford said, getting to his feet.

He moved around the table, Allison stepping out of the room as he approached. One look at her face was all it took for him to know something was wrong.

"Is the President okay?" he asked, stepping into the hall and lowering his voice.

Allison offered him the plain eight-and-a-half-by-eleven sheet of printer paper, and as soon as Rockford read the words "Alpha Flash," a sense of dread washed over him.

"I still can't get him on the phone," she said, a tremor at the corner of her eyes.

"It's fine, I will handle it," Rockford lied. It definitely *wasn't* fine.

Rockford didn't have a problem sitting in on meetings, but an Alpha Flash was a totally different ball game. *Of all the times for Cole to be out of pocket.*

An Alpha Flash was an "eyes only" statement to the President, and when they sent one to the White House it meant that in some dark corner of the world, something had gone terribly wrong.

Rockford took the paper, feeling like a second-string quarterback who had just learned he was going to be starting in the Super Bowl.

EYES ONLY

SAP (Alpha FLASH)
From: Alpha Ops North Africa
To: Cutlass Main
Subj: PRIORITY ASSET

OGA convoy traveling from AO Algiers to AO Tunis
was ambushed on yesterday's date along route
India. Preliminary battle damage assessment has
6 American Nationals KIA.

Priority Asset Breul, Ali, and one OGA **MIA**

Alpha response—URGENT.

"When did this come in?" It was the only question he could think to ask as his eyes lingered over the subject line of the paper.

"Just now," Allison replied.

"OGA convoy traveling from Algiers to Tunis, this is . . ." Rockford trailed off, not believing the words typed on the paper. "Has this been verified?"

"Yes, sir. Twice. Cutlass Main already has Stalker 7 activated and standing by."

Rockford's disbelief came from the fact that "OGA," or "Other Government Agency," was an acronym that referred to the CIA or one of its subordinate units like SOG. Rockford was an avid poker player, known for his ability to quickly calculate the odds of a winning hand. He tried to calculate the odds of a CIA team and a Program asset being ambushed in the same country on the same day. He quickly came up with the answer.

Zero.

The Vice President turned to look back into the Situation Room and found Styles observing him coolly.

He forced himself to smile and held up one finger before turning to Allison.

"Looks like this meeting is about to get cut short."

Chapter 10

Tunis

The scratching sound of the razor blades put Nathaniel West's teeth on edge. It reminded him of the basement in Argentina. He still wasn't sure how long he'd spent in the darkness. *Two weeks? Three? Sitting there with bandages over my eyes while those fucking rats tried to chew through my boots.*

He took a cigarette from his ear and stuck it between his lips. *How long does it take to get some paint off a damn window?* he wondered, looking at the two men scraping at the black paint.

He dragged the match across the striker on the outside of the box, and the flame blossomed, revealing fingers mottled with scar tissue. When he bent his neck, dropping the tip of the cigarette to the flame, the scars only got worse.

The abandoned building didn't have power, and vagrants had used the bottom floor as a communal restroom. The entire bottom half of the building smelled like piss and shit. That was why they were upstairs.

West smoked idly, watching the sunlight progress across the concrete floor. By the time he put the cigarette out beneath his boot, his men were done, and what had started out so very dim was now a spotlight that revealed two men in the center of the room.

The "package" had a black bag over his head, but was otherwise unrestrained. West knew he wasn't going anywhere the second he yanked him out of the Suburban and saw that he had pissed himself. The other man was a different story. He was a CIA contractor, and the team leader of a seven-man security detail that was supposed to transport the package from Algiers to Tunis. He was in way over his head, but just to be sure, West had him zip-tied to the chair. At first he'd planned on laying him out with the other six he had left on the edge of the highway with a hollow point through the eyeball.

Waste not, want not.

"What frequencies are you using?" the South African demanded, squinting against the beam of sunlight coming through the window while yelling at the man with the hood over his head. It acted like a spotlight, and caused the blood-splattered cricket bat he held in his hands to shimmer.

"I already told you."

West didn't blame the guy for talking, even though it had cost him a thousand bucks. Villars had bet him that he could get the guy talking in less than ten minutes. Once the bat came out the contractor would have told West what color panties his wife wore if it made the pain stop.

Villars hit him anyway, swinging at the man's shins like he was trying to send one deep over the wall at Fenway.

CRAAAK.

Good form, West thought. *Most guys are all arms, but he really gets his hips into it.*

"This guy's done, take a break, big man," he said. "Give me the cards, we have shit to do." He stripped the hood off the other man's head. "Hey, Ali Breul, long time no see."

The Iranian scientist blinked in the sudden light, and when his eyes adjusted a look of horror crept across his face. A stain appeared on his leg, followed by the smell of urine. West shuffled the cards in his hands, a twisted smile curling at the edge of his lips.

"Glad to see you remember me, buddy."

"But . . . but you're dead."

"That's what they tell me. Obviously the details of my demise have been greatly exaggerated," West taunted. "Unfortunately we don't have enough time to play catch-up, but I want to ask you something." He stepped out of the way, making room for his men to set a crate between them. "You ever play three-card monte?" he asked, switching to Arabic.

"No."

"Seriously, never?"

The man nodded. He was sweating and afraid. "Nathaniel, why are you doing this?"

"Because it's a cool game."

He knew what Breul was talking about, but didn't care. The scientist was vapor-locked, and having a hard time focusing. He kept looking toward the CIA officer tied up next to him.

"Hey." West snapped his fingers at him. "You have to pay attention if you want to win." He fanned the cards in his hands, picking out three that he wanted. "I learned the secret in Spain from a guy on the corner. Just another hustler. He called it *Encontrar la Cabrona*—find the bitch. That guy took me to the cleaners, I think he took me for a grand, but it was worth it. You know why?"

"I don't want to do this."

West ignored him.

"Because I learned something. It's what you don't see that gets you."

"Don't listen to him, Breul," the contractor said.

Thump.

West could tell it was a body shot without even having to look up. Punching someone in the body sounded different from hitting them in the face. West looked over his shoulder. The contractor's mouth was stretched in a silent scream, but he wasn't making any noise because all the air had just been knocked from his lungs.

"Like I was saying, all you have to do is find the queen. Now, usually you use a traditional deck, but that's boring. So I had one made up. Here's what you are looking for, the queen of hearts." West flipped over the first card. It had a picture of a naked woman with a big heart tattoo on her chest. It had obviously been cut out of a porno mag. "You find this one and I let you go. Pretty easy." The second one he flipped over had a picture of the contractor on it, taken from a telephoto lens. "Now, here's where it gets real. If you pick this one, he dies," West said, jerking his thumb over his shoulder.

"Don't tell him shit, Breul."

"Villars."

It was a backhand this time. A sharp pop to the face followed by a grunt of pain.

"I wouldn't listen to him if I were you. I know the CIA said they were going to keep your family safe, but guess what?" West asked, flipping over the final card.

There was a picture of a woman in a hospital with a newborn cradled in her arms, and it got Breul's attention. Pure terror crossed the Iranian's face.

"Surprise, it's a boy," West said. His whole demeanor changed in an instant. "Sorry you had to find out this way, but I want you to know that the CIA can't protect them. Not from me."

"Please, don't . . . don't hurt them."

"We are in this together, man. I believe in you, all you have to do is find the bitch."

West started out slow, hopping the queen over the card to the left, bouncing the three cards back and forth five or six times. Then he stopped and looked up.

"Where is she?"

"In . . . in the middle."

West flipped it over, revealing the queen.

"See, I told you."

Breul blew out a long breath, a look of relief.

"Don't get excited just yet. That one doesn't count,

because I was just showing you how it worked. Here we go, best two out of three."

He moved faster this time, scarred hands blurring over the box, cards jumping back and forth and Breul trying to keep up. Then he stopped.

"Find the bitch."

"I didn't see. It was too fast."

"You have to pick one."

"I don't know."

"Villars . . ."

"Wait, the one on the right."

West held up his hand and heard the South African stop behind him. He flipped the card over, revealing the picture he'd taken of the contractor.

"Nope."

He pivoted, watching as Villars produced a thick plastic bag. He shook it open and then yanked it over the contractor's head.

"His name was Jackson, father of two, married to his high school sweetheart, Janice."

Jackson tried to hold his breath while fighting against the zip ties. He banged his legs while trying to shake himself free. Behind him, Villars held the bag tight over his face. Finally the contractor's brain told him that he was running out of air and his mouth snapped, sucking the plastic tight against his lips.

"What do you want?" Breul asked.

"You know what I want," West said, hands back on the cards.

"I'll tell you anything."

"I know you will. You want to know why I love this game? It's like life. You think you are paying attention," he said, holding up his index finger like a scarred exclamation point, "but what no one tells you is that the house always wins."

Breul was weeping now, and West knew he almost had him. Just a final push to get what he wanted. He rose to his feet. "I know what you're thinking, old friend." West pointed to his arm and winked. "Eric is going to find me. Problem with those data pins is that they still work on the same frequency they did when I was an Alpha." He pulled a device the size of a calculator from his pocket and held it in front of Breul's face. "You would think they would change something like that, but oh well. It does make me wonder what would happen if I pushed this button." He pressed the key with his thumb. The device beeped twice and a message flashed on the screen.

"Jamming signal," he read. "Well, that's not good."

He saw that Breul understood what he was talking about, and a second later the Iranian began to talk.

"I left the device in . . ." he sobbed.

"You're almost there," West prodded.

Breul paused. His eyes shot to the card with his wife holding the child he had never seen and then he clenched his jaw and shook his head from side to side.

"You really want to do this?" West asked.

A tear fell from the corner of Breul's eye, sliding off his cheek when he shook his head.

"Go to hell," he hissed.

"Fine with me." West got to his feet. "I tried to do this the easy way," he said, glancing around the room. He spied a rusted toolbox left by the previous inhabitants and walked over. He flipped the toolbox lid open with the toe of his boot and bent down. "Hey, looky here," he said, grabbing a five-pound hammer and holding it aloft.

"You know what a weltanschauung is?" West asked, glancing to Villars as he walked back to Breul. "Am I saying that right?"

"No idea, boss." The man shrugged.

"Doesn't matter," West said with a wave of the hammer. "It's a personal philosophy." He knelt in front of Breul and placed his hand lightly on the man's thigh.

"So I'm lying on my back, face all burned to shit, and I start thinking about how I lived a good life and did all the right things, and it hits me. That stuff is all a bunch of bullshit. I realized something in that moment." The muscles in West's hand flexed, fingers clamping down on Breul's thigh.

"Please," the Iranian begged, trying to move his leg to no avail.

West continued talking, raising the hammer to shoulder level, where he let it pause.

"I realized that good guys always lose."

West punctuated the statement by swinging the hammer down on the top of Breul's foot, which crunched beneath the impact. The Iranian went rigid, his arms tensing against the flex cuffs holding him to the chair, a feral scream pouring out of his stretched mouth.

"We can play 'this little piggy' all day long, Breul," West yelled, hammering Breul's foot a second time, and then a third, "or you can tell me where you put *my* fucking nuke."

"Algiers," the Iranian screamed, tears running down his face.

West got to his feet. "All of that could have been avoided," he said, smirking at Breul's mangled foot. "But nooooo, Ali Breul had to be a tough guy. You and Steele deserve each other, you know that? Put ol' club-foot in the truck," he said, pointing to one of his men.

"Let's go start a war," West said to Villars on his way out the door.

Chapter 11

I nside the Osprey, Eric Steele watched the dot begin to move as the pilot cut the throttle and pushed the nose down. They were coming in hot, nap-of-the-earth, which gave the lumbering twin-engine aircraft a smaller profile.

Steele was about to let the pilot know the target location when the screen went blank, followed by the words "signal failure."

What the hell?

Breul was moving, but without the link to the pin, Steele had no idea where to tell the pilot to go. They were blind. Steele knew the manual better than the engineers who'd written it and feverishly began troubleshooting the device. He ran through the most likely problems, switching out the batteries, checking the antenna connection, and restarting the device. Still nothing.

Think, man. You have to do something.

His heart pounded in his chest. The SEALs were ready to go and he could see the coast through the cockpit. He slipped his knife out of his left pocket, flicking the blade open with his thumb. Using the tip of the knife, he pried the back plate off the unit, revealing a bird's nest of wires.

One chance.

He ignored the doubt. There was only one solution; something was jamming the satellite signal. Assuming the pin was still online, Steele was going to circumnavigate the problem. He pried one of the wires free, envisioning the wiring diagram in his head. Yellow was satellite, and he severed it from the motherboard and carefully stripped the sheath, exposing the wire's core.

"Commo cord," he said, looking at the SEAL with the radio on his back. The man nodded and rummaged in a pouch on his gear. A second later he had a two-foot section of coax cable, what radiomen called a pigtail.

Steele cut the end of the pigtail, exposing the wire inside. He deftly twisted the two exposed wires together, then connected the other end to the radio attached to his plate carrier. The radio beeped when he unlocked the face and dialed the frequency to 1003 MHz, which was the frequency assigned to Ali Breul's data pin.

Steele closed his eyes and offered a silent prayer to whoever was listening, then got to his feet. He paused at the door, thumbing the GPS's menu button until a digital compass appeared on the screen.

"No whammies, no whammies," he muttered to himself.

In theory, without a satellite connection, the modified GPS would lock on to the only signal in the city operating off of 1003 Mhz. It would think that was north, and if he was right, the compass heading would lead him right to Ali Breul's data pin.

Where are you, buddy?

The compass's index line bounced back and forth while Steele held his breath. He knew the pilots were going to start bitching about fuel soon, and while he waited for the makeshift compass to lock down, he could feel the seconds ticking away.

Please work.

He slipped a miniature spotting scope from his pack and moved to the door, and when the compass locked down, he was ready. At a hundred feet above the ocean, the city of Ben Gardane looked like a pencil smudge on the horizon. He held down on the autofocus button, and when it zoomed in he saw three Hilux trucks running north along a road. The spotting scope was equipped with a range finder, and Steele depressed the button with his index finger. He held the reticle steady on the center vehicle, the one with the hooded man in the backseat, and a second later the infrared laser bounced back, displaying the heading in red numbers at the bottom of the optic.

He yanked the pigtail from the radio and flipped the frequency back to the internal net that allowed him to communicate with the pilot and the SEALs.

"One hundred eighty-two degrees. Three trucks moving north, target is in the rear of the second Hilux."

The pilot responded by pushing the throttle forward, and Steele braced himself against the bulkhead to keep from falling out. Behind him one of the crewmen lifted a braided fast rope from a bag attached to the floor. Steele stuffed the GPS in his pocket, aware of the crewman fastening the rope to its mounting bracket.

Steele dumped the range finder into his assault pack, retrieved a pair of thick gloves from the same pocket, and zipped it up before putting them on. The H&K rifle followed, and once it was strapped to his body, he tugged the gloves over his hands and looked down through the hatch in the floor. Unlike in the Pave Hawk he would be fast roping below the Osprey instead of using the door, and when he looked down, it was immediately obvious why the aircrews called it the hellhole.

He gave the rope a tug, keeping a tight grip with his left hand while the city flashed below them. They were moving fast, and the Osprey's velocity made it almost silent. The pilot maneuvered parallel with the convoy, then at the last minute swung the bird sideways to intercept.

I'm coming, brother.

Steele kicked the rope out and the Osprey bounced and swayed from the updraft rushing off the city. The fast rope snapped wildly in the air, and that was when Steele saw the little girl.

She was standing in the middle of the street, unaware of the trucks bearing down on her. From Steele's point of view she looked incredibly small, standing there face upturned and staring at the helo. The pink ball she was carrying fell from her hands in slow motion.

She was about to be run over, and Steele knew he had to go.

The rope burned his hands and the inside of his legs. He had to hold on tighter than usual because neither the rope nor the helicopter was steady. It felt like he was trying to stay on a hurricane. The heat came through his hiking boots like his feet were on fire. He had two options: let go and break his legs, or take the pain and possibly walk away.

He hit hard, feet slapping the pavement flat and painful. The shock coursed up his legs like a bolt of lightning, and he winced at the damage his feet were taking. There was a squeal of brakes from the lead truck and he saw the front end drop low. The truck slid to a halt and the doors flew open in unison.

Steele didn't hear a command or the usual uncertainty untrained jihadists showed on contact. These men were trained and they came out shooting. He saw the girl freeze in the middle of the road, transfixed by the sudden gunfire. Steele knew he had to get her off the street, *now*.

He bent low, legs pumping, head turtled into his neck as he ran to her. He snatched her off the ground at full stride. Somehow he hadn't been hit, but he wasn't planning on pressing his luck. Without breaking stride, he swerved to the left. It reminded him of a post pattern he used to run during football practice in high school, except this time he prayed there wasn't a bullet at the end of his route.

"Gunslinger, this is Mako 2, we are taking fire," a calm voice said over the radio. The pilot hit the throttle and the Osprey's engines roared, sending it juking out of the line of fire.

Steele saw the shadow flash over him as he ran. It got smaller and smaller and he wondered where in the hell the gunship was hiding.

"Roger that, Mako, I'm coming around. You boys hold tight."

He made it to cover and set the girl on the ground behind him. He brought the H&K into the fight, tucking the buttstock into his shoulder. He flexed his deltoid into the stock, locking the rifle tight, and settled his jade eyes behind the Vortex Strike Eagle mounted to the rail.

Who the hell are these guys?

The Cobra flashed overhead, but the pilot didn't fire. "I have civilians everywhere, I'm going to need someone to mark the target," he said.

Steele had worked with the Marine aviators before and they were among the best in the world, fearless and more than willing to put their lives on the line. But like the rest of America's military, they weren't going to open fire with innocents on the ground.

It was one of the things that made Steele proud to be an American.

Steele dropped the magazine from his rifle, stuffed it into his dump pouch, and grabbed a fresh one marked with a band of red tape. He jammed it into the magwell and hit the talk button.

"Gunslinger, Stalker 7, I am marking target with tracer, stand by."

The moment he got back on target, Steele remembered why he was a big fan of the Strike Eagle. The scope's 1–6 magnification range gave him the versatility to zoom out to 600 yards, or dial down for close-in work. He had it set to 1 power, but was not ready for what he saw when he centered the reticle on one of the shooters.

The man was white, and expertly using the vehicle as cover while the rest of the convoy tried to turn around. Steele didn't have a clear shot, but that wasn't the point. The mag was loaded with tracers; all he had to do was mark the target.

He fired five quick shots, and the magnesium-tipped rounds zipped across the street burning bright. Steele sent the bullets through the door. It was the only target he had, and he prayed the 5.56 had enough ass to punch through. On the fifth shot he saw the target stumble out of sight.

The bad thing about marking a target was that it went both ways, and one of the gunners tracked the fire to Steele's position and opened up. The rounds hit the wall, throwing rocks and dust into his eyes. Steele backed up, pushing the girl deeper into the doorway.

"Little help," he said over the radio.

The shuddering *thump, thump, thump* of the Cobra's M197 20mm cannon boomed over the firefight. Steele didn't have a fix on the bird, but he had front-row seats for the damage. The rounds chewed up the vehicle and sent the men scurrying for cover.

A machine gun opened up on his right flank, pinning him deeper into the doorway. The men on the ground knew the Cobra wouldn't fire on them if they hid behind the civilians.

"Gunslinger's off," the pilot said.

Steele stripped a frag from its pouch. "Cover your ears," he told the girl in Arabic. With the Cobra peeling away, the shooters hit the streets, bounding from cover to cover.

"Frag out," Steele yelled, before tossing the grenade toward one of the positions. He needed to get their heads down and move before they pinned him.

The frag hit the ground with a metallic *tink*, bouncing into the path of two of the shooters who had just settled in behind a smoking vehicle five feet to his right. Steele ducked his head, knowing that it was going to be close.

"Stay here," he told the girl, before he pushed into the street.

One of the shooters was lying on his back, bleeding but not dead. Steele swept past him, dumping one round into the center of his head. It might seem cold, but he knew the man was still a threat. He took cover on the clean side of the vehicle and yelled at the civilians frozen around the sidewalk to get inside. He was in the open now and caught a flicker of movement from the SEALs on the rope.

"On me!" he yelled, advancing to the final vehicle, hoping Breul was still alive.

Whoever these soldiers were, they knew what they were doing. They knew there was no way out, but stayed together, trying to maneuver out of the kill zone while laying down a heavy wall of lead.

One of the men moved to the backseat of the truck and yanked open the door. Steele centered his reticle on his head. He wasn't a fan of headshots—it was the one target on the body that was always moving—but he had little choice; his friend's life was in the balance. He took a breath, letting it out slow, waiting for the crosshair to settle.

No such thing as a perfect sight picture.

He pulled the trigger, sending a single round into the back of the man's head. He dropped like a bag of rocks.

Steele conducted a combat reload on the move. He was still out in front of the SEALs and exposed, but all he could think about was Breul.

"Secure the prisoner!" one of the shooters yelled, in a language Steele recognized but couldn't place. He thought it might be Afrikaans. One of the fighters reacted to the order, turning to the open door and aiming his rifle at the hooded man trying to get out.

The rifle steadied and Steele heard himself scream.

Chapter 12

In Algiers, Meg followed Colt down a dimly lit hall to the back stairs that led up to the main floor. She knew the SOG guys called this the upper deck, and like Meg, they tried to avoid it.

The stairwell opened up to a large room with black tile that gleamed in the fluorescent lighting. To the right, a group of State Department employees were knotted together beneath the television that hung in the corner of the canteen, stirring their morning coffee. The fresh beans smelled wonderful and Meg cast a longing look at the coffee station.

Colt snorted and waved a hand at the State Department personnel standing under the TV. "Look at them. They are supposed to be our eyes and ears on the ground, and what are they doing? Watching freakin' CNN."

Meg could see where this was going and decided against stopping for a cup.

She hadn't been with the CIA long enough to develop any allegiance. She tried to keep quiet and do her job, but it was impossible not to notice the tension between the State Department personnel and the SOG teams. But she'd heard the gossip and knew that it stemmed from the 2012 embassy attack in Benghazi.

The State Department foreign staff were made up of career diplomats, men and women who believed that America's diplomatic failures in the Mideast were to blame for the war that had been going on since 2001. Because of that, many of them felt that the CIA's drone strikes in Libya had been the catalyst behind the Benghazi attack.

Meg didn't have a problem with the State Department staff, but knew better than to say that to Colt—or any of the SOG members, for that matter. Like most of his team, Colt had retired from the Navy as a member of SEAL Team 3 and served with one of the men killed in Benghazi.

They continued down another hallway to the briefing room where the rest of the team was already assembled.

The chief of station was at the front of the room reading from a sheet of paper that Meg assumed had come directly from Langley.

He looked up as Meg and Colt walked in and she caught James glance back at her from the front row. They made eye contact for a split second before he ducked his head.

God, men and their fragile egos.

"I was just reading the brief," the chief of station said. "If you want to take over."

Colt nodded and made his way to the front of the room, leaving Meg to take a spot against the far wall.

"Thank you, sir. We don't have a lot of time, so I am going to keep it short and sweet. According to the State Department there is no evidence of any civil unrest outside the wire."

A distant explosion drew Meg's attention to the far wall.

"Someone needs to tell whoever is lobbing mortars that," one of the operatives joked.

"All I know is what has been told to me," Colt said.

"The only way those goons learn about what is going on is by watching CNN," another cracked.

"Yeah, boss, why are we even going out there?" James asked.

Colt's smile fell from his face and all the jokes stopped.

"Did the new guy just ask a *question*?" one of the men wondered aloud.

Here we go, Meg thought.

Colt looked up at Meg, his eyes twinkling. "Just how hard did you hit this guy?"

The room erupted in laughter.

Thanks, Colt, that's all I need.

"All right, all right, settle down," Colt chided. "The reason we are heading out, young James, is to sanitize safehouses. And before you ask, we are bringing your sparring partner because the boss told us to."

Meg knew why she was being included. Officially the CIA had two "on the books" safehouses in Algiers. She and the chief of station knew that there was actually a third, a level one site that wasn't on the State Department list. Since she was the only one with the security clearance necessary to access the site, as well as the technical know-how to wipe the hard drives, Meg was going out.

The thought of hard drives reminded her that she had left her computer unsecured in her room. *Oh crap.* The realization sent a shiver up her neck, and she quickly slipped out of the briefing room and jogged toward the stairs.

She hit the living quarters hallway at a full run, turned the corner, and almost leveled a middle-aged man walking toward her.

"What the hell?" the man yelped as she ran into him, knocking the Snickers bar and plastic case he was carrying to the floor.

"Daniels . . . Oh my gosh, I'm sorry," Meg said, grabbing the man by the shoulders to keep him from falling.

Charlie Daniels had been with the CIA for almost twenty years and was nearing retirement. Meg didn't know much about him, other than the fact that he was the butt of most of the jokes upstairs.

"You scared me," he said, bending down with a spryness that surprised Meg and snatching the case off the ground.

Meg retrieved his Snickers, but had to wait for Daniels to shove the case into his pocket.

"Sorry, I forgot something in my room," she said. "Why are you down here, anyways?"

"I uh . . . they were looking for you upstairs and I was coming to grab breakfast." He nodded toward the vending machine a few paces away then held up the Snickers.

"That was sweet of you to think about me, thank you, Charlie," Meg said. "You sure you're okay?"

"Yeah, yeah, I'm fine. Got some padding those other guys don't have," he replied.

"Great, and thanks again."

Meg patted him on the shoulder and continued to her room, passing the vending machines on her right. She unlocked the door, stepped inside, and moved to the desk, noticing one of her pens lying on the ground beneath the chair.

Was that there when I left?

She picked it up and placed it on the desk before checking the computer. It was still locked, which was all that mattered. Meg quickly logged off the computer and checked her watch. She had been gone for five minutes.

Oh no, I need to go.

Chapter 13

Steele fired as fast as he could. He hit one of the enemy fighters in the gut before walking a second round into his chest. Behind him the SEALs engaged, their suppressed rifles making *thwap, thwap* sounds. But they were too late. The mercenary managed to dump three rounds into Breul's chest before someone finally took him down.

Steele was breathless when he reached the truck, frantically yelling Breul's name. Ali was slumped forward, the mask still covering his face, blood pouring from his chest. The SEALs set up a perimeter while Eric ripped the hood off, revealing his friend's ashen face.

"Ali, can you hear me?" Steele asked, throwing his rifle across the seat and ripping his trauma kit from his vest.

"He knew . . ." Breul said with a labored breath.

"Don't talk, buddy, I'm going to get you out of here."

Steele ripped his shirt open and knew immediately that the wounds were fatal. He pressed gauze over the holes, pushing hard to keep pressure on the wounds.

"Eric, listen to me . . ."

Steele could see his friend was dying, but refused to believe it.

"No, stay with me, man. Medic, shit, I need a medic."

Breul began to convulse, and then one of the SEALs was at Steele's side.

"I've got him, move," the medic yelled, throwing his aid bag to the ground.

Steele stepped back, his plate carrier and hands stained a dark crimson. He was helpless to do anything but watch. The SEAL laid Breul on his back and went to work. Another SEAL was calling for the helo to land, telling the pilot they had an urgent casualty.

"Roger that, stand by. Sir, Cutlass Main is on the horn," the radio operator said.

"What?" Steele asked, looking at the handmike.

"Washington, sir, they want to talk to you."

Get your shit together, Steele thought. *You have a job to do.*

"Tell them to stand by, we are not secure. I need two guys to check the rear vehicle. If there are any bags or cases I want to know." Steele moved to the front of his vehicle, searching, while in the back the medic pounded on Breul's chest and cursed.

Steele knew his friend's heart had stopped.

"Doc," he said.

The medic knew what he was asking and shook his head.

Ali Breul was dead.

"There is nothing here."

Steele stood up, moving around to the back. The team leader was standing within earshot, and Steele held up his hand and made a circling motion with his finger.

"Let's bring it in," the team leader said over the net.

Steele stared down at his friend, thinking about all the promises he'd made him and his family. Leaning forward, he brushed Breul's eyes closed with his fingertips before pulling the Spyderco from his pocket. The blade snapped open and Steele gently draped his friend's arm across his face, revealing a tiny red mark beneath the armpit. He was struck by all the things he couldn't say.

Never meant for this to happen. You know that, right?

"I'm sorry," he finally managed. "About all of it."

He made a small incision below the red mark with the tip of the blade and held the wound open until he squeezed the data pin to the surface and into his open palm. The pin looked like a silver Tic Tac. He closed his fist tight around it and made a promise that no matter what it took, or where he had to go, Steele would avenge the man who had trusted him with his life.

Someone is going to bleed for this.

Chapter 14

Washington, D.C.

Rockford walked back into the Situation Room, working hard to keep the emotion off his face. The fact that Styles had been lying to him since calling the brief infuriated him, but he knew better than to let it show.

"Is everything okay?" Director Harris asked.

"Actually, no," Rockford said.

A second door, this one on the other side of the room, came open and a man in a gray suit appeared. Rockford guessed he was in his late thirties, but as with all military men it was hard to tell.

"Sir, I need you to come with me."

"What is going on?" Styles asked, her face clouded with a sudden uncertainty.

"It seems there is a rescue operation under way in Tunisia."

"A rescue operation? Who authorized that?"

The operation was now under the Alpha Program, which meant that it was classified above even those in the Situation Room. So Rockford tried to keep his answer as vague as possible.

"Someone is missing," he replied. "Robin, you got . . ." He paused, acting as if the question pained him to ask. "You got one hundred percent accountability of your team, didn't you?"

"What are you saying?" she demanded.

Her voice had gone an octave higher, which told Rockford that his instincts were dead on. *Styles is definitely trying to hide something in Tunis.*

"Details are sketchy . . ."

"Mr. Vice President," the man in the suit warned him calmly.

"Of course," Rockford nodded.

"I'm sorry, this is now on a need-to-know basis. I have to go."

"Need-to-know basis? Who do you think you are talking to?" Styles demanded, jumping to her feet. "I called this meeting, not you."

Rockford picked up his folder and ignored her outburst. This wouldn't be the first time he had sat in on an Alpha mission, so he was familiar with what was about to happen. But it was the first time he was in charge.

"Go get 'em, Rock," NSA Director Harris said.

The Vice President nodded and headed out of the room. Styles jumped to her feet and fell in behind him. "Tunisia is *my* operation, Rockford," she shouted at his back. "If I have an agent missing, I need to be read in."

Rockford walked out of the Situation Room with Styles nipping at his heels like an annoying dog. He followed the man in the gray suit down the hall to a door guarded by two men in dark suits and leaned into the retinal scanner.

"Rockford, if you think that I am going to stand by and let Cole cut me out . . ."

What does this have to do with President Cole? Rockford asked himself.

The lock clicked and the door slid open to reveal a much smaller version of the Situation Room. Rockford stepped inside, the guards springing into action when Styles went to follow.

"This is a secure area, ma'am."

"I am the Director of the CIA," Styles said. "Get your hands off of me!" she yelled.

The door closed behind him, but not before Director Styles screamed a final warning. "Goddammit, Rockford, I don't care if he *is* the President, you tell Cole that this will not stand."

Rockford only had a moment to enjoy the silence before a voice came from an overhead speaker.

"Roger that, Variable 210, you are cleared hot."

"Sir," a man in a brown polo shirt began, "in accordance with Program protocol 1–1 it is my duty to inform you that operation 032 is in effect and that you have taken tactical control."

"I have control," Rockford said, taking the binder.

The reference number on the front of the binder read: STALKER 7/032 MAIN. It told Rockford that this was the thirty-second operation Steele had run this year, and that the operation was being controlled from Cutlass Main, the Program's tactical operations center, or TOC, at the White House.

"Here is the operation's log," the man said, handing Rockford a laminated piece of paper that listed every asset in the area.

Near the top in bold letters was VARIABLE 210: a Reaper drone that had checked on station five minutes ago.

In the center of the room there was a large screen with a drone feed that showed an Osprey disappear beneath the brownout caused by the blades. It shot clear, heading straight up.

"Stalker, stand by for rifle," the drone operator said.

The Reaper feed shook from the Hellfire leaving the rack, followed by "Cutlass Main, this is Stalker 7."

"Stalker 7, Cutlass Main switching to secure net. Stand by for authentication on frequency Bravo 2100 and wait for my traffic."

"Roger, Cutlass."

A garbled electronic squelch came from the speaker and Rockford knew they were switching to the high-frequency encrypted channel the Alphas used when talking to the White House.

"Stalker 7 on Bravo 2100," the voice said.

"Authenticate."

"Authentication confirmed. Uplink confirmed."

Rockford turned his attention to the screen and realized that he was excited. This was the first time he was getting to lay eyes on Eric Steele, the man President Cole referred to as "my boy."

Damn he looks tired.

It was the first thing he noticed, and Rockford realized that he had seen so many firefights from 20,000 feet that he had almost forgotten that there were real people on the other end of the feed.

Steele looked like a man who had just stepped out of

battle. His dark hair was matted and his face was grimy and caked with dust and grit. The sweat cut whitish lines through the dirt, and then Rockford found himself frozen by Steele's eyes. To call them green was like calling the sun bright. Rockford couldn't come up with a color to describe the shade of green; the only thing he knew was that when Stalker 7 looked at him it felt like he was staring right into his soul.

"Where's the President?"

The question caught Rockford flat-footed and his mind went temporarily blank. On the screen Stalker 7 leaned closer and the Vice President realized he was being sized up. It was an uncomfortable sensation.

"He has been held up," Rockford answered a moment later. "President Cole is en route and asked me to handle the briefing."

Stalker 7 nodded, but remained silent.

Rockford flipped open the binder and quickly scanned the brief. He came to the "mission goals" line that stated why Steele had been sent to Tunisia in the first place.

"What is your count?"

"Minus one."

Like many in the intelligence field, Rockford had heard of the Program during his time as Director of the CIA. No matter how deep you tried to bury a special missions unit, there was no such thing as a vacuum. Eventually bits and pieces of the unit made their way out of the shadows. The Program was no different. Once Rockford was sworn in as Vice President he was granted access to the Program, but most of what he knew about Eric Steele came directly from President Cole.

Rockford knew that the Program did their own recruitment and assessment of the men and women they wanted. The recruiters had watched Steele for seven months, and while he was everything the Program was looking for, it was originally determined that after only ten years in Special Forces he was still too untested for consideration.

His fourth deployment to Afghanistan changed all that. Steele's ODA, or operational detachment alpha, was hit hard near the Pakistan border. The operation was compromised and headquarters lost contact with the team. Assuming everyone had been wiped out, they sent a search and rescue team in to collect the bodies. They found Steele fifty miles south of the ambush— seriously wounded and carrying the team's captain over his shoulders.

Special Operations Command put him in for the Medal of Honor, but one call from the Program killed the award in its tracks. They were issuing him a waiver, and before Eric was out of the hospital he had been scrubbed from the Department of Defense's books. He entered Phase One in North Carolina as the youngest Alpha trainee in history, but no one would ever know because the day he became operational, Eric Steele ceased to exist. The Program called it ghosting. They erased all records that Steele had ever been born, the same way they had been doing it since World War II.

"What's the damage?"

"Ali Breul is dead."

The words hit Rockford like an open-field tackle and sent him spinning.

"How?"

On the screen Steele rubbed a blood-caked hand through his hair, a look of frustration clouding his face. It was obvious that he was waiting for Rockford to say something.

"They shot him. But that is the least of our problems, sir. This situation . . ." Steele paused. "No offense, sir, but I need to speak with President Cole, *now.*"

"Stalker 7," Rockford interrupted, his voice hard as iron. "Like I said before, the President is not available." The two men stared at each other from thousands of miles away. Rockford took a breath, and when he continued his voice was even, but firm. "Like it or not, right *now* it's just you and me. This isn't my first rodeo, so I'm not going to ask you to trust me, because I know that something like that has to be earned. You tell me what you need to get this done and I give you my word that I will make it happen."

Steele squinted at Rockford, before offering a nod.

"The first thing you need to know about Ali Breul is that there is no way in hell he would leave Iran without telling me. Either something spooked him or . . ."

"Or what?" Rockford asked, leaning toward the camera.

"Or someone pretending to be me told him to leave. Those are the only options, sir."

"How is that possible? The only things with more security than Program assets are the damn nuclear launch codes."

"You tell me, sir."

What is he implying?

"Someone cut into us, I am certain of it. But what they didn't know was that Breul and I had a contingency for this kind of thing." Steele held up a piece of metal. "This is the data pin I implanted into Breul. The same one he activated two days ago in Algiers."

"I assume that was your rendezvous?"

Steele nodded. "Only if he had the package with him."

Rockford didn't want to ask the next question, but knew he had to.

"What was the package?"

"A man-portable nuclear weapon."

Jesus.

"Sir, if I'm right and someone cut into the Program to find Breul"—Steele held up the data pin for the second time—"then I know exactly where they are going next."

"Where?"

"To get their hands on that bomb."

Chapter 15

Eastern Turkey

In Tunis, Eric Steele jumped back on the Osprey. The pilot pushed the throttle forward and Steele braced himself against the bulkhead, before making his way to the cockpit.

"How much fuel?"

The pilot checked the gauge before answering. "Eight thousand pounds."

Steele did the math in his head and knew it wasn't enough.

"We are going to Turkey. Get a tanker to meet us en route."

The flight took two hours plus thirty minutes to refuel, and when Steele walked down the Osprey's ramp, the engines were red hot. The exhaust hit Steele's neck like a hair dryer on steroids. The rotors were rotated up and the clearance was much higher than a helicopter, but he ducked out of habit.

The turbines whined behind him, and Steele turned in time to see the Osprey squat under the torque. At the door the master chief sat with his feet dangling below the skin of the aircraft. The salty SEAL grabbed the brim of his helmet and tipped his hat. It was a small gesture, but Steele got it; the chief was offering his respect.

Steele stood on the tarmac until silence returned and the Osprey disappeared from view. In his world, respect was earned, not given, and it reminded him of something his mentor, Nate West, had once said:

Lead from the front and men will always follow.

Steele's eyes slowly settled back on the airfield. The base was an isolated relic, a memory of a bygone era when Russia and the United States were locked in a pact of mutual destruction. But it hadn't always been this way. During the Cold War the airfield housed F-111s, variable wing bombers capable of carrying a nuke into the heart of communist Russia. Now it was empty except for the C-17 he'd requested idling on the sun-bleached asphalt to his left.

The aircraft reminded him of the fact that twenty-five years after the fall of the Soviet Union the threat of nuclear war was still very much alive. But instead of a bustling base and state-of-the-art bombers it was just Eric Steele. And somewhere out there was a missing nuclear weapon.

Steele knew Demo would be waiting for him inside the C-17, but instead of heading to the plane, he turned and walked into the freshly painted hangar. He needed to clean Ali Breul's blood from his hands before he went any farther.

It was cooler inside the hangar and the sudden change in temperature chilled his sweat-soaked battle shirt, sending goose bumps running up his arms. The Program had taken it over in 2001 and reconfigured it to serve as a way station. They had hundreds of them across the world, a place for the Alphas to rest or refit between missions. Each one was set up the same, a small motor pool of locally purchased vehicles, two Little Bird helicopters, and enough gear and weaponry to outfit a small army.

Since becoming an Alpha, Steele had visited most of them, and each time he did the same thing. His hiking boots squeaked over the polished floor as he walked to the back where a row of ten lockers waited in the shadows. Each locker had a section of green tape stuck to the door with the owner's call sign written in black Sharpie.

Originally the Program used a number system to

designate the different regions each Alpha was responsible for. It went from 1 to 10. During the Cold War,
Alphas 1–3 had Russia, 4 and 5 had Asia, and 6 and 7
were assigned to cover Europe, which left three operatives to watch Africa, the Mideast, and Latin America.

In 1986 number 4 was deemed unlucky after three
operatives were killed in China, and since no one would
take the number after that, higher decided to start with
0 and go through 9, omitting unlucky number 4. It was
also the year that the "Stalker" handle was first used.

Steele stopped at the third locker and placed his
hand over the tape that identified it as Stalker 2. The
locker belonged to Nathaniel West, the man who had
taught him everything.

The war had taken its toll on the Program, but the
standards remained the same. It was the one unit where
there was absolutely no wiggle room between supply
and demand. The lockers belonged to the dead, and the
strip of tape was the only legacy the Program allowed.

"Miss you, bro," Steele said before heading to his
own locker.

Inside was a variety of clothing he'd need for any
operation: battle shirts, suits, a myriad of uniforms,
shoes, boots, batteries, and a hygiene kit. A pair of
white headphones sat on the top shelf next to a folding
knife.

Steele grabbed a fresh uniform from the shelf and made a notation on the inventory list attached to the door below a small picture of his mother. He shut the locker and headed toward the restroom to take a quick shower.

He bumped the door open with his hip, and was greeted by the powerful scent of Pine-Sol. Overhead the fluorescent bulbs blinked to life, and hummed as they warmed up. The lights cast a sallow glow over the gray walls, revealing a bench and a row of showers, urinals, and sinks. Steele dropped his assault pack and set his rifle down before digging at the edge of his plate carrier.

The Velcro was rough on his fingers and made a tearing sound when he pulled it free. With ammo, ballistic plates, grenades, and a medical kit, the vest weighed almost fifty pounds. Steele's broad shoulders and lower back took the brunt of the weight, and when he lifted it free the relief was immediate.

He took a seat and tried to tug the battle shirt off, but the sweat made it cling to his skin. He gave the shirt a violent tug, temporarily losing control of the rage that he had been carrying since he left Tunisia. He felt the seam rip a second before he heard the fabric tear.

"Dammit."

He yanked the battle shirt over his head and threw it

into the corner. He lowered his head into his hands, the metallic scent of Breul's blood hammering his senses.

Eric had met Dr. Ali Breul in Stockholm a year after Nate West was killed in Algiers. The Iranian was a guest speaker at an International Nuclear Proliferation summit, and while outwardly a huge proponent of the Iranian nuclear program, he knew something the rest of the world did not.

Iran had no intention of giving up its nuclear program. In fact, Breul had proof that it was working to construct a man-portable weapon. But that wasn't the worst part. Steele vividly remembered the dinner when Breul had told him the most chilling news of all.

"So they are making a weapon and you have proof, what's the problem?"

"Eric, my friend," Breul said, leaning in with a sad smile. "Your CIA already *knows* this."

Steele got to his feet, the memory hanging there like an itch he couldn't scratch. He walked over to the sink, purposefully avoiding the mirror, and turned on the faucet.

What would make you leave Iran without checking with me?

The same unsettling tickle he'd felt regarding the CIA target package in Beirut that told him something wasn't quite right returned with the subtlety of a cattle prod to the throat. Steele realized that someone was playing him, just like they had in Algiers four years earlier.

When Nate West was killed.

The mere thought of what had happened there washed over him like a wave. Steele tried to avert the memories by ducking his face beneath the cold water of the faucet, but it was no use. The sights and smells of that day came rushing back, and he could almost taste the salt coming off the Med, mixing with the burnt-meat smell of charred flesh. What was left of Nate's boat smoldered in its slip, the gunwale burned down like a cigarette that had been smoked to the filter.

Steele knew his friend was dead as soon as he saw the smoke, and remembered the feeling of the gravel on his knees and the water soaking his pants when he collapsed near the shore. Then there was the buzzing that drew him to the connex, the scent of blood and death hanging heavy in the air. West's wife was hanging upside down from a length of chain coiled around her tanned legs. She was naked and her face bruised and swollen like a grape left in water.

But it was what Steele saw when he tracked the men south and found the tape of West's son that broke him. He would have given it all up—the Program, his hopes and dreams—and crawled back in himself for the remainder of his life if it hadn't been for President Cole.

Steele ripped himself back to the now. He knew that he couldn't change the past, but the fact that it seemed someone was using it against him sent a wave of anger washing over him. Killing Breul had made this mission personal, but the cold hand of fear tempered the fire of revenge.

His mother had told him stories of the Cuban Missile Crisis and the fear that surrounded a nuclear war between Russia and the United States. "We knew it would never happen, Eric, because after it was over there wouldn't be anything left," his mother had told him.

The tactic was called mutual assured destruction, and it promised that if any country ever hit the United States with a nuke, America would respond in kind.

Steele had grown up in a different era and never feared an all-out nuclear war. He had a different fear, and it was *one man* stealing *one nuke*. It was the scenario you could war-game to death, but never prepare for. A single nuke could literally be detonated anywhere in the world. But worse than the endless list of targets and the catastrophic body count that would follow was the moment Steele realized that right now, he was the only man who could stop it.

Chapter 16

Algiers

"You sure that's the guy?" Villars asked, taking his foot off the gas after turning the Pathfinder onto the street.

Their target, CIA officer Charlie Daniels, had pulled his vehicle to the curb and sat behind the wheel stuffing a gyro down his throat.

"Yes, Villars." West sighed.

Daniels had joined the CIA right out of college. He had given his life to the Agency, and it had cost him two marriages, three grand a month in alimony, and a junkie daughter who had recently failed out of the University of Washington. West had taken a look at his bank account and knew that Daniels didn't have enough money saved up to buy a wading pool in a trailer park.

They all have a price.

After a lifetime of service to the good ol' U.S. of A., all it had taken to turn Daniels was a million cash. West might have even let him keep it if the man hadn't fucked everything up and allowed Ali Breul to take a pit stop in Algiers.

"That fat piece of crap," Villars began, taking his foot off the gas while pointing repeatedly at the other vehicle, "works for the bloody CIA?"

West agreed that the guy didn't look the part, but his intel was solid. Daniels was the man who could get him into the CIA computer system. The problem was that Villars was beginning to make a scene and there was no way the fat man wasn't going to eventually notice the dark-colored SUV and Villars pointing at him.

"Just stop the car."

That was all he had to do, and West would handle the rest, but Villars seemed unable to stop pointing or put his foot on the brake.

"I just . . ."

They were five feet away when West lost it.

"He's a fucking slob, I get it. We *all* get it, Villars," he said with a sweep of his arm that encompassed the four men inside the Pathfinder. "Just stop the fucking car." The men in the backseat sputtered and made no attempt to control their laughter. All this did was make the big South African more angry, and West realized they were about to drive right past their target.

"For Christ's sake." West reached over and pushed the wheel hard to the left. The Pathfinder smashed into the side of Daniels's vehicle, pinning him inside. "Go!" West yelled. The men burst from the backseat, rifles in hand. West slammed the SUV into park, yanking a knife with a white handle from his belt.

Outside there was a muffled yell, followed by the sound of glass shattering. West ignored it—his hand closed around Villars's hair. He got a good grip and slammed his head against the window. He moved so fast that by the time the South African went to swallow there was a blade at his throat.

"If you ever," he hissed, "undermine me again I will cut your head off and use it as a hood ornament. Do you understand?"

Villars nodded and West slowly pulled the knife away. The truck bounced and his men threw Daniels in the back and jumped in behind him.

"Drive," West growled.

"Which way to the safehouse, Daniels?" he asked, tossing the knife into the air and catching it by the handle.

"Wh . . . what?"

"The *safehouse!*" West yelled. "I think his ears are clogged, can you guys help him out?"

One of his men smiled and then slammed his fist into the fat man's gut. Daniels deflated like a bad tire, and spent the next few minutes gasping and wheezing for breath.

"Number 12 Chemin Al-Bakir."

"Much obliged." West pointed the knife at Villars and said, "Driver, if you please."

West had been a believer once, and before his wife and son were killed he realized that if he made it to the end, all he was going to get was a shitty gold watch and a laughable pension. Just before he met Ali Breul, he was preparing to retire, and the only reason he stuck around for six extra months was to train Eric Steele. When Breul showed up, so did the heat.

Maybe I got sloppy?

I bet ol' Eric doesn't have a fucking clue.

The thought of his old protégé walking into an ambush in Beirut made him chuckle. West was confident that Steele could handle himself, but wished he could see his face when he realized that someone was pulling his strings. *Rule number one—don't get played.* That was what he had told him their first week together.

Villars turned onto the upscale street and hunched over the wheel searching for the address. West already knew where they were going, but he'd learned to take joy in the journey. Plus, it was good practice for what he had in store for his men later.

He was in his element, and just had one more detail to take care of before it was time to have some *real* fun. And that meant he was going to have to make Daniels talk, either willingly or by force.

Chapter 17

Eastern Turkey

Eric Steele was strapped in and rubbing a rag over his father's 1911. Demo had brought the pistol with the rest of Steele's gear on board the C-17. In the cockpit, the pilot pushed the throttle forward, shoving Steele back in his seat. He barely noticed because he was thinking about the first time his father let him hold the pistol. It had felt so heavy in his hands back then.

So much I never got to ask him.

He ran his thumb over the spot where the serial number should have been. It was silver and all traces of the file marks were smoothed out by years of use. The pistol was one of John Moses Browning's masterpieces, the same design that the American infantryman had carried in the Battle of Belleau Wood, Iwo Jima, Korea, and Vietnam. It was the only thing he had to remind him of the father he never really knew.

Steele had made the pistol his own by modifying it to shoot 9mm, adding a threaded barrel, and installing suppressor sights, which were taller than the factory ones. It was his gun now, and he slipped it away before taking an amphetamine tablet out of his pocket and downing it with a sip of water.

Once the C-17 leveled off, Steele checked his watch, unhooked himself, and went back to the Pelican case on the floor near the ramp to retrieve the rest of his gear. He took the tan plate carrier, checked the magazines and frags that were preloaded in the pouches and the Thales MBITR radio. He turned the radio on and conducted a check to make sure he was up on coms. The last piece of equipment in the box was the AN/PRQ-7 Combat Survival Evader Locator, or CSEL, radio. Steele called it his Amex card, because he never left home without it. The radio was small enough to fit in his chest pocket but powerful enough to call for help if things went sideways. With his gear ready, Demo helped him rig up for the fun part.

An hour later his throat was dry and scratchy from the pure oxygen coming through the hose attached to the Mark XI Advanced Jumpers Helmet. The helmet was a gift from the Defense Advanced Research Projects Agency, or DARPA. The oxygen was to keep him alive. There were no time outs at 30,000 feet, and with no doctor on board, Steele had to check himself for signs of decompression sickness and hypoxia.

Nothing ruins a mission faster than an unconscious free fall.

Demo stood at his left typing on an iPad. He was in his late fifties, short and built like a fire hydrant, with thick wrists and short hair that sported spots of gray. His right hand was scarred and missing its middle finger. A white cord stretched from the bottom of the tablet to the USB port in the side of the Mark XI.

"I am uploading the drop zone info into the navigation computer. Right now the DZ is clear, but . . ." Demo shrugged.

"I get it, I get it. If it was secure I wouldn't be conducting a HALO jump in broad daylight."

"Exactly," Demo said, closing the iPad case and pulling the cord free. "I'm not going to sugarcoat it. We have no idea what is going on down there, mano. The last cables from the State Department said the Algerian police had a legit insurrection on their hands."

"I'll be fine."

"That's my boy. Did you pack your lunch?" Demo asked with a smile.

"Shut up and give me the count," Steele said, laughing.

"Ten minutes."

Demo placed the iPad in the Pelican case, replacing it with an oxygen mask that he pulled over his head.

Steele disconnected from the C-17's internal oxygen and snapped the silicon hose into the thermos-sized bottle of O2 strapped to his side. An icon appeared on the bottom edge of the Mark XI's heads-up display telling him that he was on auxiliary oxygen and that he had thirty minutes of air.

Demo walked to the ramp and clipped his safety harness into the metal ring dangling next to the control box.

"Can you hear me?" he asked.

His voice was crystal clear through the Mark XI's internal comms.

"Got you," Steele said, tugging on a pair of thick gloves in preparation for the temperature drop that would come as soon as the ramp opened. Right now it was tolerable inside the bird because it was pressurized, but outside he knew it was freezing.

"Remember, no matter what happens your mission is to find Breul's dead drop and get your ass to the Gatehouse. The only thing that matters is securing that bomb before the bad guys do. *Comprende?*"

Steele nodded and watched his handler slam the flat of his hand on the red plunger sticking out of the control box. The ramp cracked open and with a whir of hydraulics began a slow yawn.

The jump light over Demo's shoulder switched from red to amber and Steele toddled toward the ramp. The cold air whipped at Demo's jacket and Steele felt a dagger of frigid air cut under his pants legs. His visor immediately fogged up, and when it finally cleared Demo was holding up two fingers.

The view from the back of the bird was hazy and thick graphite clouds obscured the ground. A HALO jump was a bitch in the best of circumstances. A daytime jump into a possibly hostile drop zone was like playing Russian roulette with a Glock.

At least I look cool, he thought, checking his reflection in the circular window. The helmet reminded him of something from *Iron Man.*

He checked his gear one final time and made sure the heads-up display was tracking with the altimeter and GPS on his wrist. He took the final two steps to the edge of the ramp and when he was in position turned to look at Demo.

His handler held up one finger, followed by the verbal command of "thirty seconds."

Steele was ready, and when Demo shot him a quick salute, threw himself out of the C-17.

Chapter 18

Rockford grabbed the binder and walked across the room to one of the isolation cells built off of the main floor. The rooms were known as "tanks," and were designed to give the men and women who ran the TOC a place where they could decompress. Each one had a table, overloaded with phones, a secure computer terminal, and a matching couch and recliner.

Rockford closed the door behind him and dropped the heavy binder, but instead of taking a seat he used the remote to activate the privacy shade. Behind him the window quickly transitioned from clear to opaque.

Man, Emma would get a kick out of that.

Boeing had similar windows in all of their 787s, but they took longer to transition from clear to dark green. The ones in the TOC used electrochromic material and the change was immediate.

Rockford slipped out of his suit coat and draped it over the chair. He checked his watch before sitting down, noting he had less than thirty minutes to devour the data before he had to brief President Cole.

It wasn't enough time to get a full picture of Stalker 7, but it was all Rockford had. The binder catalogued Steele's military history, Program recruitment, and operations. A tab separated each section, and the first thing Rockford noticed was that there was nothing about Steele's childhood.

Rockford had been a leader long enough to know that it was his job to learn as much about Stalker 7 as possible. He knew the binder wasn't the best way to do this, but it was the only option available. Like every Alpha recruit, Steele had begun his training at the Program's facility in Fort Bragg, North Carolina. The site was located in an area of the installation that was secure and remote, literally in the middle of nowhere. They called it the Salt Pit, a name that, oddly enough, came from an accountant.

Even secret sites had to be paid for, and the Salt Pit was no different. During Vietnam, the Johnson administration decided that the Alpha Program needed its own training site. All the president had to do was sign a piece of paper and it was up to his staff to make it happen. The project was slipped into the Department of Energy's budget and designated a salt mine, hence the name.

Rockford knew that training was broken into four phases. Phase 1, or Indoc, was at the Salt Pit and had a staggering attrition rate of eighty-seven percent. Making it to the end didn't mean a candidate got to continue, and many a heart had been broken after the review board deemed them unsuitable for the job.

Rockford skimmed the bullet points of Eric's final review, hoping to get a sense of the man.

Candidate Steele is a natural leader and is fluent in Arabic and French. His German is passable and the board recommends additional language training upon completion.

Candidate showed superior skills in weapons, communications and demolition. On training exercises he was cool under fire and has extraordinary ability to task organize and work on his own or as a member of a team. Cadre counseled candidate on 2011/07/21 after candidate halted operation to assist injured teammate. His willingness to put himself at risk to help others could have negative effect in real world operation(s).

Rockford reread the last line aloud. "Could have negative effect in real world operation?" *That's strange.*

He wondered how much Steele's altruism had led him to join the military in the first place. *Not important, I guess. After all, he made it through.*

Rockford skipped ahead to Phase 4 and the main reason he'd requested the file. A year ago, President Cole had mentioned an incident that he had forgotten about until Steele advised him that he was heading to Algiers. Rockford didn't remember how it had come up, but during the conversation Cole had made a casual remark about an incident that almost made Steele quit the Program.

He knew that there had to be something about it in the file and found it in the form of a psychological report with the heading *24 Dec 14—Algiers Debrief:*

EYES ONLY

SAP (Alpha)
From: Station 1–11
To: Cutlass Main
<AAR 241214>

On 24 Dec 2014, Stalker 7 (Steele, Eric) was conducting phase 4 operations under Stalker 2 (West, Nathaniel) in AO Algiers.

: What happened that day?

STEELE: We had just finished up and West said that he was retiring. It was the first I had heard about it, but he said that he had bought a boat.

: A boat?

STEELE: Yeah. He bought a boat and flew Lucy and Able out to meet him.

: For the record you are talking about his wife and son?

STEELE: Yes.

: What happened then?

STEELE: I took him to the marina and he asked if I wanted a beer. I had to sanitize the site and finish up some paperwork so I said no. I headed up the ramp and that's when I saw the motorcycle and the shooting started.

: What happened after that?

STEELE: I dumped the guy on the bike and headed back. There were four or five shooters, which I engaged, and then there was an explosion.

: The boat exploded?

STEELE: Yeah.

: Did you recover West's body?

STEELE: The water was on fire. I saw him floating there. He was dead.

: Tell me about the connex.

STEELE: *Do we have to talk about this now?*

: *Yes.*

STEELE: *Shit, you guys . . . There was a humming sound and then I smelled the blood. They had her strung up like a piece of meat. I could tell they had messed with her.*

: *What do you mean?*

STEELE: *They raped her.*

: *What made you cross the border?*

STEELE: *I knew Nate had brought his son Able but I couldn't find him. I spoke with one of the survivors . . .*

: *Spoke with?*

STEELE: *Yeah, I got him to talk. He told me that someone named Ali Habib was behind the hit and had taken Able.*

: *And that's when you decided to ignore the recall order and go after him.*

STEELE: *(Silence) Yeah. I found him a few weeks later . . .*

As a father, Rockford had to stop reading. The details of what had happened to Nate's son were too graphic and made him want to rush home and hug his daughter. Rockford was no stranger to the violence men were capable of, having seen it firsthand in the desert of Saudi Arabia, but this was different. Horrifyingly so, and he was relieved when he realized it was time to leave.

He returned the binder to the battle captain before stepping into the hall and the elevator. While he waited . for the car he mentally switched gears.

The situation in North Africa wasn't the only burden he had been forced to bear, but as with the missing nuclear weapon, there were only a few people he could share it with. The elevator arrived with a ding and Rockford stepped inside, preparing for the part of his day he had been dreading.

President Cole wasn't out of pocket at all. In fact he was on the next floor.

The elevator bumped to a halt and the doors slid open. Rockford stepped out and immediately took a right, finding himself in another hallway. Near the end, a Secret Service agent stood near a nondescript door. The agent nodded to the VP as he approached.

"William, how are the kids?" Rockford asked.

"Growing like weeds," the agent replied, smiling as he opened the door.

Inside, the room smelled of antiseptic, which, combined with the white floors and cream-colored walls, gave the area a clinical feel. Fluorescent bulbs burned bright in the ceiling, illuminating a mat that read: WHITE HOUSE MEDICAL UNIT.

The WHMU was responsible for the medical needs of the White House and its visitors. The doctors and nurses were the best in the business, and besides staffing the White House clinic, they ran a full-service medical suite aboard Air Force One. Rockford took the first door on his right, where he found the First Lady seated on a small tan couch.

Nancy Cole was a stunning woman, and by far the classiest lady Rockford had ever met. She was the kind of woman who'd put on makeup before going to check the mail, but today she looked terrible.

"Nancy, what is it?" he asked.

Her eyes were red. It was the most distraught Rockford had ever seen her. He tried to hide his concern, but must have failed, because Nancy's lip began to quiver, and the tears rolled down.

"We . . ." she began, her voice cracking as she got to her feet. "Just got the results back. It's terminal."

Jesus, not today.

Rockford didn't know what to say. He just stood there, watching her hands shake as she twisted a frayed Kleenex around her index finger.

He felt his heart sink.

Nancy and the President had been together since high school, and as Rockford opened his arms and scooped her to his chest, he realized that she probably didn't have a memory without her husband in it.

He held her tight, feeling the sobs. Rockford remembered a speech his wife gave at the Coles' last anniversary. She had said, *They don't make love like that anymore.*

"What am I going to do?"

Rockford patted her back. "It's going to be okay," he said, knowing that it was a lie. He waited until Nancy stopped crying and then knocked on the door and stepped inside the exam room. The President stood near the table wearing a white tank top and buttoning his pants. Behind him a nurse was taking an empty bag off the IV stand. Rockford's eyes locked on the Band-Aid taped over a cotton ball in the crook of his arm.

He didn't look like he was dying.

"John, funny seeing you here," the President said with a smile.

"I heard they had free ice cream."

Cole grabbed his shirt and nimbly worked the buttons before tucking it in. But when he began to buckle his trousers, he made a big show of laughing at the joke, while turning his body away from his VP.

Anyone else would have missed it, but Rockford knew the man too well.

He's hiding something.

Knowing that his boss was going to have to use the mirror when he put on his tie, Rockford didn't say anything.

"So, how did the briefing go?" Cole asked.

Rockford turned to the nurse.

"Claire, can we have the room?"

Cole popped his collar and reached for the blue tie draped over the back of the chair. As the nurse stepped out, Rockford used the distraction to mask him taking a small step to his left. He now had a perfect angle on the mirror.

"I got an Alpha Flash this morning, and Styles went ballistic."

Cole smiled. "Doesn't surprise me. Robin and I have never gotten along."

"Sir, I believe she thinks that you are trying to cut her out of her own operation."

"Last time I checked, John, the Director of the CIA wasn't read in on the Program. There is a reason for that."

"Yes, sir, I just feel like I am in the middle here."

"Don't worry, you won't have to deal with Styles for much longer. Now, tell me about the flash."

"Stalker 7 made contact."

Rockford made sure the president couldn't see him before looking at the belt reflected in the glass. He immediately saw what his boss had been trying to hide. The President was losing weight, and had cinched the belt two notches past the worn-out hole he usually used.

"What did he have to say for himself?"

"He, uhhh."

Shit.

Cole's back might have been to him, but there was no mistaking the sudden change in his posture. The President of the United States went rigid, shoulders locking to the rear as he drew himself up. When he turned around his blue eyes were burning like two steel ingots plucked from the furnace.

The Commander in Chief took a step closer and laid a heavy hand on Rockford's shoulder.

"Son, what did I tell you the first time we met?" he asked firmly but without raising his voice.

Rockford felt something melt in his chest, and he looked at the ground, feeling his eyes begin to burn.

"You told me . . ." His voice broke.

"Look at me, John," Cole said, squeezing his shoulder.

Rockford looked up. There was no weakness in the man standing before him—he was every inch in charge.

"You said adversity is just a challenge waiting to be answered."

"That's right. Now what did Eric Steele tell you?"

"He said we lost a nuclear bomb."

The President's response was not what Rockford expected. Instead of withering under the news, the only outward sign that Cole had heard him was a slight narrowing of his boss's eyes and a focal shift. Rockford felt that Cole was now looking through him. Other than that, there was silence.

"Sir, what should we do?" he asked like he was afraid of breaking Cole's concentration.

The President patted him and a tired smile played over his face. He turned and retrieved the jacket off the hook on the wall. Cole slipped his arms through it and finally said, "The hardest part of this job, we *wait* and remember that Stalker 7 has never failed us yet. Not once. My boy will handle it."

Chapter 19

Algiers

Outside the wire it was obvious that the State Department had no idea what was going on. The tension in the air was heavy when they pulled out of the gate. It was the same electric charge Meg had felt in Ramadi in 2006 and before the fall of Mosul in 2014, like the tingle you got before being hit by lightning.

Algiers was on the brink.

Before being recruited by the CIA, she had been a member of the ISA, known as "the Activity," one of the last truly dark units within the DOD. Her job was to collect actionable intelligence for Special Operations units like Delta and SEAL Team 6.

Her decision to leave the Army was the only time Meg hadn't listened to her father, General "Black Jack" Harden. Not only did he want her to stay in, but he was willing to call in some favors after she got passed over for major.

"I appreciate it, Dad, but I don't take charity," she had told him.

"All you have to do is keep your mouth shut and play the game. How hard is that?" he'd demanded. The Army was his life and to this day he still didn't understand why she'd left.

The simple truth was that Meg had a code, and if she couldn't earn it on her own, then she didn't want it. A day later, while she was drinking a glass of Merlot and signing the last sheet of her separation documents, the phone rang.

Her caller ID said the call was from a private number so she let it go to voice mail, and then she got the text:

I hear you need a job.

When they called back five minutes later she answered. The CIA offered her the only thing she had ever wanted—a chance to stay in the fight.

The safehouse at 12 Chemin Al-Bakir was a level two facility, a single-story building surrounded by a twelve-foot wall and a metal gate that might withstand an RPG. The main door of the house was steel reinforced and secured by two locks and a keypad.

It could take a heavier beating, but for the most part the safehouses' main defense was in remaining inconspicuous. Anyone with a Top Secret clearance could handle sanitizing them. It was the third location that was occupying her mind.

It wasn't on a map or the official list of stations the State Department had on file. In fact, besides the chief of station, Meg Harden was the only person in Algiers who knew of its existence or location. The code word for the special access site was the Gatehouse.

"Stay here," Colt told her while the rest of the team piled out to clear the house.

Meg rolled her eyes and got out of the van. In the distance an explosion rumbled like thunder off a mountain. *That's freaking artillery.*

"I bet I wouldn't be out here if I had a Y chromosome," she said to Colt's back. The only answer she got was from a roll of automatic rifle fire.

Meg tore her helmet off and threw it in the van before turning the encrypted radio to the operations channel. It was quiet and she was bored. Safehouses didn't take this long to clear and she was beginning to wonder if they had forgotten about her. She knew the SOG guys were upset that they were on babysitter detail, but since she was the only one who knew how to sanitize the mainframes they weren't given a choice.

Finally the SOG team leader came out the door and Colt waved Meg over. She looked at her watch. It was exactly 1420 hours. When she got inside Colt was already telling his men what to do. "You know the drill: collect what we need, and burn what we don't."

Meg noticed that James's eye was beginning to darken from the pop she had given him at the gym, and he was sulking around like a cat with a burned tail.

Men . . .

She walked over to the computer in the middle of the room, leaving the maps on the wall and the shelves full of binders for the trigger pullers. Colt had broken them into two teams and half were ejecting the data tapes from the storage devices.

"Red labels go in the case," Meg said, pointing to the black tote. "You can nuke the greens and blues."

She sat down in front of the computer, a tiny grin on her face. Meg knew they loved putting the data disks in the microwave. *Like little children.* Even inside the building it was obvious that the volume of fire was picking up. It sounded like someone was sitting on the other side of the wall banging on the concrete with a pair of metal drumsticks.

"Anyone going to check that out?" she asked, a frown replacing the grin when she noticed a brownish smudge on the keyboard.

Someone has been eating at the terminal again. It was one of her biggest pet peeves. Being a neat freak was not an easy job in the alpha male world. She had seen guys leave half-eaten sandwiches at a terminal for a week, and then there was the time in Syria when an operative spilled a bottle of dip spit on the keyboard. Meg had to wait two weeks to get a replacement.

After that she had instituted a strict "no eating or drinking around my crap" policy. Meg thought the stain looked like hot sauce. Her eyes went to the sign she had taped above the monitor and she wondered if anyone even noticed it.

ABSOLUTELY NO EATING OR DRINKING

That someone had drawn a penis along with the words "Eat this" answered her question. *Animals.* She woke up the computer by hitting the ctrl-alt-del keys, but instead of being greeted by the login page, there were two open files on the desktop. Someone had forgotten to lock the computer.

Using her administrator's rights she brought up the activity log. Eating she could tolerate; not securing the terminal was something that drove her ballistic. The guilty party's password popped up.

"Effin' Daniels," she said.

According to the log, Charlie Daniels had opened the terminal at 1315, a little over an hour before.

Daniels? What the hell are you doing outside the wire?

She brought up his login history and, starting from the bottom, re-created what he'd done during his session. A list of deleted documents popped up on the screen.

Deleting files, are we? Meg used her administrator rights to restore the files and saw that they were emails. She skimmed over the first couple of subject lines. Most of them were names or places that meant nothing to her. *Who is Asif Bassar?* Knowing that she didn't have time to go through them all, Meg emailed them to her secured account and went back to the history.

Daniels had spent the rest of his time going through the access logs before conducting a date search of the past week. *What happened two days ago that you are so interested in?*

She scrolled through all the keycards and key codes that had been used on that day. Card-accessed rooms in the embassy were labeled with an "E" followed by the room number. The safehouses were Sites 1132 and 1133. Everything looked normal except that her password had been used to log in to a secure subdirectory exactly thirty seconds after Daniels checked the safehouse codes.

How did that shit get my password? she wondered, her fingers flying over the keyboard to see what he had been looking at. Meg brought up the session on another screen and found one code that she knew didn't belong to anyone who worked in Algiers. There was something urgent building up in the back of her mind, but she couldn't place it.

"Tower 1, we are taking heavy fire," a voice shouted over the radio.

Meg processed the transmission distantly, the way a person hears the television in the other room, while her fingers flew over the keyboard spurred on by the fear-laden voice coming over the radio.

"We need to go," Colt said.

"What channel is that?" one of the SOG guys asked.

"Home."

The embassy.

"They are at the gate. Close it, close it!"

Her stomach knotted.

"Hey, are you bleeding?" It was Colt.

"Huh?"

"Your arm."

"What the hell are you talking about?"

Meg lifted her arm and twisted it to get a look at her sleeve. The stain looked like the hot sauce on the keyboard. She frowned, not getting it at first, but then she saw the armrest and jumped up so fast she sent the chair flying.

Oh my God, oh my God, there is blood on my arm. Her throat tightened and she fought the disgust rising up from her stomach.

Colt was so surprised by the sudden movement that his hand shot to the butt of his pistol. They stared at each other for a second and then the light-bulb went off.

"Oh Jesus."

"Boss, it is going *off* out here," one of the men said, stepping back inside. "Sounds like someone is pound-ing the Hydra district."

"You think the ALF broke the peace?" James asked, stepping over to a cabinet and reaching for the latch.

"I don't know, go get the van," Colt said. "How much longer?"

She ignored him and moved the cursor to the bottom of the screen, hitting the wrong tab by mistake. A thousand questions were running through her mind, but when the window popped up Meg found herself staring at the last face she expected to see.

Her own.

What the hell were you doing, Daniels?

Meg clicked the right window this time, accessing the security feed. The images moved backward on the screen as she backed it up to the moment Daniels had put his code in the outside door.

"I need a minute."

"We don't have thirty seconds, Meg."

The screen suddenly went blank, but the time stamp at the bottom showed that the program was still running. Someone had erased the feed and made no attempt to hide it. Everything fell into place.

"Get the UV light," Meg ordered, closing everything except the key log.

"Got it," one of the guys said, holding up the light.

"What are you thinking?" Colt asked her.

"Kill the lights," Meg ordered, hoping she was wrong. She typed the sanitize command and her password, then hit enter. The monitor went black, followed by the lights.

"If there is blood it will show up under the UV," she said a second before the ultraviolet light kicked on. "Shine it over here."

Colt's teeth luminesced in the light and when it fell over the computer everyone could see the long swipe marks that proved someone had tried to clean up after themselves. But they had missed the blood on the armrest, and when the black light hit it, the phosphors reacted, making it look dark black.

"The only way to clean up blood is with bleach and we would have smelled that."

"Look," Colt said, pointing at her feet.

Meg lowered her head and jumped back. The area below the desk was a black cloud of swirl marks and faint footprints. She knew the smaller ones were hers, but there were two larger sets that led away from the terminal. Meg followed them to one of the lockers, the man with the light tight on her heels.

She heard Colt draw his pistol, but she knew there was no need. Her heart pounded in her chest when she reached for the latch. She shot a look over her shoulder. Colt was already moving to his left, positioning himself in case he had to shoot. Meg flung the door open and stepped out of the way, letting it clang against the wall.

"Shit."

Colt lowered his pistol, and when Meg came around she saw Charlie Daniels's contorted frame stuffed grotesquely into the bottom shelf. His legs had been broken so that he'd fit, and Meg saw that he was missing two fingers on his right hand. He had obviously been tortured before someone slit his throat.

Chapter 20

Washington, D.C.

After the guards barred Styles from following Rockford she stood in the hall panting with anger. The
fact that it had been the Vice President and not Cole at
the briefing had ruined her plan, but more than that it
put her at a disadvantage.

She wanted to scream, but knew she had already
made a big enough scene. And as her anger began to
dissipate, the weight of what had happened came
crashing down.

*You got one hundred percent accountability of
your team, didn't you?* Even now it was ringing in
her ears.

Her stomach cramped and Styles tore herself away,
moving as quickly as her pride would allow to the
ladies' room. She checked beneath the row of stalls on

her way to the back, stepped inside, and without closing the door began to vomit.

She knew there was only one way Rockford could have known. Cole had told him. She had underestimated the President and once again he'd used his beloved Alphas to outmaneuver her.

This wasn't the first time Cole had used the Program to steal an operation from her without so much as a thank-you or a go-fuck-yourself. But this time it was different. This time Styles's very life was in the balance.

How exposed am I? Does Cole know about the nuke?

She flushed the toilet and went to the sink to clean out her mouth. Styles looked at herself in the mirror and began going over her options. Rockford wasn't the threat, he was an errand boy, and as the Vice President his authority came directly from Cole.

Styles knew that the animosity between her and President Cole wasn't a secret. He had a big problem with policies made during the previous administration, and since she was the only one left, he had been taking it out on her since the day he stepped into the Oval.

She was a good enough politician to have been able to play it off, if it weren't for the Iran nuclear deal.

When President Bentley first proposed the idea of a nuclear Iran it was just the two of them inside the Oval

Office. He had asked her what she thought and Styles told him the truth.

"It will never happen," she'd said.

"I see the way you look at this chair," Bentley said, getting to his feet. "You are ambitious, Robin, and I like that. Why don't you try it out?"

"Excuse me?"

"Take a seat," he commanded.

Robin had done as she was told, and when she was settled, President Bentley made his pitch. "You help me make this happen, and I will make sure you are sitting behind this desk in two years."

Styles knew she could have beaten Cole, but just as she was about to announce that she was running, everything fell apart, leaving her holding the bag.

The first sign that there was a problem came from the most unlikely of sources—her counterpart in Iran.

"Robin, one of your CIA officers is poking his nose where it doesn't belong."

"Who?" she demanded.

"A man named Nathaniel West. My people tell me he has been following one of our scientists, a man named Ali Breul."

"Will Breul talk?"

"We have his wife, but just to make sure, he is being recalled to Tehran."

"I'll handle it. There is nothing to worry about."

All Styles had to do to find out if West worked for the Agency was pick up the phone. It was immediately clear that he didn't, which meant she had to find out who in the hell he was. She started looking into the man, and it was during the investigation that followed that she first learned of the Program's existence.

But the damage was irreversible. Styles knew that with West nosing around the Iran deal, it would be impossible for her to run against Cole. If the slightest whiff of her involvement in the deal got out, it would kill her bid to become the first female President of the United States while it was still in the crib.

So Styles made the only play she could. She hired a team to take West out and hope the trail would die with him. The hit was textbook, but she knew that all it had done was buy her some time.

As long as Ali Breul was alive, and the nuke he'd built was in Iranian hands, Styles would be living in fear. The only way she knew to regain her freedom was by killing Breul and destroying the nuke. But she couldn't do either until Bentley was out of office.

Once it became clear that Cole was going to take the election, Styles realized that she was going to need to act sooner rather than later.

In light of the day's events, when Styles finally left

Langley at 6:00 P.M. she knew it was time to put her plan into action. She gave her driver an address before pulling out her burner phone and sending a text:

Down the street, can I come over?

By the time her driver pulled to the rear of the D.C. apartment building and tapped the brake before dropping into the underground garage, she had her reply:

Yes.

Styles walked across the garage, her heels clicking on the concrete, and used the access card on the elevator. The car opened and she hit the "P" that marked the penthouse.

The elevator came to a halt and the doors slid open on thick carpet and a tasteful entry room. A single mahogany door was open and music gently drifted from within. Styles walked in, closed the door behind her, and tossed her phone on the table next to the wall.

"Claire, where are you?" she asked, heading to the bar.

"In here," a voice replied from the bedroom.

Styles ignored the shelves packed with gleaming bottles. She was a Kentucky girl and that meant bourbon. In the cabinet below the sink she kept a bottle of Michter's Celebration. She poured herself a glass of the $3,600-a-bottle sour mash, turned toward the bedroom, and took a sip.

The woman standing in the door was beautiful, naked, and half her age.

"Come here," Styles ordered, her voice throaty and hot from the liquor.

The woman padded across the room, her blond hair splayed over her shoulders.

"Take off my clothes," Styles ordered, setting her drink on the bar. She watched the girl's eyes for any sign of hesitation, but the only thing she saw was lust. Her lover's hands trembled on the buttons; her breathing was fast, almost close to panting.

They had met a year ago, and while it seemed like a chance encounter, it was the culmination of eighteen months of intense search.

Styles needed someone who fit a very specific set of parameters. Male or female didn't matter—Robin swung both ways—but they had to have access to the White House and something to hide. Styles found exactly what she was looking for in Claire, a wholesome farm girl from Iowa who'd come to the nation's capital for school.

Claire just happened to be a nurse who worked at the White House, and as an added bonus, she also had a cocaine habit.

Styles made her move at spin class. It started innocently enough, some flirting and late-night drinks. Gentle kisses in the moonlight, the kind of romance that made Styles want to gag.

At first Claire refused to talk about what she did at the White House Medical Unit. So Styles took a page from the CIA and began treating her like a reluctant asset. The first step was to carefully build a level of trust between them, and after that, she could set the hook.

It took almost six months, and then out of the blue Claire started dropping little tidbits of conversations she had overheard at work, a direct violation of her security clearance. When the time was right, Styles gave Claire her personal number and told her to call her if she was ever in trouble, and then she waited.

Two months later they met for dinner and drinks in Georgetown. While they ate salmon and drank a $200 bottle of wine inside, Styles had a paid contractor break into Claire's Volkswagen and plant an eight-ball of powder in the center console.

After dinner the plan was to meet up at the penthouse, and as soon as Claire pulled out of the parking lot, Styles made a call to a D.C. cop she had in her pocket. Fifteen minutes later she got the call.

It was Claire. She was handcuffed and sobbing in the back of the squad car.

"R-Robin . . . it's me. I need your help."

"I'm on my way, darlin'," Styles had responded.

Back in the penthouse, Styles was naked. She might be twice as old as Claire, but her muscles were just as hard. Her adherence to diet and exercise was legendary and gave her the face and body of a thirty-year-old. In fact, when she was sworn in as Director of the CIA, *Time* magazine put her on the cover with a title that read, "America's Sexiest Spy."

When Claire tried to kiss her Robin backed away and headed for the bedroom, grabbing a fistful of hair as she walked by.

She liked the flicker of pain in the woman's eyes. It made her feel powerful, and was exactly what she needed after the meeting with Rockford.

"Oww, my hair."

"Do you remember the night you got pulled over?" she asked, running her free hand over Claire's arm. Claire nodded, biting her lip against the pain. "Why did you call me?"

"I . . . I was scared."

Styles let her lips brush her neck, and kissed her gently below the ear. She felt the goose bumps rushing over Claire's skin.

"I remember how scared you sounded, calling from the back of that squad car. He was going to take you to jail, wasn't he?"

Claire moaned, unable to answer, because Styles's fingers moved between her legs. But it wasn't the wetness between her legs that turned Styles on; it was remembering the helplessness in Claire's voice. "You would have lost everything, your license and your job. What would you have done if I wasn't able to help, go back to Iowa?"

"Yesss," Claire whispered.

"I might need your help for work."

"Anything."

Styles was thinking she needed to know more about President Cole. He had to have a weakness and Claire was going to help her find it.

"Promise me."

"I'll do anything you want me to."

"I need you to bring me a copy of President Cole's medical records."

Chapter 21

Algiers

E ric Steele utilized the Mark XI's voice command function by saying, "Nav," and a map appeared in the upper-right quadrant of the visor. The yellow blinking arrow told him that he needed to come left, so he lowered his shoulder and banked gently until he was locked on the correct glide path.

This thing is legit.

Steele had grown up on James Bond and thought being a spy was all about the gadgets. But in the real world batteries failed and an operator lived and died by making a plan and sticking to it. One of the main reasons Steele was still alive while so many of his friends were dead was because he didn't leave anything to chance.

He carefully brought his left arm up to eye level and double-checked the Mark XI's readings with the GPS/altimeter combo strapped to his forearm. Once he was sure that he knew exactly where he was, he snapped his arms tight and accelerated to 200 miles per hour.

The wind ripped at his clothes, buffeting the assault pack secured between his legs by a d-ring. Visibility was terrible because of the cloudbank and the rain that popped his face shield like gravel against a barn. He fell out of the clouds and far to the west he saw Algiers.

He could have been looking at L.A. in the midst of the '92 riots. The white city was wrapped and wavering in artificial smog created by innumerable fires that flickered like burning ships on the horizon. Flaming tires released tendrils of jet-black smoke, sending them skyward like offerings to the god of war. Steele knew the only reason he couldn't smell it was because he was still breathing oxygen.

"Locate."

The Mark XI's camera snapped a picture and ran it through the mapping software. In less time than it took to blink the internal computer had identified what he was looking at and a woman's voice came over the speaker.

"Houari Boumediene Airport," she began, "was created in 1924. It was the primary target of Operation Torch—"

"Mute and clear."

Steele checked the altimeter again.

Not good.

He was getting close and needed to slow down before deploying his chute. He arched his back and spread his arms and legs, creating as much surface area as possible to decrease his rate of descent. It was the worst possible situation for a parachute landing, and the second he popped the chute he knew he would present a tantalizing target.

The Mark XI identified his primary drop zone with a red crosshair, and before Steele could lock on, an orange flash blossomed near a knot of low buildings he was using as a reference point. The explosion sent a shower of yellow sparks skyward; they peaked at fifty feet before falling back to the ground. Steele was close enough to hear the growl of the explosion and immediately began searching for an alternate spot.

"Deploying chute," the calm female voice announced.

"Hell no you're—"

It was too late.

The Military Freefall Advanced Ram Air Parachute System, or MFF ARAPS, was the replacement for the older MC-4 and was basically a rectangular wing. When it ripped free of the pack tray the nylon canopy blossomed, filling each of the thirteen airfoil sections with air. The ribs were the only things keeping him from plunging to his death, and Steele checked them and the risers to make sure nothing was tangled or torn.

He grabbed the toggles running from the control lines and took command of the chute. *Well, if I'm going down, I want to do it in style.*

"Initiate iTunes. Black Sabbath—'War Pigs.' Purchase and play."

"Are you sure you want to purchase 'War Pigs' by—"

"Yes, dammit."

"Your purchase has been processed. Playing 'War Pigs.'"

The heavy guitar riff blasted through the speakers, building over the bass guitar and the haunting whine of an air raid siren. On the ground tracer fire coiled and whipped from building to building, with explosions erupting in time with the music. Steele felt like he had front-row seats to a Michael Bay movie, but then it got serious.

The woman's voice sounded calm over the music. "Taking fire. Taking fire."

"Where?" Steele frantically searched for the shooters, but the only thing he saw was a group of men running toward a truck. Most of the fire seemed to be contained near the buildings where he was supposed to land. It didn't appear that anyone had noticed him lazily descending from the darkened heavens.

No whammies, please God no whammies.

His luck failed to hold when the first red tracer zipped past his helmet. All he could do was yank hard on the toggle in an attempt to get out of the line of fire. He could handle getting shot at. It was part of the job. But taking fire when you couldn't shoot back, or even see where it was coming from, was a different ball game. The only thing he could do was extend his middle finger in the direction of the shots and hope the Mark XI really was bulletproof.

"Turn it up."

"You are taking fire."

"Yeah, I got that part. How 'bout you tell me where—"

The tug on the canopy rolled down the riser, jarring his left hand. Steele looked up and saw two jagged rips across the ribs. He pulled the toggle hard left and sent the chute into a tight corkscrew. He needed to get on the ground now, and when he was a hundred feet above it he prepared to flare by yanking both toggles as far down as he could.

There was no change in the rate of his descent.

This is not how this is supposed to go.

Steele scrambled for the reserve chute, already knowing it was too late. His hand found the ripcord and he tore it free. The reserve valiantly sought air, but Steele was already searching for someplace soft to land. The only viable option was a dilapidated chicken coop inside a walled compound. With Ozzy screaming in his helmet, *"Begging mercies for their sins, Satan laughing spreads his wings,"* Steele brought his feet up to his chest, barely clearing the wall that some asshole had lined with jagged shards of glass embedded in the concrete. He tensed his muscles, and pulled the risers down until he thought that his shoulders were going to pop out of their sockets. All he needed to do was slow down enough not to break his back. Finally the reserve thumped open and he decelerated a second before his boots hit the roof. Something hit the side of the helmet and then he punched through the corrugated tin like a lawn dart launched from space. The music cut off, followed by a second blast to the helmet that knocked him out.

Steele came to slowly. He was inside a small shed, legs entangled in the risers and the face shield cracked in front of his eye. "Are we there yet?" he groaned.

The source of the crack was a shard of metal embedded in the shatterproof glass. Steele tugged it free and tried to clear the cobwebs. The metal was hot through his gloves and he recognized the nasty sliver as a piece of an RPG's nose cone.

Everything was silent except for his heavy breathing. Steele tugged the helmet off and heard frantic voices coming closer. He hit the riser release, stripped the 1911 from his chest, and held the pistol at the ready. Outside the voices were getting closer.

"He is in here!" someone yelled in Arabic.

"Kill him, kill him!"

The door flew open, revealing a man with an AK-47 who stood there scanning the interior. Steele waited for him to step inside, then dropped him with a shot to the skull. He scrambled to his feet. There was no time to grab his rifle from his pack—the only thing he could do was press the attack. Moving to the door, he saw three more men running toward him, their chests heaving and fingers on the triggers. The closest man saw him step out. He wasn't expecting one man to attack and his eyes widened in surprise.

"Not today, boys."

Steele fired the first round too fast and it hit his target in the hip. The round spun him like a top, but Steele frowned, knowing he had rushed the shot. He settled automatically into a shooter's stance and reengaged the first target before shifting fire to the other two.

Thwap, thwap, thwap.

The suppressed 9mm bounced from chest to chest, sending a hollow point mushrooming into each. All three men were down before the first casing tumbled to the ground. Steele stepped out and finished them off with a single shot to the head. In combat there were no prizes for second place.

He checked his surroundings and shoved a fresh magazine into the pistol before heading inside to collect his gear. Outside, the gunfire slowly grew to a crescendo until it sounded like the entire city had taken up arms. Steele paused by the door, remembering a verse he'd heard a long time ago. *Yea, though I walk through the valley of the shadow of death, I will fear no evil.* He racked a fresh round into his rifle: *Because I am the baddest mother in the valley.*

Chapter 22

Algiers

Nathaniel West stood on the rooftop, picking at the blood beneath his nails with the tip of a white-handled knife.

"What's that smell?" his radioman asked, moving closer.

"Rubber," he replied without looking up from the battlefield manicure. "The rebels are burning tires to mark their positions."

"Coyote, this is Eyeball," the radio crackled. It was Villars, and West could tell by the tone of his voice that he was finished sulking. "Target vehicle is approaching Phase Line Blue."

Showtime.

West nodded, blew his fingers clean, and slipped the knife back into its sheath. He sauntered to the edge of the rooftop and surveyed the city with the bored look of a foreman at a job site. To the south, near the consulate, a cloud of dirt and rock erupted next to the wall, followed a few seconds later by a low *cruuump*. West studied the explosion like a scholar seeking meaning in an ancient text. There was much to see if you knew where to look.

The explosion bloomed outward, scorching the wall and flinging concrete and debris in an ever-widening circle. West knew it was a mortar by the blast pattern. An artillery shell traveled in a straight line from the barrel to the point of impact. You could tell an artillery round by the "splash," or the impact of the shell. The blast pattern looked just like the divots you'd find on the fairway of a golf course.

A mortar was different because they were indirect fire weapons, which meant that they went up and after reaching their max ordinate let gravity carry them down to their target. Mortars were silent and deadly, perfect for fighting in the city.

The unfolding battle sent adrenaline radiating through him. The only thing West had in common with the man he was four years ago was his name. Everything else had been stripped away by death and flame. But the change was deeper than his scarred skin. There was a time when Nate believed in childish things like justice and hope. Now violence was his only religion.

"The law of tooth and claw," he said to his radioman as he took a cigarette from behind his ear. "Do you know what that means?"

The man shook his head. He was just a hired gun and understood simple things like rate of fire and keeping fresh batteries in the radio. Like a good soldier, he left the thinking to others.

"It means that this," West said, lighting the smoke before sweeping his hand to encompass the entire city, "is the only law that matters in this world."

Everything else was empty promises and paper threats. They were illusions. A weak man had no more control over his life than a sailor in a squall. Charlie Daniels had found this out the hard way. Nate thought back to how quickly he had broken the spy.

"You like my knife?" West had asked him. "A guy in Zaire made it for me." There was fear in Daniels's eyes, and West savored it the same way he'd savored the hate in Villars's. Men were like dogs—all they really wanted was to know their place.

"I'll tell you whatever you want to know."

West continued like he hadn't heard him. "What do you think he made this handle out of?"

"I don't know. Ivory, maybe?"

"You are close, my man. He wanted to make it out of ivory, said he had some rhino horn he could use. But I wanted this knife to be special, you know, something that had meaning, and for the life of me I couldn't think of a single time a rhino had done anything to me. I'll give you another guess. Take a good look."

Daniels wanted nothing to do with this game.

"Wood?"

"Nope. It's a femur. You know what that is, CIA man?"

"A le . . . a leg bone."

"Yep. See, there are a lot of people out there who have done things to me. Like this one man, he raped my wife and kidnapped my son. When I found him I knew I wanted to remember him, so I took a little piece with me."

West was an expert at getting people to tell him things. The secret wasn't in the fear. If you beat a man he'd tell you anything he thought you wanted to know. West knew that to get to the truth you had to let them think that they had control of their own destiny.

After he cut off the first finger, Daniels started talking so fast that he had to tell him to slow down. The person West was looking for was a woman by the name of Meg Harden, and she was the only one in Algiers who had full access to the Gatehouse.

So how did Breul get inside? Daniels didn't know, and honestly it didn't matter. Breul had pulled it off and left Nate's prize inside. When he was sure that Daniels had told him everything he knew, West put him out of his misery. In a way he felt like he'd done the CIA a favor by shaving some dead weight off their books.

He smiled at his own joke. "Dead weight," he said with a shake of his head. "I crack myself up."

The sound of thumping rotor blades drew his attention to the ocean, where a pair of French Lynx helicopters zipped over the shore like a pair of green dragonflies. As usual they were late to the party, but unlike the Americans, who were still reeling from Benghazi, at least they were showing up.

West knew the helos were on station to protect his target. The Americans didn't have any assets in the area except for a drone that he knew was loitering over the embassy. He bent over the edge to spit and saw a knot of fighters milling about in the alleys.

"Tell them to get to work," he growled to one of his men, who nodded and lifted the radio to his lips.

Across the way, another of his fighters lifted a Stinger surface-to-air missile and nodded to his boss. West flicked the cigarette up at the two helos and headed for the stairs.

In the basement there were two armored vehicles waiting for him. They looked like Suburbans on steroids, and West knew they cost two hundred and fifty grand apiece. Not that it mattered, because he wasn't paying for any of this anyway. Besides the machine guns mounted to the top, West's favorite part of the trucks was the snowplow attached to the lead vehicle. He couldn't wait to see it in action.

He took a seat in the lead vehicle, and the armored door hissed closed on its hydraulic arm. Pulling a shotgun off the rack, he checked to make sure it was loaded, then told the driver, "Roll out."

Next to him Villars sat before a bank of radios. He was scanning multiple frequencies that were going in three different languages.

"I've got a lock," one of his men said over the internal radio channel.

"Tell him to send it."

The driver hit the gas while Villars relayed the message. The turbodiesel roared like a caged animal and the vehicle leapt onto the street. West had the window cracked and heard the RPGs scream skyward. He knew that his man with the Stinger had locked onto the helo and the pilot thought the RPGs were actually surface-to-air missiles. The flares spilled from the back of the Lynx, hoping to fool the heat-seeking missile. The door gunner in the trail bird fired a long burst at the rooftop before juking away. West's man knew his business; he waited for the Lynx to expend its counter-measures before firing the Stinger.

"Missile away."

West caught a glimpse of the contrail rising up and then lost it to the building.

The driver turned east, the knobby tires whining over the pavement. Up front the man in the passenger seat controlled the turret gun via a joystick tied into the targeting system. When a line of Algerian soldiers darted from cover, West was able to clearly see every detail through the monitor attached to the fire control.

Two soldiers provided covering fire while a team tried to set up a machine gun. The 7.62 pinged harm-lessly off the armor plate while the man calmly centered the reticle on the soldiers. He jammed his thumb over the button on the top of the stick and there was a shak-ing on the roof. Expended brass tinkled off the roof slats and rolled off the side. West snapped the harness over his shoulders while the first burst cut the soldiers down in the street.

"Gun truck on your right," someone called out over the radio.

"I got it," the driver said.

"Ramming speed!" West shouted.

The driver smiled and smashed the pedal to the floor, centering the reinforced plow on the Mercedes SUV painted army green. The soldier manning the DShK .51 cal machine gun in the back saw them coming and jumped clear, but it was too late for the rest of them. The impact sent the Mercedes whipsawing across the road. Inside the armored SUV West barely felt it.

The driver cut the wheel to the left, letting the trail vehicle deal with any survivors. West grabbed the handmike and depressed the talk button.

"Coyote to Eyeball, where are they?"

"Coyote, they are one block over, five hundred meters south of the target."

"You are free to engage." West clipped the handmike into the cradle and leaned up toward the driver. "As fun as this is, I have a date, and you know how I hate being late."

Chapter 23

The embassy was locked down. It was standard protocol after what happened in Benghazi. The chief
of station didn't have a choice and told Meg to get to the
Gatehouse and harden up. The only backup he could
arrange were a pair of French Lynx helicopters that
were supposed to pick the team up from the Gatehouse.

Meg wasn't worried about an extraction; she was
just hoping they could make it *to* the Gatehouse, when
the first AK rounds slammed into the van.

"Contact front!" she yelled, ducking her head.

James was driving and he jerked the wheel to the
right while she brought her rifle up and turned toward
the window. In the front seat Colt was yelling into the
radio, "Axle 1, this is Axle 3. Where the hell are those
birds?"

A bullet hit the hood, ricocheting up and through the windshield. The driver swerved, the round buzzing angrily past him and down the center aisle, barely missing Meg's head. It blew out the back window and Meg reached down for her helmet. Her head was between her legs when the team opened up.

"Mad minute, mad minute!" Colt yelled.

It was the standard operating procedure in a near-side ambush, a tactic where everyone fired even if they didn't have a target. Each member of the team had an assigned sector and their job was to lay down a wall of lead and hopefully back their attackers off long enough for the driver to get the van clear of the kill zone. The pressure from five rifles firing as one hit Meg like an openhanded slap to the ears. Besides worrying that her eardrums might burst, she had shards of glass, expended brass, and James's erratic driving to contend with.

Meg brought her rifle up and was about to fire when a casing pinged off the ceiling, hit her neck, and slid down the back of her shirt. *Ahhhhhh.* The casing was hot and the pain scalding. She gritted her teeth and tried to shake it free instead of shooting. Her eyes weren't off the street for a second before a man stepped out of an alley with an RPG raised and ready.

She fired five quick shots. Meg was so intent on

ducking her head to avoid getting glass in her eyes that she didn't bother with a sight picture, and by the time she looked up she had no idea if she had even hit the target.

You know better than that. Slow down and get a damn sight picture.

"Watch out!" someone yelled.

Out of the corner of her eye Meg saw another fighter run out into the street, a belt-fed machine gun at his hip. He wasn't in her sector, so there was nothing she could do except pray that Colt was on his game.

Staying alive in a situation like this was all about discipline and sectors of fire. Unfortunately, Meg had never trained with the team and all she had to work with was what she had done in the Army.

Bullets punched holes in the van and snapped through the interior, carrying upholstery, plastic, and bits of glass. The back of Meg's chair shuddered and behind the wheel James screamed in pain.

Meg worked her sector but felt the van was slowing. They were getting hit from all sides and it seemed like behind every door and window there was a muzzle flashing at them.

"James!" Colt yelled.

She reloaded, and looked up front, where James was falling slowly out of his seat, his hands clawed around his neck. Bright arterial spray spurted through his fingers and splashed across Colt's face.

The engine shuddered and shrieked, reminding Meg of a dying horse. She knew they were screwed if the van stopped. Flipping the rifle to safe, she climbed between the seats.

"I'm sorry," she said, dragging James, the man she had sparred with earlier that day, from his chair.

The wheel was slick with blood and vibrated wildly from shot-out tires. Before she could get it under control the van jumped the curb and crunched a wall with a glancing blow. Meg could barely see out the spider-webbed windshield and it took everything she had to get the van under control.

"Can you do something about the glass?" she yelled.

Colt had his back turned. He was passing the dying driver to the team medic.

"Hey"—Meg grabbed him by the plate carrier and shook it—"I need you up here, I can't see."

She cautioned a quick look over her shoulder and saw Colt look at her. His eyes were wide and vacant behind the bloody mask that covered his face.

"Colt, are you with me?" she yelled.

He blinked rapidly and then snapped out of it and slammed the windshield with the butt of his rifle. After three hits it popped out and slid down the hood. Meg pushed the pedal to the floor, the wind hot on her face. Shredded rubber slapped against the underside of the van as she accelerated. *Just keep going,* she thought, instinctively pulling the seat belt on.

The blood-spattered hula girl James had mounted to the dash bobbed back and forth with the vibrations of the van, and then it was gone, blasted to bits by a bullet.

"Whoa."

Despite all the damage, the Garmin GPS suction-cupped to the "A" pillar was still mapping the route to the Gatehouse. While she knew its location, the driver had not. According to the arrow, she needed to take the next right. The Gatehouse would be less than two hundred meters away.

"Hold on!" she yelled, letting off the gas and cranking the wheel as hard as she could manage. The rims screeched on the cobblestones and the back end started to slide. Meg manhandled the wheel, ignoring her burning biceps, and somehow she brought the van around like a ship in a storm.

In the rear of the van one of the men screamed in pain. Meg didn't realize she had looked back, but she must have, because when her eyes settled on the road again the last thing she saw was the sunlight reflecting off a metal plow.

Chapter 24

Eric Steele secured the Surefire suppressor to the H&K with a twist. He was a big fan of the company because they kept it simple. Unlike the Mark XI, which after two bullets was now just a million-dollar paperweight.

"Don't worry, buddy, I'll get you back to the nerds," he said, patting the helmet before stuffing it into the assault pack.

Three feet away the dead fighters lay face up on the ground. He bent over the bodies, ignoring the flies crawling over sightless eyes. They were Algerians and their AK-47s were brand-new, just like the jungle boots and Chicom chest rigs.

He went through their pockets, trying to find out who they were and where they had come from. The pocket litter wasn't much help. Together the men had a pack of gum, three condoms, and about fifty dollars American.

Steele had no pity for them. They had tried to kill him and failed. He was on his own, and the only reason he wasn't laid out on the ground was because he had been faster on the trigger. It was as simple as that. In combat he lived by three basic tenets. If you want to come home you have to be faster, louder, and more violent than your enemy.

It was a lesson he'd learned many times over.

Steele slung the H&K 416 and checked his GPS. His first stop now was the dead drop he'd instructed Breul to use in case they ever got separated. While he didn't know why the Iranian had crossed the border on his own, he knew why Breul had come to Algiers.

Because that's what I told him to do.

The spot was a low wall to the north, less than three hundred meters away. He and Breul had worked out a series of signs they'd leave on the brick with a piece of chalk, but to get there, he was going to have to cross the street.

He stopped at the gate and peeked out, clearing as much of the danger area as he could. He was on the outskirts of the city, on the wrong side of a well-traveled road that cut through a jumble of warehouses and low-rent apartments. He needed to cross and cut through the neighborhoods to get to his target location. To his immediate left a group of fighters were posted beside a Toyota pickup with a machine gun mounted to the bed. On his right side another group of fighters had their backs to him. They were talking loudly and ambling toward the city.

Steele waited for the machine gun to start firing before crossing the street, and halfway to the other side he ran across a fighter wearing a black Wu-Tang T-shirt and camo pants. They saw each other at the same time and Steele realized that the fighter had the drop on him. The fighter froze; Steele didn't.

He twisted his upper body toward the target and sent one perfect round through the man's eyeball. The fighter dropped like a stone and Steele got off the street, moving deeper into the warren of houses that grew around him as he moved to the site of the dead drop.

He rushed to the wall, keeping low while searching for the chalk mark that Breul would have placed on the brick if he had left something there. He found it after a few seconds of searching—a white line near the bottom of the wall.

Eric took a knee and pried the loose brick out with his knife. There was a sheet of paper enclosed in a

Ziploc bag and he stuffed it in his shirt pocket, before moving deeper into the neighborhood. He used the shadows of the houses for cover and finally stopped near the corner of a one-story concrete house to check his watch. *You are running out of time. Pick up the pace.*

He was about to jog off when a meaty slap followed by a pathetic whimper came from the window to his left.

Stepping closer to the window, Steele found himself looking into a living room. Inside two men were wrestling a woman half their size to the ground. One of the fighters was on his knees near her shoulders, a toothy grin spread across his face. The woman kicked at him, and earned a slap across the face for her troubles.

Steele heard a third voice. "I'm first," it said. Eric tried to locate the third man, and that was when he saw the two children huddled beneath the table to his right.

The older of the two was a boy, maybe nine or ten. His young cheeks were tear-drenched and he held his sister's head tight to his chest.

Demo's warning echoed in Steele's head.

The only thing that matters is securing that bomb.

But Steele was already pushing the door open with the muzzle of his rifle and stepped inside in time to hear a blade clearing leather.

"Put this in her mouth," the man said, handing the blade to the fighter holding her shoulders.

He placed his knee between her legs and the woman cried out, which made the fighters laugh.

"I like it when they fight," the second man said, grabbing the woman's blouse and exposing her breasts.

Steele centered the reticle on the man's left eye before pushing the door closed with his heel. The hinges squeaked and the fighter with the knife looked up.

Thwap.

The hollow point hit the man like a freight train slamming into a bowl of Jell-O and sent the contents of the fighter's head spraying across his partner's face. Not that Steele gave the second fighter long to figure out what was covering him. Steele put him down with his second shot, before stepping up to the third fighter and slamming the buttstock into the back of the man's head, knocking him off the woman. The man screamed, and crumpled to the floor. Steele locked eyes with him for a split second, then put a bullet in his skull.

"It's okay, it's okay," he said.

Steele spoke calmly, and moved to the couch, where he tugged a threadbare blanket from the arm and held it up. "I am not going to hurt you," he said in Arabic. The woman let him drape the blanket across her chest, and then Steele turned to the children hiding under the table.

The boy was still watching, and Steele shot him a smile, trying to reassure him.

"There will be more coming," Steele said, looking at the woman. He gestured to the door. "I have to go, do you understand?"

She nodded, her eyes wide and glistening like a saucer fresh from the sink.

"Do you have a back door?"

The woman opened her mouth but hadn't yet found her voice.

"This way," the little boy squeaked.

Steele followed his tiny figure through a doorway and nodded gratefully to the boy. The boy nodded back.

"Lock the door and take care of them, little man," Steele said, tousling the boy's black hair.

The back door was heavier than the front and didn't quite fit in the frame. Near the jamb the latch had been reinforced from the last time someone had kicked it in, and someone had drilled a peephole near the top. It was a rough neighborhood for a single mother and her children, and Steele wished he could do more for them. He felt especially bad for the boy, because he knew what it was like growing up without a father.

He pulled the door open. It was clear and he had to go.

Chapter 25

West casually stepped out of the armored vehicle, holding the shotgun by the pistol grip. The van was totaled, the front end crumpled from the plow and radiator fluid evaporating off of the engine block in coils of sweet-smelling steam.

"That . . . was . . . awesome," he said, admiring the devastation. "I have to get one of those."

The passenger-side door was open and West heard an electronic dinging coming from the interior. A shot rang out. It was high and the bullet sailed harmlessly over his head. West brought the shotgun up and darted wide, angling away from the door. He saw a head appear, and kept pieing the corner.

His target was ducked down, trying to clear his jammed rifle. The man was bloody and dressed in a tan plate carrier, green combat pants, and no helmet.

"Hey," West hissed.

The man looked up in time to see the barrel and then West fired. The 12-gauge tactical slug hit him in the top of the chest, right below the throat, and knocked him off his feet. He was dead before he hit the ground.

West moved closer to the van. A groan emanated from the interior, followed by glass cracking and the pop of the sliding latch. The door slid open and West swung the shotgun to bear. Bloody fingers curled around the edge of the door, followed by a curse.

"Shiiiiit," the voice groaned from the effort of sliding the door open. West stepped closer, pushing the door open with the barrel. There was another SOG man there in the same tan plate carrier. He pulled himself into a seated position one-handed, a thick stream of blood pouring from the deep laceration in his face and splattering onto the street.

"Hey, buddy, you okay?" West asked.

The man looked up, eyes focusing on the shotgun first and then squinting up at West. He tried to raise the rifle hanging from the twisted sling around his neck but his right arm wouldn't work and a look of confusion fell over his face.

"I'm no doctor, but I think it's broken," West said, nudging the bone with the barrel.

"Fuuuuck!" the man screamed. "Why did you do that?"

West shrugged. "Because I'm an asshole, I guess," he said, yanking the man out of the van and throwing him on the ground. He dumped a slug into his face, feeling nothing, and then walked around to the driver's side.

Meg was leaned forward, head resting against the wheel. For a moment West thought she might be dead, but then he saw the seat belt rising against her chest. He set the shotgun on the crumpled hood and yanked on the latch. The door was hung up, but gave way after a serious tug.

"You alive?"

"Uhhhhhh," she groaned.

"I'll take that as a yes."

West cut the seat belt with his knife and grabbed her by the hair. He was yanking Meg out of the van when she came to. She reached weakly for his hands, legs collapsing when he dropped her on the ground.

Gunfire erupted from the west, but he wasn't worried. His men were already moving to set up a perimeter, and one of the trucks was already blocking the road.

"Take her inside, and tell Villars to buy us some time," he ordered.

Chapter 26

It took Steele five minutes to reach the target location after leaving the house. He had to fight for every inch, and by the time he ducked into a burned-out shack just short of the Gatehouse there were four holes in the assault pack and the Mark XI was pockmarked with more bullet holes.

"This is the gift that keeps on giving."

He went to work refilling the magazines, replacing expended frags, and mentally switching gears. Getting inside the Gatehouse wasn't like knocking over a 7-Eleven; it was a hardened site with serious defenses. For all Steele knew it could have already fallen, so before making a move he needed to get a sense of the situation.

Inside the shredded assault pack was a Kevlar-reinforced case that housed a drone and a monitor he could strap to his wrist. The UAV, or unmanned aerial vehicle, was about the size of a clay pigeon, and when Steele pressed the flat button in the center, the drone began to hum.

He set it on the charred windowsill and waited for the screen to come alive. When it did, he was looking at an aerial photo of the Gatehouse. He used his finger to drag a geo fence around the target house. The red box marked the path he wanted the drone to take, and once he was satisfied, he hit the send button.

The UAV lifted silently from its perch on the window frame and hovered while linking with the satellites. Once it had a lock, the tiny drone whizzed toward the Gatehouse, its sensors and cameras sending real-time images back to the monitor.

The three guards at the gate and two armored vehicles blocking the street confirmed Steele's fears. He was too late.

Someone had beat him to the Gatehouse. The UAV picked up an additional heat signature on the roof, and a closer look revealed a sniper. He had seen everything he needed to, and he typed a command to the drone before taking the monitor off his wrist and shoving it into his back pocket.

Time to separate the groupies from the rock stars.

Steele climbed on top of a wooden pallet, peering over the wall at the Gatehouse. It was a white one-story building, almost like a ranch house. Except the thick walls and inset windows that marked it as a structure designed to be defended indefinitely. Steele knew that a frontal assault wouldn't work.

Let's see if we can avoid a siege.

He threw the Claymore mine over the gate toward the men and their vehicle. In his back pocket the monitor vibrated, telling him that the drone was on its way to the roof.

"Gotta love technology," he said, taking the detonator.

A moment later the drone exploded above the sniper and Steele pressed the button. The Claymore went off in a roar of smoke, spraying a thousand ball bearings in a lethal arc. Steele was close enough to hear them pinging off the armored vehicles and the screams of the men being cut down.

He stood up, set the H&K on top of the wall, and shot the first guard through the chest before he could lift the radio to his mouth. A second guard rushed toward the gate and Steele held the reticle on the leading edge of his body, dumping two rounds into his side. The man stumbled and went down, and as he turned toward Steele, Eric put the final round through his skull.

A rifle chattered near the corner of the building. Steele ducked and the bullets hammered into the wall, chipping pieces of brick into the air. The rounds cracked and whined over his head, and Steele waited a second before sticking the muzzle over the wall and returning fire.

He wasn't trying to hit the man, just hold him in place so he could get to the other position. He jumped down, prepping a grenade while sprinting to the second pallet he'd set up ten feet to his left. He climbed up, yanking the pin before peering over. The guard fired two more shots at the wall and edged forward, his rifle trained on the last place he had seen a target.

Steele let go of the spoon and lobbed the frag in a high arc. It hit the gravel at the guard's feet, and before it detonated, Steele threw his leg over the wall and jumped inside the compound.

Chapter 27

Meg came to slowly, and the first thing she heard was the voice.

It was gravelly and rough, almost like a smoker's. "You alive?"

She tried to speak, but the words never left her brain. Strong hands dragged her out of the van and flung her on the ground. Then she was being carried. Meg's senses came to slowly like a computer after a hard reset. She turned her head and pain sparked down her spine and into her shoulder, followed by a wave of nausea.

She saw the van smoking and the shattered body of her friend Colt. His face was gone and he was lying in a pool of blood. Then she passed out.

"Hey, wake up."

She opened her eyes and the man stopped slapping her. Meg's vision cleared slowly and she looked around the room. *Where am I?* There was something familiar about the white walls and stainless steel cabinets of the room. Then it hit her.

"How you feelin', tiger?" The man asked, grabbing her face and flashing a penlight into her eyes.

When he pulled the light away, Meg saw that half of his face had the lizard look of a bad skin graft. She had seen burns like that in Iraq, but it was his eyes that chilled her.

"Like someone hit me with a truck."

"You had a little fender-bender," he said with a laugh.

The memories came back in flashes, in no discernible order. They were in the van, and then she was behind the wheel. Hot brass burning her skin. The man's voice, followed by a gunshot.

"You killed them."

"Not all of them. Some of those guys were already dead."

"Who are you?"

"Where are my manners? Sorry. My name is Nathaniel West, and I need you to do something for me."

"Go to hell."

Nate grabbed a handful of Meg's hair and roughly forced her head around. She was looking at him now, and West savored the grimace of pain that flitted across her face and the fear that sparked in her eyes. When she tried to jerk free he stuck a blade against her cheek and smiled at the involuntary flinch caused by the cold steel touching warm flesh.

"Listen, girlie, I don't have a lot of time. You are going to do what I want or I will cut your fucking face off."

Meg nodded, her shoulders sagging in defeat. Nate pulled the blade away, and she was ready for it, using her forehead to ram his face as hard as she could. His nose crunched, and hot blood hit her cheek.

Nate grunted and danced backward. "Whoo-wee, looks like we have a wildcat on our hands."

His backhand came out of nowhere. Meg had never seen anyone move that fast, and after it landed, she fell out of the chair. Nate was on her in a second. He wrapped his scarred hands around her throat and began choking her. Meg grabbed at his fingers, trying to break them, or at least weaken his grip, but Nate was too strong. He squeezed so hard she thought her eyes were going to pop out.

"You think just because you are a woman I won't fucking waste you like I did your team," he hissed, squeezing tighter.

"Boss, we need her alive."

The fire in Nate's eyes dimmed, and just as suddenly as he had attacked, he let her go.

Meg fell to her knees, her vision narrowed at the edges from the restricted blood flow. Her throat felt tight and she coughed, trying to open it.

"Let's get her up."

The two men lifted her easily and pinned her arms to her sides before carrying her over to the computer. Meg saw the retina reader, and though she didn't know what they wanted, she wasn't going to give anything to them without a fight. She started thrashing, trying to break free.

"This isn't going to work. Put her down," Nate commanded.

Meg tensed, ready to fight, but never got the chance. Before her feet touched the tile Nate slammed his fist into her chest.

"Uuuuumph."

She had been hit before, but never like this. The blow was paralyzing and she was pretty sure he had broken a rib. Her ankles were pushed together and she heard the zip ties click over them. Nate dragged her over to the computer and then hit her across the back of the neck. She felt fingers prying her eyes open and saw the reader in front of her face. There was a flash of light followed by a beep, and a robotic voice said, "Welcome, Ms. Harden. Access granted."

A wall of the reinforced safe clicked open.

They dropped her on the floor, and helpless tears burned her eyes. *You have to fight.*

Meg kicked at the back of Nate's leg, a halfhearted attempt, but it got his attention.

"Damn, you don't know when to quit, do you?"

He stumbled, and she heard him laugh.

The man punched her hard in the side of the head. Meg felt the blow all the way down to her ankles, and heard her neck pop. Her scalp burned as he dragged her across the floor by her hair and threw her against the wall. He zip-tied her to a pipe with her hands above her head.

All she could feel was the burning in her wrists, when suddenly the roof shuddered violently.

Chapter 28

The explosion rolled up the man's body, severed his legs, and threw him backward. Steele hit the ground and scanned the area for any more threats before engaging the two cameras attached to the building. He climbed over the wall and took off toward the entrance, rifle at the ready. The exterior door looked flimsy, and for a second he thought that he had gotten lucky.

He delivered a powerful kick aimed at the spot just above the knob, and quickly realized his error. The shock ran up his leg, rebounding him off the door.

"Son of a bitch," he spat.

Steele backed off, angry with himself for the lapse in common sense.

This is a high-security area, do you really think they are just going to hang any old door in the frame?

He scanned the door, taking his time while looking for any markings that would tell him what he was working with. There was a small engraving of a shield near the hinges. He shook his head and began muttering to himself.

"Of course, a freakin' Shield."

Shield Security was renowned for their class 4 doors, which were used in embassies and banks all over the world. They were bulletproof and fireproof, and the glass rods running through the center made drilling the lock a nonstarter. Not that Steele had brought a drill with him anyway.

His plan was less time-consuming—he was going to blow the door through the wall.

Steele dropped his pack and dug out a canvas satchel with a cartoonish skeleton key drawn on the front. Inside was a one-pound block of C-4, a collection of metal strips cut at different angles, and a thick roll of Breachers Tape. He quickly assembled a charge, and then packed the C-4 around the door.

He ended up using more than expected, and when the charge was finally in place, it took up the entire pound of C-4.

"This is going to be *hot*."

Steele backed up well past the acceptable "minimum safe distance" before slipping his index finger through the pull ring.

Safety first.

He ducked his head, opened his mouth to avoid blowing out his eardrums, and yanked on the pin.

The first sign that he had used way too much explosives was when he found himself sitting on his ass. The extra pressure had rebounded off the wall and knocked him over like a bowling pin.

"That might have been a bit much," he grunted as he got to his feet and went to inspect the breach.

The explosion had blasted a hole in the wall big enough to ride a horse through and sent thick cracks running up toward the roof. Steele coughed at the dust and smoke and stepped inside, bits of concrete falling on his shoulders. The interior was hazy because of the low ceiling that trapped the smoke close to the ground. He worked the room from left to right, flashing his rifle light on and off to cut through the haze. A fluorescent tube swung from its fixture and the particulates the explosion had stirred up tickled his throat. He waved his hand in front of his face, hoping to clear the air, and quickly fell victim to a coughing fit.

"Damn," he croaked finally. "Where's the water fountain?"

"Look out!" a woman screamed.

Steele immediately ducked into a crouch, searching for the voice or the threat. The bulb finally fell from its ballast, and he snapped his muzzle toward the tinkling glass, sweeping the safety with his thumb.

The muzzle flash blinked at the edge of his peripheral vision, erupting through the gloom like a yellow sun. He reacted, stepping to his left, rifle swinging on target, and firing. The rifle bucked in his hands and he staggered when a round hit his ballistic plate, sledge-hammering him backward. His feet got tangled in the debris, his foot slipping on a broken tile, and he was falling.

Flat on his back, Steele knew the shooter had him, and the only thing that saved his life was the familiar *cruuump* that erupted near the wall.

Goddamn mortars.

Steele had been on the receiving end of mortar fire in Afghanistan more times than he cared to remember. He could take RPGs and 107mm rockets, because at least you could hear them coming, but the first hint that mortars were falling was when they exploded.

The impact shook the walls, kicking even more grit into the air. He still couldn't see the gunmen, but heard the rounds snapping past him. He rolled. "Son of a bitch," he swore at the searing pain that lanced his side.

Steele kicked his feet behind him, trying to crab into a shooting position. He got the rifle up just as the exhaust fan kicked on, cutting a path through the smoke and revealing the man searching for him with the rifle. Steele fired twice and the man fell. He got to his feet, ignoring the stabbing pain in his side, and then the second mortar round hit the roof and exploded.

The red strobe and the exhaust fan quit at the same time, and in the darkness Steele heard a hissing sound. He tried to place it over the woman screaming at him to "cut me loose!"

Steele moved cautiously, scanning the heaps of trash and broken sections of roof lining the floor. He picked his way toward the sound of the woman's voice, and then got his first unmistakable whiff of natural gas.

Explosion ruptured the gas line.

He knew that if the fan didn't come back on it wouldn't take long for the Gatehouse to fill up with natural gas and turn the room into a bomb.

"Hurry."

"I'm coming!" he yelled as the backup generator kicked on and the strobes and fan came back online.

But it was the flashlight that blazed out of nowhere that froze Steele like a deer in headlights. Whoever was on the other end centered the powerful beam on his face. He was blinded and was about to shoot when a voice he hadn't heard in four years froze him in place.

"Easy, kid, bullets and gas are a bad mix."

"Nate?" Steele held up his hand, trying to shield his eyes. The light dropped to his chest, and then he could see.

"In the flesh."

The light was attached to a shotgun, and with the backlight there was no mistaking his mentor.

"Shoot him!" the woman yelled.

The third mortar sparked the gas, sending orange fingers licking through the air. The heat was incredible and quickly sucked the air out of the room. Steele's chest tightened, each breath harder to draw, and what air he got burned his throat and lungs. He stared at Nate, who just stood there, scars highlighted by the flame—eyes silent and glaring like those of a wraith from the grave.

"You going to let her die too?" Nate said finally.

And then the ceiling fell in with a torrent of embers and jagged bits of metal and brick. Steele covered his head, and when he looked up, Nate was gone.

Chapter 29

I saw him die.

Steele stood fast, bolted to the floor by doubt and memory. The flames still flicking around the floor where he'd last seen Nate.

Go.

He leapt through the fire, raising his arm against the heat that cooked the sweat off his face. On the other side he found a doorway, and he was about to charge after West when he heard the woman screaming.

"Please! Don't leave me!"

Steele stopped; he was so close he could see the sliver of light outlining a door at the end of the hall. *He's right there—just on the other side. I can still catch him.*

It was a defining moment, an answer to the pain and misery that had plagued every day of the past four years.

"Please!" the woman screamed.

"Shit!" Steele yelled.

He ripped himself angrily from the pursuit and turned his attention to the woman zip-tied to the pipe. Her face was covered in soot and dried blood and her hair was matted against her scalp. She was helpless, but just for an instant, Steele considered leaving her.

"Dammit."

It took everything he had to step back into the flame, and as he did, he stripped the knife from the sheath on his chest carrier.

The flames had begun to burn out and were licking at the edges of the ceiling in search of oxygen. Steele ignored the heat, and was so angry he never heard the high-pressure hiss right above him.

"Hey, look . . ." the woman said.

"I'm coming," Steele grumbled.

"No, look out!"

He stopped and glanced toward the ceiling where she was pointing. The last thing he saw was the tail end of a flame get sucked through the crack next to the central gas line that bulged like a python after swallowing a pig.

Steele tried to jump out of the way, but his rifle got hung up. He cut the sling free, barely dodging the falling ceiling. When the dust cleared, he made his way over to the woman.

"Hey, how's it going?"

"Fine. Now cut me loose."

He hesitated a second when he brought the knife up.

"Both of you need to stand still."

"What?"

"Just kidding," he said, before turning the blade and cutting the cuff without breaking her skin.

"We need to go," she said, coughing.

The woman pushed past him without a word of thanks, but instead of heading to the doorway, she jogged over to the computer.

"What in the hell are you *doing*?"

"My job."

I've had about enough of this.

He gingerly hobbled after her and grabbed the back of her shirt. "Unless you are a fireman, we have to go right now."

She typed furiously and shrugged him off when he placed his hand on her shoulder. "Just a second."

"We don't have a second," Steele replied, snatching her off her feet and carrying her to the door. A beam fell from the ceiling, crushing the computer and sending a cloud of burning embers chasing them out the door.

He put her down once they were outside, and together they greedily gulped at the fresh air. It only took a second for Steele to realize that they weren't out of trouble yet. The alley echoed with gunfire, and when he tried to use his radio nothing happened. He looked down, trying to find the problem, and saw a scorched circle through the fabric of the pouch. He pulled the radio halfway out of it; a bullet was flattened against the metal.

"Best day ever."

"Can you be serious for a second?"

Steele ignored the question and yanked his 1911 from its holster. He was trying to keep the mood light so she wouldn't realize that they were in a bad spot. He had no idea how she had gotten into the Gatehouse, or who she belonged to. None of that mattered. The only thing he knew for sure was that she was his responsibility now.

"What's your name?"

"Meg," she answered tersely.

"Well, Meg, if you want to stay alive I am going to need you to listen. My arm's kinda messed up," he said, turning around. "But if you can grab that pistol strapped to my back and pull some security that would be great."

Meg took the Glock 26 from the holster at the small of his back and Steele continued without missing a beat. "You're with the Agency, right?" It wasn't much of a guess, seeing how she obviously wasn't with West. "So I assume you know how to use—"

Meg cut him off by press-checking the Glock, dropping the mag to make sure it was topped off before slamming it home with a smirk.

"Yeah, I got it. Got any more bullshit questions, or is macho twenty questions over? No, then how 'bout you follow *me*?"

Steele's mouth fell open and he shook his head as she walked off. "Oh, Eric, thanks for saving my life, how can I ever repay you?" he mocked while activating the CSEL's homing beacon before falling in behind her. *I hope someone has their ears on.*

"What was that you were saying back there?" she asked when he caught up with her.

Instead of replying he put his finger up to his lips. Meg opened her mouth and then her eyes widened at the sound of the voices on the other side of the wall. Steele knew they were most likely more fighters. He needed to focus, but all he could think about was Nate.

"We need a phone or something to get some help," Meg hissed.

"Man, I wish that *I* had thought about that. Do you think maybe one of these guys will let us borrow a cell phone?"

"Are you always such an asshole?" she said.

Steele stepped past her without answering and took point. The adrenaline was beginning to wear off and it took everything he had not to bite her head off.

They made it to the edge of the alley and Steele held up his hand before peering out. The street was awash with fighters and there was a flatbed truck pulled over a hundred yards away unloading more men. Half of them worked to set up a barricade while the rest turned toward the Gatehouse.

"What's the plan?" Meg asked.

Steele ignored her, but was thinking the same thing. They were in a bad way: cut off in a hostile city.

The alley blocked them from moving to the east or west, so their only options were to go back or try and get across. Steele had learned his lesson about crossing open streets, and was about turn around when he saw a man on a dirt bike puttering toward them. He had to stop and take another look.

The rider's jeans were tucked into a pair of black rubber boots that he must have stolen from the docks, and instead of a shirt, he had two bands of ammunition crisscrossing his torso. What got Steele was the pink boa twisted around his neck, and the Algerian army helmet bouncing loosely on top of his head.

It was obvious that the man was high as a kite.

"Thank you, God."

Steele stripped his last frag from his kit and handed it to Meg.

"I'm going to jack Mad Max for his bike. You throw this."

She nodded.

Steele waited until the man was just at the edge of the alley before stepping out. The suppressed 1911 spat once, and the rider tumbled over the back, his boa trailing behind him.

The AK clattered to the ground and Steele snatched it up, throwing the sling over his head before grabbing the bike's handlebars. He goosed the throttle, and the back tire got traction and spun around.

Meg tossed the grenade with a grunt, followed by a man yelling in Arabic. Steele felt her jump on the bike, and waited to feel her arms around him.

"Go, go!" she yelled.

The fighters managed to get off one shot before the frag exploded. Steele didn't bother with the effects; he twisted the throttle and the motorcycle leapt forward.

He ducked low and cut the bike in a tight turn at the next street running north. He didn't have a plan, but he knew he needed to head north—to the water. They flew through the next intersection past a group of fighters throwing Molotov cocktails at a car. They crested a small rise in the street and Meg squeezed his shoulders at the same time Steele saw a truck racing toward them.

Steele downshifted, hitting the brakes and forcing Meg's body against his. He twisted the bike through an open yard, jumping the curb before angling down the hill on the other side. He could just see the edge of the ocean, but then had to focus all of his attention on dodging the piles of trash and scraps of metal littering the hillside.

"Hold on!" he yelled.

He gassed the bike over the retaining wall at the bottom of the hill, hitting hard on the other side. The shocks absorbed most of the jump, but Steele almost dumped the bike. He was struggling to regain control when he heard a metallic banging behind him.

"Holy shit, they followed us down the hill!" Meg yelled.

Steele felt her thighs tighten around him and her right hand let go. The Glock barked twice. The road ahead was jammed with fighters and soldiers battling for control of the street. A fighter lit off an RPG and it sailed over its target and came screaming over Steele's head. Tracers coiling from a Browning .50 cal mounted to a soft-skinned jeep punched through a knot of fighters before sparking off the ground.

"Take the alley, it cuts through," Meg yelled into his ear.

Steele ducked off the road and into the alley and found a row of stairs. He had too much momentum to stop and only enough time to yell, "Stairs!"

"No, don't take the . . ."

"Hold on."

The front tire dipped and Steele held on for dear life, trying to keep his weight centered.

"I said *don't* take the stairs," she yelled again.

Steele white-knuckled the handlebars all the way down and miraculously kept control of the bike. Finally the front tire hit flat ground and he let off the throttle. Steele hadn't realized he was holding his breath and started breathing again.

He hazarded a smile, gently took the corner, and was just turning to check on Meg when a man stepped out of the shadows, pointing a rifle at his face.

Chapter 30

Nate West stood on the deck of the container ship watching Algiers burn. *Didn't lose as many as I thought.* West had known that he was going to take casualties in the city and had been prepared to lose half of his men. It was an incredible number, one the U.S. military would balk at these days, but it was all part of the plan.

In the end he had only lost six, and all of those were at the Gatehouse.

Eric, you lead-shootin' bastard.

West had thought that sending Breul north would keep Steele off his tail long enough to hit the Gatehouse and slip away. But that was before he learned about Meg Harden. Having to track her down cost him time, and if Daniels had been able to do what West had paid him for, he had no doubt that his men would have gotten away scot-free. Not that it mattered.

He had already lost everything that he cared about, so in a way death was a release.

"You should have killed Steele," Villars had chided him.

"Leave the thinking to me," West replied.

He knew how the U.S. intelligence apparatus worked. The CIA and NSA were a bunch of bureaucrats who had to get permission to take a piss. The Program, while faster and more agile, had its own rules.

"Steele is alive because I want him to be," West said. "Right now I need you to contact Baudin. Tell him I need him to find someone for me."

"Then what?" Villars had asked.

"Then we sit back and watch the fireworks."

Chapter 31

B ack in Washington, D.C., John Rockford was poring over the reports coming out of Algiers. Intel was sketchy, and while he had ordered UAVs and satellites to be directed over the city, it would take time for them to provide any usable intelligence.

What was worse was that Rockford hadn't heard anything from Stalker 7 and Styles had pulled a Houdini. Instead of coming to brief the Vice President and the chief of staff, the Director had sent one of her lackeys. Rockford knew the drill. The only reason Styles hadn't shown up was because somehow the CIA was exposed.

Right now the best intel the White House was getting came from the networks. The television inside Cutlass Main was tuned to CNN and the network was painting a stark picture. Algiers was in chaos. The rebels had stormed the city, destroyed the power grid, and were digging out the secure phone lines. Communications with the U.S. embassy were spotty and Rockford knew it was the same with the French and British.

The satellite uplinks were overloaded and the rebels were besieging the airport. After their impromptu meeting in the White House Medical Unit, Rockford had followed President Cole to the Oval Office. The President went to his desk and casually began looking over some paperwork while Rockford paced.

"John, sit down, you are making me nervous," Cole said without looking up.

Rockford forced himself to take a seat on the couch.

"So, John," the President began, "how do you feel about taking point on the Algiers situation?"

"Sir, I do not think I am qualified for that."

"Why not? You were there when it kicked off, and it *is* in your wheelhouse," Cole answered, coming around the desk.

"Well, first of all there is Styles."

President Cole held up his hand. "John, we have been over this. I will handle Robin when the time is right."

"Well, sir, I guess—"

"Great," Cole said, slapping his hands together. "I know you will do an excellent job."

And just like that, the issue was settled. Rockford was taking point on Algiers. The problem was, the answers he needed were supposed to come from the CIA, but Styles was stonewalling him.

If Rockford waited on the CIA there was no doubt in his mind that Styles would make sure there was nothing linking her to what had happened before she told him anything.

Back in his own office, Rockford picked up the phone and dialed his chief of staff, Ted Lansky.

"Teddy, before you head home can you come down to my office for a second?"

"On my way."

Rockford had worked with Lansky when he was the Director of the CIA, and they had been friends for almost twenty years. But the two men were polar opposites. Rockford was the practical one and prided himself on being able to detach from even the most passionate situation. It was the reason he had risen through the ranks of the CIA while Lansky stayed out in the cold, relegated to the clandestine services. When Rockford became the Director, one of his first moves was to fire the head of the clandestine services and appoint Lansky in his place. The job came with the unofficial title of "spymaster."

During his tenure, Lansky made his share of enemies, and it was said that when he was finally forced out of Langley he had more vendettas than the Sicilian Mafia. Rockford knew that it was his friend's fierce loyalty and the tendency to say exactly what was on his mind that got him in trouble.

In fact Lansky had so many enemies that before he cleared his personal effects from his office the powers that be had already made sure that he was blackballed inside the Beltway. If it hadn't been for Rockford tapping him as his chief of staff, there was no doubt in the Vice President's mind that Ted would have ended up in Boca Raton playing cribbage with a bunch of geezers.

A knock at the door signaled Lansky's arrival.

"Come on in," Rockford said, getting to his feet.

"You needed to see me, boss?" Lansky asked.

Rockford waved him in. "Shut the door behind you," he said, bending down to open the shelf at the bottom of the minibar. He pulled out a bottle of Blanton's Special Reserve and held the bottle so Lansky could read the label. "You want a drink?"

Lansky studied the bottle from behind the pair of leather chairs in front of Rockford's desk, eyes narrowed like a deer smelling a hunter in the woods.

"Blanton's—what's the occasion?"

Rockford knew where his mind was going. Lansky was still as cagey as ever.

The Vice President chuckled softly and popped the cork. He poured two fingers into each glass and set the bottle down. When he turned, Lansky had a worn pipe in his hand, the stem scarred with teeth marks.

He quit smoking ten years ago, but still carries that damn thing around with him.

The pipe was a crutch, an object that had been part of Lansky's life for so long that he found himself unable to think without it. Lansky stuck the pipe between his teeth, a sign that he had his guard up, and asked:

"What is going on?"

Rockford handed one of the glasses to his chief of staff before lowering himself into one of the leather chairs. He took a sip and savored the liquor's burning march down his throat while Lansky sucked on the empty pipe so hard it caused the bowl to whistle.

"Who told Ali Breul to leave Iran, Ted?"

The sound of Lansky's teeth grinding on the pipe stem told Rockford that the question had caught him off guard.

"That is a complicated question," he finally answered.

"Complicated questions are the reason you have a job."

"One of the reasons," Ted admitted.

"This isn't the Inquisition, Ted. I called you down here because even though you are an angry bastard, you happen to know more about clandestine operations than anyone else in the country."

Lansky relaxed and took a seat. He pulled the pipe from his mouth and finally took a sip of the bourbon. "The official word out of Langley is that the convoy was hit by a terrorist group out of Tunis. Some ISIS offshoot."

"You buy that?"

Ted rolled his eyes.

"So what really happened?"

Lansky set the glass on the end table.

"Boss, my advice is that you leave this alone. Let the old man handle this one."

"Let's say I can't leave it. What would you say if I told you that the President put me in charge of this one?"

Rockford watched his chief of staff and could swear that he saw the wheels turning in his head.

"Now why in the hell would he do something like that?" Ted asked, leaning forward.

Rockford saw the intensity in the man's eyes, a brief glimpse of the old spy now fully engaged.

"What do you know about the Program?"

Ted winced at the mention of the classified organization. He ran his hands through his hair. They had both cut their teeth in the intelligence game, and had run across the Alpha Program more than once. It was hard to hide missions from men trained to bring the secrets into the light of day. But when questions were raised, a simple cease-and-desist notice would show up from the White House.

"Where are you going with this, Rock?"

"I think Styles is dirty." He let the statement hang there. "I can't prove it, but I believe that she had something to do with getting Breul to leave Iran, and I need you to help me prove it."

"Shit." Lansky got to his feet. He started pacing, and Rockford could tell he was walking through the particulars in his mind.

"She definitely has the ability to pull it off. I mean, she is the Director of the CIA. Robin might be a cold-hearted bitch, but she isn't stupid. Why would she do something like that?"

"That is what you are going to find out."

"Rock, it isn't that easy. I'm not with the Agency anymore, and it's not like there are a line of people at Langley lining up to help me."

"Just get it done," the Vice President said, rising to his feet.

It was the universal sign that the meeting was over. Lansky nodded and headed to the door, but stopped when Rockford said, "And, Ted, the clock's ticking."

Chapter 32

M eg's head was still throbbing from the beating she had taken at the Gatehouse. She was holding on to Steele's back for dear life on the motorcycle and when he slammed on the brakes, Meg looked up to see a man pointing an AK-47 at her. She knew she had to do something.

Shoot, shoot, her brain commanded.

The tires squealed in the confines of the tight alley. Meg smelled the smoke from the burning rubber as the back end of the motorcycle whipped around.

She shut her eyes and waited for the chatter of the AK. Instead she heard:

"Good to see you, mano. You didn't tell me that you were bringing a friend."

What the hell?

Meg cracked her eyelids. She was alive and the only

sound was the gentle *blub, blub, blub* of the engine vibrating against her legs. The man with the AK had brown eyes that twinkled like they were waiting to deliver a punch line.

"Hey," Steele said, shaking his shoulders from side to side in an attempt to get her attention.

"Huh, what?" Meg came out of the nightmare slow but defensive.

"Can you . . ." The words came out through gritted teeth, short and choppy. "Can you let up? I think my ribs are broken."

"Oh—sorry," she muttered, unlocking her arms.

"Oh God, that feels good."

"You look like hammered shit," the man with the Kalashnikov said to Eric.

Meg hopped off the bike, the blood flowing back through her oxygen-starved muscles with a tingle. *Does he know this guy? What in the hell is going on?*

"Tell me something I don't know," Steele said.

She stumbled but caught herself before the man with the rifle offered his hand. Steele pushed the bike farther into the alley, making the introductions while he moved. "Meg, this is Demo; Demo, Meg."

He extended his hand, which swallowed hers.

"Now that we have that straight, we need to get the hell out of here."

A heavy roll of automatic fire coupled with an explosion from a block away highlighted his point. Demo climbed into a van and it took Meg a second to realize it was actually an ambulance. Inside she saw that there was blood on her hands. She wiped them on her pants legs, before patting herself down, checking for broken bones or bleeds.

"It's not me," she said aloud.

"What?" Steele asked.

Meg held up her hands, showing what was left of the blood. "I think you are hit. Do you have a med kit back here?" She immediately realized it was a stupid question. *It's a freaking ambulance.*

"Yeah, behind the seat."

"Take your plate carrier off." Meg grabbed the orange bag.

"I'm fine," Steele lied.

"No you're not." She pushed on the plate carrier to prove her point, noticing the grimace of pain. "You said your arm was messed up back at the Gatehouse. Let me take a look."

"I'm—"

"Just shut up and do it," she ordered.

Meg took the headlamp from the bag and stretched it over her head while Steele lifted the armor free. She found the source of the blood. The wound had clotted, and when the fabric fell away, revealing Steele's well-defined torso, a section still clung to him. Meg concentrated on cutting around it while Steele talked to Demo.

"Primary exfil is blown."

"Yep, but don't worry, I know a way around. You know, mano, it seems every time the CIA comes out to play, a nice spot like this goes from cool to scorching in a blink of an eye."

The CIA comment drew Meg's attention away from her work and toward the cab. She looked up in time to see an orange fireball blossom skyward. Out of habit she counted the seconds until she heard the explosion. *One Mississippi, Two Mississippi, Three—*

The low rumbling told her that the blast was two and a half miles away. *The Hydra district.* "They are hitting the embassy."

"One of them," Steele said.

She looked up at Eric. His face was soot-stained and his hair singed from the flames. Meg remembered a Bugs Bunny cartoon where a bomb blows up in Yosemite Sam's face. Steele had the same blackened look, except his green eyes were red-rimmed and watery from the smoke.

They were the kind of green that made "piercing" seem an understatement, but the way his pupils reacted to the light troubled her.

"You get hit in the head?" she asked, abandoning the shears for the moment to reach for his skull.

"Why? You want to bag on my jokes again?" He grinned. "Or do you want to play doctor?"

"I get it, you don't want to look weak in front of a girl so you make jokes. Well, jokes aren't going to help you if you have a concussion."

"A concussion?" Demo snorted. "Ain't nothing hard enough to hurt his *cabeza*. Damn thing's harder than an anvil."

"Hey, no one pulled your chain, *ese*," Steele said. Meg thought he seemed all too eager to switch the focus off of what she had just said.

Meg tiptoed her fingers across his head, and let a triumphant smile spread across her face. When her fingertips stepped on the knot protruding from the side of Steele's head, she gave it a little push.

"Owwww, damn it."

"Don't be a baby."

"It hurts."

She *tsked* at him like her mom used to do to her brothers and continued her inspection. There was another knot on the back of his head, but this one was harder—older.

"That's old."

"How old?"

"A night. Hell, what day is it?"

"Just how many times have you been hit in the head lately?"

"Uhhhh, a couple."

"I don't think you have a skull fracture, but you can't ever tell with head trauma. Your pupils are irregular, which suggests that you have a serious concussion."

"Drink water and drive on."

Meg rolled her eyes and squatted down to finish cutting the wound free. "We've got all the balls in the world in here," she muttered. Another few seconds of cutting and the shirt was free. Meg knew the next part was going to hurt and tried to distract Steele with some questions.

"So how was the embassy when you left it?"

"No idea, haven't seen the Algerian embassy in four years."

"Wait, what?"

"I'm not from the embassy."

Meg's brain fumbled over the statement. She understood the words by themselves, but when she tried to make sense of the sentence as a whole her mental gears began to grind. She recognized what was happening. She had been riding the crest of adrenaline since getting off the motorbike. The aches and pains erupting along her synapses told her that she had reached the end of the line.

"You mean, you guys *aren't* with the CIA?"

"Do we *look* like Christians In Action?" Demo belly-laughed from the front.

Shit, of course.

Meg had assumed Steele was with the CIA, because it made sense. Upon closer examination she couldn't believe that she'd missed the signs. She'd worked with every Special Operations unit under the sun and could easily pick out a SEAL from a Ranger just by the way they acted. Steele, on the other hand, was unreadable. He had the quiet reserve of a Green Beret, but the macho nonchalance of a SEAL mixed with the skill set of a Delta operator.

"Who do you work for?" she asked, picking the edge of the shirt free with her fingernails.

"That's classified."

"Good thing I'm cleared all the way up to Top Secret."

"Not for this," Steele said.

"Hmmm." Meg pursed her lips and ripped the shirt free with a violent tug.

"Holy shit . . ." She tossed the cloth away and took her time collecting a handful of gauze before pressing against the wound.

"Damn, woman."

"Sorry," she lied. "Demo, I hope you know how to suture, because I was never cleared for that class."

Meg saw Demo's shoulders bouncing over the edge of the seat in her peripheral vision. He made no attempt to hide his laughter and she accepted it as a sliver of acceptance. "I—I think we can work something out."

"Judas."

Steele put his hand on top of hers and they locked eyes. The simple skin-on-skin contact was nothing special, but Meg swore she felt a tiny charge.

"You are definitely going to need stitches," she said.

Demo chimed in from the front seat. "Try to stay out of sight," he said, flipping on the ambulance's emergency lights before making another turn. "There is a checkpoint ahead."

He rolled down the window and shouted, "I have to get through."

It was too dark for Meg to see without the head-lamp. Her heart pounded in her chest then she heard the *snick* of a safety catch. She squinted and was able to make out the outlines of a 1911 in Steele's hand. Eager voices began shouting over the engine noise.

"Yes, yes, I have money. Here, take it and move."

"Good, very good," a voice said in Arabic. "Twice this much if you come back."

"Fine," Demo replied, and then they were moving again. "Holy shit, I didn't think that was going to work."

You weren't the only one, Meg thought.

"Got to have a little faith," Steele replied with a wink.

They finally cleared the city and Demo pulled the ambulance off the road, gravel popping beneath the weight of the tires. Meg looked through the windshield and saw the headlights play over an empty lot with a wall running half of its length. Demo wheeled the ambulance in a wide arc, cut the lights, and pulled up to the dark side of the wall.

"And we are good," he said, cutting the engine and hopping out.

"What's up?"

"Changing cars," Steele explained.

Meg slid the door open and stepped down, with Eric grumbling on her heels. Behind the wall there was a battered sedan that looked puke yellow in the moonlight. Demo was already at the trunk. He popped it open and pulled out a black duffel.

"Got you some clothes," Demo said to Steele, dropping the bag and turning to Meg. "And if I'd known you were bringing a plus one I could have brought you something."

"It's fine," Meg replied, glancing toward a roll of gunfire. A line of tracers shot skyward like a row of bottle rockets, and she knew they had gotten out of the city just in time. "I'm sure I can . . ." she began.

The words froze when her eyes made contact with the .40 Sig Sauer Demo held at her chest. "What's going on?"

Steele was the first to answer. "Meg, you've been around the block, so I assume you know the rules." His voice was ice cold and she knew he wasn't waiting for an answer. The anger flared inside her like flash paper. She was tired, beat up, and the only thing she wanted was a cold beer and a handful of aspirin.

"This is bullshit."

"No," Steele replied, "this is *business*. You don't know me, and I sure as hell don't know you. Any other time and we could sit around and figure it out, but as you can see"—he stopped and pointed at the tracers arcing skyward—"time isn't something we have right now. So it is up to you. Do you want to do this the easy way or the hard way?"

Meg had to draw the last drop of reserves from the tank to keep from losing her shit. Her mind told her that Steele was making the right call, but her frayed emotions were focused on the betrayal polluting the bond that she *thought* they had formed.

"I like you, *chica*, even if you are with the CIA," Demo said.

Meg looked at him. His eyes were flat black, like a shark's, and it didn't take a genius to figure out that if she made the wrong call he wouldn't hesitate to put her down.

Steele pulled a fresh shirt from the bag and slipped it over his head. Next he took a black box and held it up. Meg recognized it as an RF scanner. She had used them herself, and when he flipped the switch she waited for the red lights to boot up.

"You think I'm bugged, or maybe the spooky CIA is tracking me?"

Demo shrugged. "Just following the book."

Steele stopped an arm's length away and wanded the box from her head to her feet. When it didn't beep, he nodded and flipped it off. "Almost done." He switched the RF scanner out with what looked like a Polaroid camera.

Give me a break. He's going to retinal-scan me now? What in the hell happened to him to put these guys on edge?

"Hold still and give me a smile."

"Fuck off."

The scanner beeped, telling them that it had captured the image.

"Are we done?"

"Almost," Steele replied, waving a pair of zip ties and a black hood.

Meg knew that the time for action had passed. If she bolted now there were two outcomes. Either Steele would take her to the ground or Demo would put a bullet in her head.

These are serious men, girl. Get hold of yourself.

She looked into Steele's eyes and for some reason knew he wouldn't hurt her.

"Let's get this over with," she said.

Steele gave her a wink and then pulled the bag over her head.

Chapter 33

Eric strapped Meg into the backseat and set a pair of headphones over her ears. He held the iPod up, noticing that the screen was broken, which meant he couldn't tell what songs were on it.

"What's on here?"

"The usual mix," Demo said laconically.

"Are you kidding? She isn't a detainee."

"Mano, you're the one who brought the fucking spook with you."

"Hope you like Metallica," he said, hitting the play button and turning up the volume so that it was loud, but not deafening.

Steele closed the door and gingerly took a seat up front. Demo put the car in gear and made a few wide circles around the gravel lot. The idea was to mess up her internal navigation, and when Steele flashed the thumbs-up, Demo bumped onto the road.

He used the rearview to check on Meg. She looked so frail sitting there with the bag on her head. *Man, this feels shitty.* But he knew that if she were a dude he wouldn't even be thinking about it. He left the thoughts and plugged the retinal scanner into the laptop and uploaded the data. It would take some time before he got a response from the database.

"So what happened?"

"*West* happened."

"West? You mean Nathaniel West?" Demo asked.

Steele caught the *are you crazy?* look Demo shot him.

"You are going to have to explain that one, my man, because last time *I* checked, Nate West was dead."

"I saw him. He was at the Gatehouse, which means he was the one who punched Breul's ticket."

They rode in silence, with the only sound coming from the steady hum of the tires and the music bleeding out of the headphones. From the front seat it sounded like there was a tiny concert going on in a soup can.

"What about the package?"

"Breul must have stashed it at the Gatehouse."

"Which means that ol' Lazarus West has that too?"

"I could have gotten it, but . . ."

"But let me guess, our damsel in distress needed a knight in shining armor." This time the look was full-on disappointment, and the only thing Steele could do was wait for the lecture. "What did I tell you during the counseling board at the end of Phase 1?"

"You said selflessness is not a virtue."

"Annnnd?"

"I think it was along the lines of, 'This is going to bite you in the ass one day.'"

Demo held both of his hands up. "You can't save everyone in this business, mano . . ." It was the same exasperated look Eric's mom used to give him. Then Demo chuckled and said, "Look at us now, just two lifers in a world of shit."

"Just like old times."

Ten minutes later Demo cut the lights and snaked the sedan off the road, stopping in front of a metal gate. Steele hopped out and spun the combination of the lock. The chain rattled when he pulled it free, followed by the grating of metal hinges. He pulled the gate open and stepped out of the way, thinking about what Demo had said. *He's right. We would be mission complete if I had just left her.* The sedan cruised through and Steele manhandled the gate closed and secured it.

He stepped to a frazzled scrub bush and knelt down

instead of heading back to the car. The dull red brake lights offered enough illumination to find the wire that snaked out of the ground. Steele twisted off the plastic cap and connected the end to the firing device staked inside the bush.

Demo took security seriously, and Steele knew that on the other end of the wire he had buried a pressure pad lengthwise beneath the drive. All Steele had to do to arm the explosives was pull the safety pin, which he did. Typically Demo bought local, so if things went kinetic no one could trace it back to the United States. *Probably three 122 shells daisy-chained together. Simple but definitely not subtle.*

Steele knew from Indoc that the man didn't do subtle. When Demo was still an operational Alpha he had been an "8," which meant he worked in Latin America. Fighting the rebels gave him the opportunity to develop his love of explosives from a hobby to high art. He hit labs, safehouses, training sites, and logistic hubs until a nasty bit of business in Colombia put him in traction and almost cost him his hand.

But instead of hanging up his cleats, Bobby "Demo" Cortez became an instructor at the Salt Pit. By the time Steele came through Indoc he was the lead cadre.

Steele hustled back to the car, hopped in, and they continued down the road.

"How much you got on the gate?"

"A pound of C-4 and three 122mm mortar rounds."

"Jesus."

"Yep, go big or go home."

The computer beeped from the floorboard when Demo finally made it to the end of the drive. Bathed in the yellow glow of the headlights, the structure before them reminded Steele of something from a horror movie.

"This is *it*?" Steele asked, picking the device off the floor.

"Yeah, she's perfect. Just make sure you stay away from the bushes, got a few Bouncing Bettys that I just set out."

After Demo did his time at the Pit he switched over to the support side of the Program. Steele knew that it had been hard on him staying out of the action, but the only job that would get him back in the field was if he became a handler. The official Program term was "Housekeeper," but the Alphas called them "keepers." It was the last step before retirement and their job was to support the Alphas in the field by maintaining the safehouses and waypoints in their area of operations.

"Maybe it's time for you to—"

"Listen here, I remember when you were wet behind the ears. Why don't you do yourself a favor and save all comments until the end of the tour, young pup?"

"Fair enough." Steele smiled.

"What they say about our girl?"

"Went to the University of Florida, majored in psych, graduated ROTC top of her class. She got commissioned and sent to MI."

"Military Intelligence?"

"Yeah, did a pretty good job according to this. Got sent over to Fort Meade to do some secret squirrel work with the NSA and managed to get invited to the Activity."

"The Activity? Worked with them in Colombia when we were going after El Padrino in Medellín. I think they were calling themselves Rivet Joint back then. They do good work."

"So what do we do?"

Demo pulled a stub of a cigar out of his shirt pocket and jammed it in the corner of his mouth. Steele had never seen him smoke, but Demo loved to gnaw on them like his idol Telly Savalas. "I don't think the Program has a policy on taking in strays. But hell, nothing wrong with giving her a bath and a saucer of milk."

"You sure?"

"Screw it, what's the worst they can do, send us to find a missing nuke?"

Steele stepped out and opened the back door. He

gently lifted the headphones from her head, followed by the bag. Meg blinked in the dim light of the garage.

"Are we there yet?" she asked.

"Sorry about the theatrics. I checked you out and know you understand the game."

Demo plodded over to a bench and lifted a pair of wire cutters from the pegboard. He nudged Steele out of the way with his hip. "No hard feelings?" he asked, holding the snips aloft.

"Never been a big fan of Metallica, but other than that, we're good," she said.

Demo cut the flex cuffs and both men stepped back, giving Meg room to get out. Steele thought she seemed wrung out, but even with the grime and dried blood she managed to look regal. *I bet you're one of those girls who looks good right when they wake up. Whoa, where the hell did that come from?*

Steele hadn't been around a woman in a long time. It wasn't by choice, just one of the by-products of the job. Working in the Middle East didn't help his cause. The notoriously male-centered world kept the fairer sex behind closed doors. He wasn't sure what to do with Meg besides making sure she got food and a shower.

"I like what you've done with the place," Meg said when they stepped inside.

"Is this because of the Metallica?" Demo asked.

"No, it's because this place looks trashed. I'm not an interior decorator, Demo, so you are going to have to help me out. What exactly do you call this décor? Crack house chic?"

"I think it's modern art," Steele added.

At first glance Steele thought the walls were painted yellow, but on closer inspection it was obvious that the pallor was wallpaper adhesive that had yellowed over time. The floor was bare concrete. If Steele had to pick the worst part, it would have been the furniture. The couch and battered chair had seen better days and smelled as though bums had used them for urinals.

"Keep laughing. You guys ever heard of camouflage? Wait till you check this out."

Demo moved the edge of the rug out of the way and pressed on the floor with the toe of his boot. There was a click, followed by a section of floor popping up half an inch.

A trapdoor. Sneaky Mexican bastard.

Demo lifted up the rug and the section of the floor it was attached to opened to reveal a rickety flight of stairs.

"Cool, a *basement*," Meg said.

"If you want, I can take *you* back to the city," Demo huffed.

"And leave without the tour? Hell no."

Demo headed down, with Meg and Steele bringing up the rear. By the time Eric got to the bottom, Demo had a small generator running. A set of workers' lights illuminated a roughly cut tunnel, the sides reinforced with wood.

"You *can't* be serious?" Steele asked.

"Used to belong to some money guy who handled all the finances for Al-Qaeda in the area. Ran across it while going through the database and thought I'd check it out. Wait until you see what's on the other side."

"Okay, so are you going to tell me who you guys work for or are we going to play ignore the elephant all night?"

"How 'bout that beer?" Steele said.

"Good call, right this way," Demo said.

They both ignored Meg's protests and walked down the hallway. Steele tracked the distance they walked by counting every time his left foot hit the ground. He guessed the tunnel was fifty yards long, with another rickety set of stairs at the far end. At the top was a trap-door that was secured with a combination lock.

The interior was well lit and tastefully furnished.

"Whoa."

"Yeah, apparently funneling money for jihadists pays pretty well."

"I'll say," Meg agreed. "Whatever happened to the previous owner?"

"Oh, they cut his head off for embezzling. Go figure."

"Even has an ocean view," Steele said, making his way to the plate glass door that overlooked the sea.

"Only the best for you, my friend."

"Meg, if you will follow me I will show you your room. I might even have some clothes around here that will fit you."

Steele dragged himself to the kitchen, cracked the fridge, and snagged a beer from the shelf. He twisted the top off and drained half the bottle before finding the trash can. The brew was ice cold and Steele couldn't remember one ever tasting this good. He savored what was left at the window, staring out at the ink-black ocean. The rhythmic crash of the surf lulled his weary mind, reminding him that he was exhausted.

"When was the last time you slept?" Demo asked. Despite his size the old man had a silent step and the question startled Steele because he hadn't heard him slip in.

"Had a nap on the helo out of Libya."

"Real sleep, mano. When was the last time you had some real sleep?"

"Three, maybe four days."

Demo nodded, clanked two fresh ones from the refrigerator, and motioned Steele to follow him. Eric drained the last of his beer and fell in behind his keeper. From the hallway he heard the shower running and the smell of shampoo. They passed another bedroom before ducking into the infirmary.

"Drop everything but your skivvies," Demo ordered, setting the beers on the stainless steel table next to an exam chair.

While Steele stripped, his keeper disappeared through another doorway, followed a moment later by the sound of running water and the rattle of ice on metal. With his clothes on the floor, Steele dropped himself into the exam chair. Demo appeared a minute later and began collecting medical supplies. He placed the tray on the table, cracked both beers, and after handing one to Steele, snapped on a pair of latex gloves.

"Walk me through it," he said.

"I got the call that Breul had left Iran when we were exfilling Lebanon," Steele began.

"Any idea why?"

"Someone had to reach out, that is the only thing that makes sense, because he took the device and went to Algiers. Somewhere along the way he got picked up and transported to Tunis."

Demo nodded. "So you go to Tunis, Breul gets whacked, and no nuke?"

"Yeah, and now Nate has it." By the time Steele had brought his keeper up to speed he had a new set of stitches in his side.

"I know some guys at the Agency who will find out what's going on at Langley," Demo said, picking up a penlight and checking his pupils.

"I've got to call in. POTUS is due for a situation report."

Demo stripped the gloves off and got to his feet, taking his first pull of the beer.

"C'mon," he said, walking toward the doorway he had disappeared through earlier.

Steele knew what was coming and wasn't looking forward to it. "I'd rather take a shower."

"I bet you would, but you need the tub."

The galvanized tub was Demo's prescription for everything, and Steele hated it. His keeper stuck his hand in the ice water while Steele dropped his underwear and eyed the blocks of ice floating on the surface. There was a stopwatch on the wall, a rectangular digital number with thirty minutes already punched in.

"Well, get in," Demo said.

"Shit."

Steele stepped in and felt his feet go immediately numb. He took a deep breath and slowly lowered himself through the water until it was up to his chin.

"You know that if Rockford follows Alpha protocol he is going to pull you out, right?" Demo said.

"We will see about that."

Chapter 34

On board the cargo ship bobbing in the Mediterranean Sea, Nathaniel West pulled the shower door open and twisted the knob all the way to the left. The pipes bucked and shuddered against the bulkhead, before belching an intermittent stream of brown water.

He tore at the wrapper, but the soap was wet and the packaging slippery. The wax paper refused to come off. He gave up on the soap, letting it fall as he stepped under the nozzle, face upturned. "Dammit." The smell of his burnt clothes was alive inside him and the only thing he could think to do was suck water up his nose.

It burned, but not enough. He groped for the knob, found it, and maxed out the heat. He opened his eyes, water going from lukewarm to scalding, chill bumps spread across the patches of unscarred skin—the ones that he could still feel. West was losing control, he would have puked but hadn't eaten anything all day, and as hard as he retched, the only thing to come up was a little bit of bile.

He'd been here before and knew there was only one way out. Pain, and lots of it. The burning in his eyes and nasal cavity wasn't enough, but, unable to see, he pawed for the wall with his left hand, rage scorching the fear.

He steadied himself, and a second after his left hand found the tile wall, he launched a jab with his right. It was a solid blow, the impact rushing up his arm and into his shoulder, but it wasn't enough. He hit it again and again until his chest heaved and his arm was sore. He backed up to the tile on the opposite wall, cold on his ass. It sent a shiver up his spine that spread until he was sitting on the floor of the shower.

Nate sat there, calm now despite his shoulders, which rose and fell rapidly. "You're good, it's all good," he self-soothed before sucking on his bloody knuckles. The blood rolled down his forearm, mixing with the water—reminding him of the oil that floated on the sea. He closed his eyes and leaned his head back like a junkie who had just spiked a vein. The hot water beat down on his face and rolled over the scars.

The memories were still just as vivid, but he could take them now.

He remembered swimming toward the light, lungs burning, arms and legs heavy—lead-filled. When his head broke the surface all he could think about was getting some air, but the world was on fire. He took a deep breath, sucking in a lungful of the black, acrid smoke. It tasted caustic and West realized he'd surfaced in the center of a large puddle of oil and gas. Horrified, he saw a wall of flame barreling down on him, orange and yellow fingers clawing at his gas-soaked face. He was burning, and his shirt had become a torch. He flailed at the flames and his last thought before sinking below the surface was his family.

Unable to breathe and too tired to swim, he let himself go.

Nate saw his wife in the blackness. She looked so beautiful and waved at him to join her. *I'm coming,* he said. *Wait for me.* He was moving toward her, feeling warm and at peace, drifting forever, it seemed.

And then strong hands were lifting him out of the water.

West didn't remember much after that except screaming at the men to let him die. They ignored him, heaved him over the boat's gunwales like he was some charred fish, before tossing him flopping onto the flat bottom.

A vile mix of oil and water came rushing up, and he turned his head and caught a glimpse of the coastline.

Where am I? he wondered.

One of the fishermen came into view holding a bottle of brandy. "Dear God," he said in Spanish. He crossed himself one-handed before leaning down to cradle West's head, bringing the bottle to his lips.

The brandy burned going down his throat. Everything burned—his skin, his stomach, but most of all his heart.

"You are safe now," the man said, but that was a lie.

But they're dead, West thought before passing out.

Back in the shower he opened his eyes. The door was frosted with steam and his shoulders were red from the hot water. His hand closed around the knob and he twisted it to the right. The water turned cold in an instant, and the undamaged parts of his body grew tight with goose bumps. It was freezing, but West didn't care.

Pain had been his only companion for so long that he missed it when he started to feel comfortable. After the explosion the current had carried him out to sea. He later learned that two fishermen from the island of Mallorca found him in the open water. They pulled him into their boat and rushed him to the local doctor.

The man kept him alive, but only barely. The first week was the worst. In and out of feverish dreams, he'd wake up to feel his skin crawling—the doctor was using maggots to eat the dead skin, and there was nothing he could do about it because the man had secured his arms and legs.

When West slept he dreamt about the moments before the blast. He paused before getting onto the boat and turned to wave at Eric. He noticed the figure on the motorcycle looking down at him from the entrance of the marina. They made eye contact and West noticed that he was holding something in his hand.

What is that?

He turned to get a better look, and in that instant his mind identified what the man had in his hand.

A detonator? Why would he . . . ?

The figure depressed the trigger on the top of the object and West's insides went cold. He turned to yell a warning to his family, and then the world went black.

West spent every waking hour examining the operations he had conducted as an Alpha. He knew for a fact that his cover had never been blown, and since all of his targets were dead, that left only one option. The people who murdered his family had been on the inside.

Then it hit him.

Breul.

West realized he must have made a mistake when he approached the Iranian. He had been using a CIA cover that worked well in Europe, and slowly the pieces began to fit.

Breul had claimed that the CIA knew what Iran was doing, so if someone in Iranian intelligence thought that a CIA agent was bothering their man, they would reach out to . . . Styles.

It made sense, but it was only a theory, and once West got back on his feet he knew that he had to stay underground to prove it.

The only money he had was in a safety deposit box in Cyprus. He spent most of it buying false papers to South America, finally ending up in Ciudad del Este, the gateway to the triple frontier. It was a beautiful and dangerous place where Paraguay, Brazil, and Argentina came together in a teeming mass of drugs, guns, and money.

The perfect spot to start over.

Nate spent the rest of the money getting skin grafts in Brazil. The first operation was shit, and he almost died from infection, a painful introduction to black market medicine. Later, when he'd gotten settled, he went to a doctor in Argentina who cost him nearly ten times what he had spent in Brazil. The man was worth every cent.

West tracked down one of the men who had killed his family. He took his time getting the information he needed, and in the end the man confirmed his suspicion.

Robin Styles had contracted a team to kill his family.

With that fact at the forefront of his mind, Nate West patiently planted the seeds of his revenge, nurturing them until the time was right. And now that he had the nuke, he was going to destroy everyone who'd been remotely involved in the death of his family.

Chapter 35

It was too quiet in the safehouse and Eric Steele didn't sleep well when it was quiet. His body had become accustomed to noise and movement from years of catching naps en route to drop zones or nodding off in the back of trucks. When it was quiet his brain drifted back to the places he'd rather forget, like the first time he was in Algiers, when Nate West was training him to be an Alpha.

"I'm done after this," West said out of the blue.

"What do you mean, done? You can't just leave."

"Watch me."

They were following a van and Steele was trying to keep his interval, watching for any signs of counter-surveillance and chatting to West at the same time. Talk about sensory overload.

"You are going to miss it. I know you are."

"What have we been talking about these last four-teen days?"

It was the same question over and over. Steele answered without having to think. "Staying alive and accomplishing the mission."

"That's right. You want to know the real secret, the one they don't teach you at Indoc?"

Steele nodded.

"Always go out on top."

Steele opened his eyes, leaving the memories behind. He stared at the ceiling and remembered the note that Breul had left for him at the dead drop. He sat up slowly and swung his legs off the bed.

He got to his feet and half limped, half walked to his plate carrier, bending to retrieve the Ziploc bag, which he carried back to the table. He laid it there, next to the remains of last night's dinner and his father's 1911. He picked up the pistol and ran a rag over the slide, feeling with his fingernail the five notches cut into the metal. He had never gotten the chance to ask his dad what they meant, but he had a good idea. The notches were memories from another war.

Steele tore the baggie open and removed the folded sheet of paper. A part of him hoped that the answers to all his questions were here. He stared at the single word in Breul's distinctive handwriting.

"Cobalt," he read aloud. "What the hell?"

He flipped the paper over, wondering if he was missing something. The note didn't make any sense. Cobalt was a code name assigned to an SAP, or special access program. Steele could count on one hand how many people were read in on that operation, and Breul wasn't one of them.

Steele pulled the computer over, logged in to the Program's intelligence database, and typed "Cobalt" into the search bar. A second later a list of hits popped up. He read through the operation brief, noting the CIA heading and the SAP classification.

He dressed quickly and went into the kitchen, where Demo and Meg were chatting over breakfast.

"You talked to the boss yet?"

"I wanted to run something by you first. The last time I spoke with Ali Breul I told him that he was going to have to stay in Iran for a bit longer. Breul was ready to leave. He felt that things were getting too hot."

It was a painful conversation to remember.

"I have a family, Eric," Breul pleaded.

"Do you trust me?" Steele asked. It was a liar's question and it burned Eric's tongue, but he uttered it all the same.

"Yes, of course I trust you."

"Then you have to believe me when I say that nothing is going to happen to you, or them."

"But what happens if . . . ?"

"We have covered that. If you think you're burned, grab the package and get to the border. There is a man there who will get you across, and you know what to do from there."

"Breul's job was always to grab the nuke. We had gone over the plan a few times and the Gatehouse was the only place safe enough to stash the device. The questions we haven't answered are *why* he left Iran and how anyone knew he was going to the Gatehouse."

"I think I know the answer to the last one," Meg said. "There was a CIA officer in Algiers named Charlie Daniels." She filled them in on leaving her computer open and passing Daniels in the hall before leaving the wire.

"Did Daniels have access to the Gatehouse log?" Demo asked.

"If he had my password," Meg replied.

"Would your password let him see that an Alpha code had recently been used at the Gatehouse?" Steele wanted to know.

"He would be able to see *any* code," Meg said, the embarrassment evident on her face. "Before we found his body I was checking the computer. Daniels had deleted a bunch of recent emails. I restored them and emailed them to myself. Daniels sent a message to Director Styles. The gist of the memo was a meeting between a guy named Ronna and—"

"Burrows," Steele finished for her.

The links were starting to fit. The cover-up, getting Steele out of position while someone lured Breul across the border. Everything pointed to the CIA. West had let them do the dirty work and then slid in to grab the payoff.

He still had no idea who got Breul to leave Iran.

"All that is great," Demo said, "very informative. But the question is, where is West going with the nuke?"

"Breul left me a message at a dead drop. A piece of paper with the word 'Cobalt' written on it."

"Cobalt as in Dr. Bassar?" Demo asked. "Isn't he dead?"

"I have no idea who you guys are talking about," Meg said, holding up her hand.

"Dr. Asif Bassar. He is a Pakistani who developed their nuclear program. During the Iran nuclear deal, President Bentley decided it was a good idea to grant him asylum in Iran."

"Best idea ever," Demo quipped.

"And the Bentley administration kept the move quiet too. Didn't want to have to deal with the backlash from the people."

"So Bassar is a nuclear bomb expert, who is supposed to be dead. Just like West?" Meg asked.

"Yep," Steele replied. "I just don't know why Breul would leave that message."

"Maybe he knew Bassar wasn't dead."

It's possible, Steele thought.

"Even if that were true, why is it important?"

"Mano, it is way too early for all these questions," Demo said, turning his attention back to his bowl of Cocoa Krispies. "All these dead people suddenly alive. Running around with a nuclear bomb and shit."

"What are you muttering over there?" Steele asked.

"It's like one of those Netflix Steven Seagal movies. Dead scientist isn't really dead, and just so happens he is the only one who knows how to make a nuclear bomb detonate."

"Wait, what was that?" Steele asked.

"The new Steven Seagal movies, they all go straight to Netflix," Demo said. "Sad, really. *Under Siege* was a classic."

"No, you moron, the other part. About making a nuclear bomb explode."

"Dude, did you even read Bassar's file? That's what he did. He built the triggers for the bomb."

The statement hit Steele like a ton of bricks. "How the hell did I miss that?" he demanded aloud.

"Because you hate reading. Or you have been hit in the head too many times." Demo grinned at Meg and winked.

"Don't you get it? That's why Breul left the message. He knew someone would have to build a trigger."

"Oh, damn. Did I just crack the case?" Demo said, shooting another smile at Meg.

"We have to find Bassar."

"What's this *we* business? *You* still have to call POTUS, and when you tell him about West . . ."

The rush of adrenaline that had built with finding Bassar's link in the operation dissipated in an instant.

"What is he talking about, Eric?" Meg asked.

"I've got to update the President," Steele said with a shake of his head.

"Well, he should be happy that you have this figured out."

"I'm sure he will be," Demo broke in, "but that doesn't matter. Steele and West had history."

"So?"

"The Program has rules," Steele said. "If an Alpha has any type of relationship with a target . . ." He paused, the rest of the sentence like ash on his tongue.

"If they have a relationship, what?"

"The Alpha gets taken off the op."

Chapter 36

S teele sat in front of the computer, bracing himself for what he had to do.

"Code in," the electronic voice said.

He leaned into the camera and let it scan his retina. "Identification complete, Stalker 7 is now online," the robotic voice said. "Please stand by."

Steele knew that inside Cutlass Main, someone was alerting the President that an Alpha was online. Depending on where Cole was, it could take a few seconds or ten minutes. In less than thirty seconds the screen came alive. Once again it was Rockford, not Cole, who appeared.

"I was starting to wonder when I was going to hear from you," the Vice President said. "Getting out of

Algiers was a hell of a thing. I'd give you a medal, but looking at your file"—Rockford held up the binder— "the box appears to be full."

Steele knew that if Rockford was reading his file it meant the Vice President had taken a sudden interest in this operation, which was a change from the norm. Steele knew from experience that changes didn't happen in a vacuum. Something was going on.

"Is something wrong with President Cole?"

Steele watched his reaction closely, looking for any hint of a lie. The first sign was the micro tic under his right eye, a tiny tremor caused by sudden stress. In itself it was nothing, but when linked with Rockford looking away from the camera followed by a gentle clearing of the throat, deception was indicated.

"The President is fine. He is, however, indisposed for the moment."

Indisposed. Ali Breul is dead, the Program has been breached, and Nathaniel West has an untraceable nuke. What could possibly be more important than taking this call?

"What's your count?" Rockford asked, clearly trying to steer the conversation.

"Plus one."

"You grab a tango?" Rockford asked, hope sparking in his eyes.

It was time for Steele to come clean, no matter the consequences.

"Negative, sir. The plus one is a friendly, a CIA operative named Meg Harden." Steele had her file waiting and sent it to Rockford's screen with a touch of a button. "I checked her out, and she is legit. Army Intelligence, a couple tours with the Activity, and then the CIA."

"Any idea what she was doing there?"

"The chief of station sent her out to sanitize the safe-houses. Purely precautionary, but after Benghazi it is the State Department's standard operating procedure when credible intel points toward a possible uprising."

"The CIA is being close-lipped about this one. I smell a cover-up. What's your take on the ground?"

"Sir, we have a problem."

Rockford frowned. "What is it, son?"

Steele took a deep breath, knowing that he could lie and stay on the operation, or tell the truth and get pulled. He already knew what he was going to do, but the temptation was still there.

"Nathaniel West. He isn't dead. I saw him with my own two eyes at the Gatehouse."

"What? How is that possible?"

"I don't know. What I do know is he has an untraceable nuclear device and I think he is on his way to get it armed."

Vice President Rockford was stuck on Steele's last words. *He is on his way to get it armed.*

The fact that West was still alive explained the aura of defeat that hung over Steele.

I've got to pull him, but it's best to wait until he lays everything out.

He knew Alphas were completive by nature, so having to disengage from an operation was incredibly difficult. Steele had a personal interest in this one, which was going to make it damn near impossible to make a clean break.

"Ali Breul left a message for me at one of our dead drops," Steele was saying. Rockford had to force himself to focus on the piece of paper he held up to the camera. On it Rockford could see the word "Cobalt" scrawled in black ink.

"You know what I am talking about, don't you, sir?"

The first time Rockford heard of Cobalt was during a series of transition meetings held for President Cole's incoming administration. It was boring stuff except for the daily intelligence briefs. Cobalt was the code name assigned to a scientist named Dr. Asif Bassar—the man who had made Pakistan a nuclear power.

"What do you know about him, sir?" Steele asked.

"First time I heard the name was during an after-action report that followed a drone strike." He swiveled in his chair and grabbed a binder from a stack on the edge of the desk. The binders had date labels in their upper-right-hand corners and Rockford quickly found the one he wanted.

"The Director of National Intelligence just threw it out there," Rockford said, turning back to the screen, "like it was the most normal thing in the world to allow the one man who knew how to build a nuclear weapon safe travel to Iran. Cole went ballistic. First time I have ever seen him truly angry. Demanded to know why they waited two years to take him out."

"Did they have an answer?" Steele wanted to know.

Rockford shook his head and flipped through the binder. "All they wanted to talk about was the drone strike." He found what he was looking for and started reading aloud from the text. "Reaper was called on station and fired two Hellfires into target house. SOG team was sent in to collect DNA. Lab results taken from scene provided a positive match."

"And you took their word for it."

"No. I definitely did not." Rockford flipped to the end of the binder and traced his finger down the page. "Secondary test of lab results taken from scene . . ." He skipped over the collection date, chain of custody, and test site, and searched for the result. Rockford turned the page, lips moving as he read everything but the one thing he wanted to know—the results. "Here it is, secondary sample was tested against primary DNA sample and results came back inconclusive . . ."

He trailed off, the weight of the word pressing him to his chair. "Wait, there has to be a mistake." Rockford flipped back to the previous page, wondering how he could have missed this critical piece of the puzzle. " 'Inconclusive.' How could I have missed that?" he hissed.

"You didn't miss it, sir," Steele said, voice flat through the computer speaker. "That information was withheld from you."

Rockford looked up and the blood drained from his face as he realized that suddenly their CIA theory didn't seem so farfetched.

"Cobalt . . ."

"Isn't dead." Steele finished the sentence for him before falling silent.

Rockford knew that he was waiting for the inevitable.

"The org chart says that Stalker 8 is the closest Alpha to you. He is in Syria running with our Spec Ops boys. How long do you think it would take to pull him out, get him recocked and redeployed?"

"Fighting around Wadi Barada is bad. Real bad. Probably take a few hours to get enough ass in the air, maybe send an SF team from Italy, that's another couple of hours. Come up with a plan, launch airstrikes, and send in the troops." Steele looked at the ceiling and Rockford figured he was doing the math in his head. "Eight, nine hours. Depending on how long he has been out and how much rack time he's gotten, you could have him at my location in a day, day and a half."

We don't have half that much.

Rockford swiveled his chair to get a look into the TOC. He scanned the row of clocks on the wall. Each one was counting upward, and below the red numbers was the name of the Stalker element each mission clock corresponded to. Steele's was at seventeen hours and counting.

"If the CIA is in on this we can't let Ms. Harden go, you realize that, right?"

"I was just thinking the same thing," Steele replied.

Rockford leaned closer to the computer. "I need a no-bullshit assessment," he began. A blind man could have seen the hope ignite like a match head in Steele's eyes. "This is a defining moment for both of us. You are the man on the ground, and waiting isn't an option. Before I decide, I want to know, just how good is he?"

"West?"

"Yes."

Steele didn't hesitate. "He's the best there is."

Jesus. It was not what he wanted to hear, but Rockford kept a tight hold on his disappointment. He knew that whatever rapport he had built up with Steele could come crashing down if the Alpha saw him falter. "What would it take to stop him?"

"If we had everyone—and I'm not just talking about our guys, I mean Interpol, MI6, French DGSE, CIA, NSA, the whole ball of wax—working round the clock with every asset at their fingertips, I'd say fifty/fifty."

"Well, we don't have those assets or the time. You know Nate West better than anyone else alive."

"What are you saying, sir?"

"I'm saying that there is an untraceable nuclear weapon in the hands of one of the best-trained operatives in the world. I don't know about you, Eric, but I don't think a bunch of rules are going to stop that threat right now."

Steele's mouth fell open on the screen. "Are you leaving me in play?"

Rockford nodded.

"The only caveat is the girl. She goes too. I can't afford to tip Styles off."

"Roger that, sir. What are your orders?"

"We need to locate Bassar and then I want you find Nathaniel West as fast as you can and then I want you to kill him."

Chapter 37

Robin Styles stood at the window, looking over D.C. It was her ritual anytime she stayed at the penthouse. She found the Capitol building with its white dome gleaming in the early morning light and then let her eyes drift west.

The apartment was high enough to get a good look, but she knew it was there, the one thing she desired above all else.

"You do that every morning and I always wonder what you are looking at," Claire said, bringing her coffee into the living room.

"The White House," Styles mumbled.

Claire came up beside her, squinting against the sun. "Where is it?"

"You see where the treetops open up right there?" She pointed.

"Uh-huh," Claire replied.

"Right there."

Claire didn't seem to be paying attention, and Styles could tell there was something bothering her.

"What's on your mind, darlin'?"

"I couldn't get his records, but I looked inside."

"And?" Styles turned, giving the girl her full attention.

"I could get in trouble for this, Robin. Don't you care?"

"Oh, darlin', I would never ask you to do anything that would hurt you."

Claire lowered her eyes for a moment and Styles resisted the urge to say anything else. *You can't appear desperate.*

"He is sick. His doctors are keeping it real quiet, but I saw his lab tests . . ."

"And?"

"He's dying."

Styles had never been religious, but at that moment she almost dropped to her knees and offered up a prayer.

"He came down to the hospital unit for a blood draw. His usual nurse wasn't there, so I did it, and when the results came back they accidentally sent them to me."

That's why Cole wasn't at the briefing.

"Do they know what's wrong with him?" Styles asked.

"He has cancer, and it's terminal."

This is it. This is your opportunity.

"Can you get a copy for me?"

"I think the Secret Service took all of his files and lab results. The only thing we have is his medication list."

"Remember when I said I needed you to do something for me?" Styles asked, turning on all of her charm.

"Yes, anything, you know that."

"I need you to get me a copy of the medication list."

"But I could lose my license."

"Darlin', I would never let that happen. Remember, I work for the CIA, which means that if you are helping me, I can protect you."

Claire nodded her head like she understood. Styles couldn't believe how easy it was to manipulate her. She might have felt sorry for Claire, except that Robin was walking on a razor's edge and did not plan on getting cut.

"Don't you worry, little lamb, I promise that nothing is going to happen to you."

It was a lie and Styles knew it.

Chapter 38

Smoking a cigarette, West looked at the black nylon backpack. He realized that he had just made history. When he was an Alpha, the Program's code name for a man-portable nuclear weapon was "Sasquatch." It was a fitting name, because while everyone claimed they existed, no one had ever seen one.

There were rumors that a few had gone missing from East Germany after the fall of the Berlin Wall, but no proof. West was tempted to take a picture and send it to Robin Styles, and he would have except that it would spoil the surprise.

The bag was exactly like the one his son had carried back and forth to school, except instead of books this one had a nuclear weapon inside. Holding the cigarette between his lips, West bent over and lifted it into the air.

It was lighter than he had imagined. According to one Soviet defector he had tracked from Berlin to Libya, the Russian variant was supposed to weigh fifty pounds, and only had a six-kiloton yield.

The first bomb dropped on Japan had been almost three times as powerful, but that wasn't really the point. The key to the Iranian bomb was that not only was it untraceable, but it was built inside a vacuum compartment that kept sniffers from being able to detect it.

But there was a problem. West had assumed that Ali Breul would be able to arm the weapon. He learned during the interrogation that he was wrong. Breul's job was to build the bomb, a job he could do. To make it go boom, Iran had to bring in outside help.

"So you built the damn thing, but don't know how to blow it up? Are you fucking serious?" West had demanded.

"The Pakistani built the trigger," Breul blubbered, thinking he could still save his own life. "The chain reaction needed to make the bomb detonate has to be exact. One break in the chain and . . ."

"And what, it won't explode?"

"Yes . . . yes, it will still explode, just not at its full potential," Breul stammered.

It was not what West wanted to hear. He wanted

maximum effects and the message only a towering mushroom cloud could convey.

The computer on the desk came to life, showing the outside of the cabin. West had installed a motion camera above his door, and the picture showed one of the crewmen. West knew he was safe, but he had learned what happened when you trusted someone other than yourself. Grabbing a pistol from his waistband, he took up a position next to the door, waiting for the knock.

"Yes?"

"The captain, sir," the crewman began in French, "he would like a word if you have the time."

"Tell him I am on my way," West replied.

"Yes, sir."

West watched the computer until he was sure that the man had gone, then slipped the pistol back into his pants. The road that led him here had not been easy, and he wasn't taking anything for granted.

West had a vast network of spies and informants, and the most important of them was a man named Henri Baudin.

Baudin was born in Paris. His father was a German engineer and his mother a teacher. After a stint in the military, Baudin began a career with DGSE, the French version of the CIA, but had gotten the boot for arming fighters loyal to Syrian President Bashar al-Assad.

While the French government was quick to publicly denounce the Syrian dictator, behind closed doors they were making a fortune off of him. It was an old game, but what got Baudin into trouble wasn't what he was doing, it was who the Frenchman wasn't paying off.

So Henri took his skills to the private sector and became a serious player in the illegal gun trade. He was the man who could get you what you wanted, no matter the price. But his good fortune came to an end when a rival hired West to liquidate him.

Instead of a bullet, Nate made him a deal. He let Baudin know that a very valuable commodity was about to come on the market. The buyer would foot the bill for whatever West needed and he and Baudin would split the proceeds.

Baudin found a buyer in twelve hours, which didn't surprise West in the least. An untraceable nuclear weapon was a hot commodity, but now the Frenchman was eager to collect his end of the deal and disappear.

On cue the computer chirped. West brought it to life by hitting the space bar. The desktop wallpaper was a picture of an old barn covered in kudzu. He had seen the picture in a bookstore in Prague and later downloaded it off the Internet. The photo reminded him of his wife. She had taken a similar picture years ago of a place he'd never see again.

The message was from Baudin.

Is the package ready?

Yes, West typed back.

Big mess in Algiers. You said to expect a CLEAN operation.

"Fucking French," West snorted. He had just pulled off the impossible and his employer was bitching about the damage.

> Got to break the egg to make an omelet. You just do your part. Send papers through Interpol and stay out of the way.
>
> *Anything else?*
>
> Have you found Bassar?
>
> *Yes.*

An address popped on the screen and West exited the messenger and clicked on Google Earth. He typed in the address and found himself looking down on an isolated house in the middle of the country.

He had carefully choreographed what would happen next. Baudin's contact at Interpol would send an official request for information to the CIA. The request would be the match and Director Styles was the fuse.

As much as the Program wanted to believe that its existence was a closely guarded secret, West knew for a fact that the Director of the CIA had been nosing around for years. The request from Interpol would appear to be manna from heaven: a once-in-a-lifetime opportunity to catch an Alpha totally unaware and in the midst of an op.

West knew that Styles would be unable to pass it up. In fact, she would move heaven and earth to grab Steele.

And that was exactly what West wanted.

West calculated the distance from his current location to Bassar and knew he had the time. He had to move fast, and if he pulled it off, by the time the nuke was armed, the Director of the CIA would have shifted every asset at her disposal to Europe in pursuit of Steele.

This really is too easy.

He typed another address into the search bar and waited for the map to come up. This was his endgame— the place where he would take the bomb once it was armed.

The map came up pixelated, and slowly cleared until Washington, D.C., covered the monitor.

"Daddy's coming home."

Chapter 39

M eg stood on the deck looking out over the ocean. She hadn't slept well the night before, kept awake by nightmares from the Gatehouse. The images that plagued her sleep were unrelenting snapshots of horror and abject terror. Daniels's mangled body balled up in the wall locker. The firefight in the street. West yanking her from the van by her hair, the helpless feeling of her boot heels bumping off the pavement. Colt Weller's faceless body. The beating before they forced her eyes open in front of the retinal scanner.

And then Steele showed up.

Meg had known the moment she saw him appear through the smoke that she wasn't going to die.

Steele and Demo had spent the previous hours refining the plan and now were waiting for Rockford to tell them where to find Bassar. Meg had gotten restless waiting inside, and the salt air helped clear her head.

Once they had the location, Demo would file two separate flight plans, using unencrypted channels. Steele had told her that the CIA would be tracking all of the flights coming out of Algiers and that Demo knew a local who acted as a CIA snitch. Once they had their destination, Demo would leak the tail numbers to the local. He would add that the people on the plane were involved in what had happened in Algiers.

The snitch would send a priority cable to Langley and the game would be on.

"We are going to Spain." Steele's voice cut through the darkness.

Meg jumped; she hadn't heard him come outside.

"You scared me," she admitted.

Steele walked over, leaned against the rail, and took a moment before he spoke.

"Demo is sending the flight details now. One plane will go to Paris and the other to Cyprus. The CIA will use every available asset to lock down the two areas. It's an old trick I learned from West."

What if I screw this up? Meg asked herself.

"I know what you are thinking," Steele said, "and you don't need to worry about it."

"Worry about what?"

"If you can hack it. We will be traveling under a cover I have used a hundred times. His name is Max Sands and the legend is solid."

"I've run ops before," she said, wincing at the way her voice sounded. "I can do this."

"I wouldn't be bringing you along if I didn't know that."

"Are you always so damn confident?"

Steele grinned. "My mom raised me after my dad left. She worked as a data processor during the day and at this shitty diner at night. Sometimes I'd hear her crying late at night when money was tight, but in the morning you'd never know. She taught me that you have to be strong even when things aren't going your way."

Meg was surprised by the admission, but it made sense. If Steele was raised by a woman, it explained his big heart and protective nature.

"I bet that was tough."

He shrugged. "You do what you have to. Changing subjects, Rockford told me that Styles was the one who pushed for Bassar to get religious asylum. Said he was being persecuted in Pakistan, whatever the hell that means. She even signed off on the deal when Iran offered him refuge."

"Why would she do that?"

"Let's go ask Bassar."

Chapter 40

S tyles was in her office reading an official cable re-counting what the CIA knew so far in regard to the situation in Algiers. All night long, CIA assets, State Department officials, and various other intelligence assets controlled by Langley had been firing cable after cable to the States. Some were short, others long, but each represented a fragment of the chaos.

Styles was trying to make sense of the mess. She had two plastic boxes, one for the cables that contained something useful, and one for the trash.

Garbage, she thought, tossing the cable into the trash pile, which she noticed was almost full. *This is ridiculous.*

She hadn't gone home last night and Claire had been blowing up her phone. She decided she was at a stopping point and was about to return her call when her aide said:

"I've got something."

The Director looked up at the man who had just barged into her office.

Fucking Jamie.

Styles speared the intercom button on her phone and heard the line ring outside her door on Jamie's desk. There was no answer.

What part of do not fucking disturb is she not getting?

It was the second time this morning. The first came when Jamie walked in to let Styles know that Rockford had asked for a briefing.

"She wasn't at her desk a second ago, boss."

Styles sighed. "What is it, Dan?"

"I wouldn't bother you if I didn't think it was important," the aide said, holding up a brown folder with SECRET stamped across the front. Styles held out her hand and Dan dutifully placed the folder in her fingers. She opened the file and rolled her eyes.

"Dan, what is this?"

"A Blue Notice, ma'am," he replied, padding to the table in front of the couch and tidying up the empty coffee cups and detritus left over from his boss's dinner.

"I see that," Styles said, taking her reading glasses from the desk and placing them on her nose. The readers were new. A year ago her eyesight was 20/20, but the late hours spent reading emails or the damn cables had wreaked havoc on her vision. Yet another unwelcome reminder that Robin Styles was not as young as she once had been.

Interpol was the largest law enforcement agency in the world, but unlike the FBI and its European counterparts, its agents didn't have authority to make arrests. In essence, they were an administrative liaison, watchdogs for the 190 member countries that made up the agency. The lifeblood of any good bureaucracy was paperwork, and Interpol shed it by the quart. A Blue Notice was an official request for additional information. The CIA got hundreds of these memos a day. Very few ever made it up to Styles's office.

The Director scanned the origin line and saw that it was from an agent in France requesting information regarding two aircraft that had flown out of Algeria. One was heading to Paris, the other to Cyprus. Both tail numbers were highlighted.

"Tell me about the planes."

"Both flights originated in Chlef, an hour's drive from Algiers. The source intel came from an asset we have on payroll. According to him the people on the planes had something to do with the attack on our SOG teams."

Finally a stroke of luck. "Tell me you are tracking them?"

"Yes, ma'am. The flight to Cyprus landed thirty minutes ago. A man got off and we have an agent following him. His name, we think, is Roberto Cortez." Styles flipped the page and found a Department of Defense "DA photo" showing a man wearing Class A's, the Army's dress uniform.

"Stocky son of a bitch," Styles murmured.

Her eyes went to the stack of medals on his chest, topped by the Combat Infantryman Badge, or CIB. The award told her that Cortez had been to combat. The Army used the DA photos to quickly determine a soldier's professionalism and military bearing. It was a career in a snapshot.

Cortez cut an imposing figure, and in addition to two Silver Stars, Airborne Wings, and Ranger Tab he also had the distinctive "long tab" and combat patch of the Green Berets.

"That photo is the original. According to a friend at the Pentagon, everything else had been erased. It was almost like Mr. Cortez never existed."

The next page showed a woman, the angle and clarity telling Styles that the photo had been taken from a security camera.

"Meg Harden. That picture is from the safehouse

where Charlie Daniels's body was recovered. She is one of ours, but came out of the Army. Used to work for the Activity. The SOG team that was escorting her was wiped out."

Styles flipped the page. This photo was hazy, but she knew it came from a Reaper drone. Someone in the imagery department had tagged the building in the center with an ID number. The Director didn't need it. She knew it was the Gatehouse and it was a mangled, sagging wreck. There were jagged holes in the roof, and the wall had been blown out and blackened by fire. In the far right of the frame there was a van. The next couple of images were close-up shots of the van. The front end was a twisted, crumpled mess. All of the windows were shot out and the metal pockmarked with bullet holes. Inside, expended brass shone golden atop pools of congealed blood and bits of flesh. There was a headless body leaning against the door, the flesh around the neck flayed bits of reddish meat.

"Not for the faint of heart, is it?" Styles asked.

"No, ma'am. The final page I believe will interest you the most."

It was another Blue Notice. Styles had never seen the man before, but was struck by his dark green eyes. He was a hard-looking man, someone you would not fight unless you had to.

"Who is this?"

"He is the man traveling with Ms. Harden, and we assume they are both on the aircraft heading to Paris."

"What's his name?"

"That's just it. According to Interpol that man is Max Sands, a businessman from Toronto. I think it is a shell."

"An alias? Why do you think that?"

"I ran him through the systems. Sands has a passport, tax information, and a driver's license, but no tickets or debt. His passport shows that he travels exclusively to Europe, but when I ran his face through facial recognition I got hits in Tunis, Algiers, Iraq, even a hit in the Ukraine. Places Max Sands has never been."

He's an Alpha.

Styles couldn't prove it, but the best part of her job was that she didn't *have to.* All she needed to launch an operation was actionable intelligence and a target. The Blue Notice, combined with the tail numbers sent from the asset in Algiers, gave her exactly that.

She had run operations on much less.

"I want everything we have on this. Tell Interpol to update this to Red," she said, tapping at the notice, "and send it to customs and Homeland Security. They go on the no-fly list within the hour, do you understand?"

"Yes, ma'am."

"Send a team to Cyprus and have them keep Cortez under surveillance. The priority is Harden and this guy. I want all available SOG teams in Paris before the plane hits the tarmac, and tell NSA we need eyes in the sky. Dan, I need you to listen to me," Styles said, talking over her glasses. "This is priority one, everything we have goes to nailing this guy, do you understand?"

"Yes, ma'am."

"I mean *everything*. You have my direct authority to pull anyone from anywhere."

"I was going to issue a BOLO and send it to Europe," Dan added.

A BOLO stood for "Be on the lookout" and was sent to local police forces and anyone else not connected to the national database.

"Do it.

"And, Dan, I don't care if you bring him back in a body bag, just get him."

Chapter 41

"A legend is like a second skin, you have to know it inside and out," Steele said, shifting to take the pressure off his lower back. Economy class was not built for comfort, and Steele was getting a crick in his neck from facing Meg.

She rolled her eyes, venting her frustration. Steele was beginning to figure her out in bits and pieces. Meg was used to being good at things and he imagined she was the kind of person who latched on to a new idea the first time. He was sure that she knew what a legend was, but Steele wasn't the kind of guy who settled for mediocre.

This is exactly why I work alone.

"Let's take a break, I have to pee anyway," she said, snapping the seat belt free and flinging it into the seat.

They had flown from Chlef, a city two hours south-west of Algiers, and boarded a flight that was sched-uled to land in Seville in an hour. Steele could feel the minutes slipping away. The papers they were using to get into Spain were disposable, and Steele had every intention of dumping them after clearing customs. Once they cleared the airport, he would become Max Sands and Meg would be his wife.

Adding a wife hadn't been a problem. He chose the name Caroline because it reminded him of his mother. They were newlyweds from Toronto on their way to the Riviera for a honeymoon. He had been hammering Meg with the details, ignoring Demo's warning to start slow.

"Where do we live?"

"1901 Bayview Avenue, Toronto."

"Do we rent or own?"

"Rent—it's a condo. We moved there because of the view and because they allow dogs."

When Meg came back she was holding two min-iature bottles of vodka and a can of Sprite snuggled atop two plastic cups. "Thought we could use a study break." Steele took the airplane vodka and twisted the top. He wasn't a vodka man and would have preferred to shoot it straight, but he waited dutifully for Meg to crack the Sprite and mix her drink before following suit.

"You sure this is what you want? The boss said I had to take you with me, he didn't say you had to play. Seville has some nice shopping, you could look around—"

"What happens when we hit the ground?" she interrupted.

"Been wondering that myself," he said, adding a drop of Sprite for "flavor."

Flying commercial was the only way in. They were trading security for time. What was nagging at him was the realization that he had no idea where West was.

Steele needed an edge, either speed, surprise, or violence of action, but right now he didn't have any of them. "Always chasing the rabbit," he mused aloud.

"What?"

"When I was in Special Forces we'd go down to Mississippi and train."

"Shaws?" She asked, referring to the nickname given to the Mid South Shooting Institute.

"Yeah, you been there?"

"Once or twice."

"Ever meet Ronnie?"

"No." Meg's eyes rotated up, accessing her memory. "Don't think so."

"Ronnie was an old Team guy, a SEAL from Bangor, Maine, I think." Steele smiled, remembering the old salt's raspy accent. "He'd set up these scenarios where you'd end up chasing a guy who was sucking you into an ambush. We were using sim guns, and after we got shot to shit he'd say, 'Ain't no fun when the rabbit's got the gun.' After that we called it 'chasing the rabbit.'"

Steele paused to take another drink. "I heard Ronnie took a contract in Afghanistan. Teaching guys how to shoot just wasn't enough," he said wistfully.

"What happened to him?"

"Took an IED outside of the Bermel District Center, blew him right out of the Hilux and into a ditch. He bled out before they found him."

He could tell by the way she brushed the story off that she had plenty of her own. Death was nothing new to a soldier.

"You ever gone in blind like this?" she asked.

He nodded and finished the drink with a long pull. The vodka burned the back of his throat and warmed his face. "I've gone in blind and I've gone in dark, but never at the same time. An 'empty quiver' tends to change the rules."

"Empty quiver?"

"A missing nuclear weapon." He fell silent, sensing Meg's eyes on him.

When they landed in Spain, Steele pulled a hat low over his face. He'd put brown contacts in to hide his eyes and followed Meg to the baggage carousel. Before 9/11 you could travel light, but these days security tended to pay attention to people who traveled without luggage, especially on international flights.

They stood together in the customs line, and Steele brought his mouth to Meg's ear and whispered, "We are just two lovebirds on their honeymoon." He gave her a kiss on the ear and stepped forward.

The agent looked at their Canadian passports and asked, "Mr. and Mrs. Sands, what brings you to Spain?"

"It is our honeymoon," Meg answered, looping her arm around Steele's waist.

The agent glanced at their passports before waving them over the scanner. Eric felt Meg stiffen and knew she was holding her breath. He gave her a gentle squeeze and said, "This is her first time in Spain. I know she is going to love it."

"I hope so," the agent said, handing the papers back and motioning them through the line.

Outside the terminal they headed to the long-term parking garage and Steele pulled a universal key fob out of his pocket.

"How do you have a car already waiting?" Meg asked.

Steele smiled in response and pushed the button. The line of cars closest to him all unlocked with a beep. "You mean to tell me the CIA doesn't have these?"

"Show-off."

He needed a newer vehicle, one that didn't have a key, and luckily found a BMW that fit the bill right away.

"Okay, I have got to see this. My dad is a car guy and he swears that you can't hotwire the new Beemers."

"Hotwire, what is this, the nineties?" Steele asked, tossing their luggage in the trunk. He walked around to the driver's side and put his foot on the brake. "No one boosts cars like that anymore. Wait, please don't tell me they are still teaching that at the Farm."

"What are you going to do, smartass?"

"Uh, I'm going to start the car." He jabbed the push-to-start with his index finger and the sedan came to life. "Gotta love technology."

Steele had already memorized the route from the Seville airport to the Palacio de Congresos train station and headed west, bypassing as many road cameras as possible. It took a bit longer, but nothing blew an op faster than having your picture taken for running a red light. He parked the car at the station and wiped it down the best he could.

"You good, baby?" he asked, coming up behind Meg and grabbing her butt with a roguish smile.

She jumped and slapped his hand away with a surprised yelp. "What the hell are you doing?"

Steele was still grinning and held up his hand, waving his ring finger back and forth like an exclamation point. "Caroline, baby, you have *got* to relax."

"Shit." Meg hid her face behind her hands, but Steele could see her cheeks redden.

He got serious real fast. "That's how it happens," he began. "You drop your legend for one second and"—he snapped his fingers and Meg jumped—"you're dead."

Maybe this was a mistake.

Even if it was, Steele knew it was too late to switch her out. The best he could do was keep her on the sidelines as much as possible. Hopefully that *might* keep her alive.

She was tired, he could see it in her eyes, so he decided to give her a break and turned his attention back to the situation at hand and the added stress of traveling "clean." He didn't have a weapon, cover, or any backup. Besides Meg, his closest help was Demo, and he was in Cyprus. A slip here could cost the mission.

No matter how fast they ran, there was no way Steele and Meg could outrun a Motorola, the radios the police

used in Europe. The digital age had changed everything, and while it made life easier for civilians, the
opposite was true for Steele. The Internet connected
everything and there was no doubt that someone was
watching. Every cell phone came with a camera, and
when you added traffic cams and video feeds it was
impossible to stay out of the light.

"This is the time we are most exposed. I have a
locker in the train station that has my gear. We have to
get to it or it's game over."

Meg grabbed his hand. The touch was both un-
expected and electric, and this time Steele was caught
by surprise. She felt him flinch and grinned from ear
to ear.

"Relaaax, hubby," she taunted, "we are just a married couple heading for a train ride."

The station's security was serious. Overhead, tinted
globes hid surveillance cameras, and soldiers with fully
automatic weapons guarded the exits. A teeming mass
of families walking hand in hand with young children
and businessmen glued to smartphones formed a crowd
that stretched the terminal to bursting.

The first thing Steele did was clear the door and
move to the wall. He ambled over to a gift shop with
Meg in tow and pretended to peruse the shop. He used
the glass to scan the faces, looking for anyone who

might be watching before focusing on a table cluttered with envelopes and postal supplies.

"You see the table?" he whispered, without looking at Meg.

"Yeah."

"Walk over to the envelopes and stand on the far right. You are going to mask me."

Meg did as she was told, weaving through the crowd until she was standing where he wanted her. Steele took a piece of paper out of his pocket, just another traveler with something to put in the post. He kept his head down, eyes on the paper, checking his flanks out of his peripheral. He sidled up to the table, patting his pocket like he'd forgotten something, and let Meg know to block the camera. Reaching below the table, he found the key right where it was supposed to be and palmed it.

"Let's go."

Steele looked at the number engraved on the metal. The key belonged to locker 103, which sat on the far side of the platform. There were too many faces to watch and he knew that if they were going to take him down they would do it now. Getting hit wasn't his only worry; he also had to be on the lookout for counterintel.

He waited for the next train to pull in and let the squealing brakes cover his move. The crowd jostled for position, creating a human shield, and he flashed to the locker, inserting the key into the lock and swinging the door open deftly. The bag inside looked exactly like the one he was carrying and he made the switch and secured the locker in less than ten seconds. He placed his arm around Meg and guided her back to the bathroom, gently nuzzling her neck as they moved.

"Go change, dump your clothes. I'll be waiting here."

"Okay."

She was following his lead and Steele couldn't ask for anything more. The bathroom was packed, but luckily one of the stalls near the end was unoccupied. He ducked inside, locking the door behind him. Unlike American stalls, the European ones had floor-to-ceiling cubes surrounding the toilets—perfect for changing. Steele opened his luggage and changed into a pair of dark jeans, work boots, and a gray shirt. He took Max and Caroline Sands's passports from the bag he'd retrieved from the locker and checked the entry stamp. It was from Heathrow Airport and dated the day before.

Satisfied, he stuffed his old passport and dirty clothes into a bundle and flushed the toilet. On his way out, he dumped the wad into the trash can.

Meg came out in a pair of formfitting pants and a cream top. *Wow, she cleans up nice.* She had even touched up her makeup, effectively hiding the circles under her eyes. Steele handed Meg her ticket just as a train pulled up in a squeal of brakes and a press of eager travelers. Steele and Meg joined the rush, but didn't relax until they pulled out of the station.

The private compartment was small and the blue interior and recycled air reminded Steele of the plane they had taken from Algiers. There were two bunk beds, a small bathroom, and a desk near the window.

Meg threw her bag on the top bunk and kicked off her shoes. "Are you going to get some sleep?"

"In a minute," Steele lied, stepping into the bathroom.

He popped an amphetamine tab and turned on the sink to wash his face. Recycled air always made his skin greasy, and the short scrub was a welcome luxury. By the time he had wiped off the sink, used the toilet, and stepped out, Meg was snoring lightly.

She's all tuckered out.

He took a blanket from the closet and draped it over her, realizing that besides what he had read, he didn't know one common thing about Meg. The first question that popped into his mind was whether she was single.

Easy, buddy.

The one thing he did know was that a girl like Meg didn't belong in this world. He locked the door and slipped the chain in place, then kicked off his shoes, grabbed the bag, and padded to the desk next to the window. He used his fingernail to find the hidden seam in the bottom of the bag and found a stack of cash, credit cards, a computer, and a .38 Smith & Wesson revolver. The serial number had already been filed off and the cylinder release, just like the trigger, was covered in surgical tape. *Don't have to worry about prints if I toss it.*

After ensuring that the pistol was loaded, Steele flicked the cylinder into the battery with a snap of his wrist, and opened the computer. He logged in and brought up the browser that linked him to the Keyhole Surveillance and Global Target System. At the top was a tab with the mission reference number Rockford had assigned to Bassar, and Steele clicked it and waited for the uplink to establish.

The only reason the Keyhole wasn't leaked by Edward Snowden was because he didn't know it existed. Like the Program, Keyhole was a special access program, highly compartmentalized to keep it from prying eyes.

Finally the computer dinged at the same moment

Steele felt the amphetamine creep into his blood-stream.

He opened a second window and logged in to the Program's debriefing files. He typed in West's name and a list of audio files popped up. He selected one from the list and hit the play arrow.

"Alpha Debrief 19072004 conducting After Action Review with Stalker 2," a voice began. "Stalker 2, what was your mission?"

"On July 19, 2004, I—" Steele ignored the chills that came from hearing Nate's voice and placed the cursor over the audio bar that corresponded with what West was saying. He knew he needed at least a ten-second sample for the best possible voice match and was forced to listen as West spoke.

"I was conducting close target reconnaissance on high-level members of Al-Qaeda in preparation for the second battle of Fallujah. My primary concern was identifying IED cell leaders . . ."

Steele had what he needed. He hit the pause button and cut the audio sample he needed. After closing the window, he dragged the new file over to the Keyhole's audio targeting platform and dropped it into the search parameter bar.

The file uploaded and all Steele had to do then was hit enter. Keyhole's targeting software would take care of the rest. It fed the audio sample into the system, linking it with every satellite, phone tower, repeater, or listening post in the world. If West uttered a word anywhere near a radio, cell phone, or computer with a microphone, Keyhole would mark the hit and send it to Cutlass Main, where Rockford had authorized one of the targeting teams looking for Bassar.

Nate, unless you are hiding in a hole, I'm going to see you real soon.

Chapter 42

I t was dark on the stern of the longboat and Nathaniel West heard the cigarette boat before he saw it. The thirty-eight-footer came out of the shadows. Its hull was painted with a radar-dampening epoxy and tinted a dark gray. It looked almost black in the moonless night, like blood on the water.

The smugglers called them Picudas, and with the Twin Mercurys putting out 450 horsepower per engine, they were the fastest things on the water. West snugged the pack tight on his shoulders and waited while the pilot cut the wheel and drifted the boat alongside the container ship's longboat. He stepped on board without a word.

"*Vamonos.*"

Yeah, let's go.

The pilot waited for West to take a seat before advancing the throttles. The engines growled and lifted the prow skyward. West hit the start button on the Casio G-Shock strapped to his wrist. *Plenty of time.*

He sat slightly behind the pilot, but close enough to the glass to avoid the salt spray cascading over the bow. The Spaniard piloted by GPS, and beside him, a second smuggler kept his face pressed to the rubber boot covering the radar.

On the container ship, he and the captain had traced the route West would take into Spain. The smugglers would not use the traditional lanes used to ferry drugs from North Africa to Spain. West couldn't afford to hug the coastline, so he paid extra for them to make most of the trip across the open ocean. Getting caught in the open was a smuggler's worst nightmare. On most nights, the narrow channel was packed with helicopters patrolling in conjunction with a fleet of small cutters. Working in tandem they had a better chance of stemming the tide of heroin coming from North Africa. But palms had been greased and those who would not comply had been silenced. There would be no coast guard on his route tonight.

Still, West didn't leave anything to chance.

The Picuda traveled at 90 miles per hour and at that speed the engines sucked fuel like a drunk during happy hour. Not long into the trip the pilot throttled back, slowing the boat enough for the first mate to top off the tanks from one of the fuel cans packed in the back.

In an hour they had to stop to refuel. While the captain piloted the boat, West slipped a handheld GPS from his pocket. The Garmin Rhino looked like a walkie-talkie, which in a way it was, but he had the radio option turned off. Instead of beeping when West depressed the transmit button, the GPS sent his location to his men who were waiting somewhere over the horizon. Once he was satisfied that they had a lock, he shoved the GPS back into his pocket.

Five minutes later the pilot once again cut the throttles.

"How much farther?" West asked in Spanish, standing up to stretch his legs. The navigator moved to the rear for the final time and filled up the tanks.

"Forty-five minutes, I'd say. Let me go help Miguel."

West watched the two smugglers work, their backs to him the entire time. It was a simple operation except when they had to switch the refueling hose from one can to the next. When that happened Miguel needed the pilot's help.

West waited for the pilot to lift the hose free and slipped behind him, the blade silently coming out of its sheath. He jammed it into the base of his skull and twisted. *Lights out, hombre.*

He eased the pilot to the ground and crept forward to the mate, who was bent over the fuel tank. "Emilio, the fuel cap," he said, stretching his arm out behind him.

West grabbed him by the hand and torqued it, wrist and arm as one, exposing the side of his neck. He spiked the blade sideways through Miguel's neck, severing the artery, and savagely yanked it free. The blood sheeted across the gunwale with a wet splat and the smell of raw meat. Miguel clawed at the wound with his right hand, trying to stem the red tide.

"Don't fight it, amigo."

But the wild-eyed mate wanted to live and tried to jerk his hand free, forcing Nate to let go of the knife. He knew it would have been easier if he'd just shot them both, but even with a suppressor the sound would carry over water. West didn't know who else was lurking in the darkness, but more than that, he *liked* using the blade. A bullet was impersonal. It meant nothing.

He thought all of this while forcing Miguel into a wristlock. In aikido they called it *nikyo,* or "the second technique," and it was one of the first moves West had mastered as a student of the martial art. It was a simple movement, and when he locked it down, Miguel had to stand up or let West break his wrist.

"It's nothing personal, I just need to borrow your ride."

The mate was shaky on his feet, the lost blood over-coming the shot of adrenaline. West stepped in close. He could smell the man's breath, see the shimmer of the black blood on his shirt and the dumb deer look in Miguel's eyes that told West he knew he was about to die.

He guided him toward the edge of the boat and with a final twist and shift of his hips, flung Miguel into the sea. He retrieved the knife, wiping the blade on the dead pilot's shirt, and then secured the cap. The boat bobbed beneath his feet, and after stepping behind the wheel, West dialed the radio to the frequency he wanted and pushed the handmike.

Out of the corner of his eye he saw Miguel reach skyward for a God that wasn't there for him and then sink below the waves.

"Eagle 1 to Nest," West said.

"Go ahead, Eagle."

"I am moving to the rendezvous point."

"Roger, Eagle, we will see you there."

West pushed the throttles forward and brought the boat on line with the GPS. Ten minutes later he double-clicked the transmit button, signaling that he was in the area, and cut the engines. With the engines off the silence was deafening. The only sound came from the wake lapping against the fiberglass hull. Off to the port side a light flashed once, twice, and then a third time. West responded with two flashes of his own and an engine started up.

A Zodiac inflatable boat appeared, trailing a white wake, and as it drew closer West could see three heavily armed men aboard. The rubber boat drew alongside and Villars was there with a line. He tossed it across while the other two pulled security.

"How was it?" Villars asked.

"Too easy."

West sent the bomb across first and Villars secured it with straps and then tossed a package the size of a paperback book across. West caught it and moved swiftly to the back of the boat. He yanked the fuel line free, made sure the gas was flowing, popped the igniter, and set the explosive next to the tank. After tossing off the line, he climbed on board the Zodiac.

"Let's roll."

The Zodiac surged toward the shore and when it was a quarter mile away an orange fireball lit up the darkness.

Chapter 43

Meg Harden woke up without a hint of jet lag, which surprised her. *I always get jet-lagged.* There was a note on the table from Steele.

"I'll be waiting in the dining car," she read aloud, grinning at the smiley face he'd drawn at the bottom. She jumped in the shower, the water making her flinch when it hit the scrapes and bruises West had left on her body. She wondered if Steele had slept. *Probably not.* She could see him in her mind's eye, keeping watch while she was passed out on the bed. He had pissed her off on the plane and hurt her feelings when he yelled at her, but after the nap Meg was able to put things into perspective.

"What would I have done in his shoes?" she wondered aloud, already knowing the answer.

From what she had gathered, he had been on the go for almost four days, and sleep deprivation had a way of cutting even the toughest men down to size.

Meg had seen every shade of the male ego. The screamers, the bullies, and the ones who treated her like a china doll. Steele didn't fit any of these categories. He was a rarity, a man who actually checked his ego at the door.

Will wonders never cease?

She hopped out of the shower and found a pink toothbrush and a tube of toothpaste waiting on the sink. She had missed them before and was wondering what she was going to do about her kitten breath. After brushing her teeth and fixing her hair, she stepped out of their compartment, checked the sign, and swayed through the shifting cars until she saw Steele sitting at a table, a half-empty glass of wine before him. He looked good in a navy button-up that complemented his eyes, and as she approached he got to his feet.

"You look great, darling," he said, stepping close and brushing his lips lightly against hers.

The operational side of Meg's brain said the kiss was nothing, strictly business. But the woman in her, the side that had abhorred the isolation and loneliness she'd endured in Algiers, desperately *wanted* the kiss to mean something. *And why shouldn't it? He did save your life.*

The kiss lasted a microsecond, but before Steele could pull away, Meg was kissing him back. *I have to know.* She pressed her lips against him, felt his strong arms slip around her waist, and allowed herself to forget everyone and everything except the feel of his lips and the rugged, manly scent of his cologne.

Her heart hammered in her chest, carrying the electricity of the kiss all the way to her fingertips. It seemed to last an eternity, and then Steele pulled back. Meg opened her eyes. His face was hot and his pupils dilated with desire. A hungry, eager look replaced the usual predatory stare, and then just as quickly as it appeared, the look was gone.

"Sleep well?" he asked.

She blushed and took her seat. *What the hell was that?* She watched him sit, noticing the waiter observing them. She wasn't a fan of public displays of affection, but something about Steele made her reckless. It felt like . . . *feels like you can be yourself.*

The waiter came over with the menu and a carafe of water.

"She is just as beautiful as you described, Monsieur Sands," he said in French. "You are a lucky man."

"Yes, I am," Steele replied in flawless French before giving her a wink.

"Madame, would you care for anything besides water?"

"Ummm . . ."

"She'll have a glass of red," Steele said.

He watched her, checking her approval, and when she nodded the waiter scurried off. There was something sexy about a man who took charge. *Jesus, is this the first time you've been around a man?* she chided herself, looking at the menu.

The dining car was not what she expected at all. It was clean, with tables laid out with fresh linen and silverware that sparkled under the lights that vibrated with the train's movement. Meg studied Steele over the top of her menu. He was physically attractive, what her girlfriends back in the civilian world would call hot. She had never seen eyes as green as his, but oddly enough what stood out was how neat he was.

How neat he is, really? First date you have been on in two years and you are checking out his silverware? What is wrong with you, girl?

"Anything look good?" Steele asked.

"Uhhh, yes the . . ." Meg realized she was holding the menu upside down. She flipped it over, scrunching up her face in embarrassment, but there was nothing but warmth in Steele's eyes.

"That's how I do it too."

She settled on the chicken and green beans, and when the waiter returned with the wine, Steele ordered for them both. Meg had spent a semester in Normandy during college and noticed that his accent was perfect.

"I didn't know you spoke French," she said when the waiter was gone.

"We've been married for how long now and you didn't know that?"

"We still have a few hours until we hit Spain."

"I'll give you that."

"You realize I don't even know your first name?"

"It's Eric."

"Really?"

"Yeah, why?" He frowned for a second. "You think I'd lie about my name?"

Meg smiled. It was a loaded question.

"Isn't that what you are trained to do?"

"I'm not my job."

"So you can just shut it off? All the training, the missions, everything, just flip it like a light switch?"

"Well, it may be hard to believe, but I was a person before all of this."

"Oh, I can't wait to hear about young Eric Steele."

"Let's get a bottle of wine."

Halfway through the bottle, Meg realized she was

tipsy. It wasn't just the wine, and she realized that she was enjoying pretending to be married.

"You think we'd work, you know, in a different situation?" she asked.

The question caught them both off guard, obviously flustering Steele, who took a sip of water to compose himself. *Dammit, am I drunk? Why did I ask that?* The question brought the fear of rejection and the fact that he could be simply playing his part.

"I like kissing you," he said honestly.

Meg bounced her eyebrows up seductively and reached for his hand. It was a start, and she'd take it. "You said you looked into me, but never told me what you found."

"I was impressed."

"I bet you thought I was just another pretty face, what you guys call tab sniffers."

"Never heard of that one."

"Really? The guys at Bragg called some of the girls who tried out for the Activity tab sniffers. Kinda like a Special Operations groupie."

"The thought never crossed my mind."

"Really?"

"Yeah, you want to know the first thing I thought when I saw you?"

"Sure," Meg replied, playing it cool.

"You really want to know?" He took a painfully slow sip of wine, before lowering his voice to a whisper.

Meg nodded, grabbing her own glass, savoring the tang of the alcohol on her tongue. Steele made a big show of checking his surroundings like he was about to let her in on a secret and she leaned in as he whispered:

"I thought you were a lesbian."

The comment caught her off guard, and Meg almost spit the mouthful of wine across the table. She choked, trying to laugh and catch her breath at the same time.

"Really? That's what you thought?"

"Scout's honor," he said, holding up his hand.

The dining car was almost empty now and the waiters were busing the tables, the lights low. Meg knew they would leave soon, and the realization tugged at her heart. There were some moments you wished would last forever, and this was one of them.

"Do you need me to carry you back to the car, Mrs. Sands?"

Meg smiled at him, finished her glass, and got to her feet. She held out her hand, waiting for her "husband" to stand, and when he did, Steele took it.

"I think that it will take more than a bottle of wine before I let you carry me to bed," she teased.

"Well, I think the bar is still open."

Chapter 44

The Zodiac dropped Nathaniel West on the shore at dawn. The sun peeked over the horizon and the sky was the color of static on a television. The crew headed back out to hide the boat, leaving West and Villars to trudge toward the jeep waiting for them. West stopped to light a cigarette before getting in.

"What's the status?" Villars asked in Afrikaans.

"Two recon teams are watching the house," the driver replied. He handed Villars a radio and put the jeep in gear. "Call signs are Ghost 1 and Ghost 2."

"Stand by," Villars said, offering the radio to West.

Nate took the radio and pressed the transmit button. "All teams, status report."

"Ghost 1, no movement on target."

"Ghost 2, we are moving to relieve Ghost 1."

West knew that even if Steele knew where to look, which he didn't, his old protégé was too far behind to catch up now. Baudin had made sure of that when he sent the Blue Notice, and if that idiot Styles did what West assumed she would, the Director would quickly upgrade it to a Red.

It really is too easy.

The jeep's knobby tires kicked up a mix of gravel and sand, the engine whining as it groaned up the hill. West was left alone with his thoughts. The drive took an hour, and halfway through the terrain changed from coastal scrublands to hills covered in chaparral, yellowed grasses, and dark red earth that reminded him of Texas. It was a hard land, pristine yet devoid of both movement and wildlife.

The landscape also reminded West of the contract he'd taken after recovering from his first surgery. He had needed money fast and found the perfect employer in Los Urabeños, an offshoot cartel that had popped up after the death of Pablo Escobar.

Los Urabeños knew that to draw the ire of the United States meant certain death, and the only way they were going to stay in business was if they evolved. They left Cali and set up shop in Paraguay. They also abandoned the *plata o plomo*—silver or lead—style of negotiations Escobar employed. In its place Los Urabeños paid senators and judges to do their dirty work.

One senator in particular, a man named Miguel Alba, became very valuable to their organization.

Alba was a local legend and devout Catholic who donated generously to the community. However, Los Urabeños weren't the only show in Ciudad del Este. The Russians had decided that the death of Escobar was the perfect time to get into the cocaine business.

But the Russians had their own style of play. They offered Alba triple what the cartel was paying him, and just to make sure he couldn't refuse, they kidnapped his wife and daughter. West was hired to take care of the situation.

It took him three days to find Alba's family. They were being held in a hacienda by the river and guarded by a group of tough-looking professionals. West didn't learn that they were Russians until he grabbed one on his way into town.

"Who hired you?" he demanded.

The Russian knew the game. He wasn't saying a word. West wasn't a fan of torture, because it took too long, and in his experience a man would tell you anything he thought you wanted to hear to make the pain stop.

But there were other ways. West made a call, and an hour later he heard the vehicle pull behind the empty shop he was using as a makeshift prison. To his surprise, the person who got out carrying a brown paper sack from a local pharmacy was a young woman. The cartel had all types of people on their payroll, but this one wasn't the usual thug. She was well dressed and carried herself with a quiet confidence. Instead of the gaudy jewelry the *cholas* loved, she wore a few simple gold pieces.

"Where is the patient?"

"In there."

"How far along is she?"

West smiled. The world made sense again. She was a doctor, most likely an OB-GYN, and she assumed that the oxytocin he had requested was for a woman in labor.

"Not that kind of patient."

"I see."

West knew she didn't.

"I'll take it from here. Wouldn't want you to ruin your shoes."

Before she was in the car, West was drawing up the injection. Oxytocin was used in labor and delivery either to start contractions of the uterus or to stop bleeding, but it had a more sinister application. Scientists called it the "trust drug" because of the way it affected the brain. West had used it in place of sodium amytal, the so-called truth serum, and found it much more effective.

He gave the Russian twice the recommended dose and settled back on his haunches to enjoy a cigarette and wait for the drug to kick in. It didn't take long.

"O true apothecary, thy drugs are quick," he said.

"What did you say?" the Russian slurred in Spanish.

"It's from Shakespeare, but don't worry about it," West replied in kind, getting to his feet. He switched to Russian when he was closer. "You and I have more important things to talk about. Let's start with your name."

"Aleksandr, but my friends call me Sasha."

"Are we friends?"

"It could be," the Russian replied with a shrug. The big man was flushed and tipsy, as if he had just left a bar. He leaned forward with an embarrassed look and whispered, "Your face is rather hideous. Were you burned in the war?"

"No. The war hasn't started *yet*, Sasha, but it will, and very soon," West replied.

"I went to war. I was with the Spetsnaz in Grozny, do you know where that is?"

West nodded. "Yes. It is in Chechnya."

"We did horrible things there. Our commander told us that the rebels were not human and we should not feel bad. But I did."

West knew all about the atrocities the Russians had heaped upon the Chechens, mostly their women and children. It was a savage war, reminiscent of Stalin's purges, but West planned on doing much worse when the time was right.

"Tell me about the family at the *estancia*," he said, checking his watch.

The oxytocin had turned the ex-soldier into a babbling drunk and he willingly complied with West's commands. Nate took notes while the man spoke, and Sasha even helped him draw a map of the estate.

Thirty minutes later, when the drug finally wore off, he was not so jovial.

"You have been a big help, Sasha."

"What did you give me, you asshole? My head is pounding."

"Yeah, that's the drug wearing off," West replied. "You want something for the pain?"

Sasha glared at him and looked like he was going to tell him to piss off, but decided an aspirin couldn't hurt.

"Yes."

"Okay." The pistol appeared out of thin air. West drew so fast that Sasha didn't have time to blink before the round punched through his eyeball and blew his brains over the dusty floor.

That night West rescued Alba's family, leaving nothing behind but a stack of bodies and a note for the Russians to clear out. The job set his reputation as a man who could get things done, and after that he found his skills in high demand. There was so much work that he started charging exorbitant rates for his services, but there was always someone willing to pay.

The command post in Spain was an old villa that had once been white. The sun and elements had taken their toll and some of the terra-cotta tiles were missing. It sat on the peak of a low hill and had an excellent view of the road. The jeep climbed the steep drive and paused at an iron gate bolted to a crumbling brick wall. Two armed men guarded the entrance beneath camo netting they had stretched over a machine-gun position.

West carried the bomb inside, where cots were lined neatly on the tile floor. The men not on duty were cleaning their weapons, and near the far wall a communications area had been set up. West handed the pack to Villars and walked behind the radioman, checking the map pinned to the wall.

"Ghost 2 is set. Ghost 1, returning to base," a voice came over the net.

"Roger, 1," the radio operator replied.

West looked at the map. Blue pushpins marked the overwatch position the recon teams were using. It was in a depression on the downslope of the hill. *A good spot,* West thought. From there the team had a clear line of sight to their east and were able to observe the gravel drive that paralleled the rows of olive trees before dropping into the low ground.

At the end of the road lay the final piece in West's plan, and once he had it, he was going to make the United States bleed.

Chapter 45

Málaga, Spain

It was midafternoon and the Mediterranean sun lay low in the sky when Steele and Meg arrived in Málaga and walked out of the train station. Keyhole had picked up a weak hit on West, but the signal was mobile and the program lost the track. While Steele didn't have an exact fix on his mentor, Keyhole confirmed that he was in the area.

"Is this the right place?" Meg asked, looking up from the travel guide she had bought on the train.

Steele glanced at the page. It showed a professional-grade photo taken from the citadel—a big difference from the row of apartments peering above an eight-foot wall in front of them.

He could feel her disappointment and looped his arm over her shoulder. "This is the industrial area.

Wait until we get the car before being too hard on her."

Málaga was one of the oldest cities in the world, and from the train station it appeared grimy, like a rumpled suit. Meg slumped her shoulders and followed Steele toward the rental lot. He angled toward a row of luxury vehicles glinting in the sun, digging his passport from his pocket. He had arranged a car while on the train, booking it under the import/export company Max Sands owned and operated out of Paris.

"*Buenos días,*" he said, handing his passport to the man in the glass vestibule. The man smiled, checking Steele's name against a piece of paper on a battered clipboard. He took a set of keys from a board and, after comparing the picture on the visa to the man before him, handed them over.

"Your keys, Mr. Sands," the attendant replied in Spanish.

"*Gracias.* This way, darling,"

Meg appeared to perk up at the sight of the brand-new Land Rover. They loaded their bags and got inside.

Steele started the engine and left the train station, heading toward the commercial district. They drove east, and just like he'd said, the view changed accordingly. The architecture was a perfect blend of Old

World charm, whitewashed adobe, and swaying palms, mixed with the new style of mirrored glass. When they were close to their hotel the Med appeared off to the right, crystal clear, just like the picture in Meg's guidebook.

Steele pulled the Land Rover up to the Room Mate Larios Hotel and hadn't put it in park before a valet was running toward them.

"Good evening, *señor y señorita,* welcome to the Mate Larios," he said, opening the door. "I hope you had a pleasant trip," he stammered.

Steele, now Sands, nodded and got out of the SUV without saying a word. He was an important man here on business and didn't talk to peons like valets, but he was a good tipper. He handed the valet a hundred-dollar bill and walked around to open the door for Meg. With enough cash you didn't have to be polite, and Steele knew that Max Sands could drag a body through the hotel foyer and no one would bat an eye. This was the swagger he had been trying to impress on Meg.

"We will be down in thirty minutes. Have the car ready," he said in Spanish.

"Yes, sir, of course."

Steele helped Meg from the SUV, looking at her legs as he did. "Make it an hour," he said to the valet with a wink.

"Will you stop?" she said, blushing.

"Just playing the newlywed part, my dear." Steele leaned in close to whisper his final instructions in her ear. "The manager's name is Tano. He is going to make a big scene. Just remember who you are supposed to be and, oh yeah, what size do you wear?"

"Huh?"

"What size clothes do you wear?"

"Oh, I wear a six."

"Shoes?"

"An eight, why?"

Steele didn't answer. Tano had seen him through the door and immediately begged the pardon of the young European couple he was speaking with and came skimming across the marble floor.

"Ahh, Señor Sands, what a wonderful surprise."

Tano was short and balding, dressed in a dark blue suit with a smiling but pockmarked face. He mopped his brow with a white handkerchief before extending his effete hand. "This must be Caroline. Enchanting, just as I imagined."

"Excellent to see you, Tano," Steele said, dropping his bag. The manager searched for a bellhop and Steele gave Meg a gentle nudge. "You don't carry your own bag anymore," he whispered.

Tano found who he was looking for and snapped his

fingers at the closest bellhop, and Meg dropped her bag as bidden.

"This is my nephew, Mateo. He will take excellent care of you. Shall I show you to your rooms? I am sure that you are very tired."

Tano chattered like this all the way to the rooms, which he unlocked with a keycard, stepping out of the way to let Meg in first. Steele had booked the best rooms and smiled to himself when she walked to the open balcony and stepped out to look at the ocean.

"She is very beautiful, Señor Sands."

"Thank you, Tano. I ordered some clothes. Have they arrived?"

"They are already in the closet."

Steele tugged the wad of dollars from his pocket, stripped two crisp hundred-dollar bills off the top, and pressed them into the manager's hand. "I need you to send the shopgirl up with what she has in a size six for the clothes and eight for shoes."

"Very well, Mr. Sands. Will you be dining with us tonight?"

"No, we have an engagement."

"A girl could get used to this," Meg said, throwing herself on the bed and stretching out.

Steele thought she looked beautiful lying there, and Meg flashed him a hungry smile. He found himself at the edge of the bed looking down at her. Meg rolled over on her stomach and reached out for his belt, pulling him close.

"What are you looking at, Mr. Sands?" she asked.

"I'm looking at you."

Eric lowered his face to hers. He could smell her perfume, feel the warmth of her skin on his. The kiss was passionate, charged with the intensity and fear of the unknown. Steele traced his hands down Meg's back and she sat up, raising her arms over her head so he could take off her shirt. He tossed it on the floor and Meg wrapped her arms around his neck and pulled him on top of her.

"A girl could *really* get used to this," she whispered into his ear.

Chapter 46

Director Styles plotted all the way to the White House. She had put off the briefing for as long as she dared. *What a fucking asshat.* Styles hated the Vice President despite their shared past. Though she'd never admit it aloud, the root of her rancor was simple.

She was jealous.

Rockford had come to an Agency in flux, desperately in need of a hero. The Cold War had mired the CIA in scandal after scandal and new blood was desperately needed to brighten its tarnished reputation.

"I had to work for everything I got, and *he* comes in and everyone thinks he's a goddamn war hero," the Director grumbled to herself.

Styles blamed both the Program and Rockford for her current woes. Rockford had forced her into a corner and the damn Alphas had cut her out of the operations loop.

In hindsight she admitted she had made mistakes, but action was always faster than reaction. Going up against the Program had been ill-advised and the only way she was going to live to fight another day was by forcing Rockford to back down. She hoped threatening to expose the Alpha operation in Europe would do just that.

Rockford silently waited for Director Styles to finish, his eyes focused on the face staring up at him from the Interpol notice. It was Eric Steele.

The picture was enough for Rockford to realize that Steele had been right about the leak.

He could fade a Blue Notice, brush it off until after the meeting, then make some calls. The immediate problem was with Director Styles. Rockford glanced at his chief of staff sitting silently in the corner. Lansky's face was impassive, but Rockford knew he was trying to figure out the Director's angle.

"You play cards, *Director*?" he asked. Dropping a title was an old-school power play, a verbal cue that Rockford was in charge and Styles was here to answer questions.

"Are you asking if I gamble?" Styles replied, brushing off the barb.

"Sure."

"Depends on the game and the dealer."

"I get it. Control as many unknowns as possible. But you are familiar with the adage 'the house *always* wins'?"

Rockford watched Styles's eyes slip to the picture before her. He put himself in her shoes. *She is pretty sure Steele is an Alpha, but can't prove it. If she could, we wouldn't be here.*

Publishing the Red Notice could potentially sabotage a major operation and open the Program and the Cole administration to all kinds of trouble. To hang the Director, Rockford would have to prove that Styles knowingly leaked classified information, which would be hard to do. It would be even harder still to prove that the Director of the CIA had committed treason.

"My job is to protect the United States of America from foreign threats no matter who is pulling the strings. I have reason to believe that this man"—she tapped her finger on Steele's picture—"is part of an off-the-books kill team whose mere existence is unconstitutional. I also believe that President Cole has authorized *you*, a dutifully elected official, to run this team."

Dammit, the State of the Union address is tomorrow night, isn't it? Rockford had been so caught up in what was going on with Steele that he had totally forgotten. *The timing makes sense now, little snake.*

"Let me get this straight," Rockford said. "The Director of the *Central* Intelligence Agency suspects that the President of the United States has a top-secret unit that somehow has managed to stay off the radar of everyone in Washington, D.C.?"

"Yes."

"Why would President Cole want the liability that comes with such a unit? If anyone found out, he would go to jail."

"You tell me," Styles said.

"Well." Rockford leaned back in his chair. "I would assume that if such a unit existed there would have to be one hell of a reason. Maybe certain people realized a long time ago that the CIA has its head up its ass and didn't realize there was a revolution brewing in Algiers. What do you think, Ted?"

Lansky shrugged. "The only thing I know is that in the last week the CIA lost a team in Tunis, and a safe-house and SOG team in Algiers."

"That is ridiculous. The CIA—"

"The CIA what?" Rockford demanded, sitting forward in his chair and lasering in on Styles. "The CIA thinks that it is a *good* idea to put a Red Notice on a man who may or may not be tracking an untraceable nuclear weapon that could be headed anywhere? Hell, Robin, it could be heading to the States for all we know."

Styles went bone white with anger. "Don't you dare lecture me. President Cole is running his own unsanctioned kill team and you want to lecture me? Give me a fucking break, John. You can sit around kissing Cole's ass and pretending that no one knows about the Program all you want, but guess what. It is all bullshit. The Program is real and it is illegal as hell, and this"—Styles jabbed her finger at the Red Notice—"proves it."

"Robin, are you sure you want to play it this way?" Rockford asked.

"I am ready to play it to the bone. Are you? Is Cole?"

"Fair enough," Rockford said, getting to his feet. "But whatever happens to you after I put this in the President's hand is on *your* head."

"Well then, you better be getting a move on, *boy*," Styles sneered before turning to the door.

Chapter 47

Meg and Eric decided against going out for dinner, ordering room service instead. Afterward, neither one wanted to leave the room, knowing what lay outside the door. But finally they had to go.

Steele piloted the Land Rover toward the docks, while Meg basked in the salt-laden air coming through the open window. Overhead a passenger plane swooped in, the air passing over its extended flaps with the whine of incoming artillery.

Steele turned off the street, pulling up to a gate where a serious-looking guard with a Beretta strapped to his waist blocked their path. Steele flashed the man his passport and the guard replied with a light to his face before studying the photo.

"Very good," he grunted, opening the gate.

There were more guards on the inside, armed with pistols and rifles. One of them led a Belgian Malinois on a leash. The working dog, often confused with a German shepherd, tugged against the leather when Steele cruised by.

"I've seen those land sharks do a number on the insurgents in Syria," Meg said. "That is one dog I never want to meet in a dark alley."

Special Operations used the Malinois for a multitude of applications. They were called dual-purpose dogs, good for bombs and people, and typical of the breed, they were single-minded in their day-to-day life. When they were working it seemed they were always looking for something soft to sink their teeth into.

Steele stopped at a corrugated warehouse and hopped out to type in the code. The door rolled open and he got back in and pulled inside the warehouse.

"What is this place?" Meg asked once they were inside.

"We call them way stations. The Program has them set up all over the world."

Meg nodded and walked over to a stack of crates that had the shipping bill already filled out and attached to the side. "Tractor parts," she read, "and they are heading to . . . of course. They are heading to Yemen."

She flashed Eric an *are you serious?* look, before opening the clasp that secured the lid. "Oh, look, Kalashnikov makes tractor parts now, how nice."

He walked over, fighting the urge to grin as she placed her hands on her hips. Inside the crate was a row of AK-74s, still gleaming with packing grease.

"How did *those* get in there?" he said.

Meg didn't smile.

"C'mon, Meg, you know the CIA does the same thing. I can't tell you how many Agency shipments of opium I have run across in Afghanistan."

"So that makes it okay? You are sending automatic rifles into a war zone? You can't tell me that these guns don't end up in Syria, because I know they do. A year ago when I was over there we found a stash of brand-new AKs just like these."

"Don't worry, most of these guns come with a tracking chip."

"Wait, what?"

"Unlike the Agency, the Program doesn't profit off of people's misfortune." He reached over and tapped on the fore end. "It was Demo's idea. He figured out how to embed them in there. Leads us right to the bad guys."

"Okay, you've got guns and a cute little minivan with antennas all over it," Meg said, pointing to the dark-colored Ford Transit Connect sitting in the center of the warehouse. "But where is this secret weapon?"

"Well, I'm glad you asked," he said, walking over to the Transit. "And it's not a station wagon, it's a leisure activity vehicle." The Transit looked like an engineer had put a courier van in the dryer and shrunk it. At first glance it was nothing to write home about.

Steele swung the back door open and stepped out of the way. "Allow me to introduce you to Johnny Number Five."

"You have got to be kidding," Meg said, looking inside.

"What? This thing is awesome."

"That thing is your secret weapon?"

"Yep," he said.

Steele was making his way to a large metal locker when the computer terminal beeped from the table to his right. His fingers flew over the keyboard, and after accessing the mainframe he found a message waiting for him.

"What's going on?" Meg asked.

"C'mon, c'mon," Steele said, waiting for the message to be run through the decryption software. Finally it popped up, showing him an authentication pin number along with a note:

From everyone at Cutlass Main, happy hunting—Rock.

Steele typed the pin number into Keyhole and a moment later a photo of a man's face looking up at a stoplight appeared on the screen.

"Who is that?"

"That is our friend Bassar," Steele answered. He clicked on the data tag, which provided the date of the image capture. It was two weeks ago, and Steele knew the only way the boys back at Cutlass Main could have found it was by running a sweep of every traffic camera along the coast.

Got to love those guys.

"Okay, next question . . ."

"Meg, you definitely don't have the clearance . . ."

"Really, Eric?"

Steele knew it wasn't a fight he could win.

"It's called Keyhole," he began. "This picture was taken two weeks ago."

"Okay, how does it help us find Bassar?"

"By itself it is worthless. A good analyst might be able to pull some metadata off the file. But the guys we have . . ." Steele pointed to the screen as additional text boxes started popping up.

"How are they doing that?" Meg asked, obviously in awe of what she was witnessing.

"According to the this"—Steele moved his cursor over one of the boxes—"they used the ATM camera to get the plate off the car." He moved to a second box. "They traced the plate to a dealership, and finally"—a red dot appeared on the map—"they got a phone number from the dealer's hard drive and located the phone."

"How many man-hours did that take?"

"What do you mean?" Steele asked.

"To do all of that. It must have taken them days."

"No, you just watched them do it."

"Wait, that was in real time?"

"Uh, yeah, you just watched it."

"Are you guys hiring?"

"Just so happens," Steele said, moving back to the locker, "that we have an immediate opening." He placed his palm on the reader and the locker's heavy doors clicked open, revealing a weapons vault. "Timeline has changed. We are going now. C'mon, it will be fun. We get to hang out, shoot some guns, and save the world."

The locker was packed with guns and gear. Steele grabbed a set of cammies and held them up in front of Meg. They were a bit long, but would do in a pinch.

"Eric, we are going right now? What about West?"

"No time, we have to go," he said, handing her a pair of boots. "Those might not fit, but it's all I've got." He picked a set for himself and, not one to worry about modesty, started changing, a sly grin playing across his face.

Meg just stared at him openmouthed.

"I can take you back to the hotel if you are scared," he quipped.

"Really?"

She kicked off her shoes, careful not to scuff them, and Steele watched her undress.

"Are you just going to stare at me, or do you want to hang this up?" she demanded, stepping out of the dress.

"I'm just going to stare at you," Steele joked.

"Men."

Steele hung up her dress, pulled a combat shirt over his head, and began collecting the tools of his trade. He took a Milkor MGL, a South African 40mm grenade launcher, from the rack and placed it in a bag. Behind him, he could hear Meg pulling on her clothes. The launcher looked like a revolver with a stock and fired 40mm grenades. In the Army, they called them 40 mike-mike, and they were a force multiplier in combat. He took a 5.56 SCAR with a Vortex Razor HD 1–6 and a suppressor attached to the barrel. Preloaded magazines were hanging in a pouch and they all went into the bag.

Meg slipped up behind him. She ran her hand up his back, looking over the contents. Steele handed her a Glock 19 and a holster.

"Grab the shotgun. It's time to go to work."

Chapter 48

Rockford found President Cole in the White House Medical Unit hooked to an IV machine. He looked gaunt and exhausted but smiled weakly when Rockford stepped into the room.

"Claire here was just telling me that I need to watch my sodium, do you believe that?" he joked.

Rockford noticed the smile didn't go to Cole's eyes and knew that the President was putting on a show for his benefit. He wasn't sure what to say, so he looked at the nurse and asked, "What are you giving him?"

"Just some fluids and a few other things to keep his immune system up."

"Got to look good for the people," Cole said.

Rockford saw the yellow label stuck to the bag of

fluid. He recognized it from his aunt's battle with breast cancer, and didn't need to read it to know that it said:

Chemotherapy—Dispose of Properly

Cole caught him looking and offered an apologetic shrug. "I can only assume by the look on your face that your meeting with Director Styles didn't go so well. I'd offer you a drink, but all we have is saline."

Rockford smiled and was about to ask Claire to leave the room, but she was already heading for the door. Usually he would wait to hear it close, but Cole was already asking:

"How bad is it, John?"

"It isn't cancer, but . . ." He handed the paper to his boss.

Rockford watched Cole's tired eyes tick over the heading and then shift down to the picture. "Jesus Christ, Robin," Cole said warily. "A Red Notice? What the hell were you thinking?"

"Sir, she hasn't passed through security yet. I can have Secret Service grab her."

"So I can face her like this?" Cole asked, holding up his arm and jiggling the clear tubing. It was the first time Rockford had seen him feel sorry for himself, and it cut him to the core. Cole was a strong, proud man, and being laid low by such an insidious disease was heartbreaking.

The President paused and took a sip of water, and when he had finished, Rockford saw that the leader of the free world had composed himself.

"John, I am not a vindictive man, but when I am forced to take scalps, I take 'em on my own two feet."

"So what do you want me to do?"

The machine beeped and Claire stepped into the room, another bag of fluid with the same yellow label in her hand. Rockford thought that Cole would wait to give his answer, but he was wrong.

"We stick to the plan. I want her at the State of the Union so she can hear how this country is going to get back on track after she and Bentley tried to destroy it. When I finish the address I will have her brought to the Oval, and then I am going to bury her."

Styles and Claire had dinner brought in from Marcel's. It was a silent affair with Claire drinking freely, while Styles nursed the same glass of wine she had started with. She wanted to get drunk, but after the call she had gotten from Claire earlier in the day, she knew she needed a clear head.

"He said he is going to bury you," Claire had said.

Finally Styles broke the silence. "I need you to do something for me."

Claire looked up at her, eyes glassy and wet from

the wine. "Sure, anything." Styles got to her feet and walked around the table, reaching for Claire's hand. She looked so innocent sitting there, and a lesser woman might have faltered, but not Robin Styles. She had been planning for this eventuality since the first day they met.

Styles knew that Cole was in bad shape, because she had already taken to an oncologist she knew the list of medications that Claire told her the President was taking. Cole's cancer was terminal.

"Prolaxic is the outlier here," the oncologist had said. "The FDA has been sitting on it for a few years because of the side effects."

"A friend of mine is taking it. Is there anything she should be worried about?"

"Not if she keeps taking it. The problem is when you miss a dose. Prolaxic has an extremely short half-life, and the research has shown that you can miss one dose and be fine, but the second typically causes seizures."

Styles knew that if she couldn't convince Claire to switch the pills before the State of the Union address, her life was over.

"I need you to switch his Prolaxic."

"Wait, what?"

Claire pulled her hand away. She was drunk, but Styles's request had a sobering effect.

"Look, it won't kill him, I already checked."

"You told someone? Robin, that was confidential, I could lose my license."

"Do you trust me?"

"Of course . . . but I . . . I can't do that."

Break her now.

Styles stood up. It was time Claire learned the hardest lesson there was. Nothing in this world is free.

"Claire, I've taken care of you and never asked for anything but your love in return."

"I won't do it."

"I want you to think about the consequences, darlin'." Styles's voice turned to ice. "You have put yourself in a terrible position, and if you—"

"Go to hell, Robin."

Styles got to her feet and backhanded Claire across the face as hard as she could, knocking Claire to her side. Styles wasn't finished. She grabbed a handful of her hair and yanked her head back, ready to beat her to death if she had to.

"I saved you from going to jail, you little coke whore. The only reason you aren't in jail, fighting off a bunch of butch bitches in the shower, is because of me," she shouted. "You are going to do what I tell you and you are going to do it tomorrow or I *will* destroy you."

"Why are you doing this to me?" Claire cried.

Styles dragged her to the floor and lifted her foot. Her fury was a living thing and she was ready to stomp Claire's face into the ground if she had to. But further violence wasn't needed; Claire was broken and sobbed uncontrollably.

"Stop. Please. Stop. I'll do whatever you want," she bawled.

Chapter 49

According to the map the target house had been a farm and was well outside the city. Steele had Meg drop him off south of the house on the edge of an olive orchard. He knew that at this time of year the olive trees would be untended and he could use them to make his way to the house unseen.

It also gave Meg access to a gravel road that looped through the low ground before coming up on a ridge. He waited for the sound of the van to fade before checking his compass and moving north through the trees.

Steele stayed low, moving slowly and keeping a lookout for any tripwires or anti-intrusion devices. In fifteen minutes he had made it to the edge of the clearing.

The night was still and silent, the moon partially obscured by a cloudbank, and he adjusted the PSQ 36s until he could see the back of the house. The goggles were the best of both worlds, fusing the night amplification capability of traditional NVGs with thermal imaging. Traditional night vision needed ambient light to work properly, which the cloud cover interfered with. To compensate, Steele adjusted the thermal setting and the residual heat left over from the day gave him a clear, greenish picture of the house and the low wall ahead of him.

The layout was a tactical nightmare. Steele was surrounded by high ground, which he was sure West's men had locked down.

"Make the call," he said over the radio.

"Copy that," Meg answered.

Steele was counting on her to convince Bassar to play ball, otherwise Steele was going to have to breach the house and force the man to comply. Getting inside and setting up the ambush on his terms was the only way the operation was going to work.

"Making the call."

Steele wasn't sure exactly where Meg had chosen to set up, but he had given her explicit instructions. If things went south she was to head back to the hotel and get the hell out of Spain.

A flicker of movement on the edge of the property grabbed his attention and Steele pressed the SCAR's buttstock into his shoulder. Finger on the safety, he watched and waited.

Just a damn deer.

"Okay, I made contact. Bassar sounds cagey, but he is coming to the door. The proword is 'Raven,' your answer is 'Sparrow.'"

"Got it."

Steele moved to the wall, the bag of gear shifting awkwardly on his back. The side door cracked open, hinges whining in the dark, and a sliver of yellow light trickled out. Slowly a head appeared. It was Dr. Asif Bassar's, and he squinted through the darkness. Steele knew he couldn't see him, but he felt exposed.

Let me see your damn hands.

He raised the SCAR, ready to put a bullet in the man's head if he made the wrong move. They didn't necessarily need him alive, so whether the doctor lived or died was up to him.

Waiting was always the hardest part, but patience had kept Steele from gathering more holes than he had started with more times than he could count. Finally, Bassar crossed the threshold and Steele could see that he was unarmed.

"Raven," the doctor whispered. It was the signal that Steele could approach.

Steele crept silently through the darkness. He had the rifle up, trained on his target, with his thumb on the safety.

"Raven," Bassar said again.

Steele was a foot away when he answered:

"Sparrow."

Bassar jumped, eyes big as saucers, when the barrel came to a halt a few inches from his face.

"You move and I will burn you down," Steele said in Arabic. "How many people are inside?"

"My wife an . . . and daughter."

"Ali Breul sent me, and you have five seconds to make a choice."

"Oh, God."

"Men are coming for you and your family. I don't know exactly what they want, but I can promise you that when they leave, you and your family will not be breathing."

"Please don't hurt me."

"Turn around and put your hands behind your back."

Bassar did as he was told and Steele slipped a pair of flex cuffs over his wrists and pulled them tight. He nudged Bassar forward with the barrel and closed the door behind him with his foot.

"Where is Ali?"

"He's dead."

"What? How?"

"Don't worry about that."

"Papa, who is that?" a timid voice asked.

"Go back to sleep, my angel," Bassar said. To Steele, he pleaded, "Do not kill me in front of my daughter. She has done nothing."

Steele saw a tiny head peering around the corner and lowered his rifle. A woman appeared behind the little girl, Bassar's wife, he assumed.

"We don't have time to talk right now," Steele said. "Do you have a safe room?"

"Yes, of course."

"Show me."

"Asif, what have you done? Why is this man here?"

"Everything is going to be okay, I am here to help you," Steele replied in Arabic.

"Just do as he asks," Bassar pleaded.

"Move," Steele ordered, prodding the man with the barrel.

Bassar led him around the kitchen and into a room that looked like a closet. "In there," he said.

"What is your wife's name?"

"Esta."

"Esta, I am here to protect your family. If there is anything the child needs, headphones, a toy, get it now, but do not do anything stupid."

She nodded and rushed out of the room, leaving her daughter looking up at Steele with curious eyes.

"How do you know Ali Breul?" Steele asked.

"We went to the university together," Bassar answered.

"You are supposed to be dead."

Bassar looked confused. "Dead? I have been living here since your CIA smuggled me out of Iran. They paid for all of this," he said with a sweep of his hand that was meant to encompass the house. "In fact, the United States pays the Spanish government to let me live here."

Steele wasn't sure what to believe. He didn't have time to conduct a proper interrogation, but little bits and pieces of Bassar's story filled in the gaps of what he already knew.

"Do you have any idea why Breul would give me your name?"

"I can only think of one reason, and that would be the weapon we worked on."

"You worked on it together?" Steele asked.

"Parts of it, yes. It was just a prototype at first,

something the leaders in Tehran could use to threaten Israel if they launched an attack on our reactors like they did in Iraq."

"You expect me to believe that?" Steele demanded.

Bassar shrugged. "As a Muslim it was my duty to protect Islam from the infidels."

"You said *was*. Are you not a Muslim anymore?"

"Of course I am, but things have changed. If this bomb goes off the war between America and Islam will never end. Millions of innocents could die."

"Tell me about the device."

"Like I told you, it was a prototype, the core is unstable."

"But it will still explode?"

"Yes, if it is armed it will explode."

Esta appeared with the girl's headphones and unlocked the safe room door. Steele ushered them inside and before shutting the door handed Bassar a cell phone.

"There is only one number you can call on that phone. I have put a charge inside it, so if you do anything stupid"—he made an exploding motion with his hand. "In a few minutes, you will get a text. Call the number. A woman will answer saying she is with a security company. Do you understand?"

Bassar nodded.

"Do not come out until I get you. It is going to be loud, but if you trust me, you will live.

Steele waited for the door to lock and then set a motion detector near its edge. If Bassar tried to come out, he would know. Once that was in place, he went upstairs. He picked the room with the best field of view and worked quickly to build the hide site.

He cracked the first window. This was where he planned to use the rifle, and he quickly constructed an impromptu hide site with a sheet of rolled-up screen he had brought with him. When it was secured across the opening he pulled a chest that came up to his knees in front of the window and then checked his field of fire with the SCAR.

Satisfied, he went to the second window and pushed it open all the way. He couldn't use the screen technique here because it would deflect the trajectory of the 40mm grenades, so he pulled the curtains closed, leaving a small slit to see through. When he was good to go he took the MGL and a bandolier of the 40mm grenades out of the bag and laid them on the floor.

"I'm set. Do you have the scanner working?"

"Yes."

"Let's rock and roll."

Meg had turned out to be worth her weight in gold and gave Steele the chance to test out a piece of gear he'd never had a chance to use. Unlike the scanner he'd taken with him in Beirut, the equipment Meg had with her was designed for military-grade cryptology. Not only could it break encrypted frequencies, but it could also lock the signal at the source.

"Bassar is waiting for your text."

"Got it."

Steele took the MGL and went through the plan in his head. He snapped the grenade launcher's breech open and examined the grenades he had brought with him.

The most common round used by the U.S. military was the M381. It looked like a fat, stubby bullet and was designed to explode on impact. Steele had managed to get his hands on a case of the brand-new Rheinmetall airburst grenades, which were perfect for catching a team out in the open. He slid the projectile into the slot, followed by a 381. The third round was an M583 parachute flare, a nonlethal gamble he prayed was worth the risk.

Outside the floodlights came on first, illuminating the yard and pushing the shadows back a few feet. Now the only thing left for Steele to do was wait.

Chapter 50

"Sir," the radio operator said, interrupting West in the middle of the brief.

"What?"

"Ghost 1 and 2 are reporting activity around the target location."

There had been nothing since the doctor went to sleep an hour ago. West was planning to wait until 0200 to launch the raid because the pattern of life his recon element established pointed to this time being when the target would be in his REM. If they were right, West knew his assault team would be in the house before the man woke up.

"Get them ready to move," he told Villars, and then turned toward the communications desk.

"Ghost 1 to Eagle," the recon team leader said.

West had put another one of his men on the radio

in preparation for the assault. One monitored the net, and tracked everything the overwatch team sent in on a sheet of paper taped to the wall, while the other monitored the phone and radio lines.

"Go for Eagle."

"The exterior lights just came on, followed by the interior lights on the bottom floor."

It was a deviation from the norm, but nothing to worry about yet.

The second man at the commo station pressed the headphone closer to his ears. "He is making a call."

"Cut the line," West ordered. His men had already captured his cell phones and landline for just this reason.

"We don't have this one."

"Who the hell is he calling?"

West waited for the answer, wondering if he had missed something

"I think he is calling a security service," the man said, obviously confused.

"Put it on the speaker.

Bassar's voice came through. He was agitated and spoke quickly in heavily accented English. *"There are men outside my house."*

"Find out what team is moving around out there."

"Eagle to Ghost elements . . ."

West tuned him out, listening to the operator Bassar was talking with. He had sent a team inside the house not only to trace and tap the phone lines, but also to check for any unwanted surprises. *Lazy shits.*

"*Sir, I need your identification code,*" the female operator said.

Bassar rattled off a number and West heard the sound of computer keys.

"Villars, go now, and hurry."

"Both teams advise that they have not moved."

"Well, something spooked him."

"What is it?" Villars asked, walking over.

"We are blown, Bassar is talking to a bodyguard service . . . I thought you handled this."

"He doesn't have security, we checked, but even if he does we are ready for that contingency."

"That's not the point, Peter," West said, pointing at the radio where the woman was asking, "*We have your location, what is your emergency?*" "There is a record now."

"*I already told you there are men outside my house. I need you to come and get me, right now.*"

"*Yes, sir, a team is on the way. Go to your safe room and stand by.*"

West wanted to shoot someone, but instead grabbed his gear and rifle. "Let's go," he said, pointing at Villars.

Chapter 51

In the van Meg hung up the phone and pulled the screen back on the dark box she had built in the back. She used a red lens flashlight to find the power on the Foster-Miller SWORD. The unmanned robot that Steele referred to as Johnny Number Five looked like a mad scientist had gotten hold of some kid's radio-controlled car, given it a cycle of steroids and rubber tracks, and added a 240 Bravo machine gun. Once it was ready to roll, Meg opened the back door and hit the deploy button on the controller. The robot squeaked over the metal, rolled down the ramp and out into the night.

"SWORD is deployed."

Before closing the door she unlatched the ramp just in case she had to take off, and then it was back to her cave. The phone bit was right out of the Activity's playbook—an oldie but a goodie. Steele didn't want her on the ground throwing punches with West's men, but he knew she was an asset. Inside the van she was just as lethal, but just in case anything went wrong she taped an M67 fragmentation grenade to the post next to the computer and had the shotgun ready to go.

She made sure the SWORD's uplink was working on the laptop, ran a sensor test, and then turned to the scanner.

It had already identified the three radio positions and their point of origin, or POO. The interface marked the two scout positions with a red "X" and connected the lines of transmission with blue lines. Even better, it gave the grid of each one, and as more of West's people got on the radio she would track them as well.

"SWORD deployed. I am sending you the commo grids," Meg told Steele, giving him time to write them down and read them back.

"Okay, you know what to do. Be careful."

"Don't worry, hubby, I've got this."

Chapter 52

Steele lifted the FLIR, or forward looking infra-red, binoculars to his eyes and switched them to "black hot." Unlike night vision, FLIR worked off of heat, and hot objects appeared black through the scope, while rocks and trees, which lost heat faster when the sun went down, appeared gray.

Where are they?

The men coming out of the rocks were hot from moving down the hill and gave off a powerful heat signature compared to the ambient terrain. Steele knew there were two teams in the open, but he could only see one.

These guys are good.

His plan revolved around getting as many of West's people as possible into the kill zone, with Meg and the

SWORD holding the rear. Steele knew that even if he executed a textbook ambush, some of the men would get away. And then there was the possibility that West might not even be with the assault team.

There were too many things that could go wrong, but Steele had to try. It was the only shot he had at recovering the bomb.

Chapter 53

"All elements, this is Eagle, I am en route." It was West, and Meg quickly locked the transmission on the computer.

"You hear that?"

"Yeah. He's here and he's moving toward our location now."

Meg plotted the azimuth on the SWORD's tactical console and hit send. The robot's internal navigation system, connected to GPS, whizzed into action, and the feed on the computer began to bounce as it moved out.

The setup was like a video game, with the majority of the screen split in half to show two camera views. The SWORD's main camera was on the gun, facing forward with crosshairs that were red, telling the operator that the master arm was off. A heads-up display told Meg how much ammo was on board, and a row of numbers gave the heading, speed, and location in latitude and longitude.

Meg clicked the second screen on the satellite overlay map she had downloaded from Google Earth and found a dirt access road running down from the ridge, toward the target house.

I bet that's where he is going. She used the joystick to shift the robot's path to the southwest in hope of intercepting the vehicle. The robot had rolled a hundred feet when light played across the camera. Meg stopped the vehicle and activated the second camera situated atop a mast. This camera was equipped with a wide-angle lens, and when the mast began extending she rotated it in the direction of the light. The vehicles bouncing over the road were unmistakable.

"I've got three jeeps coming your way. No idea which one has West."

"Let's find out."

Chapter 54

S teele flipped off the safety and looked through the leaf sight attached to the launcher. The sight was simple to use, and all he had to do was raise the muzzle of the launcher until he could see his target through the aperture. At this range he had to kneel to clear the top edge of the windowsill, and when he was sure the round would clear, he sent it.

The launcher thumped the round skyward. It sounded like a potato gun going off, a gentle *thoop.* The lands and grooves on the casing of the round forced the 40mm into a tight spiral, arming the fuse after a factory-set number of rotations. The cylinder rotated and he fired the second round and then waited, counting slowly in his head.

Steele knew that if these men were as well trained

as he assumed, they would hit the deck, assess casualties, and then decide to break contact or move out. He needed to keep them in the kill zone, which was the reason he'd loaded the flare.

The explosion blossomed over their heads, raining razor-sharp shrapnel down on the recon team. A moment later the sound hit the house. *Cruuump.* The screams followed, sharp and pitiful like a wounded animal, and then the second round went off.

"Eagle . . . Ghost 2 . . ." There was anguish in the man's voice and he lapsed into a language Steele thought was Afrikaans. The radio stayed open—no doubt the wounded fighter had left the talk button mashed down and everyone listening got a taste of what was going on.

Someone was moaning and a second voice was pleading with the man to hold on. "We've got to get him out of here."

"Break, break, break," West snapped, breaking through. "Ghost 2, give me a sitrep."

"A mine . . . I think we stepped on a mine."

"Ghost 1, what is your location?"

"Coming in from the east. Did he advise the area is mined?"

Steele couldn't believe his luck. Things were working out better than he had imagined. The fear of mines would make the recon teams hesitant to attack.

"Meg, where is Ghost 1?"

"Forty-five degrees magnetic from your position, about two hundred yards out."

"What about West?"

"He is either in the first or second vehicle. I'm about to go loud."

"Got ya, make 'em count."

Steele stayed low, rotating his torso in the direction the second recon team would be traveling, and got as much elevation as he could. He wanted the flare as high as possible. He fired and quickly lined up a 200-yard shot before sending two more HE rounds. He dropped the launcher and scrambled to the second position, grabbing the SCAR and lying out on the chest.

Chapter 55

"Fucking mines?" West shouted, hammering the dash with his fist. "I thought you assholes checked the damn terrain." The mission was a simple snatch and grab, but it was falling apart because he hadn't been there to make sure Villars did it right. If the South African had been riding with him, West would have killed him right there. Luckily for Peter, he was in the lead vehicle.

"Why are you slowing down?" West asked the driver.

"Mines, boss," the man replied.

West drew his pistol, flicked off the safety, and went ballistic. "You *might* hit a mine, but I promise that if you don't get your ass moving you *are* going to get a bullet."

The driver floored it and then a blinding white light blossomed in the sky.

Is that a parachute flare? What the hell is . . .

West never got a chance to finish his thought. A line of tracers cut through the night and stitched Villars's vehicle from hood to trunk.

"Contact left!" the driver screamed, cutting the wheel. In the backseat someone fired out of the window, brass spinning off the roll bar. The jeep hit a rut, bouncing it skyward. The lead vehicle was on fire, and West dropped the pistol.

Chapter 56

Meg tracked the reticle across the lead vehicle, the camera so clear she actually saw the round hit the driver in the head and blow his brains across the man sitting next to him. A tracer round hit the fuel tank and then the jeep was on fire.

She let go of the trigger and checked the ammo count, letting the gun fall. The first burst had sent a hundred rounds into the vehicle and Meg had two hundred left in the can.

"Where the hell do you think you're going?" she asked, tracking the second vehicle, which cut across the open ground, muzzle flashes erupting from the back window.

She centered the crosshairs on the driver and ripped a fifty-round burst just as the jeep got air. Tracers hit the hood, deflecting skyward. Dammit. The gun's tracking system was powered by a small motor that wasn't powerful enough to make fast corrections at close range. It was lagging, so Meg let off the trigger, working to get back on target while trying to zoom the camera out. The driver corrected, steering the jeep right at the SWORD. Meg wasn't sure if he'd spotted it or was just taking evasive maneuvers. Either way, all she could see was the grille.

With no other option, she jammed the trigger down and fired head-on into the jeep.

Chapter 57

"Watch out!" West yelled, catching sight of the muzzle flash fifty feet in front of the speeding jeep. The rounds punched through the engine block and the SUV sputtered, as fluid splashed over the windshield. The dashboard sparked, bullets zipping through the hole and activating the airbag.

The interior filled with the acrid stench of the airbag's propellant mixed with blood and antifreeze. Something was warm on West's face and when he saw his driver slump against the window he knew it was blood.

He grabbed the wheel and fought to center the bumper on the gunner. The front tires exploded, jerking the wheel free from his hand. He saw a small ditch coming up and without hesitation shoved the door open and threw himself from the jeep.

Chapter 58

The flare burned with the power of 90,000 candles, and Steele didn't need night vision to see the point man freeze. All he had to do was center the reticle on the man's leg and fire. The suppressor spat and Steele's target went down, a gaping hole in the back of his thigh.

This was how the insurgent fought, shooting to wound instead of kill, because to evac a comrade took three men out of the fight. One wounded and two to carry their brother.

Brrrrrrp. Brrrrrrrrrrp. The 240 Bravo thundered to life, spiking Steele with a shot of adrenaline. Before becoming a Green Beret, he had been a machine gunner with the 10th Mountain Division at Fort Drum, and like any infantryman he loved the staccato cadence of the heavy machine gun.

He settled behind the glass and lined up his next shot. The recon team had four men—one was wounded—and just as he pulled the trigger one of them looked directly at the window.

The round hit him low in the hip and knocked him on his ass. Steele saw him pointing at the window. *Shit.* He sent the second round through his throat, but it was too late.

"Shooter in the second story of the house."

Steele rolled off the chest a moment before a burst of automatic rifle fire chewed up the desk. He clutched the SCAR tight against him, ignoring the wood and glass splintering through the room, and dashed to the other window. He scooped the grenade launcher off the ground and stuffed 40mm grenades into his pocket.

Out in the hall he snapped the breech open, extracting the husks of the fired grenades, and threw them on the floor. He had one HE left in the launcher, plus two more in his pocket. Everything else was nonlethal: a flare and three CS gas canisters.

He kept the flare in his pocket and loaded the HE, followed by the CS gas, and moved to find a better position. He could tell he was taking fire from two sides and needed to think about getting out. If he couldn't kill West and his men he was going to have to get Bassar and his family out of the house.

"Meg, how's it looking?" he asked, running to the end of the hall.

"One of the jeeps hit the gun, it's offline."

"Are you good?"

"Yeah, I got the first two vehicles, not sure on—"

Whatever she was about to say was cut off by the sound of bullets shrieking through metal.

"Meg! Meg, do you copy?"

Chapter 59

Nathaniel West didn't have time to tuck and roll. He hit the ground awkwardly, skidding ass over end until finally coming to a halt on the lip of the ditch. He snatched the pistol from his holster and pushed himself to a knee, his profile illuminated by the burning truck to his right.

He limped over to the machine gunner, ready to put him down in case the jeep hadn't killed him.

What the hell is this?

The SWORD lay mangled at his feet, tracks hanging off the robot drone like unused rubber bands. West knelt down to inspect the 240 Bravo. The machine gun appeared undamaged, and he unbolted it from the mount, pulling the belt of 7.62 free of the ammo can.

From the looks of the burning jeep he concluded that his men, including Villars, were either dead or too messed up to be useful. His vehicle had continued rolling down the hill, smoke emanating from the hood and the horn blaring long and loud through the night.

It was a shit show. A year of planning and hundreds of thousands of dollars wasted. West scrambled up the hill and was fumbling with his radio when he noticed a van a hundred yards away. He knew from the antenna array that it had controlled the robot.

Eric.

At fifty yards West thought he could hear someone talking. The voice was coming from the van. "Fuckers," he yelled, bracing the machine gun against his hip and holding down the trigger.

The 240 bucked in his hand, the muzzle rising skyward, turning the back of the van into Swiss cheese. West let off the trigger after a five-second burst, angling to the left. His ears were ringing, but he heard something thump against the metal and yanked the trigger to the rear, leaning all his weight into the gun to keep the rounds on target.

Chapter 60

M eg recognized the 240 Bravo by the sound and knew she was in trouble. The van's thin skin wouldn't save her from the 7.62 rounds the machine gun fired. The bullets tore through the vehicle, shattering the computer she had just been sitting in front of. The cramped confines of the Ford filled with a fog of upholstery, bits of plastic, and padding. Meg grabbed the controller, threw it at the back wall, and scrambled toward the front, protecting her eyes from the shattering glass.

The shooter reacted to the sound and started working over the back of the van.

Meg thought her eardrums were going to rupture. She wanted to curl up into a ball and pray everything would just go away. Instead, she pushed through the fear, blocking out the bullets digging ragged stars in the metal and buffeting the van on its springs.

The firing stopped as suddenly as it started.

He's out of ammo.

She grabbed the shotgun lying next to her head and waited, blood hammering in her ears. She racked the slide, the sound impossibly loud inside the van. A pistol snapped nearby, the shooter firing at the sound. The bullet hit her in the shoulder and Meg bit down on the pain.

It shoved the air out of her lungs and brought tears to her eyes. She held them shut, wanting to cry out, but she knew what would happen if she did. Her hands shook on the shotgun when she lowered it, sighting over the barrel.

She could hear footsteps outside, crunching the glass and bits of metal torn off the van. A light washed over the exterior, filtering in through the holes.

"Eric, come out or I will burn you out."

The sound of West's voice sent a trembling up Meg's spine. The shotgun wavered in her hands, tears burning hot down her cheeks. Her shoulder sparked with white-hot pain, but she knew to move or speak was to die.

"Have it your way."

Meg caught movement, a flitter of a shadow through the bullet hole and the whisper of metal on nylon. She could see him, pulling a frag from his vest.

Now.

The shotgun bucked in her hands, a guttural shot that echoed for an eternity in the metal confines of the van. Meg worked the pump and fired again. The buckshot blew a hole the size of a dinner plate in the skin on the van, and Meg racked the slide, sending the empty shotgun husk flipping through the air. There was a grunt of pain.

I hit him.

She was lining up her next shot when the van bucked upward, filling the interior with black smoke. The concussion hit Meg like a baseball bat to the head, shoving her against the wall of the cargo compartment. She lost the shotgun and her ears rang from the blast, but there was no time to regroup. She smelled the distinctive odor of leaking gasoline, followed by orange flames clawing up the hood.

She searched for the shotgun, holding her breath against the black smoke pouring through the shattered windshield. The heat was unbearable, and even though she had no idea if West was out of the fight or simply waiting for her to show herself, she had to get out of the van or she was going to burn to death.

Chapter 61

E ric Steele slipped through the kitchen and found himself in a tidy dining room. He was looking for the stairs and still trying to raise Meg on the radio when headlights played across the wall. He glanced through the open window and saw a jeep bouncing toward the house with a man hunched over the roll bar.

"Pop smoke . . . !" a voice screamed, the rest of his transmission cut out by the gunner, who opened up on the second floor of the house.

The stream of high-velocity lead cut through the outer wall and into the bedroom. Little puffs of white dust began sprouting all around him, but it wasn't until he felt a stream of air past his face that Steele realized that the bullets were coming into the hall. He threw himself to the ground a moment before a line of neat black holes appeared over his head. Masonry dust and insulation rained down on him and the only thing he could do was grab carpet.

The MGL took a round to the stock, knocking it from his hand. Steele caught sight of it tumbling down the stairs but was in no position to retrieve it. *Hope the safety's on.* The thought of an HE round going off in the house was not how he wanted to end the night.

He took a moment to ponder the situation. He knew how he reacted would be the difference between life and death. *Worst case, Meg is dead and I'm cut off. Either way I have to get the hell out of here.* Steele had no idea how well constructed Bassar's safe room was, and swore at himself for not taking more time to find out. Once again he found himself faced with the choice of who lived or died.

Across the hall he saw the window where he had set up his first position. A salvo of lead came diving through the window and Steele realized the gunner was using plunging fire, letting gravity carry on an arc into the room in hopes of hitting anyone on the floor. A tracer round came in too low, hit the windowsill, and flashed toward the ceiling in a line of orange. Balls of insulation drifted down from the hole, and Steele thought he saw a tendril of smoke.

Well, that settles that.

He pushed with his toes and reached out for a handful of carpet. As he dragged his belly across the ground he felt one of his stiches tear. By the time the gunner stopped to reload, Steele smelled the acrid scent of burning insulation and knew that in minutes the attic would be on fire.

For some reason Rock Master Scott's classic "The Roof Is On Fire" popped into his head, and when he jumped to his feet he realized he was humming the chorus.

The roof, the roof, the roof is on fire.

He took the stairs two at a time, stopping only to snatch the MGL from the ground and rub his hand over the gouge in the plastic. Not only was the launcher functional, but the safety was still on. *That's what I'm talking about. Can't put a price on good gear.*

He jogged to the kitchen, the SCAR bumping against his leg, and when he rounded the corner he saw the silhouette of a man with a rifle at the window. Experience told him that he was good to go, so he thumped a 40 mike-mike HE through the glass and was already turning the corner when it hit his target and exploded.

Steele found the safe room door and hammered on it with the ball of his fist.

"Alamo, Bassar, Alamo!" he yelled, giving the signal that the Iranian needed to hurry his ass up.

The door cracked open and the doctor looked out. Behind him, his terrified wife clutched their daughter to her chest.

"Do you have gas masks?" Steele demanded.

The smoke was thicker now, and he looked over his shoulders to see gray fingers clawing across the ceiling.

"Here," Bassar's wife shouted, reaching for a panel with her free hand. The panel hinged open, revealing one child-sized and two adult masks.

"Put them on, we have to go."

Steele went to the door leading out to the garage, snatching the keys of the Peugeot off the ring. He threw the driver's-side door open and started the car without getting in.

"C'mon," he yelled, heading back inside.

Bassar had the mask on his daughter, but she was fighting to pull it off. "No, you must keep it on."

"She cannot breathe," his wife said in Arabic.

Steele pushed Bassar out of the way and stepped closer. His daughter's eyes were wide with fear and the mask was collapsing around her face. She wasn't getting any air. Steele immediately saw the problem and remedied it by tearing the shipping cap off the end of the filter. Immediately it ballooned back to normal and the little girl took a long breath.

"Is that better?" he asked with a smile.

She nodded.

"A lot of good that would have done," he snapped, yanking Bassar's mask over his head. "You are the father, it is your job to protect your family." He could tell the doctor was too freaked out to understand that he had almost suffocated his child.

Steele knew how he appeared to them, incredibly calm and in control, but inside his mind was whirring. He needed to get them out and then go after Meg, all without collecting any additional holes.

He grabbed Bassar by the shoulder, hustled him to the car, and pushed him behind the wheel. He snatched the garage door opener off the visor. "I am going to cover you. When I open the door, you go."

Bassar reached for the car door handle and Steele stopped him, making sure he understood what was going on.

"I open the garage door, you go, do you understand?"

"Yes . . ." Bassar said, trying to take the mask off.

Steele slapped his hand away and leaned in. "You are going to need that. Don't stop for anyone. They"—he pointed to his wife and child—"are counting on you."

He slammed the car door and headed back inside the house. Visibility was starting to get worse and the air was thick and gray. He could hear the machine gun going off and even though it seemed like forever since he had come downstairs, he was sure it hadn't even been five minutes.

Steele inspected the ceiling for any signs of flame. So far the only sign of fire was the smoke, but he was about to change all of that. He wrenched the stove from the wall, pulling it back far enough so he could hammer the gas line free, and then took the flare from his pocket. He set it in the center of the microwave, turned the power to high, and pressed the button that looked like a turkey. He left the 40mm round revolving on the glass turntable and stepped out into the hall.

The layout was simple and he followed the hall to the master bedroom. From the doorway he aimed at the top of the window, where the frame was reinforced with brick, lined up the shot and fired. Steele had deflected bullets before, but had never tried it with a grenade. Before the analytical side of his brain could talk him out of the plan, he fired.

He shot was on the money. The grenade hit the mark, ricocheted off the frame, and popped through the glass like a line drive in backyard baseball. Steele tensed, opening his mouth and turning his head in preparation for the explosion.

Cruuump.

The grenade hit close enough to blow the entire frame from the wall, creating a perfect breach. Steele switched the MGL to his left hand and lifted the SCAR. He fired the first CS gas grenade through the smoke, and sprinted after it. He cannonballed out of the house, right in the middle of a firefight.

Blindly Steele snapped the final CS canisters to his left, sending them in the general direction of the driveway. He dropped the MGL and with both hands on the SCAR engaged the man to his left, firing a center shot while sidestepping behind a tree and dropping to a knee. Leaning out, he sent a second round before pivoting for a headshot on another shooter.

Backing around the house, Steele unloaded half the mag into the jeep as fast as he could pull the trigger and ducked out of sight. Changing magazines on the run, he was planning to cut wide, avoiding the CS gas, and after he was sure it was clear hit the garage. But Bassar had other ideas. No sooner was Steele to the driveway than he saw the Peugeot backing out.

"Son of a bitch."

Bassar had obviously panicked and was leaving without him.

Steele took a deep breath and charged straight into the gas, his only thought getting to Meg.

Chapter 62

Meg pulled the pin on the grenade taped to the computer and clawed at the door handle, needing to get out of the van before it exploded. Her left arm was useless, and even with the adrenaline rushing through her veins and the strength that came with wanting to stay alive, it was hard to manipulate the handle.

Her fingers slipped off the plastic, leaving crimson streaks on the metal. Another shot from outside accompanied the spoon clattering against the floor. West was screaming at the top of his lungs, threatening to flay the skin from her body, and finally the door slid open. Meg jumped from the van, clutching the Glock in her right hand, running hard. Headlights bumped across the uneven ground, playing across her face, and Meg blindly fired at the vehicle that was angling to the east.

Beneath her feet the ground began to rise, another small hill she hadn't known was there. Her leaden thighs strained while she fired at the jeep, and then she was at the apex, looking down at the house. It was on fire, smoke billowing from beneath the eaves, orange flames leaping and falling in the night.

A machine gun opened up, and bullets cut across her path, kicking up dirt and grass. Meg knew that she was about to die. The Glock locked back on the empty magazine, but she kept running, and then the van Meg had just been in exploded behind her.

Chapter 63

The gas burned Steele's eyes and was seeping into his pores. His face was on fire, but he pushed through the pain, his heart thundering in his chest as he held his breath. To his left Bassar's car shot up the drive, the back end fishtailing on the gravel.

He had to get to Meg—the thought was as loud and undeniable as his need to take a breath. A man appeared out of the gas haze, hacking and spitting against the CS. Steele didn't have time to do anything but lower his shoulder. He bulldozed the fighter off his feet, slamming him hard to the ground. His momentum sent him rolling, the SCAR ripped from his grasp and knocked the air out of his lungs.

Steele sucked in a short breath, the CS scalding his lungs. The man got to his knees and he threw himself at him. The fight was close and dirty, all knees and elbows. Neither man could throw a full punch or see the other through tear-soaked eyes. It was like fighting underwater, dark and claustrophobic.

Steele slammed his forearm into the bridge of the man's nose and took a loping right hand for his trouble. There wasn't any time for pain, just the primal urge to live and to kill. Steele fought like a feral animal, using every part of his body as a weapon. He managed to land a solid blow to the jaw and rose to his feet. The man sprawled for his legs and grabbed him near the knees. Steele hammered at the back of his neck, stretching against the stitches like he was about to split a piece of wood with an axe.

The blow crumpled the man, folding him in half the same way you'd close a lawn chair. Coughing and sucking air, Steele retrieved the SCAR and put a bullet in him.

Chapter 64

The jeep sped away from the burning van a moment before Steele appeared out of the shadows, the gas still burning in his lungs. Winded from the run, he raised the rifle, desperately wanting to take the shot, but the flames flared out his NODs.

His thoughts immediately turned to Meg. He ran toward the van on rubbery legs, his muscles burning like battery acid. The vehicle burned hot, the blaze stoked by the rubber tires and flammable upholstery.

"Shit."

He fumbled the Nalgene bottle from the pouch and poured it over his face, hoping the water would let him get closer. Tugging his battle shirt over his mouth, he approached again. The air shimmered from the heat and silver tendrils of liquefied aluminum rolled off the

rims and down the slope. The water evaporated immediately and Steele paced around the pyre like a wolf on
the edge of a campfire, but he could get no closer.

"Meg!"

Unable to take the heat anymore, he backed off, still
screaming her name, and it was only when he stopped
to take a breath that he heard her moan.

"Uhhhh, Eric . . ."

"Meg?"

He turned his back to the van, making ever-widening
circles, scanning the ground through the night vision.
And then he saw her, lying in a crumpled heap next to
a rock. Steele stumbled to her side, falling to his knees.

"Meg, hey, talk to me."

"It hurts," she moaned.

The blood on Meg's plate carrier reflected in the
firelight and the placement of the wound sent a chill up
his spine. It was close to her heart and Steele jammed
his hands beneath the armor, probing for the entry
wound.

"I've got you," he said, because he couldn't think of
anything else. He stripped his knife from its sheath and
sliced the retaining straps, pulling the vest free before
ripping her shirt to get a better look at the wound.

"Oh, thank God."

The bullet had hit her shoulder.

"Did I get him?"

"Don't worry about that now," Steele answered, unbuckling his trauma kit. The first things he took out were a fentanyl lollipop and a roll of tape. The fast-acting painkiller was used widely in the war on terror for gunshot wounds, and he taped the stick to her right hand and brought it up to her mouth.

"It's fentanyl, just suck on it."

"That's what *she* said," Meg joked. The smile turned to a frown when Steele began probing the wound.

"You scared the hell out of me, do you know that?"

"I think I hit him."

"Good girl, I should have been there."

"No, it's fine."

Steele unwrapped the XSTAT hemostatic injector from his packaging. It looked like a giant syringe filled with tiny white pills. The pills were actually sponges, and when injected in the wound they would expand, forming a clot.

"This is going to hurt," he said, jamming the tip into the wound and pressing the plunger.

"Son of a bitch," Meg cried, attacking the fentanyl pop with a vengeance.

Steele pulled the injector out and watched the wound bulge from the inside as the sponges expanded. In seconds the bleeding stopped, but just to make sure,

Steele pressed a gauze pad over the wound, securing it with a square of tape.

"Is . . . is that guy moving?"

"Where?"

He turned to see a man struggling to get to his feet. "Hold tight for me." Steele drew his Glock and walked toward the wounded fighter.

"Let me see your hands," he commanded.

The man looked up. His face was a mess and blood poured from his ears and nose. Most of his hair had been burned away and his scalp was pink with patches of charred skin. The man reached for his pistol but Steele held his fire. He knew by the crooked angles of his fingers that the man's hand was broken.

Steele swept his legs, slamming him to the ground. The man cursed in Afrikaans, and Steele jammed the pistol into the center of his forehead.

"Give me a reason."

The man tried to fight, but was in no condition, and after a halfhearted effort he gave up and lay on his back.

"Kill me," he whispered.

"What's your name?"

"Just kill me."

Steele knew this was one of West's men and he seriously thought about putting a bullet in his head.

"He might know something," Meg said, her voice strained from standing.

"I ought to . . ."

Meg placed her hand gently on his shoulder.

She was right and he knew it. Steele slipped the pistol into its holster and got to his feet. He looked around. The field was on fire just like the house, and there were no vehicles for him to use. In the distance he thought he heard sirens.

How the hell are we going to get out of here?

"What are we going to do?" Meg asked, swaying where she stood.

Steele grabbed her and helped her to the ground. Once she was set he took the remaining fentanyl pop from his kit and shoved it in the wounded man's mouth. He didn't answer right away because he didn't know yet. The only thing that was for certain was that there was no way they were going to get away with Meg and the wounded man.

"I don't know."

He didn't realize he was bandaging the man's wounds until the patient started struggling. "Just kill me, for fuck's sake," he groaned.

"Shut up and suck on your lollipop, asshole."

"Eric, do you hear that?"

Steele's ears were still ringing and he could barely hear Meg's voice, let alone anything else. He strained his ears, looking up from the man he was working on.

Rotors—shit.

He grabbed the SCAR, switching out the magazine, while searching for a place to hide. "We need to go, can you move?" he asked, gently helping Meg to her feet. *The rocks, we can hold out there for a little bit.* He was almost out of ammo and had one frag left. The fight would be short, but Steele had no other options.

"C'mon."

The sound of the rotors got louder—they had been masked by the hillside—and before they were halfway to the rocks the bird was overhead. "Get down," Steele said. He pushed Meg as gently as he could into a hollow, planning to draw the helo's fire away from her.

The helo came in fast and settled in a tight orbit overhead. A spotlight clicked on, illuminating every-thing, and Steele broke into a run, hoping to draw them away.

"Where ya goin', mano?" a voice boomed from the bird.

Chapter 65

In the wings of the House of Representatives chamber, Rockford stood in front of President Cole while the sergeants at arms of the Senate and the House cracked jokes. It was 8:28 P.M. and in two minutes they would move to their seats. He could hear Cole's strong voice as he joked in the hallway, seemingly at ease and giving no outward sign that he was sick.

I have no idea how he does it. Yesterday he was up all night puking from the chemo, but you sure as hell couldn't tell.

"One minute, gentlemen."

Rockford turned and locked eyes with his boss. Cole gave him a wink.

At exactly 8:30, the deputy sergeant at arms announced the arrival of the Vice President and Rockford walked through the hall and into the Senate, taking his seat. Lisa beamed at him from her box, where she sat with Emma.

Rockford scanned the faces of the men and women who ran the United States. The general attitude toward Cole was one of respect. Even though the President's approval ratings were strong, there was a feeling that America was ready for a change. They had been at war since 2001, almost sixteen years, and Cole showed no signs of letting up. He viewed the world as a realist and saw an enemy that refused to admit defeat.

Rockford noted that Styles was conspicuously absent.

At 9:00, President Cole entered the chamber and the assembly got to their feet as "Hail to the Chief" boomed from loudspeakers. Rockford found himself nodding as Cole pressed the flesh, all smiles and the picture of health. The President shook hands with friend and foe alike. Tonight wasn't about the partisan politics that dominated the capital, it was about America. Cole was gracious, humble, and well liked. The left could say what they wanted on TV, but it was generally accepted by both sides that Cole was a good man.

The President was slowed by endless handshaking and pausing for pictures with members of Congress. It was a lesson Rockford took to heart every time he saw his boss in action. Cole was a fair man, and that went a long way in this day and age. His ability to remember everyone's name and something about them was both astounding and endearing. Rockford still had no idea how he did it.

It took ten minutes for him to get to his chair, and when Rockford took his hand, with a "Good evening, Mr. President," he felt a tremor in the usually iron grip. Cole was sweating around his hairline and Rockford could see that they had caked the makeup on, but there was still strength in his eyes, and that was enough for Rockford.

"Members of Congress," the Speaker began after taking the podium, "I have the high privilege and distinct honor to present to you the President of the United States."

Finally Cole took the podium, the flashes from the press pool erupted, and he nodded as his party showered him with adoration. Eventually the applause died down enough for him to speak.

"Ladies and gentlemen, I stand here both humbled and in awe by your gracious show of support and the weight of the occasion. Being the President of this great nation is the highest honor of my life and a sacred duty that I hold most dearly.

"As we close in on the end of my first term I am happy to say that our great nation is stronger now than it was when I took office. It is more profitable, secure, and respected than it was four years ago, and while we still . . ."

Rockford knew his knees would be hurting when the address ended in an hour. It was like church—sit, stand, sit, stand—but it was worth it. He hadn't seen Cole this happy since before he was diagnosed with cancer.

"I want the American people to know . . ."

The first time Cole faltered, Rockford thought that the emotion of the moment had gotten to him. Cole was an excellent orator and memorized his speeches, which meant he didn't need the teleprompters.

He saw the tremor start in Cole's leg.

"I want the American people to know that I will always put the needs of . . ."

Rockford moved to the edge of his seat. There was something very wrong. Cole raised his hand to his ashen face. It was shaking, and he was sweating profusely now. Rockford's eyes shot up to the monitor hanging from the ceiling, and his mentor suddenly looked tiny and frail. The First Lady saw it too and they locked eyes.

"Help him," she mouthed, but there was nothing Rockford could do.

What the hell is going on?

"Nancy . . ." Cole said suddenly. It wasn't a whisper, more of a gasp.

And then President Cole collapsed onto the podium.

Chapter 66

Robin Styles sat on the couch watching the State of the Union, her hand cramping around the phone. President Cole had just taken the stage and she caught herself breathing in short expectant gasps, like a dog tugging on a leash.

This is it.

Cole began to speak, and Styles leaned forward, taking a sip of wine while searching the President's face for the signs she had been told to expect.

He looks fine. Did she do it?

She set the glass back on the table. Her hands shook and it vibrated slightly, sending red wine cresting up toward the rim.

"There," she said, pointing at the TV even though she was the only one in the room. The camera angle switched and showed Cole from the side. Behind the podium his leg was twitching. He stumbled over his lines, seemed to recover, and then all the blood rushed from his face.

You don't have to die, just collapse right here on national TV.

"Nancy . . ." the President moaned. He reached for his face and then he was falling.

"Yes!" Styles screamed, jumping to her feet.

Triumphantly she watched Vice President Rockford hurdle the edge of the stage and scramble to his boss, the camera catching everything. Chaos exploded in the room, Secret Service coming in from all angles, flashing lights erupting like fireworks, blinding the camera.

It was better than she ever could have imagined.

Chapter 67

Henri Baudin's Gulfstream was waiting for West at the airfield. His men had failed to grab Bassar, which meant West had lost the initiative. But there was a silver lining.

At least Steele is dead.

West carried the bag up the stairs and was just about to step into the cabin when the engines began winding down. The pilot stepped out of the cockpit, his blue bus driver's hat cocked to the side and his hands held out in front of him like he was shooing a flock of geese.

"What the hell are you doing? Get this bird in the air."

"I'm sorry, sir," the pilot said in accentless English, "but Mr. Baudin has informed us that you are no longer authorized to . . ." He grunted and lowered his hands. A wrinkled confusion spread from his forehead over the cocky look he'd worn when he came into the cabin.

The pilot looked down at his stomach and touched the crimson stain spreading over his white shirt like spilled wine on a tablecloth. His mouth formed a silent O and he shuddered when West yanked the knife.

West held the man upright with his left hand and wiped the blade across the pilot's collar, leaving two bloody smears.

"I'm sorry, what were you saying?" he asked, letting go of the man's shoulders. He turned sideways and let gravity carry the pilot out the door.

"Jonas, get this plane in the air," he said.

The South African marched into the cockpit, pistol in hand. He jammed the barrel into the copilot's ear. "You've been promoted," he said, cocking the hammer. "Get the engines lit."

"Of course, sir."

West sheathed the blade and carried the device into the cabin. He took a seat on the leather sofa and groaned appreciatively.

"Boss, you're bleeding," Liam said.

West looked down at his arm, noticing the blood

for the first time. The nerve endings in his left arm were dead and he hadn't even realized that he had been shot.

Liam, like his brother Jonas, had served with Villars in South Africa. West called them the "platinum twins" because of their white/blond hair and love of outlandish jewelry that they referred to as "flash." West watched Liam cut his shirt away with a precision that Nate had come to expect from the former combat medic.

Liam inspected the wound and said, "Let me give you a shot for the pain."

"Don't need it. Be a good lad and grab that bottle," West said, motioning toward a bottle of Chivas Regal that sat in the cabin. "Best part about third-degree burns, they kill the nerve endings." He took the bottle and popped the stopper with his teeth. He spit the cork on the ground and took a long pull, pausing to take a breath and check the label. "Never was a scotch fan, but this stuff ain't bad."

He leaned back, letting Liam bandage his wound and listening to the engines powering up.

"So Steele is dead?" West asked.

"That's what Jonas said."

"Did he see the body?" West demanded.

Liam nodded.

Like Liam, his brother Jonas was a pro and if he said that Steele was dead then West knew he had one less thing to worry about.

"I'd pour some out for him, but why waste good booze?" He handed the bottle to Liam, who put down the shears and took a hit.

"Enjoy it, we are about to make history."

Chapter 68

M eg came to slowly, blinking up at the white ceiling and listening to the heart monitor beep. She had no idea where she was.

"Welcome back," Steele said.

Meg looked over at the chair, her vision blurry from the pain meds. She tried to lift her arm but it was tied tight to her body in a sling. The pain lurked beneath the surface, dulled by whatever they had given her.

"Where am I?"

"Morón Air Base."

"Still in Spain?"

"Yep."

"Hey, *chica*, looking good," Demo said, stepping in the room.

"What took you so long? We thought you were dead."

428 · SEAN PARNELL

Meg noticed Demo had a fresh bandage on the side of his neck, but other than that he didn't appear any worse for wear.

"Rest now, I'll check on you later."

"Don't you leave me here, Eric."

"Wouldn't dream of it."

"I want your word. Promise you will not leave me here."

He gave her a kiss instead.

Steele stepped out of the room and nodded to the MP who was leaning against the nurses' station flirting with a brown-haired girl in white scrubs.

"You ready to go talk to our friend?"

Demo rubbed his hands together before picking up an attaché case from the chair. "I cannot *wait*."

The nurse saw them coming and whispered something to the airman, who stood upright, smoothing his uniform top and adopting an official-looking scowl.

"Serious little guy, isn't he?" Demo joked in Arabic.

"And a major to boot. This should be fun."

"Gentlemen, I am Major Taylor, and I will be accompanying you to the security ward." There was something familiar about the man's face that stirred Steele's memory.

"I knew a Taylor in the Army. You don't have a brother, do you?"

"Yes, sir, I do."

"Damn, you're right. He looks just like ol' Brad, except *his* hair," Demo said, pointing at the airman, "isn't all gray."

The major grinned and ran his hand over his jet-black hair. "Do you know him, sir?"

Steele nodded. "I was with him in Afghanistan when he was a major. His team HALO'd into Kandahar, word is he killed fifty Taliban with an E-tool. Good man."

"I heard he is writing romance novels now, is that true?"

"That's him." Taylor chuckled. "Writes under the name Ray Ironrod."

The major badged them through a few doors and into the secure wing of the hospital.

"He's in room 201."

"Major, if we could hold up a second," Steele said, looking at the desk where three beefy-looking airmen sat in front of computers. There were cameras everywhere and Steele needed to set some ground rules.

"Yes, sir."

"I assume you were given certain orders regarding us."

"Yes, sir. I was told by the base commander to help you in any way possible."

"Major Taylor, do you plan on making a career out of the Air Force?"

"Plan on staying as long as they will have me."

"Excellent. The reason I ask is there are some questions we are going to ask the prisoner, and it is probably best if you and your men have plausible deniability."

"Okay . . ."

"What I'm saying is, I need you to cut the cameras in the room and make sure you erase any pictures of us."

Steele and Demo waited in the hall, just out of sight of the cameras, for Major Taylor to brief the men at the security desk. Steele watched the nearest camera, focusing on the red power light, and when it went out they continued down the hall.

They stepped inside the room and Steele looked at the man he had saved in Málaga. He was heavily bandaged and secured to the bed by handcuffs and leg irons. Demo set the attaché case on the chair and popped the locks, causing the man to look over at his guest.

"Remember me?" Steele asked.

"Piss off."

Demo took a black object from the case while Steele

walked to the head of the man's bed and looked down at him.

"Before they took you to surgery I went ahead and ran you through the database," Steele began casually. The man watched him, but remained silent. "Fingerprints were a bust." Steele grabbed the man's hand, which was balled into a fist, and slowly worked his fingers open.

The man fought against him, beads of sweat forming on his forehead. It wasn't long before he was sucking air. "Nurse, nurse!" he yelled.

"Nobody here but us," Steele said, peeling his fingers back until he was looking at the white scars where his prints should have been. "Lye?"

"You're wasting your fucking time with me," the man huffed, pain clouding his eyes. The IV machine beeped, administering a dose of something that instantly relaxed him in the bed. He smiled up at Steele, the pain evaporating.

"Have it your way."

Steele let go of his hand, turning his attention to the bags hanging from the hooks at the top of the pole. The larger bag was saline, and he ignored it, knowing that the doctors had hung it for hydration purposes. Next to it was a smaller bag with a label identifying it as morphine.

"Put thirty minutes on the clock," Steele said.

Demo nodded, fingers clicking on the plastic, and then set the object on the bed next to the patient. The digital readout was already counting down.

"Do what you want, I'm not telling you a damn thing."

Steele unlocked the IV pump and disengaged the morphine drip. It wouldn't take long for the last shot to wear off, and he knew the pain would change the man's mind.

"The thing is, I already know who you are. Peter Villars, age thirty-nine, from Pretoria, South Africa," he said. "In South Africa they might still use prints, but the rest of the world knows that it's all about the eye," Steele said with a wink. "I know you were with the South African Defence Force and spent seven years with the 5 Special Forces Regiment. The only thing I want to know is where the hell West is going."

Steele moved to the door, pausing before stepping into the hall.

"Loyalty is a strange thing, Pete, and it only works if it goes both ways. When the pain starts, I hope you remember that you are suffering for a man who left you to die."

"You think they have coffee around here?"

"We have thirty minutes to find out."

―――――――

They were on their second cup when Demo's watch beeped. Steele's keeper hit the button without looking up from the old magazine he'd found in the break room.

"Says here Brad and Angelina are breaking up."

"Everybody knows that," Steele lied, not really sure what he was talking about.

"Oh really?"

"Yep. Man, look at the time, we probably should get going."

Demo leaned back in his chair and shook his head. "Not until you admit that you have no idea who I'm talking about."

"Brad what's his name. The basketball guy, right?"

"Nope."

"Okay, I have no idea who you are talking about."

"Brad Pitt, the actor," Demo said getting to his feet.

"Never heard of him."

Steele held the door open for his keeper and followed him down the hall. When they turned the corner Villars was screaming for the nurse.

"That didn't take long."

"Dude is burned up like a fish stick, should have put fifteen minutes on the clock."

"Nah."

Steele cracked the door and stuck his head in. Villars's face was bathed in sweat and his bandages were soaked through.

"You ready to talk?"

"Turn the fuckin' drugs back on, mate. I'll tell ya whatever ya want to know."

Demo slipped into the room, heading for the IV pump.

"Please," Villars begged.

"You know the game. Where is West?"

"I don't know the exact spot, but he is headed to the States."

"Yeah, I figured that out myself," Steele said, picking up the stopwatch. "Hey, Demo, how do you bump this up to an hour?"

"The button—"

"I'm serious, he never told me shit. West is a fuckin' bastard, mate. I would have killed him myself if I didn't need the money."

"So you expect me to believe that you have been working with West, but have no idea where he's going?"

"The States, mate, that's all I know."

"Where in the States?"

Steele punched the button and called off the numbers as they increased. "Thirty-five, forty, forty-five . . ."

"Okay, okay. I don't know the target, but I know there is a house somewhere near D.C. The guy Baudin owns it and it has a landing strip West was going to use."

It made sense, but before Steele put his trust in Villars he was going to check it out himself.

"I am going to see if you are telling the truth," he said, holding up a phone. "If I find out you are lying I am going to come back in here and put two hours on the clock."

Chapter 69

While President Cole was being transported to Bethesda Naval Hospital, the Secret Service drove Rockford and his wife back to the White House.

"Poor Nancy," Lisa said.

Rockford wasn't listening, his mind still replaying the moment Cole went down, the memory repeating over and over on an endless loop.

Rockford took the steps two at a time. Cole was falling, but somehow Rockford got there before the President's head hit the ground, masking his friend from the cameras with his body.

"Sir, sir, can you hear me?"

His voice bounced off the ceiling, magnified by the microphone connected to Cole's lapel. Rockford ripped it off and threw it away, aware of the flurry of movement around them.

Cole's eyes rolled back, lids fluttering and face white as the grave. He started to seize, the tremor shaking him from foot to head. There was white foam forming at the edge of the President's lips, which were turning blue. Rockford's grandfather had suffered from seizures, and he remembered how the old man lisped because he had once bitten off the end of his tongue.

Get something between his teeth.

Rockford yanked a pen out of his pocket, the one Emma had given to him when he was sworn in, pried the President's jaw open, and jammed it between his teeth.

"I've got him, sir," a man said, dropping a large red bag on the ground.

Rockford recognized the White House medic, but couldn't make himself let go of his friend.

"Sir, I've got him."

Rockford sat back, watching the medic pull an oxygen mask over the President's face. The agent in charge of Cole's security detail was there, leaning over his boss. He was asking the medic something Rockford couldn't hear, and then he turned and looked him straight in the face, a hand moving up to his mouth.

What is he saying?

More agents arrived, but instead of circling Cole as they were supposed to, they formed a perimeter around Rockford. "Sir, we need you to come with us."

"Not until I'm sure he's okay," he snapped.

"That wasn't a question, sir." Strong hands slipped under his arms, lifting him off his knees.

"Let's go, let's go."

"Denton!" he yelled.

The phone in the center console rang, pulling Rockford from his thoughts. It was Lansky.

"Boss, I found something."

Rockford knew his chief of staff wouldn't be calling right now unless it was vital. "What is it?"

"Styles had a girlfriend, she just got picked up by the Capitol Police for public intox."

"Okay."

"I've got a guy who works in central holding. He says that she is talking about poisoning President Cole."

"Ted, I'm not following you. What does this have to—"

"Boss, she was Cole's nurse."

"I want her in federal custody in the next five minutes. Take her to the black site in Bethesda and wait for me there, do you understand?"

"They are already on their way."

Chapter 70

Rockford couldn't get used to the idea of being addressed as Mr. President. The hospital called him regularly, updating him on Cole's condition. His friend was in a coma, hanging on, but it was obvious he would never be the same. The phone on the desk rang and Rockford snatched it up.

"Yes?"

"Mr. Vice President," Eric began.

Steele's voice hit him like a stab to the heart. *Shit, he doesn't know about Cole.*

"Sir, are you there?"

"Yes . . . yes, Eric, sorry, we almost lost the reception."

Tell him, you selfish asshole. But Rockford knew he couldn't, not now at least. He needed Steele to be thinking clearly, not on the man who meant so much to him, who was at the moment lying in a coma. *Yes, it is selfish, but that's the job.*

"What do you have?"

Rockford listened while Steele filled him in. It wasn't the news he'd been hoping for, but right now as long as the nuke hadn't been detonated, he considered that a win.

"What do you need?"

"I need to know if Henri Baudin has any property that fits what this guy is saying, and if so I am going to need a ride."

Rockford jotted the name on a piece of paper and handed it to his chief of staff. Lansky read the name, nodded, and headed for the door to check.

"I don't like this," Rockford replied.

"Me either, but as long as we have a trail we have a chance."

"Do what you have to do."

"Yes, sir, I am going to need you to make a call for me. Are you familiar with the Skunk Works?"

"Lockheed Martin's advanced test lab?"

"That's the one. They have an aircraft, the SR-92 Aurora. Would you mind giving them a call and telling them that I need a ride to the States?"

Chapter 71

The Gulfstream G650 had the speed and the range to make it to the States in ten hours, which gave West plenty of time to think. Proper planning and good luck had gotten him this far and proved the merit of keeping the operation compartmentalized. Everyone under him was on a need-to-know basis, and that included Villars and especially Henri Baudin.

It was a lesson West had learned the hard way when his family was killed.

The only person you can trust is yourself.

It turned out that he had received two wounds, both superficial. The shotgun pellets had grazed his arm, and the first one made a big tear that looked terrible, but Liam had sewn it up without any problem.

The second pellet must have hit his vest, because

when Liam pulled it out of his pectoral the lead shot was flattened. "I hope your tetanus is up to date."

"When we land I'll be sure to go to the emergency room."

Liam pumped him full of antibiotics and offered a shot of Novocain. The medic couldn't believe that his boss didn't feel the scalpel or the needle.

West stopped drinking and left a few fingers in the bottom of the bottle. He had a nice buzz and his eyes were getting heavy. But before he could rest there was something he needed to do.

Going after Bassar had been a risk, West knew that on the front end, but it was necessary. Breul had designed the bomb around a fusion booster, which allowed him to make the device small *and* powerful. West had read about boosting and knew that the idea was to fire a small amount of fusion fuel into the core prior to detonation. The fuel created a two-stage thermonuclear device, which increased the yield by 27 percent. The bomb dropped on Hiroshima had wasted 80 percent of the plutonium packed into its core, and now West faced a similar problem. His failure to grab Bassar meant that his device would be inefficient. Instead of using the booster, he was going to have to rig the core to detonate.

It will still be nuclear, he thought. *But instead of killing millions, looks like I'll have to settle for a few*

hundred thousand, at least until the fallout starts kill-
ing everyone.

West tottered to the workstation and logged in to the encrypted computer mounted to the mahogany desk. Baudin had everything a man could need on the plane, and after the pilot helped Jonas disable the transponder, West knew the Gulfstream was untraceable. He easily reconfigured the computer terminal, locking Baudin out of his own network, and logged on to one of the public forums he used to communicate with his network of sources and fixers.

The men weren't cheap, but West had thought of that one too. Baudin had bankrolled the operation out of the Caymans, giving West access to the money he'd need. Knowing that he might need an emergency fund, West had been secretly siphoning cash from the myriad of accounts, hiding them in a rainy day fund of his own. He knew the balance was two million dollars, and with that kind of money he could get anything he needed.

The first thing he did was drop a handful of bread crumbs among a group of sources he knew were on the payroll of the U.S. government. West knew from years of experience that the American intelligence apparatus had a network of spies and informants who worked for money and that even after the failures in Iraq and Afghanistan the United States would rather pay for information than train its operatives to get their own.

All he had to do was whisper in the right ears.

Time to drop some dimes.

He sent four messages, all relating to Baudin, the only one left who could really hurt him. West knew it was only a matter of time before they linked him to the Frenchman. The key was to keep the "unblinking eye" looking somewhere else.

He told the snitches exactly where to find his employer. He knew by the time they checked the intel out, sent a team to grab him, and transported him to a secure location, West would be in the States. Even *if* Baudin knew what he was planning, there wasn't enough time left for him to do anything about it.

When he was done, West brought up Skype and logged in. It was a favorite means of communication all over the world because of its sophisticated encryption package. He dialed the number but kept the camera off, and after a few rings a man with a southern accent answered.

"Yeah?"

"I need a team and they need to be heavy."

"Jesus, do you know what time it is?"

"I don't give a shit what time it is. Do you want the money or not?"

"How soon do you need them?"

"Right now the location is stateside, so you won't have far to go."

"It's going to cost you."

"I'll give you two million if you can have them there in the next three hours."

There was silence on the other end.

West was paying three times the normal rate, and that kind of money meant big risk. It also meant that the man could retire as soon as the wire hit his account.

"Done."

"I'm sending half now, the other half on delivery. You good with that?"

"Yes."

"One more thing, I only want the pipe hitters. If they don't have confirmed kills, don't bother bringing them."

Chapter 72

"Welcome home," the pilot of the SR-92 said as the jet slipped over the coast, feet dry for the first time since leaving Spain.

"It's been eighteen months," Steele said.

The pilot nodded.

Steele looked over his shoulder. Demo was passed out in his seat and Meg was chewing on her bottom lip, enjoying the view. From their altitude the Capitol building was lit up like a pale yellow jewel and he remembered Ronald Reagan's final words before leaving office. *America is a shining city upon a hill.*

Steele believed it all the way to his core, just as the President had. It was why he'd made the decision on the way over that whatever it took, he was going to finish this.

The Aurora touched down and taxied to the waiting hangar. Ground crewmen chalked the wheels, the hangar's heavy doors closing before the pilot cut the engine. Standing by himself at the nose of the plane was a man he didn't recognize dressed in a faded pair of cammies with a pistol strapped to his hip.

"Sir, my name is Captain Starl, I will be transporting you and . . ." The captain stopped speaking and a confused look fell over his face.

Steele turned to see Meg and Demo approaching.

"Sir, I was told that I was transporting two, not three."

"You are."

"What?" Meg demanded.

"Demo, get with the captain here and figure out where we are going."

"Got it, mano."

"You told me that."

"I told you that I wouldn't leave you, which I didn't."

"This is bullshit, Eric."

"This is a Program mission," Steele said, grabbing her by the elbow. He was trying to pull her off to the side, but Meg wasn't having it.

"Get your hands off me," she snapped.

"You want to throw a fit here? Now? Why, because I don't want you to get hurt?"

"I wasn't in the Program in Spain, but that didn't stop me from getting shot," Meg replied.

"Yep, and you aren't a hundred percent. Plus this isn't Spain—this is the U.S. and you are in the CIA."

"Shit."

"Yeah. Even if I wanted you to, it is against the law for you to operate here."

"Asshole," she sulked, but he could tell she was easing up. She was angry, but wasn't going to go to war over it.

"Maybe, but you love it."

Meg smiled and pretended to pout. "Go play with your friends," she said. "But, Eric, you better come back in one piece."

"Yes, ma'am."

Steele walked over to a dark blue Bell 407 where Demo was waiting for him at the edge of the spinning rotors.

"Was she pissed?"

"Kinda, but then I told her it was illegal for the CIA to operate in the U.S. and she calmed down."

"She believed that?"

"Looks like it."

Steele hopped inside the helo, followed by Demo. They took a pair of headphones from the hook on the ceiling. Starl motioned for the pilot to take off and turned around so he was facing Eric and Demo.

"I was told to give you this," he said, handing Steele a case that obviously held an electronic tablet.

Eric cracked the security seal taped across the case with his fingernail and pulled out the tablet. He typed in a security code and centered his eye on the built-in camera. A moment later the device was unlocked and the briefing packet from Cutlass Main began to play.

"Stalker 7," a robotic voice began. "Your target is a ten-acre estate on Kent Island." An aerial shot of the house was followed by satellite imagery that showed an expansive estate surrounded by a thick wall of pine trees. Steele zoomed in on what looked like the backyard.

"Bingo," he said, tapping the airstrip.

"Cutlass Main has confirmed the deed holder to be Henri Baudin," the narrator continued. A photo of a middle-aged man dressed in a dark suit, gold-rimmed shades, and flowing silver hair appeared. Steele tapped the picture and Baudin's bio popped up.

"Says here Henri was French special forces and then went to the DGSE. He was relieved of duty October 14, 2014, on bribery charges. Two years ago he transferred a total of six million euros to an unlisted account in the Caymans. Looks like someone sent an anonymous tip to the Joint Special Operations Command. SEAL Team 6 just conducted a maritime assault on Baudin's boat. They have him in custody."

"Wow," Demo replied, "aren't we lucky."

Steele exited the window and went back to the brief. A photo of Baudin's airfield showed a C-130 backed up to a barn. A large tarp had been strung over the ramp, so Steele couldn't see what was being unloaded, but they had failed to cover the tail numbers.

"The plane belongs to Kinetic Solutions, a PMC out of Virginia."

"Private military contractors?" Demo said.

"Yep, no idea how many, though."

Steele and Demo had gone through the brief twice by the time the pilot lined the helo up on a small square clearing cut in the midst of a forest of pine. Steele saw an aluminum building with a helipad already filled with three Little Birds and a modified Black Hawk known as a Direct Action Penetrator, or DAP, whose pylons bristled with rockets and miniguns.

"This is as far as I go, sir," Starl said as they landed. "There is a NEST team and a Delta troop fresh from Syria waiting inside. "The Air Force also sent a present—check out the DAP before you go in."

Steele extended his hand. "Thanks for the lift."

"Roger that, and sir, good hunting."

Steele and Demo followed the captain's advice and got a closer look at the DAP before heading inside the pole building.

Demo let out a long whistle of appreciation. "I had heard they were building these bad boys, but never actually thought I would see one."

Steele looked at the missile attached to the pylon. It looked like all the other Hellfires he had seen, except this one had a bulge in the middle—like a boa that had just swallowed a goat.

"Help me out here, Demo?" Steele asked, wondering what he was missing.

"That, my friend, is a Hellfire III. The little bulge is the thermite payload."

"So if worst comes to worst . . ."

"You can put one of these puppies on the nuke and no big boom."

"What happens if you aren't clear?"

"You get turned into a charcoal briquette. Now let's go inside."

The interior of the pole building was as simple as they came: concrete pad for a floor, two bathrooms, a kitchenette with overflowing coffeepot and plenty of open space for the Delta operators to check their gear and conduct pre-mission checks.

To the untrained eye there was little difference between the operators and the NEST techs other than the gear they carried. Both took advantage of the relaxed grooming standards and had long hair, beards, and top-of-the-line kit. That was where the similarities ended.

The NEST, or Nuclear Emergency Support Team, were specialists whose only job was to deal with nuclear weapons. In Steele's eyes they were like doomsday Special Forces, and while the operators checked and rechecked their lethal loadouts the NEST guys were poring over charts and computer models.

Steele found it hilarious how Hollywood typecast the D-boys. Every movie that had a Special Operations lead was played by a towering, thick-necked body-builder type. In reality the operators came in three universal sizes: short, tall, and wide. They were raw-boned tattooed warriors who had an average body fat index of eleven percent and couldn't wait to get in the fight.

Up front the Delta team sergeant and their commander studied the Reaper feed, and the imagery pinned next to it. They paused now and then to jot a note in their green-covered books, snapping them closed when Steele and Demo approached.

"Demo, how the hell are you?" one of the men said as they drew near.

"They made you a sergeant major?" Demo replied with a laugh.

"I've got them fooled."

"Eric, this is Sergeant Major Ron Siler. I worked with him back when he was a young private."

"Pleasure," Siler said. "This is my commander, Major Jay Thompson."

"Howdy," the major said, extending his hand.

"This is for you," Siler said, picking up a duffel and handing it to Eric. "If you wouldn't mind getting dressed, maybe we can get this show on the road."

Demo shot Steele a big smile. "Hurry up, we are waiting," he said with a laugh.

Eric headed to the bathroom to change. Everything he'd asked for was in the bag, and after slipping out of the flight suit he suited up, laced his boots, and strapped the Winkler combat knife to his belt. Finally he clipped the pistol to his waist and pulled the plate carrier over his head, tightening the straps over his torso. When he was done, he jumped up and down to make sure nothing rattled.

Once he was satisfied he headed back out to the bay. Siler and Major Thompson were standing up front and the two teams were now formed into one.

"I'll keep it brief," Steele said, stepping up to the front of the room. The chitchat stopped immediately and pads and pens came out. "I know you guys are switched on, so I'm not going to belabor the point. This is a straight search-and-destroy mission. Anyone on that strip is fair game. We aren't taking any prisoners."

There was a murmur of approval from the men and Steele allowed himself a smile. "I want to be very clear about this, Nathaniel West is a bad mofo. If you see him, you *put* him *down.* West will have a bag with him. That is the package." Steele paused. This part of the brief was classified even for Delta, but the men had a right to know what they were getting into.

"The package is priority one," he said, looking at the NEST team. "The proword is 'Jackpot.' Delta will clear the path, you guys get the package and get the hell off the X."

The men nodded.

"If you haven't figured it out yet," Steele said, addressing the group as a whole, "Nathaniel West has brought a nuclear weapon into our backyard. He wants revenge; we are going to give him lead. Any questions?"

There were not, so Steele grabbed his kit and rifle and headed outside.

He took his rifle, checked the optic, and dropped his night vision over his eyes to test the infrared laser. When he was satisfied he racked a round into the chamber. There was a modified ATV puttering silently in the dark with a Delta sniper and his spotter in the front.

"Be careful, mano," Demo said.

"Yes, Mom."

"I'm serious. If things go sideways, I will be a phone call away," he said, pointing to the DAP. "Just get your ass out of the blast area and give me a call."

Eric nodded and got in the back of the ATV, flipped his night vision down, and flashed Demo a thumbs-up. "See you on the other side, brother," he said.

And then the driver hit the gas, speeding silently into the night.

Chapter 73

Rockford could see the lead vehicle, a gray Sprinter van, from the backseat of the Suburban. Instead of the usual motorcade, he had convinced the agent in charge of his Secret Service detail to let them travel low-profile: three up-armored Suburbans.

Mike hadn't been happy about it at first.

"Mr. President, I don't think that is a good idea."

"Figured you would say that. Ted, do you have that video?"

"Right here, sir," Lansky replied, placing the laptop on the seat.

"Mike, I know you guys have a hell of a job and I am appreciative of all you do. I'd like you to watch something for me."

"Uh, yes, sir," Mike replied.

The video began to play. It showed a young woman in an orange jumpsuit sitting at a table. A chain ran up from the floor, through the manacles around her feet, and up to the handcuffs on her wrists.

"This is from an FBI detention facility. That woman is—"

"Claire," Rockford interrupted. He recognized her as Cole's nurse from the White House Medical Unit.

"Yes, sir, Claire Moore."

A second woman walked in wearing a blue polo and a pair of khaki pants. She carried a folder to the table and took a seat.

"Audio and video are rolling," she said. "Ms. Moore, my name is Jane and I am with the FBI."

"What is this about?" Claire asked meekly.

"I will get to that," Jane said. "According to the report provided by the Capitol Police, you were found near the Lincoln Memorial and appeared to be under the influence of an intoxicant. The officer approached, and after you attempted to assault him, you were placed under arrest. Do you remember that?"

"No, I had taken some medicine. I don't remember much of what happened."

Jane nodded and flipped a page. "During transport you made a spontaneous utterance, and I quote: 'The President is dead because of me.'"

Rockford was watching Mike for his reaction and saw that the statement hit home.

"Due to the severity of the statement a blood draw was authorized, and according to the toxicology report you had cocaine, three times the recommended dosage of Zoloft, and alcohol in your system."

"I think I might need a lawyer," Claire whispered.

"Claire, you are not in jail," Jane began. "And I am not a cop. I work for a unit called the High Value Interrogation Group, and while I am technically with the FBI, I actually work for the Department of Defense. Do you understand what I am telling you?"

"I . . . I really think I need a lawyer."

On the screen, Jane leaned forward, her lips thin and serious. "Claire, when I said that you were not in jail, what I meant was that because of the seriousness of this situation, the rights that come with the typical arrest of an American citizen have been revoked. You are being charged with treason, and attempted murder of the President of the United States. You will not stand trial and you will not be serving a sentence in the United States."

Claire burst into tears and after a minute of intense sobbing she began to talk.

The story was simple but damning. Claire admitted to administering a placebo to President Cole instead of the prescribed dosage of Prolaxic, the drug that he was taking for cancer.

Halfway through, Mike looked at Rockford and said, "President Cole had cancer? How did I not see it? I was around him every day."

Rockford laid his hand on the man's shoulder. "He didn't want anyone to know."

On the video, Claire was still talking.

"It was Robin Styles, she made me do it."

"You are referring to Director of the CIA Styles?" Jane asked.

"Yes, she . . . she said she loved me and if I—"

Rockford had hit the stop button and pulled a sheet of paper out of his jacket pocket.

"Mike, the rest of the video is top secret. But I am going to tell you what Claire says so that you will understand why I am asking you to take me to Georgetown." He handed the agent the piece of paper.

"That is a federal arrest warrant. It charges Director Robin Styles with treason, terrorism, and about a dozen more crimes. In exchange for leniency, Claire agreed to give a written affidavit to the judge. She admitted her role in all of this and explained how Director Styles used her office as Director of the CIA to coerce and manipulate her. The judge agreed that Claire's statement was enough to issue the warrant, and while it doesn't change the fact that President Cole will probably never come out of the coma, I am asking you to allow me to be there when justice is served."

In the Suburban, Rockford watched the van's brake lights illuminate before making a right turn into a neighborhood.

"Here you go, sir," Mike said, handing Rockford a small television screen. The monitor showed the inside of the van. "It is linked to the team leader," Mike said.

Inside the van was a group of agents assigned to the FBI's Hostage Rescue Team, or HRT. It was the most elite counterterrorism unit outside of the military, and the agents who made it through selection routinely trained with Navy SEALS and Delta. They were in high demand all over the world, and while serving an arrest warrant in Georgetown wasn't their most glamorous assignment, it was hard to say no when the new President of the United States asked for your help.

The lead Suburban pulled to the side of the road with Rockford's vehicle right behind it. The drivers cut the lights and the interior went dark, except for the light emanating from the screen in Rockford's hands. He watched the van's taillights grow smaller and turned his attention to the screen.

Inside the van a red dome light bathed the heavily

armed men in an amber glow. The helmet cam gave Rockford the feeling that he was sitting among them, and the video was so clear that he could make out every detail.

"One minute out," the team leader said.

Rockford heard the sound of weapons being checked and saw the men tug the balaclavas they wore over their faces.

The camera turned to the door and a gloved hand reached for the handle.

"Cut the lights, we are going green."

The screen went black for a moment, but then the infrared lens came on, giving the appearance that someone had put a green filter over the camera. Rockford watched the door slide open, and heard the sound of wind whipping past the microphone as the team leader got to his feet and stood in the door.

"Silver 1, I am marking the house," a second voice said.

"Silver?" Rockford asked aloud.

"It is the call sign HRT uses for their snipers," Mike answered. "They set up early."

Rockford saw IR laser shine on the target house and nodded his head. *Smart. Makes sure everyone knows which house to hit.*

The team leader bumped the aiming laser on his

own rifle at the house and made a figure eight with the beam.

"Confirm laser," he said.

"You're on it."

The house was a modest brownstone fifteen yards from a streetlight. There were no other lights, but Rockford could see that it had a balcony on the top floor. There was a gentle hiss of brakes and the team camera bobbed as the team leader stepped out of the way and his men jumped from the van. He was the fourth man, and by the time he was on the ground his men were already jogging toward the target. Rockford saw a flash of light and heard the *thwap* of a suppressor. Glass tinkled from the shattered light and darkness fell over the street.

"Thermals are up. I've got one heat signature on the second floor. Room with the balcony."

"Got it," the team leader said, breaking into a jog, heading toward the corner of the house where his team was stacking up. "Ladder up."

"Moving, boss," a fresh voice said.

The team leader met up with his men and turned to the van, allowing Rockford to see an agent running toward him with something over his shoulder. The agent stopped under the balcony and expertly deployed a collapsible ladder. He had almost gotten it fully extended when a motion light on the other side of the house came on.

"Hold," the team leader said. "Silver, what do we have?"

"A dog, looks like a Lab."

Rockford watched as a light came on in the room attached to the balcony. The HRT agent with the ladder pulled it down and flattened himself up against the house.

"Thermals show movement. Target is up."

Rockford had told the team leader that he wanted a quiet operation, which was why they had attempted to use the ladder and go through the window. But with Styles awake he knew he needed to give the team leader full control. He picked up the radio sitting beside him on the seat.

"HRT is Blue," he said, using the code word the team leader had given him for just this situation.

"Roger, Blue. Silver, sitrep."

"Looks like the target is in the hall, heading for the stairs."

"Copy that. Breachers up."

Rockford watched two men creep to the door, one covering while the other stuck what he knew to be the breaching charge to the iron on the door. It took them less than five seconds to set the charge, spool out the blasting wire, and make their way back to the team.

"Silver, we are going loud. You have the eyeball."

"Copy. Target is at the top of the stairs. Stand by for count. Five . . . four . . . three . . . two . . . Burn it."

The camera shifted to the ground, followed immediately by a flash of light and a deep boom.

"Positive breach, go."

"FBI! Robin Styles, let me see your hands!" a voice yelled, followed by a woman's plaintive screams.

"Do you know who I am?"

"Get on the ground, now!"

By the time Rockford walked into the house the smoke had dissipated and HRT had finished clearing the structure. He found Styles on the couch, her hands zip-tied behind her back, the soot on her face streaked with tears.

Rockford's feet crunched over the broken glass as he walked over, and she looked up at him as he approached.

"You," she spat. "I should have known. I don't know what kind of bush-league power play you have going on here, but I can promise you—"

"That's enough, Robin," Rockford interrupted, coming to a halt a foot away. He reached into his pocket and took out a sheet of paper. "This is a warrant signed by a federal judge."

"For what?" she sneered.

"For the attempted murder of the President of the United States, and aiding and abetting a terrorist," he said, tossing the warrant on her lap.

"I want a lawyer."

"If you had done all of this as just a plain old citizen that would be your right. But since you used your office in the CIA to conduct your affairs, well, that changes things."

Rockford stepped out of the way and motioned to two men in black suits. "These men work for the Justice Department. I am sure they will be happy to answer any questions you might have."

Chapter 74

The driver stopped the ATV three hundred meters south of the estate. He cut the engine and slowly the night sounds returned. There were no lights this far out in the country, and Steele motioned for the sniper to lead them in. Working with Delta made everything easy; they were the best soldiers in the world and Steele had no problem following the point into the woods. He moved quiet as a shadow and Steele let him get a ten-yard lead before following. The space was in case they were ambushed or took a grenade.

The branches and deadfall made for slow moving, and twice they startled deer lying in a thicket. Both times they took a knee, waiting, watching, and listening. When it was clear the point man motioned them forward until they could see the lights of the estate.

The point man clicked his radio, breaking squelch and pointing to a spot on the ground where they would stop. Steele knew the drill and passed the arm movement back to the spotter who was bringing up the rear. Instead of going to the spot, they patrolled past it, cloverleafing through the woods until they had made a complete circle. The reasons were evident only to those who had worked behind enemy lines.

Steele had seen good and bad recon teams in his career. Good teams had one thing in common—they never forgot the basics. In Iraq, Steele had watched a reconnaissance team use the same position on three different operations, and if that wasn't bad enough, they occupied the position the same way each time. On the third outing the law of averages caught up with them. The team had just set up their position when they came under heavy mortar and small-arms fire from a firing point fifty meters away. The entire team was wiped out.

A simple cloverleaf would not only have revealed the ambush, but would have put the team in position to flank their would-be attackers. Steele had taken this lesson to heart, and halfway through the cloverleaf he called a halt to watch their back trail. Only when he was certain that they were alone did he signal the point man to move out.

Finally they returned to their original position and the three men established a tight perimeter. Steele set up next to a tree and made sure one of the operators was watching his area before digging a poncho out of his kit. He draped the poncho over his head, using it to block the glow from the ruggedized tablet that connected him to the drones overhead.

The Reaper feed confirmed that the area was hot. Light towers had appeared along the edge of the strip, illuminating the outlying buildings. Steele counted way more than ten armed men and noticed they had four patrols running the perimeter.

It made him wonder if they had been tipped off.

Could West know that we were coming?

The Delta spotter activated the digital camera and started clicking away. Steele studied each picture, noting the night vision, gear, and posture of the men. They were heavily armed and well trained and when the last picture hit the tablet, Steele attached them to an email and shot them off to Demo. He turned the tablet off, stowed the poncho, and flipped his night vision over his eyes. He forced himself to relax and was waiting for his eyes to adjust when a dry *snap* shattered the silence.

Someone's coming.

Steele froze, his vision blocked by a stout tree. He could move but knew any movement or sound could blow their cover. He had to trust that the operators were covering his ass. The spotter raised his hand an inch from the ground, and an upside-down pistol, pointing his index finger to Steele's left. It was the signal for enemy front.

A deafening silence fell over the position. Steele's senses were maxed out and everything from his breathing to the hammering of the blood in his ears sounded like a brass band. He took a deep breath, held it for ten seconds, and let it out. The concert in his ears slowly subsided to a dull roar, and then he heard the dog.

Steele could tell by the light footfalls that it wasn't a German shepherd. *Most likely a Belgian Malinois.* The K9 didn't make a sound, not a groan or a whine, and Steele knew in that instant that he was up against some serious hitters.

There was only one way to keep a dog that quiet, and that was by removing its vocal cords. A barking dog was good for static security, but in the bush a wayward growl could get you killed. Steele hadn't heard of a company that cut their dogs' vocal cords since . . . *Africa, shit.*

The company was called Dynamic Effects back then, and Steele had run across them while tracking West's son. He'd heard they had been forced to close down after a particularly nasty massacre in Central Africa.

Steele inched his hand to the radio and pressed the transmit key down two times. One short and one long—the signal for possible compromise.

Back at the base a radio operator responded with three long breaks: *Roger. Standing by.*

Steele knew that right now the operators were grabbing their gear and the pilots had the blades spinning up. He had ten minutes to check in, and if he didn't the strike team would rain hell on the estate.

A low wheezing sound slithered into the tiny perimeter. Steele knew that the dog was pulling hard on the lead. He had found something that he wanted and was so locked in that he was choking himself to get to it.

He must smell us.

Heavy footfalls marched closer. It sounded like a giant was crashing through the brush, pulverizing leaves and sticks beneath heavy feet. Over the sound the man's radio squawked to life and a voice exclaimed, "Package inbound, all elements sound off."

"One-zero clear. One-one clear. One-two all clear . . ."

The sentries were calling in from their positions around the edge of the airstrip, and Steele breathlessly waited for the handler to key up. The entire operation balanced on a razor's edge. If they were compromised now, West would disappear. The strain of the moment caused sweat to start dripping down Steele's face.

"One-three, stand by," the handler said, his accent marking him as either from Boston or New Hampshire.

He is right on top of us.

"What is it, boy, you gotta take a dump?"

Steele cursed himself for not bringing a "hush puppy." *Stupid.* The suppressor on his rifle was too loud and if *he* fired the shot would definitely give them away. He made a trigger motion to the spotter, hoping the operator was more squared away than he was. As usual, Delta saved the day.

The spotter pulled a long-barreled pistol from his kit and one look told Steele that it was an integrally suppressed .22. The spotter pointed at the ground, signaling that he would take the dog. Steele gave him a slight nod and reached for the knife at his back. He slipped it from the sheath, keeping the blade up and trying to get a fix in his mind on the handler.

"One-three, are you good?"

The movement stopped and Steele took a deep breath, getting ready for the shot. Instead of the whisper of the .22 he smelled shit and knew the dog was relieving himself.

"Roger that. Ol' Spike had to drop the kids off at the pool."

"Good copy."

Steele relaxed his shoulders and his heartbeat was just returning to normal when the radio came to life once again.

"SAM team hot and ready to rock."

Did he say SAMs, as in surface-to-air missiles?

If the men on the ground had the ability to bring down the helos, Steele was going to have to find and neutralize them before the strike team could hit the objective. He felt the spotter's eyes on him and was turning his head when the man's suppressed .22 spit in the darkness.

Chapter 75

Steele came around the tree like a sprinter from the blocks. He could see the handler clearly in the night vision's emerald glow. The man was frozen in place, left hand holding a limp lead, brow furrowed as he tried to figure why his dog had decided to take a sudden nap.

Steele didn't give him time to figure it out. He drove his hand into the man's throat and swept his legs out from under him. The handler didn't have time to say or do anything before Steele had the blade to his neck.

"Where are the manpads?" he asked, using the slang for surface-to-air missiles.

The man's reply was choked and whatever he said was lost under the chirp of the Gulfstream touching down. The pilot smoothly applied the reverse thrust and the engines howled.

"Where are they?"

"The . . . roof."

Steele looked up, focusing on the roof, and the handler twisted beneath him, making a play for his pistol. "Don't." The man ignored him, and Steele didn't have a choice. He drove the blade into the base of the man's skull and felt him go limp beneath him.

Steele looked at the sniper, then back at the body. It was the first time he had killed a fellow American and he fought the urge to vomit. *Damn you for this, Nate.* He felt dirty, like he had betrayed a sacred trust, but what nagged at him the most was the sense that he was going to have to do much worse before the night was over.

"Nothing you could have done," the sniper said simply. "You did what you had to."

The three of them were warriors, men who protected their countrymen, not killed them. Theirs was a deadly business, one that broke the most sacred of all commandments: Thou Shalt Not Kill. They were the men who went out and took the lives of those who would harm America and her citizens' way of life, but killing one of their own was something they never signed up for.

"That plane doesn't get off the ground," Steele said, breaking himself from the moment.

"Roger that. We've got your back."

"Atlas, this is Stalker 7. The package is on the ground. New intel suggests they might have manpads."

"Say again, Stalker."

Steele had to make a choice. He knew it would take the helos seven minutes to get from the rally point to the target, and if he called them now and didn't find the surface-to-air missiles the helos wouldn't stand a chance. On the other hand, he knew that West wasn't just going to stick around.

No matter what.

"Atlas, I will mark the manpads with an IR strobe. Advise you launch now."

"Good copy."

Steele set his stopwatch to seven minutes and looked at the operators.

"No matter what happens, that plane doesn't leave," he told the snipers.

"Easy day, brother."

It was the typical Special Operations response.

Steele stripped the radio from the dead handler and clipped it into his vest. Before stepping off he hit the start button on his watch.

7:00, 6:59, 6:58 . . .

He moved counterclockwise through the wood line, using the trees to mask his approach. The Gulfstream had already reached the end of the tarmac and the pilot goosed the engine, swinging the jet around and toward the hangar.

"Let's get a perimeter set up," the voice on the radio said.

Steele crouched low, scooting in and out of the shadows, frantically searching the roofs for any signs of the missiles. *They would want the tallest building, to clear the trees.* He keyed in on a two-story building two hundred yards away that appeared to be made out of corrugated steel. *That's where I'd be.*

Ten feet from the building there was a shimmer of movement at the corner. Steele dropped to the ground. *Dammit, can I get a damn break?* He rolled the H&K to his back and slowly drew the Glock 34 from its holster and clipped the suppressor on the end of the barrel with a twist.

Lying there, Steele thought he heard the gentle scrape of metal on metal, but that could have been his ears telling him what he wanted them to hear. He hazarded a glance at his watch and his heart sank when he realized the strike team was three minutes out.

The shape was moving toward him and Steele raised the pistol but was unable to see the sights without sitting up. The blood was pounding in his ears again. He ignored everything but the shot. He pressed his thumb firmly on the back of the slide. By locking it forward he was trapping the gas created by the fired bullet inside the breech. The gun wouldn't be able to cycle, and while it would be silent, he would only have one shot.

Aiming from the chest was not a guarantee. He was going to have to go for the head, and without the use of the sights. *Maybe he will turn around.* It was a pipe dream. All he could do was wait, and the seconds felt like they were stretching into hours. He fought the urge to check his watch. *Who is this guy, Betty White? Slowest walker I have ever seen. Jesus man, shake the lead out.*

At five feet Steele knew he couldn't wait any longer. He steadied his hand and gently squeezed the trigger. *Pffft.* The Glock coughed weakly and the figure stopped in his tracks. *Shit, I missed.*

He was about to rack the slide when the figure wavered and dropped face-first into the dirt. Steele silently racked a fresh round into the chamber, holstered the Glock, and dragged the body to the edge of the building. After turning off his radio, he checked his watch.

1:30, 1:29.

Steele turned the volume all the way down on the radio he'd taken from the dead K9 handler and, straining his ears, pressed the transmit button. Above him a radio chirped, confirming that there were men on the roof.

He tore the strobe from his pocket and covered it with his hand before flashing it three times. He was shoving the strobe back into his pocket when a voice said:

"Did you see that?"

Chapter 76

West had switched clothes with the pilot and stood at the window waiting for the Gulfstream to come to a halt. He watched the contractors from Kinetic Solutions with a keen eye, hoping to divine their intent from their posture.

The reason he had changed clothes was because he didn't trust them. They were mercenaries, men who sold their skills to the highest bidder. Their loyalty was to the almighty dollar, and he knew the only thing that decided if they would protect or betray him was the number of zeros at the end of the check.

The engines whined down, followed by the squeak of the cabin door. West turned to see the copilot appear, dressed in West's clothes, arms at chest level, palms facing out. Jonas was behind him, a pistol jammed in the small of his back.

"Do you know what to do?"

"Yes."

"You better," West growled, opening the cabin door and unfolding the stairs.

On the tarmac the mercs ignored him, just like West knew they would. He was the hired help and the only looks shot his way were in reference to the scars on his face. He pretended to inspect the plane, letting his stand-in descend the stairs with Liam and Jonas.

"This way, sir," one of the contractors said, motioning to the old barn. "I hope you had a pleasant flight."

When their backs were turned, West jogged back up the stairs and grabbed the pilot's flight case. It was just big enough to hold the device.

"We are about to go," a voice yelled from the tarmac.

"Thank you," West replied.

He grabbed the bag and moved to the door, stuffing the detonator he'd attached in flight into the inner pocket of the pilot's jacket. He hustled back down the stairs. The contractors had collapsed the perimeter and were heading back to the barn. West tugged the pilot hat down over his head and was going to follow when a distant sound stopped him dead in his tracks.

"What is it?" Liam the medic asked.

West held up his hand for quiet, ears straining in the dark.

Then he heard it again, clearer this time. Helos, and they were close.

Steele sucked up against the building, his heart pounding in his ears. He could hear the men above him walking around and prayed they didn't look over the side. He glanced at his watch—the numbers were all zeros.

"Hey, pay attention," a voice snapped.

"I thought I saw—"

"Who cares what you saw, watch your sector."

Steele let out a sigh of relief and watched. The perimeter had collapsed around West and was moving toward the barn when the tactical radio came alive.

"Atlas 1–2 inbound from the south."

"Roger that, Atlas. The target is marked by infrared beacon," the sniper said.

He couldn't hear the DAP but knew it had to be close, the gunship pilot keeping the helo close to the ground to mask the sound of the rotors. Steele activated the beacon and dropped it at the base of the building, scurrying back into the shadows to get away from the explosions that he knew were coming. When he was safely behind the pump house he took a length of electrical tape he kept attached to his gear and wrapped it around the transmit button of the stolen radio.

The red transmit light was the only thing that told Steele it was working; other than that the radio was silent. But he knew that the rest of the radios were hissing from the static of the open channel.

"Atlas 1–2, I have the target."

Steele could hear the helo now. The blades made a distant buzzing, which he knew to be deceitful since the DAP was actually moving faster than the sound. He glanced over his shoulder in time to see the Hellfire light off from the pylon, followed by a second missile.

Someone shouted atop the target building, but it was too late. Steele ducked behind the pump house, opening his mouth against the detonation he knew was on its way.

Boooom.

The Hellfire pulverized the building, the explosion flaring out Steele's night vision. The pump house shook under the shock wave and he kept his head down, wincing at the shrapnel banging against the sides of his makeshift shelter.

He flipped his night vision up and cast a tentative look around the pump house. All that was left of the building was on fire, twisted beams and a gaping hole in the ground. Automatic rifle fire erupted near the barn, the contractors caught out in the open with their package. Some of them stood to fight; the smart ones ran for cover. Steele jumped into action, his only thought finding West.

He ran toward the orange tracers pouring down from the DAP, a finger of death cutting through flesh and bone like a knife through butter.

The heavy machine gun Steele hadn't noticed earlier waited until the Little Birds appeared from the north before opening up on the DAP. Steele heard the gun chugging away and saw something spark off the DAP.

"Got a heavy in the tree line, boys," the pilot advised calmly.

A trail of smoke appeared behind the gunship just as the first Little Bird touched down short of the barn, and then a second gun opened up in a small shed twenty yards from Steele.

He knew that any moment the two guns would interlock their fields of fire. He had to do something or there was no doubt in his mind that they would shoot down one of the birds.

He took a grenade from his kit and stepped into the open, fully aware that the fire from the burning building gave him away.

You can make it, he told himself, opening his legs into a run.

He hadn't gone ten yards when a line of tracers zipped over his head. Caught in the open, he threw himself to the ground. He rolled left, barely avoiding the line of bullets that slapped the grass in front of him. Blinking the dirt out of his eyes, he frantically searched for cover and prayed for a miracle.

Chapter 77

Nathaniel West ducked beneath the Gulfstream, using the jet to shield him from the fireball growing from the destroyed building. The flame backlit the gunship that came racing over the landing strip, its dual .50 caliber machine guns chattering beneath the wing mounts.

"Son of a bitch." He'd known it was Steele the moment he heard the blades. *That asshole has more lives than a fucking cat.* The contractors grabbed the pilot, who was dressed in his clothes, so they naturally assumed he was their "principal," and formed a scrum around him. They herded him toward the barn, leaving West and a handful of extra contractors to fend for themselves.

"We have to go!" Liam the medic yelled.

"I need to get to the barn, you moron!" West yelled.

"Let's fucking do it, then," Liam shouted back, stepping out into the open.

West was about to follow when he heard the round snap past his head. The shot was followed by a meaty slap that sent Liam tumbling to the ground. A jet of blood and gore spurted from the exit wound and splattered over the nose of the jet.

Sniper.

West ran for the barn, zigzagging back and forth, away from the minigun buzzsawing above him. He fully expected each step to be his last. There was no way to outrun a helo, but when the big gun the contractors had hidden in the woods chattered to life, it forced the DAP to peel off.

A string of tracer fire flashed from a gun pit and West saw that the gunner was firing at a lone figure caught dangerously in the open. *Is that Steele?*

Even in the dark West knew it was Eric. *No place for you to hide this time,* he realized as the tracers whipped past Steele's head, forcing him to throw himself to the ground.

He's done.

With Steele caught in the open, West stopped and waited for the inevitable. He was sure the next blast would cut into Steele's back, but then a lone Little Bird dropped out of the darkness. The pilot dipped the nose and fired a burst from the .50 caliber machine gun. The bullets slammed into the gun position, saving Steele's life.

"Are you fucking serious?" West screamed as the Little Bird leveled off at the last minute, cut hard right, and came to a hover next to the barn. The men on the benches jumped off and started engaging the contractors.

West snatched a submachine gun from one of the dead contractors and checked the chamber. Jonas was yelling at him to "follow me." If West hadn't needed the man he would have cut Jonas down for lying to him. Instead he pointed the submachine gun at his chest and yelled, "Take this!" He tossed the pilot's case to him and pointed at the barn. "Go get the ride."

West watched Steele fling something toward the gun emplacement, and then throw himself to the deck.

He doesn't see me. West realized he had the drop on Eric and held his fire. There would be no mistakes this time. He slung the submachine gun behind his back and started toward Steele.

"It's just you and me now, boy."

Chapter 78

I owe *that pilot a case of beer for saving my life,* Steele thought as the grenade went off, silencing the gun. He got to his feet, his body bruised from diving into the ground.

I might be getting too old for this shit.

A flare hissed skyward and when it burst Steele saw the operators leaping into action. They worked in tandem, firing and maneuvering closer to the contractors, who were forced to break contact or be cut down.

Steele sensed movement to his right. *Is that the pilot? What the hell is he doing?* "Hey, you need to get down!" he yelled at the man. The pilot kept walking and Steele was about to run over and force him to the ground when he noticed the strap running across the front of his shirt.

A sling?

He turned his body like someone behind him had tugged on his shirt. The hairs on the back of his neck stood up and he threw himself toward the damaged gun emplacement as an MP5 appeared in the pilot's hand.

A tongue of flame leapt from the barrel and Steele hit the ground. Bullets snapped over his head, followed by West's voice.

"No use hiding, Eric."

"I didn't recognize you in your little costume, Nate," Steele yelled back.

The first wave of contractors made it back to the barn. They threw grenades and switched out magazines, but the explosions did little to stop Delta's assault. One of the men took a round and dropped to his knees. Steele saw all of this while working his way to the edge of the barrier. He fired a shot at West, who dropped to a knee. Steele was leaning out to line up a shot when the side of the barn ruptured outward. "Holy shit . . ."

Jagged splinters and severed planks scattered in all directions, followed by an MRAP clawing free of the barn. The mine-resistant vehicle reminded him of a prehistoric beast, yellow headlights for eyes and chest-high knobby tires for claws. It gained momentum with a belch of diesel smoke and sent the kneeling contractor flying through the air.

A head appeared in the turret, followed by the chatter of a machine gun. The armored vehicle made a beeline for West, blocking him from the operators' fire when it came to a halt. The ramp was down and three contractors jumped out, laying down covering fire for West, who jumped to his feet, angling for the ramp. Steele rushed after him, but had to sweep wide when one of the gunmen saw him coming and opened up.

He knew that since West didn't have the device on him, it had to be inside the MRAP. One of the contractors shielded West with his body so he could climb up the steps cut into the ramp. Overhead the gunner worked short, accurate bursts into the operators, and from the radio traffic Steele knew they were taking casualties.

Do something, God damn it.

Steele was sucked up against the MRAP, too close to get a shot off but close enough that he could hear the crew yelling out targets for the gunner. He wanted to lob a frag through the turret, but couldn't risk detonating the bomb. His only option was a flash-bang, and luckily he had just the ticket.

Calling the ALS Magnum a flash-bang was like calling Babe Ruth a baseball player. The Magnum was twice the size of a standard munition, and while it wouldn't kill the gunner, Steele had seen grown men shit themselves after being hit with one. He quickly prepped the flash-bang, and just as he was about to lob it into the turret, the contractor peeked his rifle around the corner and capped off five rounds.

Steele took one in the plate, and the force shoved him face-first into the armor. He cursed because the bullet had found the same exact spot he'd been hit in the Gatehouse. Sucking air and cursing through gritted teeth, he managed to toss the Magnum in the turret.

I was just starting to breathe normally.

The driver gunned the engine impatiently, and a cloud of diesel belched from the tailpipe near the back wheel. The only thing that kept Steele from sucking the acrid smoke into his lungs was that he couldn't take a full breath. He transitioned the rifle to his left shoulder, wishing he could make a wide sweep to the left. Pieing the angle would have given him a better shot on target, but the machine gunner made that impossible.

Counting down from five in his head, Steele advanced on the ramp, waiting for either the flash-bang to go off or the contractor to try and take another shot. The contractor got sloppy the second time. Steele saw his foot appear, followed by his shin. The rocking motion of foot and leg told him that the gunman was pumping himself up—trying to get the courage to step around for another shot.

I'll take it.

Steele knew that West had to be at the top of the ramp by now, and he couldn't waste any more time. He centered up on the man's shin and fired a bullet through the bone. The contractor screamed, stumbling forward. Steele put his follow-up shot through the man's forehead and grabbed hold of the armor.

"Grenade!" someone yelled.

Steele swung himself up on the ramp, grabbed a handhold, and was trying to climb aboard when the driver gunned it. The MRAP surged forward, dragging Steele behind it. His feet bounced off the ground, jarring his shoulder socket, and then his grip began to slip.

Chapter 79

The only reason West knew it wasn't a grenade that exploded inside the MRAP was because he was still alive. His brain told him that it was a flash-bang, but he had never felt one that powerful.

The coffinlike interior magnified the concussion and it bounced off the wall, hitting West in the face like a haymaker from Mike Tyson. The concussion rattled his teeth and turned the breathable air into a scalding vapor. He stumbled backward, arms flung wide and all of his senses offline.

He knew he was falling and grabbed for anything that would keep him inside the MRAP. His fingers brushed skin, cloth, and metal, but he couldn't get a grip on anything. The driver stomped the pedal to the floor and the armored vehicle bounced over an incline.

West was weightless in the back and felt air beneath his feet.

At the last second his left hand found the fire extinguisher mounted next to the ramp hinge. He clamped down, holding on for dear life, willing his vision to come back. Slowly his eyes focused; everything appeared blurry and spotted around the edges, and the first thing he saw was the gunner hanging upside down in the hatch. A trickle of blood oozed from the bullet hole in the man's forehead before dripping to the floor.

Everything else inside the MRAP was chaos, and when West's hearing slowly returned he heard the men cursing and coughing.

Check the device.

It was the only thing that mattered.

He took a step forward, wavering like a reed in the wind. He could see the pilot case containing the device just out of arm's reach. He finally had his legs beneath him and was reaching out for the case when a hand closed on the back of his shirt.

"No . . ."

West was jerked backward and knew without having to look that it had to be Steele. He fired an elbow behind him, his head snapping toward his shoulder to find his target. He knew it was a solid blow from the impact rolling up his shoulder and the warm blood he felt on his arm.

He turned and stood toe to toe with Steele, who looked battered, but definitely not out of the fight.

"You just won't give up, will you?"

Steele answered by ripping his pistol from its holster and flicking off the safety. He brought the pistol up, his arm still numb from being dragged behind the MRAP. "This ends now," he said.

Off balance and with blood dripping into his eyes, Steele fired. He knew immediately that he'd rushed the shot. The bullet sparked off one of the metal braces inside the armored vehicle, barely missing the man holding the case. He saw the driver lurch forward, the insides of his skull splattered across the windshield.

And then West was all over him.

"You think you can stop me?" West screamed.

Steele managed to block the first kick, but West ducked and smashed an elbow across his chin. Steele's legs went soft, and he felt West grabbing his wrist.

"You never had what it took," Nate taunted, slamming Steele's gun hand against the wall.

Steele's knuckles hit armored plate and he was losing the feeling in his hand. He managed to drive his knee into West's gut and tried to bounce his head off the armor plate, but West managed to land a tight hook to his side.

Huuumph.

Steele doubled over, the air rushing from his lungs. The man holding the device had moved to the front and was trying to wrestle the dead driver, whose foot was pinning the accelerator to the floor, off of the wheel.

The MRAP's turbodiesel screamed and the heavy APC began to swerve back and forth across the road. West was thrown off balance, giving Steele a moment to yell:

"Nate, you don't have to do this!"

But West wasn't listening. He sneered at Steele, his face twisted, eyes filled with fire. "You think you can save me?" he screamed.

Steele knew at that moment that the West he had known was gone. The man in front of him was some twisted version of Nate, and he was absolutely right, Eric *couldn't* save him.

The only way this was going to end was when one of them died.

Chapter 80

Steele managed to jam his thumb down on the radio while West prepared himself for another attack.

"Demo, the device is in the MRAP."

"Nooo!" West screamed, throwing himself at Steele.

"Take it out," Eric managed to say before West landed a shot to the nose.

Steele felt the cartilage give and tasted blood. His eyes watered, forcing him to yield ground.

"Are you clear?" Demo asked over the radio.

Steele slipped to the side and whipped a back fist across West's face, pressing the transmit button for the final time.

"Yes, I'm clear," he lied. "It's over now!" he screamed at West, who lowered his shoulder and launched himself at Steele.

West slammed into him just as the MRAP bucked and went airborne. Steele felt himself falling and the only thing he could do was hold on to the back of West's shirt. He looked through the windshield as the MRAP came crashing back to the ground and saw the glint of water yawning before them.

And then he was falling.

Chapter 81

As Eric fell from the MRAP, everything froze. There was no sound or pain, and in that moment he could see everything.

In front of him, the MRAP dashed forward, hit the lip of the embankment that separated the earth from the massive pit that housed the lake, and launched itself into the air, momentarily weightless. The knobby tires spun furiously in the air, and then the front end began to nose downward.

A flash of light erupted overhead, and Steele saw an orange finger of flame rushing through the sky. He knew it was a Hellfire being fired from the DAP. He also knew that he was too close.

The explosion created a tornado, sucking everything inward, and when it reached critical mass, it abruptly shifted gears. The overpressure rushed from the core, moving faster than the speed of sound. A wall of super-heated air grabbed Steele and javelined him through the air.

He was helpless to do anything but take the ride and brace for impact.

This is going to hurt.

He had just enough time to tuck his head, and force his muscles to go limp. His instincts screamed for him to throw out his arm and stop himself, but he knew better. If he did that, it was a sure way to break a wrist or a forearm. Shrapnel from the blast hissed over his head and bits of metal and tire rained down all around him. And then he hit the ground.

Steele landed harder than he ever could remember, and heard the vest's ceramic back plate crack before he bounced off the ground. He skipped and then skipped again, like a flat stone across the surface of a lake.

He forced his head up.

The landscape was on fire, green grass smoldering and trees scorched and leafless. A slight breeze caused broken tree limbs to sway, while a cloud of billowing smoke rose from the pit, carrying the smell of burnt rubber mixed with the caustic taste of Composition B and magnesium.

Pain radiated in time with his pulse, every breath an effort, and when he finally opened his eyes he could smell the blood on his face. Steele shook the cobwebs off and took stock of the situation. His ears were ringing and the fire made it clear as midday.

Someone was calling his name.

"Eric, Eric, talk to me."

It was Demo, but Steele couldn't figure out where his voice was coming from.

He forced himself up to his knees and unclipped the plate carrier. It fell free and he felt his ribs. They screamed at the touch, and the fingers of his gloves came back red with blood. A shadow fell across his field of view, and when he looked up he saw Nate walking out of the flames.

"Jesus Christ . . ."

Nate opened his mouth to yell, but choked instead. His face was bathed in blood from a laceration that started at his scalp and went down to his jaw. He tried to speak again and failed. He stopped and calmly held up a finger, like he was asking Steele to give him a second, and then opened his mouth.

Steele watched West fish around inside of his mouth, and when he pulled his fingers out there was a shard of metal clutched between them.

"That's better," he said, holding up the inch-long piece of shrapnel. He bent over and spit a long stream of blood on the ground and then said, "Get the fuck up."

If Eric still had his pistol, he would have shot him dead. But he had lost it in the MRAP and the only thing he could do was get to his feet. "Nate," he grunted as he stood up and opened his arms wide to encompass the scene, "it's over, man."

"It's not over until I say it is," West lisped, slipping his knife from his belt.

You have to kill him, Steele thought.

He drew the Winkler knife from his belt and stepped forward. "What would your family think if they could see you now, Nate? You ever wonder about that?"

"Don't you talk about them."

"They'd be ashamed of you, just like I am ashamed of you."

"You don't know what you're talking about."

"I've seen enough of what you've done to know it's true. Your wife and son get killed, so what do you do? You kill a bunch of innocents who had nothing to do with it?"

Nate screamed like an animal and lunged with the knife, feinting a slash, replacing technique with rage. Steele slipped to the right, trying to change direction. West drove the blade toward his gut, and when Eric twisted away, West turned left into a wild kick aimed at his knee.

The blow numbed Steele's leg, causing it to buckle. He started to fall and West hammered him in the face with a left hook.

"Keep your guard up, boy."

God damn, he's fast.

Steele wondered for a moment if he could beat him, but forced the thought out of his mind. He let himself fall, tucked into a roll, and came up in a crouch, off to Nate's right side.

"I went after your son."

"Shut up."

West kicked at his face, but Steele was ready. He caught the leg, shoving upward, and sliced the back of West's leg with the blade. "I put everything on the line to find him."

Nate screamed in pain, but didn't slow down. He came in a second time, seemingly unfazed by the jagged tear to his calf. He stabbed at Steele's face, forcing him to backpedal. Eric wasn't quite quick enough and the knife caught his chest and cut through fabric and the skin.

They locked up, exchanging elbows and knee strikes, a close, dirty fight. West stuck him in the leg and tore the blade across his thigh, leaving the back of his arm exposed in the process.

Steele brought the blade up and dragged the edge across the back of his tricep.

Nate fired a loping elbow into Steele's already bruised ribs, knocking the breath out of him.

Fight through it.

He didn't have a choice. To let up now was to die. He stayed in close, slicing West across the jaw and driving his knee into his groin. West gagged, slowed for a moment, and Steele drove the blade down through his shoulder, aiming for the heart. The tip hit the collarbone and blood gushed out onto the handle. Steele tried to bury the blade deeper, but West pulled free, taking the knife with him.

The DAP came roaring overhead, the spotlight blazing down on the two men. West shaded his eyes and staggered back. Steele looked up to see Demo hanging out the side with a rifle.

"No, he's mine!" Steele yelled.

Steele buried his fist in Nate's stomach, folding him over like a La-Z-Boy. He hit him again and again, driving him backward. West threw a wide loping punch and Steele blocked it easily and drove his forehead into Nate's nose.

"Aaaagghhh."

"You want revenge, Nate? Is that it?"

"Fuck you, boy," West gurgled.

Steele hit him in the throat with the web of his hand. West ducked his head in response, and Eric grabbed him with his left hand, pulling him close. With his right he reached over and ripped the blade from his back. Nate tried to push him off, but Steele had the leverage.

"Goodbye, Nathaniel," he said, forcing West to look at him.

And then he drove the blade straight down into his chest.

West spasmed, eyes locked wide and mouth open in a silent *O*. Steele held him close, hand on the hilt of the blade, which he drover deeper and deeper until he felt West's legs weaken and finally give out.

He grabbed him in a bear hug and gently lowered him to the ground. He laid his mentor's head on the earth as the DAP circled and came in for a landing.

"Holy shit, mano," Demo said as he ran to Steele's side.

Eric waited until the life finally faded from West's eyes.

"Get me out of here," he said.

Chapter 82

E ric Steele stared out the window while the doctor continued to tell him why it was a bad idea to leave the hospital.

"The MRI confirms the concussion. You got lucky, doesn't look like you fractured your skull. X-rays found two broken ribs, a broken left wrist, and a separated shoulder. We sewed up the laceration to your chin and forehead, and I doubt you will have a scar."

Eric wasn't listening. He was looking at his hands, and the dried blood beneath his fingernails. It was West's blood.

He knew that killing West had been the only option, but he didn't feel good about it. In fact, he felt empty. Nate hadn't always been a monster. At one time he had been the most patriotic man Steele knew.

A damn shame.

"Mr. Steele, are you listening?"

"Yeah, I need to rest up," Steele replied.

"I'd love to see that," Meg said, smiling by the door to the room.

Steele looked up to see her standing there with a bouquet of flowers and the brightest eyes he'd seen in days. "Eric, you look like hell."

Steele cracked a grin. "I fell off my bike," he joked.

Meg stepped into the room, followed by Demo, who was eating a bag of chips.

"Excuse me, visiting hours are over."

"Don't worry, Doc," Demo said through a mouthful of chips, "that nurse with the blond hair said it was okay."

"Well, she was wrong."

"How about you and me go talk to her, then," Demo said, placing his hand on the doctor's shoulder and urging him toward the door. "These two have some catching up to do."

"Well, don't we make a good pair," Meg said, gesturing to the sling on her arm.

"Two cripples. I was going to call, but—"

"You don't have my number," Meg finished. She set the flowers on his chest, then leaned over and pressed her lips to his.

It was a long, starved kiss, and for a moment Steele forgot all about his injuries and tried to pull Meg up onto the bed. His broken ribs reminded him with a jolt of pain.

"Damn, that hurts," he said.

"Easy, turbo, what's the rush?" Meg joked before sitting beside him. "I'm glad you're not dead, but I'm still pissed you didn't take me with you."

"I told you, it's illegal."

"Nice try. I looked it up."

Steele pulled her close and kissed the top of her head, taking in her smell and warmth. He closed his eyes and allowed himself a second to savor the moment.

"President Rockford wants to give you a medal. Says you are a hero."

"I don't feel like a hero."

"You saved thousands of innocent lives. West made his choice." She looked up at him, her eyes soft and caring. "And you did what you had to."

Steele nodded. He knew she was right, but it still wasn't easy.

"The way I see it is, you can either sit here and feel sorry for yourself, or . . ."

"Or what?" Eric asked.

"You can get your ass up and buy me dinner."

Acknowledgments

Eric Steele has been in the works for almost ten years now. I remember thinking about him on late nights in Afghanistan. Wondering if there'd ever be a moment in my life when I'd get to share him with you. Wondering if I'd ever make it back from Afghanistan at all.

Well, eventually I did make it home. And I owe my former soldiers a debt of gratitude that I'll never be able to repay. You had every reason to marginalize me, a young second lieutenant with zero experience. Put me in a remote office somewhere and bury me with paperwork. But you didn't do that. Instead you took me in. Made me a part of the platoon. You taught, coached, and mentored me on what it meant to be a leader in the United States Army Infantry. When we landed in Afghanistan you had my back for 485 days of absolute hell. It's because of you, the soldiers of Outlaw Platoon, that I am alive today. Without you, Eric Steele never makes it to the page, because I never make it home. So even though this seems so insignificant, thank you all.

Just because the idea for Eric Steele was rattling around in my noggin didn't mean he would ever come to life on the page. To accomplish that mission, I knew I needed an agent. Not just someone to help me sell a book. I needed someone who truly believed in me as a storyteller, and Eric Steele as a character. Scott Miller is that someone. If you're in the publishing industry, you know his name. It's gold and there's a reason why. Scott pushed me to get the story right. The rest, as they say, is history. Serious writers have serious agents. Believe it. Scott, thank you for taking a chance on me.

At some point during the writing, authors always reach out to people they trust for help. And that is a damn good thing, because these people normally make decent stories good and good stories great. Josh Hood is that person for me. He's an Iraq and Afghanistan combat veteran who served with the 82nd Airborne Division. He was on a full-time SWAT team in Memphis, Tennessee. He wrote two great thrillers. The list goes on and on for this guy. Why he decided to help me I'll never know, but I'm glad he did. He speaks my language, the language of the military. Like my best noncommissioned officers, Josh never holds back and tells me exactly how he feels one hundred percent of the time. He knows his guns. He understands tactics. And he's a good friend who's always been there for me. Josh, thank you.

Plotting is difficult work. Crafting a story that moves with a sense of urgency is everything in the thriller world. Like all new fiction writers, I struggled with it. Thankfully I had John Paine and his sage wisdom in my corner to help me. John has a knack for telling a good story and he was able to make concrete suggestions that made this book far better.

A day after *Outlaw Platoon* was published, David Highfill told me that if I wanted to try to write fiction, he would help me. I was blown away. To have one of the best, most accomplished editors in the business offer to help me realize one of my lifelong dreams was a blessing that's difficult to articulate. Here we are six years later, and not only did he help me publish this book, he brought a cast of characters to life that existed only in my head for over a decade. What a gift. In fact, the entire team at William Morrow are top-notch publishing professionals. They are the best in the industry. Tavia Kowalchuk, marketing extraordinaire,

Danielle Bartlett, publicity guru, Chloe Moffett, jack of all editorial trades—thank you all from the bottom of my heart.

To my great friend John Rokosz. We had many conversations about Eric Steele and Nathaniel West. We also had many glasses of whiskey and bourbon in the process. We've been friends since high school, we went to college together, and you're the godfather of my youngest son. I consider myself lucky to have such a great friend in my life. You are a fantastic storyteller in your own right, and one day the world is going to see that. Thank you for helping me get this story right.

Mom and Dad. You raised an incredible family. I want you to know that I consider myself lucky to have had such amazing parents. All those years raising me. . . . Looking back, being a parent myself now, I realize that I must have been a colossal pain in the ass. Thank you for being so patient with me. And tough on me.

For the last five years I've had the honor of working with Fairway Independent Mortgage Corporation. They fund a charity that I cofounded called the American Warrior Initiative. Over the years Fairway has given AWI millions of dollars and only asked one thing in return—that we go out and do some good in the lives of our nation's veterans. What's truly amazing is that every single person who works for the company shares similar character traits. They're kind. Generous. Loving. Caring. Humble. Smart. I've never in my life seen a company operate like this, and it is a blessing to be a small part of the Fairway family. I have the CEO of Fairway, Steve Jacobson, to thank for that blessing. He is the definition of a servant-leader. He embodies excellence and service to others in everything he does. He's the hardest worker I've ever met and someone I aspire to be like someday.

I would also be remiss if I did not thank Louise Thaxton, the Director of the American Warrior Initiative. She is the most passionate supporter of our nation's veterans. She leads a mortgage branch with over seventy employees and runs a national nonprofit that does nearly forty public events per year. She truly is a force to be reckoned with, and I am blessed to call her a friend. Louise, thank you for the support and guidance you've given me over the years. I am forever grateful.

Finally, I'd like to thank Ethan, Emma, and Evan. Every day I wake up and thank God that I have you. Watching you grow up has been the honor of a lifetime. You are so unique in your own ways. Every day you make me proud to see the people you are becoming.